BALTIMORE

Chapel of Bones

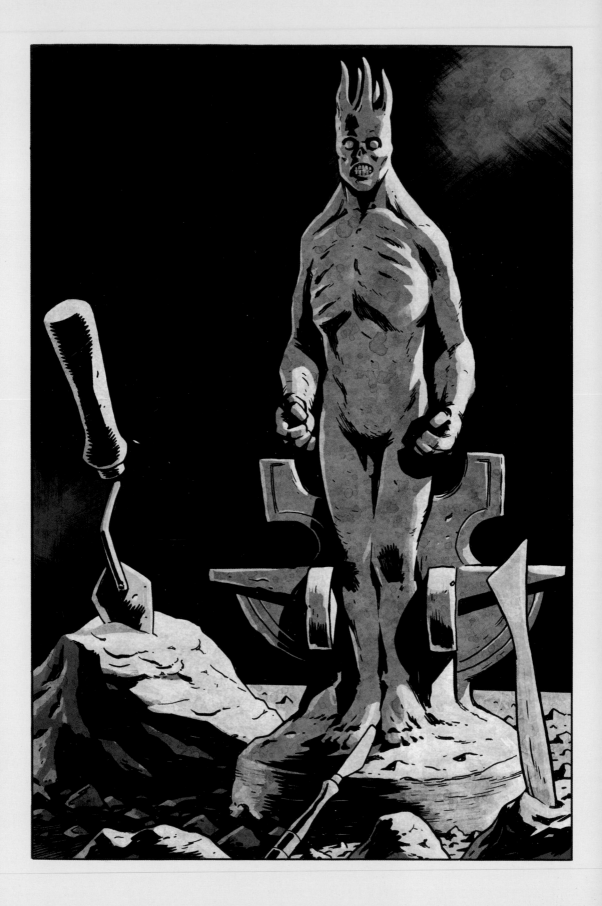

BALTIMORE™
CHAPEL OF BONES

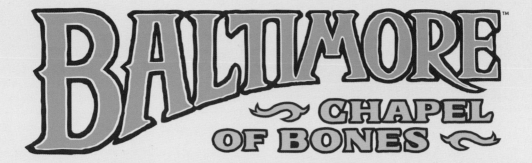

VOLUME FOUR

Story by
MIKE MIGNOLA
CHRISTOPHER GOLDEN

Art by
BEN STENBECK

Colors by
DAVE STEWART

Letters by
CLEM ROBINS

Cover Art by
MIKE MIGNOLA with **DAVE STEWART**

Editor SCOTT ALLIE
Associate Editor DANIEL CHABON
Collection Designer AMY ARENDTS
Publisher MIKE RICHARDSON

®
DARK HORSE BOOKS

For Hans Christian Andersen—Heart and Soul.
—Mike Mignola

In memory of Bob Booth, who loved stories more purely
than anyone else I've known. He understood.
—Christopher Golden

For Geof Darrow.
—Ben Stenbeck

Neil Hankerson *Executive Vice President* • Tom Weddle *Chief Financial Officer* • Randy Stradley *Vice President of Publishing* • Michael Martens *Vice President of Book Trade Sales* • Anita Nelson *Vice President of Business Affairs* • Scott Allie *Editor in Chief* • Matt Parkinson *Vice President of Marketing* • David Scroggy *Vice President of Product Development* • Dale LaFountain *Vice President of Information Technology* Darlene Vogel *Senior Director of Print, Design, and Production* • Ken Lizzi *General Counsel* • Davey Estrada *Editorial Director* • Chris Warner *Senior Books Editor* • Diana Schutz *Executive Editor* • Cary Grazzini *Director of Print and Development* • Lia Ribacchi *Art Director* • Cara Niece *Director of Scheduling* Tim Wiesch *Director of International Licensing* • Mark Bernardi *Director of Digital Publishing*

Special thanks to Szukits Gábor

DarkHorse.com

Published by Dark Horse Books
A division of Dark Horse Comics, Inc.
10956 SE Main Street
Milwaukie, OR 97222

First edition: June 2014
ISBN 978-1-61655-328-9

1   3   5   7   9   10   8   6   4   2

Printed in China

This volume collects *Baltimore: The Infernal Train* #1–#3 and
Baltimore: Chapel of Bones #1–#2, published by Dark Horse Comics.

"It's a day for remembering things best forgotten."

—Thomas Childress Jr. in *Baltimore; or,*
The Steadfast Tin Soldier and the Vampire (2007)

IT BEGINS HERE; IT ENDS HERE. With this volume, Captain Henry Baltimore resolves (for a second time) his quest to avenge his personal loss while confronting the plague of vampirism sweeping the Continent at its source, the bloodsucker Haigus. How that resolution plays out, I leave to you to discover in the pages that follow.

That's as much of a spoiler as you'll get from me; this I vow.

Like all contemporary vampire tales, *Baltimore* owes a primary debt to Bram Stoker's *Dracula* (1897). The structure of Mike Mignola and Christopher Golden's original novel (published in 2007) blended Stoker's epistolary narrative—various first-person and newspaper accounts of disparate events strung together into a whole—with the Chowder Society of Peter Straub's *Ghost Story* (1979)—into a collective of apparently disassociated, unrelated supernatural tales that culminate in a catastrophic finale. The *Baltimore* novel's central cast are here relegated to supporting roles: Dr. Lemuel Rose, Thomas Childress Jr., and Demetrius Aischros. There is much of Stoker and Straub in their characterizations (of Stoker above all, echoing *Dracula*'s Dr. John Seward, Quincey Morris, and Arthur Holmwood). And, yes, Captain Baltimore himself is a clear echo of Professor Abraham Van Helsing, the first of all obsessed vampire hunters. By backdating

Baltimore's suck-stalker saga to the First World War and its wake, Mignola and Golden conceptually place him in the first generation of Van Helsing's successors.

The pitch-black heart of *Baltimore* is the conceit of vampirism as contagion, synonymous with a plague, herein named the Red Death (handily referencing Edgar Allan Poe, who makes a guest star appearance; more on that in a bit). This (invented) Red Death pandemic is contemporary to the early twentieth century's smallpox epidemics, siring villages of Renfields. But there are all kinds of epidemics: Stoker, after all, succumbed to tertiary syphilis, according to some biographers. Why not invent new ones? Vampirism as contagion was an undercurrent of Stoker's novel (where vampirism and plague were implicitly linked, crossing the Channel into the heart of England), but as long as aristocratic counts *personified* the contagion, extending only as far as their individual appetites, the disease was contained. It took the cinema to manifest the metaphor in more concrete terms, via F. W. Murnau and Henrik Galeen's illegal adaptation *Nosferatu: Eine Symphonie des Grauens* (1922), and the viral metaphor was more emphatically showcased in Werner Herzog's 1979 remake. Stoker placed rats among Dracula's familiars; Galeen and Murnau had their taloned, rodent-faced Count Orlok (Max Schreck) moving with swarms of rats, toothy harbingers of one another, coffins their crop as they nested to breed and feed.

For my generation, it was Richard Matheson's novel *I Am Legend* (1954) that popularized vampirism as an apocalyptic infection. In Matheson's wake came a dour international-coproduction adaptation of his novel, *L'ultimo uomo della Terra* (*The Last Man on Earth*, 1964), Mexican vampire movies like *El mundo de los vampiros* (*The World of the Vampires*, 1961), and especially Roman Polanski and Gérard Brach's *The Fearless Vampire Killers* (1967), all codifying vampirism as blight as a new genre norm. I can still hear the final narration of Polanski and Brach's masterpiece in my head, almost half a century later: *"That night, fleeing from Transylvania, Professor Abronsius never guessed that he was carrying away with him the very evil he had sought to destroy. Thanks to him, this evil would now be able to spread itself across the world . . ."*

It has spread ever since, a pox central to much in our pop culture. Vampirism as disease spawned zombies as disease, via George Romero and John Russo's low-budget revamp of *I Am Legend* into *Night of the Living Dead* just a year after Professor Abronsius unleashed the contagion of vampirism. In *Baltimore*, the novel and the comic series, Mike Mignola and Chris Golden and their artistic partners Ben Stenbeck and Dave Stewart have synthesized both vampirism and disease (and oh, so much more) into their own revisionist World War I scenario. For Mignola, Golden, and Stenbeck, European villages and ports are populated by zombie-like plague victims, gray-skinned and dead-eyed cues or familiars for a plague of vampirism awakened by their singular hero in the bloody trenches of the Great War. The vampires themselves are foul, sentient leeches, loathsome humanoid vermin malingering in shadows.

Kim Newman wrote eloquently about the Great War and the genre roots of *Baltimore* in his fine introduction to the previous volume, *A Passing Stranger and Other Stories* (2013). Let us go deeper . . .

———

More than the novel, *Baltimore* the comics series is a European western, with Captain Baltimore an ingenious fusion of pirate, smuggler, highwayman, and bounty killer. In all these genres, surly locals fester about the pub, the inn, or the saloon while strangers wait for the arrival of a missing character. In this very installment of *Baltimore*, the witching hour (and a mad artist's garret) supplants *High Noon* (oops, second spoiler—my bad).

With his false leg (in the novel it bristles with nail heads, one for each vampire extinguished) and seaworthy, self-contained armory, Baltimore is as much Sabata as Ahab, with a bit of Russell Thorndike's Reverend Doctor Syn (a.k.a. Captain Clegg) in the mix. And oh, that leg—*"a curious appendage,"* Captain Baltimore's friend Aischros notes in the novel. *"Not some sea-dog's peg, but a hinged, jointed limb carved from the finest wood."* If the wooden-legged captain had a theme song, it would be more Ennio Morricone than *Have Gun—Will Travel*. Captain Baltimore echoes Captain Ahab of Herman Melville's *Moby-Dick*, yes, along with Sterling Hayden's harpoon-wielding sheriff in 1958's *Terror in a Texas Town* (who was as much a "novelty character" in his genre and day as Mignola and Golden's harpoon-tossing hero) and Brian Clemens's delicious Hammer Films swashbuckler in *Captain Kronos—Vampire Hunter* (1974). Buffy, mind your elders.

Melville's Ahab is consciously referenced in Baltimore in numerous ways, but the whole of *Baltimore*—the novel and the comics that followed—refutes Melville's own stance on Calvinism and Christian hellfire and brimstone. *"The hairs of our heads are numbered, and the days of our lives,"* Melville wrote in his short story "The Lightning-Rod Man" (1854). *"In thunder as in sunshine, I stand at ease in the hands of my God. False negotiator, away! See, the scroll of the storm is rolled back; the house is unharmed; and in the blue heavens I read in the rainbow that the Deity will not, of purpose, make war on man's earth."*

Such is not the case with *Baltimore*, I assure you. As in most post-Stoker vampire sagas,

Christian symbols—the crucifix, Holy Water, churches—are lethal tools. However often he may rage (Ahab-like) at God and God's role for himself as God's avenger, Captain Baltimore embodies *and* interrogates rigid moral ideals. Mike recently answered a devoted fan who referred to Baltimore as an amoral character; Mike disagreed, saying he "never thought of Baltimore as 'amoral,' " and that speaks volumes.

Mignola cites the 1970s Marvel monster comics as favorites of his own formative reading years (*Tomb of Dracula*, Mike Ploog's issues of *Werewolf by Night* and *The Monster of Frankenstein*, and the Jack Kirby/Stan Lee/Steve Ditko monster-reprint titles like *Where Monsters Dwell*). Like those series, the *Baltimore* comic hits the key genre notes within its cartography of the damned. Some of these horror touchstones date back to the Universal horror films Joe Lansdale mentions in his introduction to the second volume in this series; others do not. After all, Mike and Chris (and I) grew up with very different terror totems. For every venerable nineteenth and early twentieth century genre archetype, there are those from later, tougher, post–JFK assassination fare: here a surrogate Erik, the Phantom of the Opera (*The Play*), there a Witchfinder General (Judge Duvic of the New Inquisition), an eruption of Ray Harryhausen or Guy N. Smith–inspired outsized crustaceans (*Dr. Leskovar's Remedy*), followed by a nasty bit of nunsploitation (*The Curse Bells*) as redolent of Matthew Gregory Lewis's *The Monk* (1796) as it is of Aldous Huxley and Ken Russell's soul-searing *The Devils* (1971). If we bring Mike and Chris's original *Baltimore* novel into consideration—as we must, since this chapter of the *Baltimore* comics saga re-creates the final chapters of that seminal book (oops, was that another spoiler?)—there are more references than we have room to detail here. Savor them, from evocations of H. P. Lovecraft's "Pickman's Model" to Mario Bava's wispy, flitting, swarming bloodsuckers in *Hercules in the Haunted World* (*Ercole al centro della Terra*, 1961), to the monstrous lake dweller El Cucro, recalling countless pulp magazine blobs (see Anthony M. Rud's "Ooze," Joseph Payne Brennan's "Slime," etc.), the amoeba-like Mayan "god" of Riccardo Freda and Mario Bava's *Caltiki, the Immortal Monster* (1959), and the all-devouring whatsit feeding on teenagers lazing on a Maine pond in Stephen King's "The Raft" (1982). Mike and Chris aren't merely cribbing: these are primal elements, distilled into new forms, the wing of bat and eye of newt for these fresh brews.

That's how horror works. The genre is rich in ways both conscious and unconscious. Neither Mike nor Chris has seen either version of Abel Gance's antiwar *J'accuse* (1919 and 1938), yet both movies ring as loudly as the curse bells over the whole of the *Baltimore* battlefields. *"Wherever the darkness touched, the soldiers began to rise from muddy trenches where they had been left to rot,"* Mike and Chris wrote in the novel *Baltimore*; *"Graves split open and cadavers crawled free."* This passage describes the climactic imagery of both versions of Gance's *J'accuse* (in the first, a mad soldier-poet's vision; in the remake, a real march of the war dead conjured by a desperate, infuriated WWI veteran-scientist-inventor). For his first *J'accuse*, Gance cast soldiers on leave from the WWI trenches; many marched off to die after appearing before Gance's camera and were long dead before their cinematic images kissed movie screens around the world. This was a haunting real-and-reel-world form of resurrection, undeath, and vampirism. Gance knew it and was greatly troubled by it, folding his emotions profoundly into the narrative of his harrowing, heartfelt 1937 remake, wherein the dead of WWI march on the living to try to stop, in vain, what soon would become World War II.

We all know how that turned out, don't we?

In this, we must note that the whole of *Baltimore* reflects the genuine time of war in which Mike and Chris and Ben have been working. The post-9/11 Afghanistan and Iraq

Wars, inquisitions, and economic implosions are the real-world backdrop, and the apparent plague of apathy that brands the decade-plus in which military families have given everything (a mere 0.7 percent of the population serve), while most Americans have sacrificed little or nothing. I'll leave it to future scholars to tread those thematic minefields after the fog of war has passed, if ever it will.

————

This volume would seem to wrap up the *Baltimore* saga, but only Mike, Chris, Ben, editor Scott Allie, and their coconspirators in the vampire malignancy know for sure. Even if I could tell you, I wouldn't.

I should quote a smattering of Poe here, but Bluto (John Belushi) in *Animal House* (1978) said it best: *"It ain't over until we say it's over!"*

But I will say this:

I bring your attention to the quote that opens this introduction, about "things best forgotten." The only thing missing from an ideal volume of *The Compleat Baltimore*, for me, remains the guest appearances from H. H. Munro (Hector Hugh Munro, a.k.a. Saki), William Hope Hodgson, and Abel Gance.

Yes, yes, Mike and Chris have given us Poe's head as a character, and grievously maligned Russian occultist Елéна Петрóвна Блавáтская (Helena Petrovna Blavatsky) as well. Thus do one century's visionaries become the next century's hell spawn. A mutual hero of ours—the late, great Ray Harryhausen—found Blavatsky to be an intriguing historical figure, and no doubt Ray would *not* have approved of her demonization as a resurrected malign presence. Alas, less than two decades after her death (in *Baltimore*'s narrative chronology), Mike, Chris, and Ben depict Blavatsky being conjured forth from the beyond as a wizened, dwarfish, power-hungry blood sponge. So much for Theosophy in the *Baltimore* universe; could the slander of Theosophy cofounders Henry Steel Olcott and William Quan Judge be far behind?

But Poe's and Madame Blavatsky's appearances only beg the obvious.

Hopefully, you can see the grand and glorious potential of weaving Abel Gance's filming of *J'accuse* into a *Baltimore* segment. After all, the seed is already planted (see page 22 of *Baltimore: The Plague Ships*). Make your move, kind sirs; I will happily arrange for you to see the film(s) for yourself, if you doubt the potential.

Baltimore: The Plague Ships already owes so much to William Hope Hodgson's fiction, including its titular infection (initially coming across as a continental inflation of the fungal horrors of Hodgson's "The Voice in the Night" or *The Boats of the "Glen Carrig"*); why not a glimpse of his death at Ypres in April 1918? Reportedly it was an artillery shell that took Hodgson out, but who's to say it wasn't *something else*—or that *worse* happened in the wake of his demise? The newspaper accounts of that spring were notoriously vague.

A gay Tory like Saki could add some spice to the *Baltimore* brew as a character, but it's the last words ascribed to him while in the WWI trenches—*"Put that bloody cigarette out!"*—that I scoured the *Baltimore* panels for, in vain.

Is it too much to ask?

Really, just one word balloon—and three images: a crack of German sniper fire, a puff of smoke, a splatter of something dark in the mud.

C'mon, Mike and Chris and Ben. Get on it.

I will have satisfaction, gentlemen.

Stephen R. Bissette
Mountains of Madness, Vermont
The final day of the Year of Our Lord AD 2013

THE INFERNAL TRAIN
Chapter One

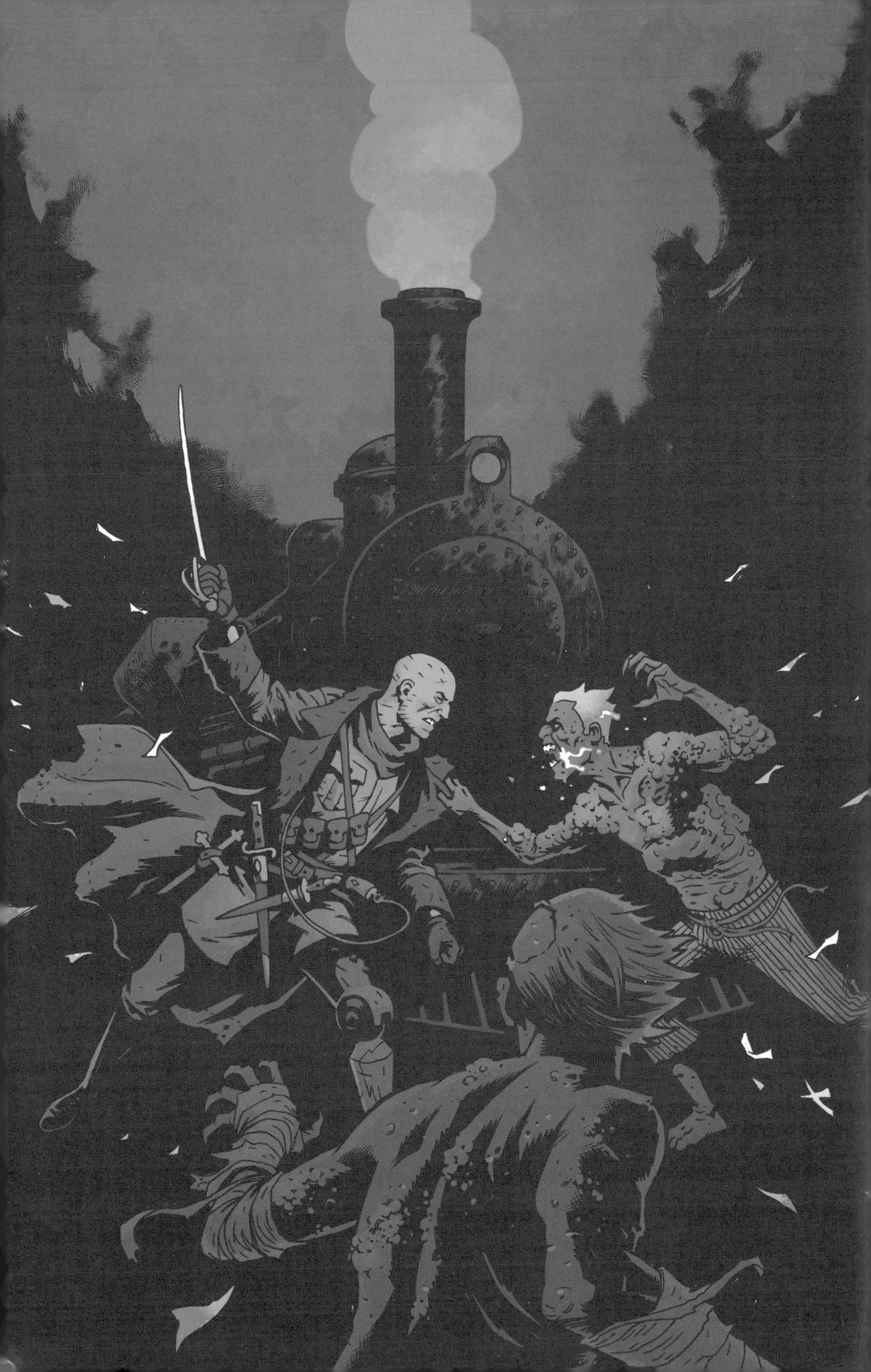

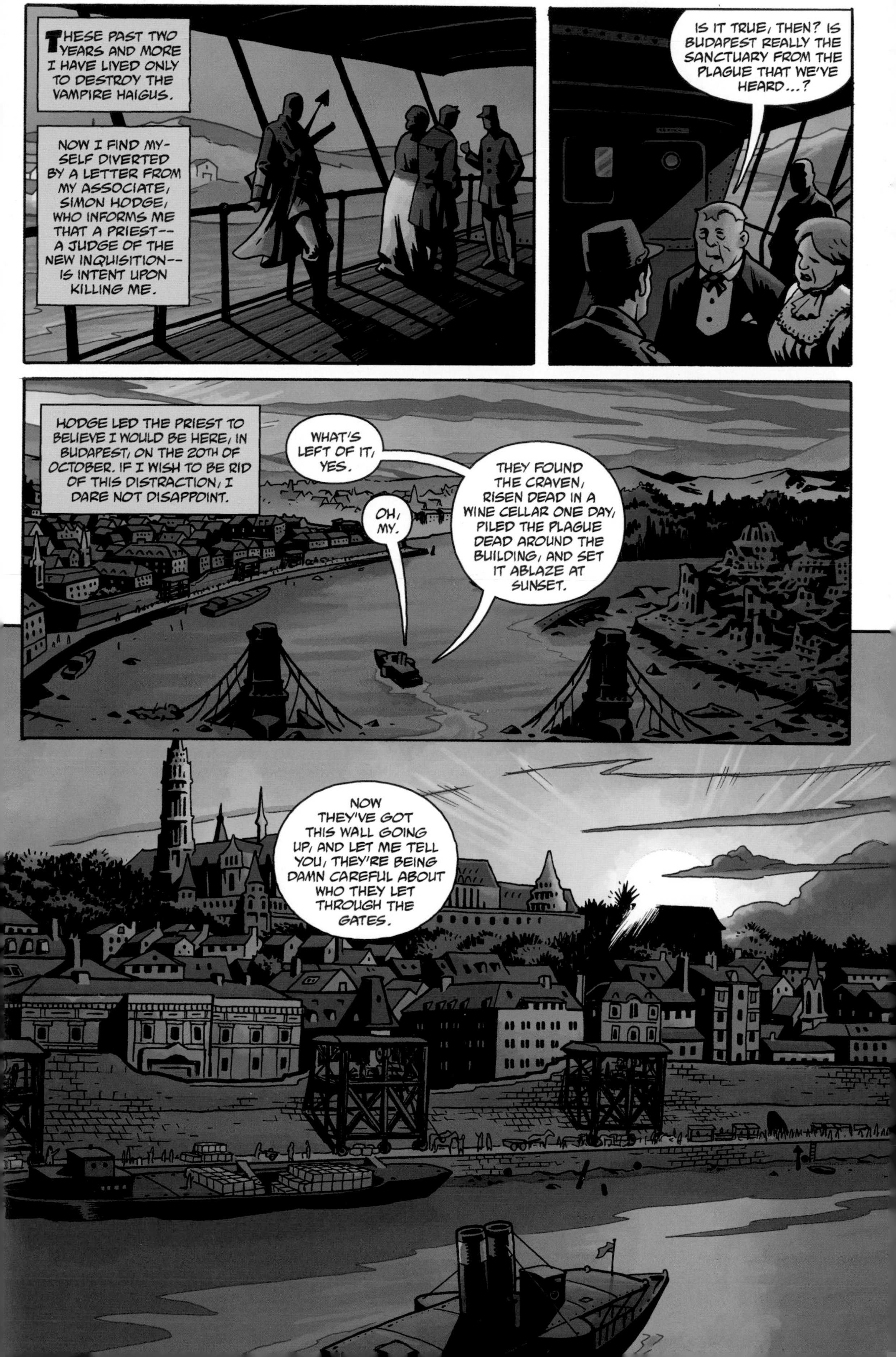
THESE PAST TWO YEARS AND MORE I HAVE LIVED ONLY TO DESTROY THE VAMPIRE HAIGUS.
NOW I FIND MYSELF DIVERTED BY A LETTER FROM MY ASSOCIATE, SIMON HODGE, WHO INFORMS ME THAT A PRIEST-- A JUDGE OF THE NEW INQUISITION-- IS INTENT UPON KILLING ME.
IS IT TRUE, THEN? IS BUDAPEST REALLY THE SANCTUARY FROM THE PLAGUE THAT WE'VE HEARD...?
HODGE LED THE PRIEST TO BELIEVE I WOULD BE HERE, IN BUDAPEST, ON THE 20TH OF OCTOBER. IF I WISH TO BE RID OF THIS DISTRACTION, I DARE NOT DISAPPOINT.
WHAT'S LEFT OF IT, YES.
OH, MY.
THEY FOUND THE CRAVEN, RISEN DEAD IN A WINE CELLAR ONE DAY, PILED THE PLAGUE DEAD AROUND THE BUILDING, AND SET IT ABLAZE AT SUNSET.
NOW THEY'VE GOT THIS WALL GOING UP, AND LET ME TELL YOU, THEY'RE BEING DAMN CAREFUL ABOUT WHO THEY LET THROUGH THE GATES.

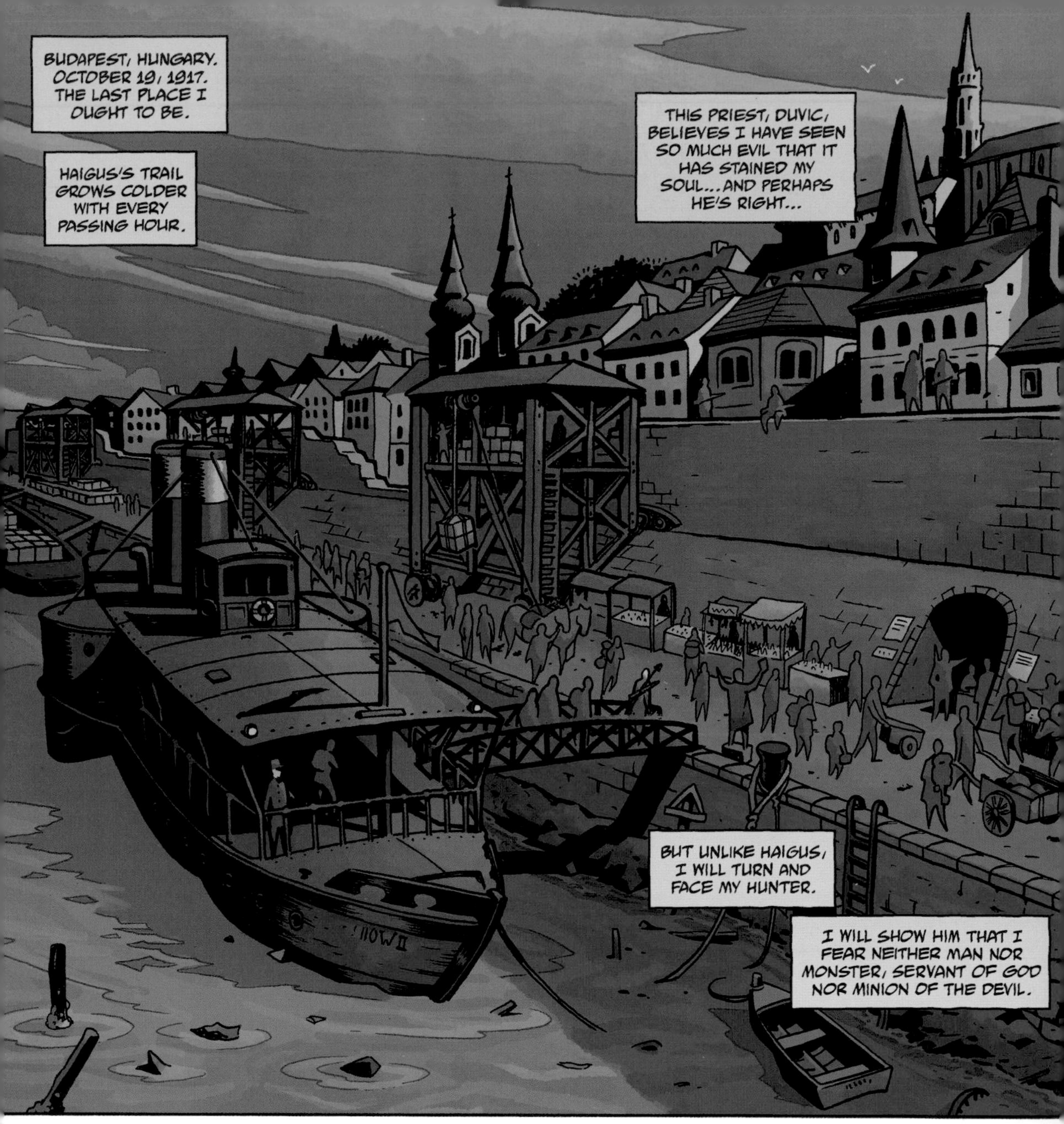
BUDAPEST, HUNGARY. OCTOBER 19, 1917. THE LAST PLACE I OUGHT TO BE.
HAIGUS'S TRAIL GROWS COLDER WITH EVERY PASSING HOUR.
THIS PRIEST, DUVIC, BELIEVES I HAVE SEEN SO MUCH EVIL THAT IT HAS STAINED MY SOUL... AND PERHAPS HE'S RIGHT...
BUT UNLIKE HAIGUS, I WILL TURN AND FACE MY HUNTER.
I WILL SHOW HIM THAT I FEAR NEITHER MAN NOR MONSTER, SERVANT OF GOD NOR MINION OF THE DEVIL.

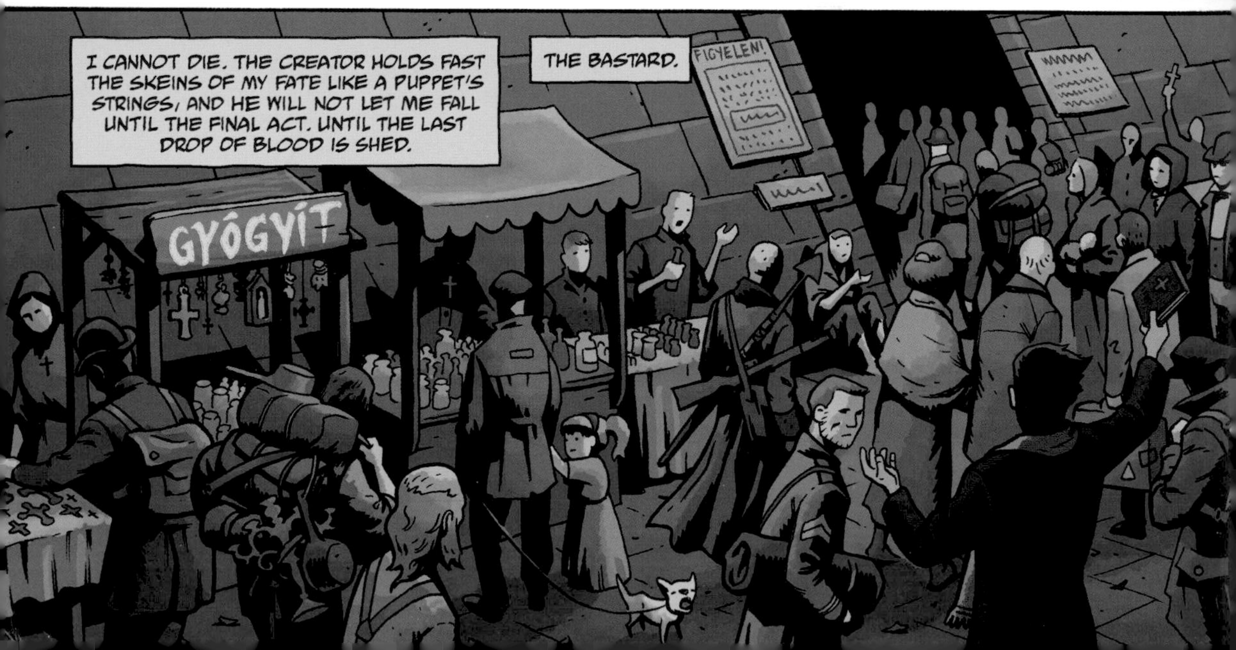
I CANNOT DIE. THE CREATOR HOLDS FAST THE SKEINS OF MY FATE LIKE A PUPPET'S STRINGS, AND HE WILL NOT LET ME FALL UNTIL THE FINAL ACT. UNTIL THE LAST DROP OF BLOOD IS SHED.
THE BASTARD.
FIGYELEN!
GYÓGYÍT

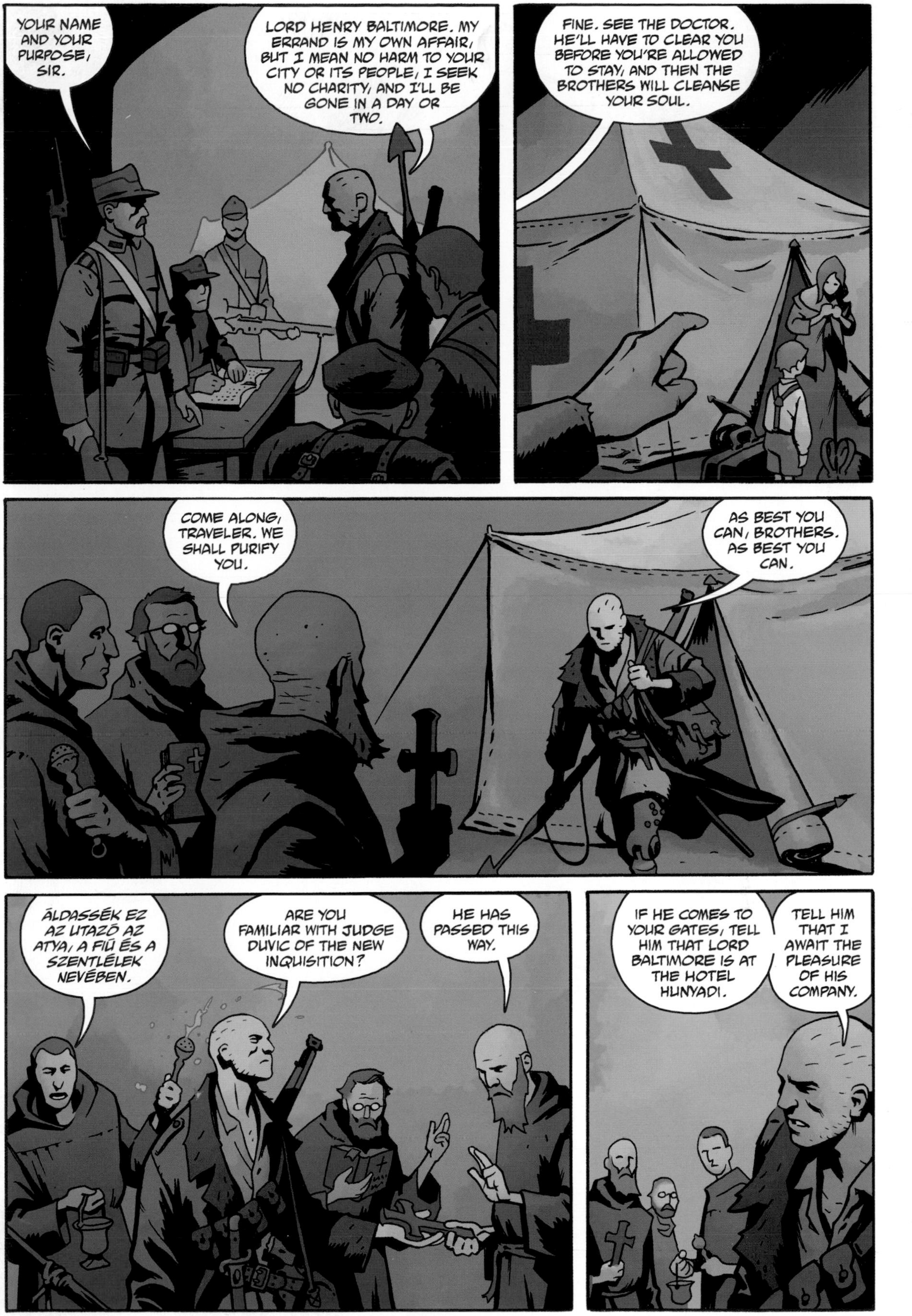
YOUR NAME AND YOUR PURPOSE, SIR.
LORD HENRY BALTIMORE. MY ERRAND IS MY OWN AFFAIR, BUT I MEAN NO HARM TO YOUR CITY OR ITS PEOPLE, I SEEK NO CHARITY, AND I'LL BE GONE IN A DAY OR TWO.
FINE. SEE THE DOCTOR. HE'LL HAVE TO CLEAR YOU BEFORE YOU'RE ALLOWED TO STAY, AND THEN THE BROTHERS WILL CLEANSE YOUR SOUL.
COME ALONG, TRAVELER. WE SHALL PURIFY YOU.
AS BEST YOU CAN, BROTHERS. AS BEST YOU CAN.
ÁLDASSÉK EZ AZ UTAZÓ AZ ATYA, A FIÚ ÉS A SZENTLÉLEK NEVÉBEN.
ARE YOU FAMILIAR WITH JUDGE DUVIC OF THE NEW INQUISITION?
HE HAS PASSED THIS WAY.
IF HE COMES TO YOUR GATES, TELL HIM THAT LORD BALTIMORE IS AT THE HOTEL HUNYADI.
TELL HIM THAT I AWAIT THE PLEASURE OF HIS COMPANY.

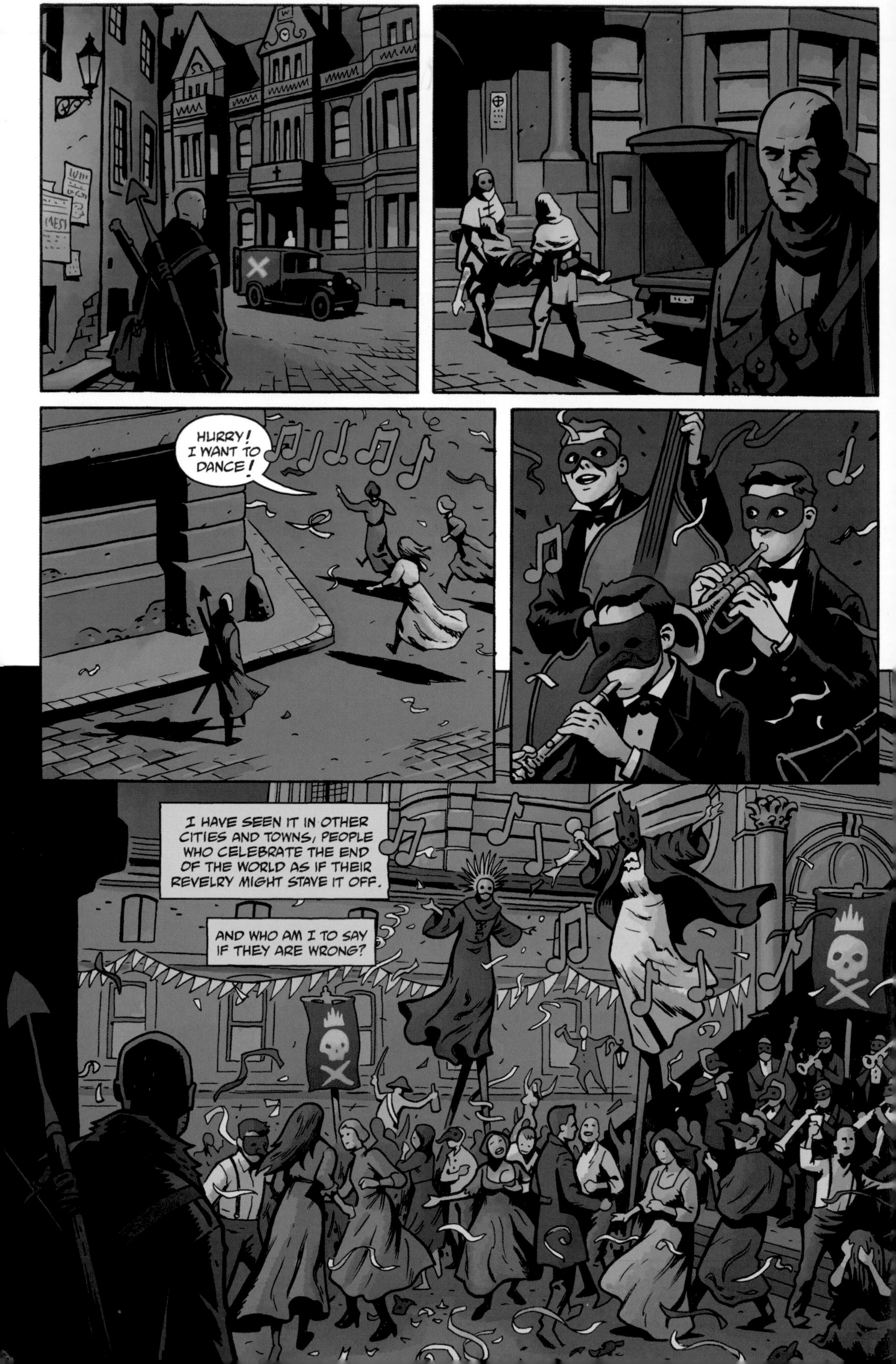
HURRY! I WANT TO DANCE!
I HAVE SEEN IT IN OTHER CITIES AND TOWNS, PEOPLE WHO CELEBRATE THE END OF THE WORLD AS IF THEIR REVELRY MIGHT STAVE IT OFF.
AND WHO AM I TO SAY IF THEY ARE WRONG?

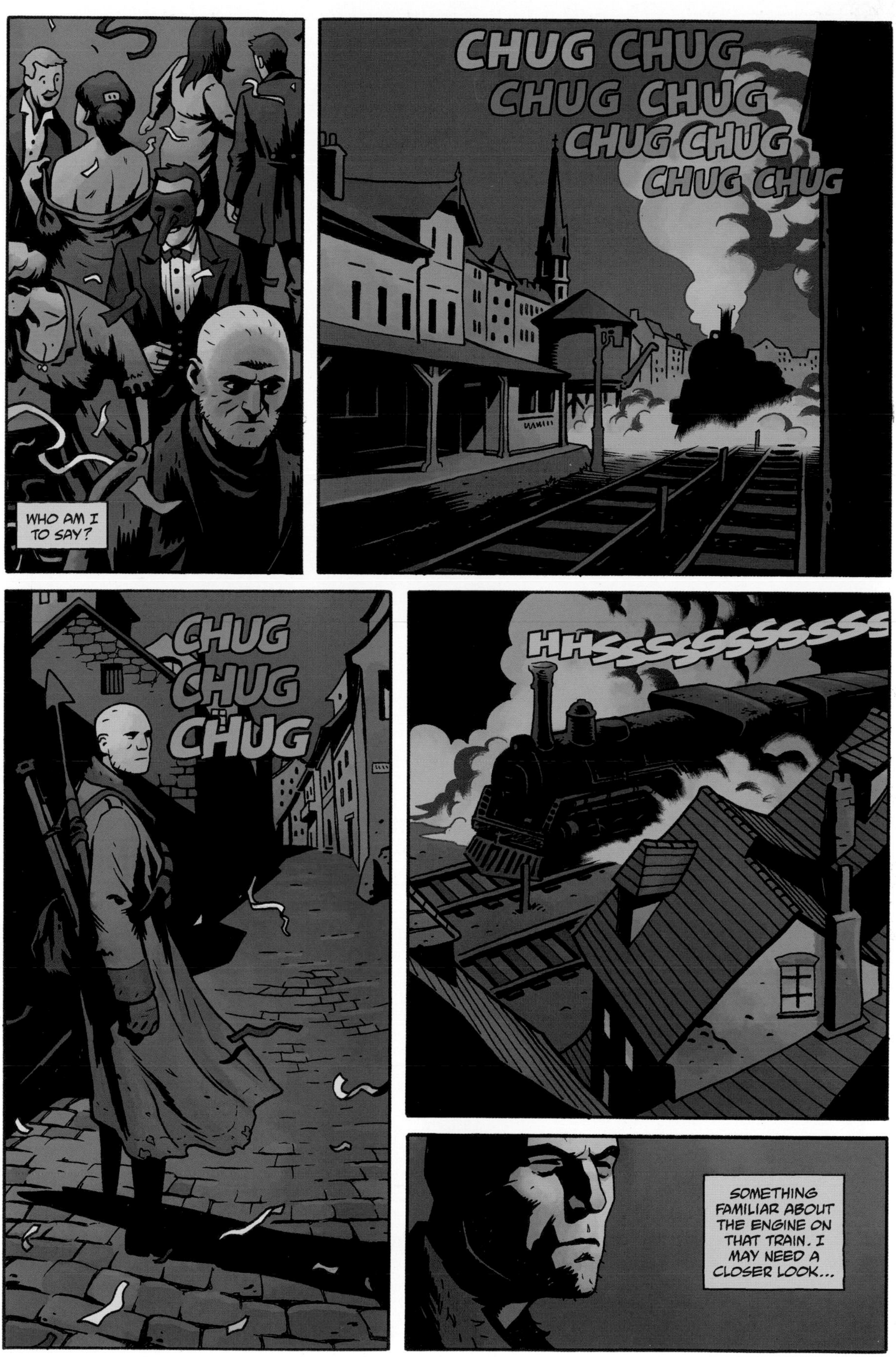
WHO AM I TO SAY?
CHUG CHUG
CHUG CHUG
CHUG CHUG
CHUG CHUG
CHUG
CHUG
CHUG
HHSSSSSSSSSSSS
SOMETHING FAMILIAR ABOUT THE ENGINE ON THAT TRAIN. I MAY NEED A CLOSER LOOK...

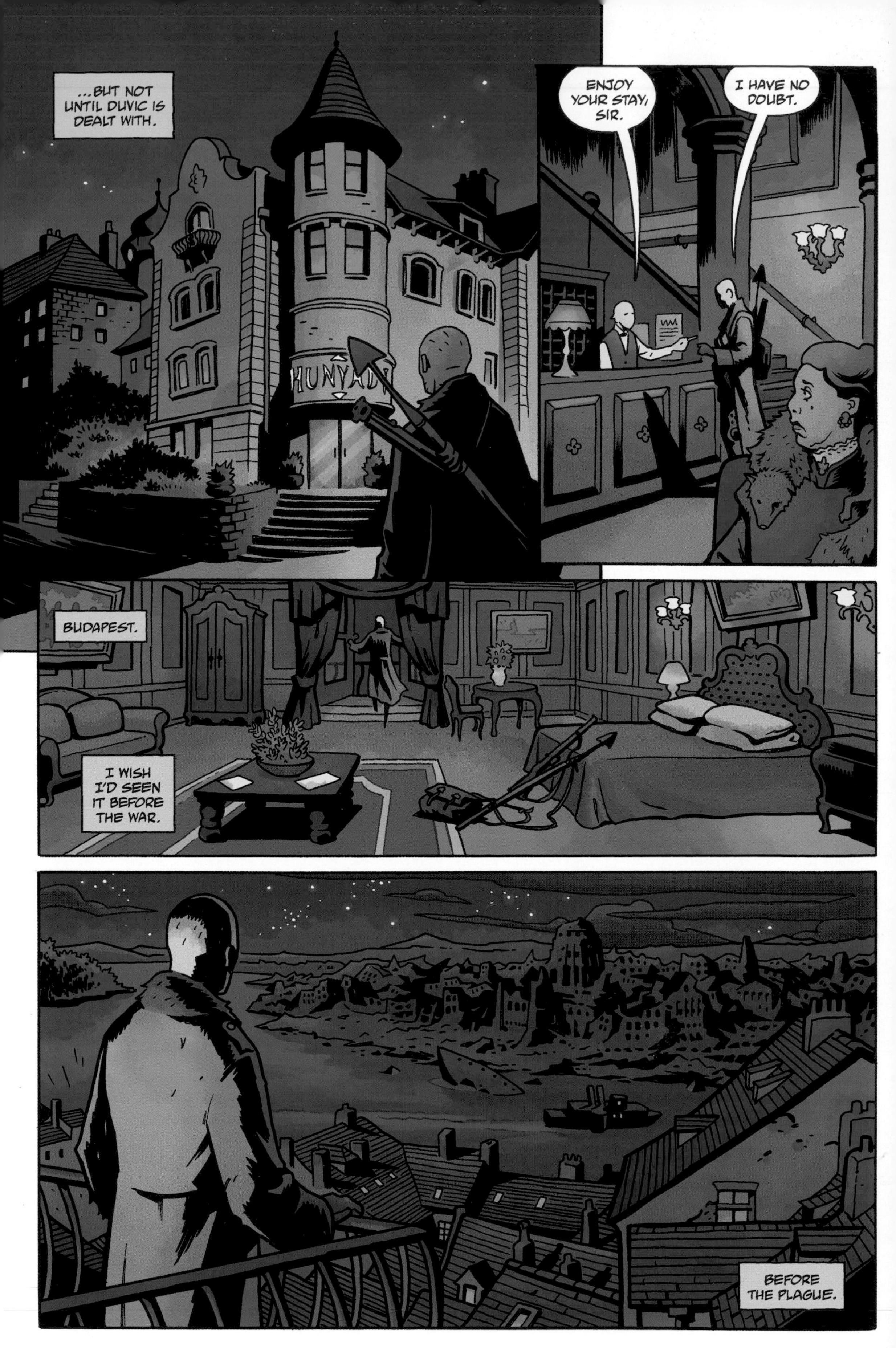
...BUT NOT UNTIL DUVIC IS DEALT WITH.
HUNYADI
ENJOY YOUR STAY, SIR.
I HAVE NO DOUBT.
BUDAPEST.
I WISH I'D SEEN IT BEFORE THE WAR.
BEFORE THE PLAGUE.

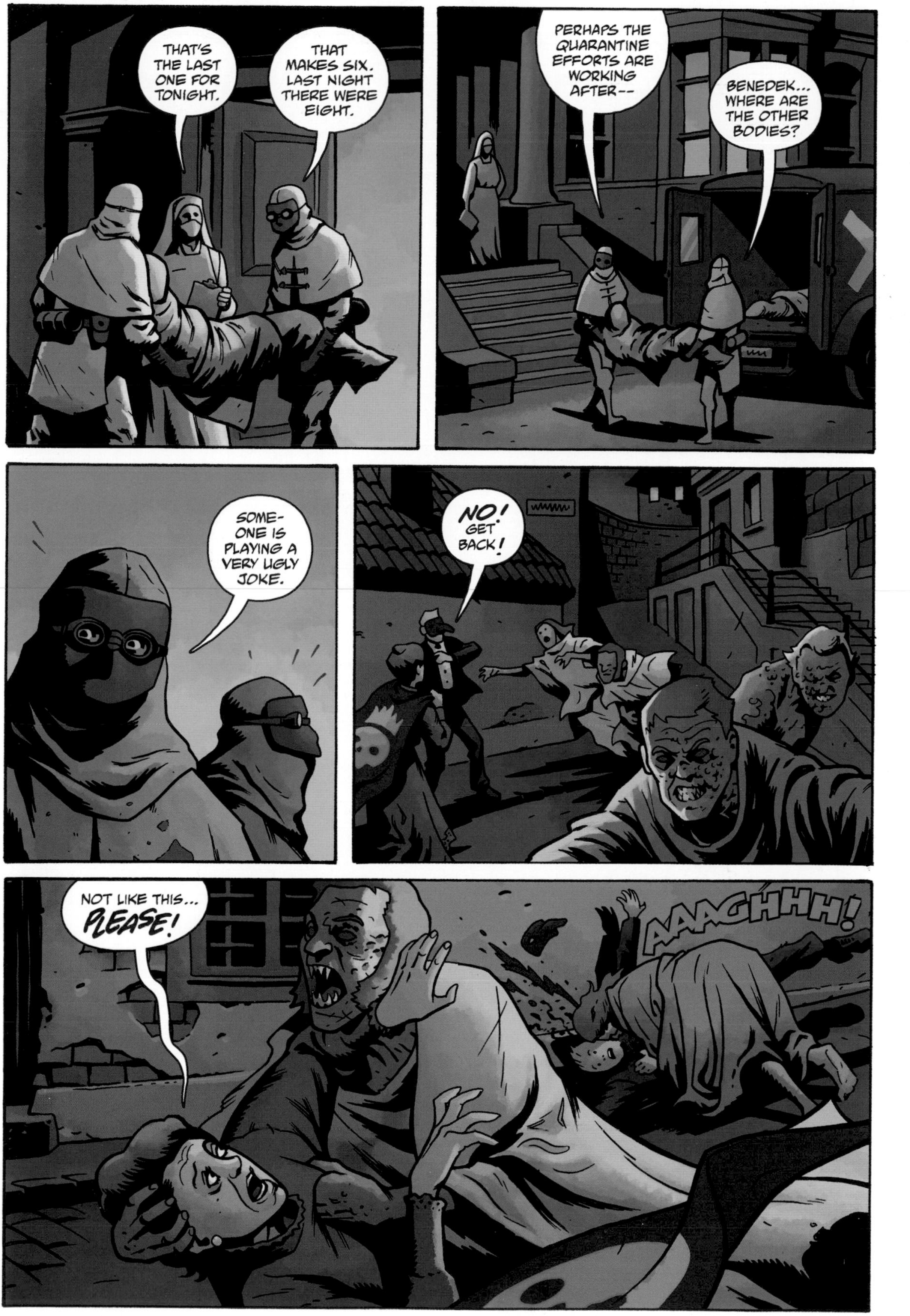
THAT'S THE LAST ONE FOR TONIGHT.
THAT MAKES SIX. LAST NIGHT THERE WERE EIGHT.
PERHAPS THE QUARANTINE EFFORTS ARE WORKING AFTER--
BENEDEK... WHERE ARE THE OTHER BODIES?
SOME-ONE IS PLAYING A VERY UGLY JOKE.
NO! GET BACK!
NOT LIKE THIS... PLEASE!
AAAGHHH!

WELCOME, MY FRIENDS.

I'M SO PLEASED THAT YOU COULD JOIN US.

NOW, FEED THE FLAMES.

REJOICE AND BE GLAD

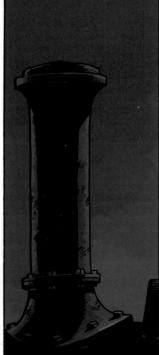

FEED YOUR FATHERS.

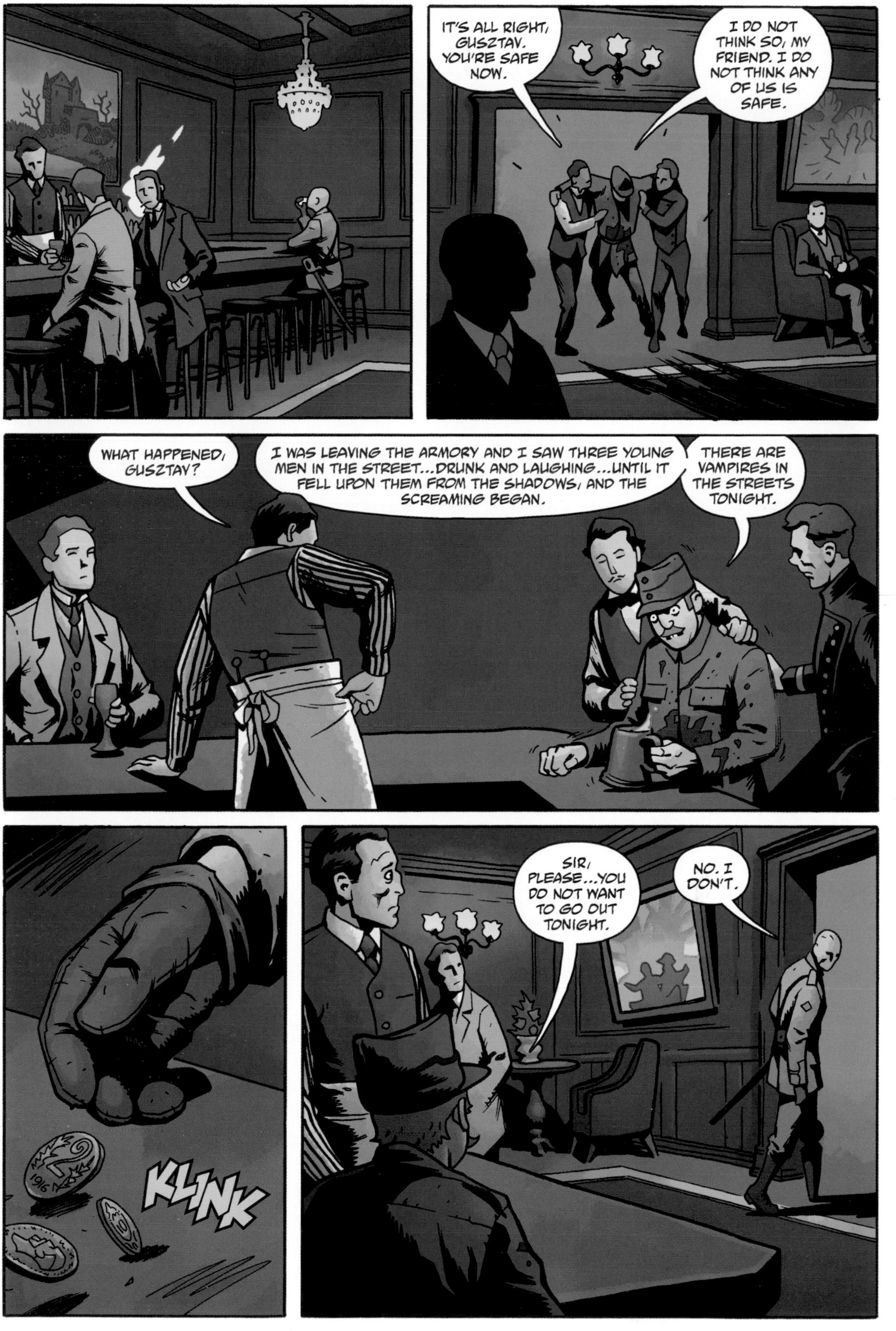
IT'S ALL RIGHT, GUSZTAV. YOU'RE SAFE NOW.
I DO NOT THINK SO, MY FRIEND. I DO NOT THINK ANY OF US IS SAFE.
WHAT HAPPENED, GUSZTAV?
I WAS LEAVING THE ARMORY AND I SAW THREE YOUNG MEN IN THE STREET...DRUNK AND LAUGHING...UNTIL IT FELL UPON THEM FROM THE SHADOWS, AND THE SCREAMING BEGAN.
THERE ARE VAMPIRES IN THE STREETS TONIGHT.
KLINK
SIR, PLEASE...YOU DO NOT WANT TO GO OUT TONIGHT.
NO. I DON'T.

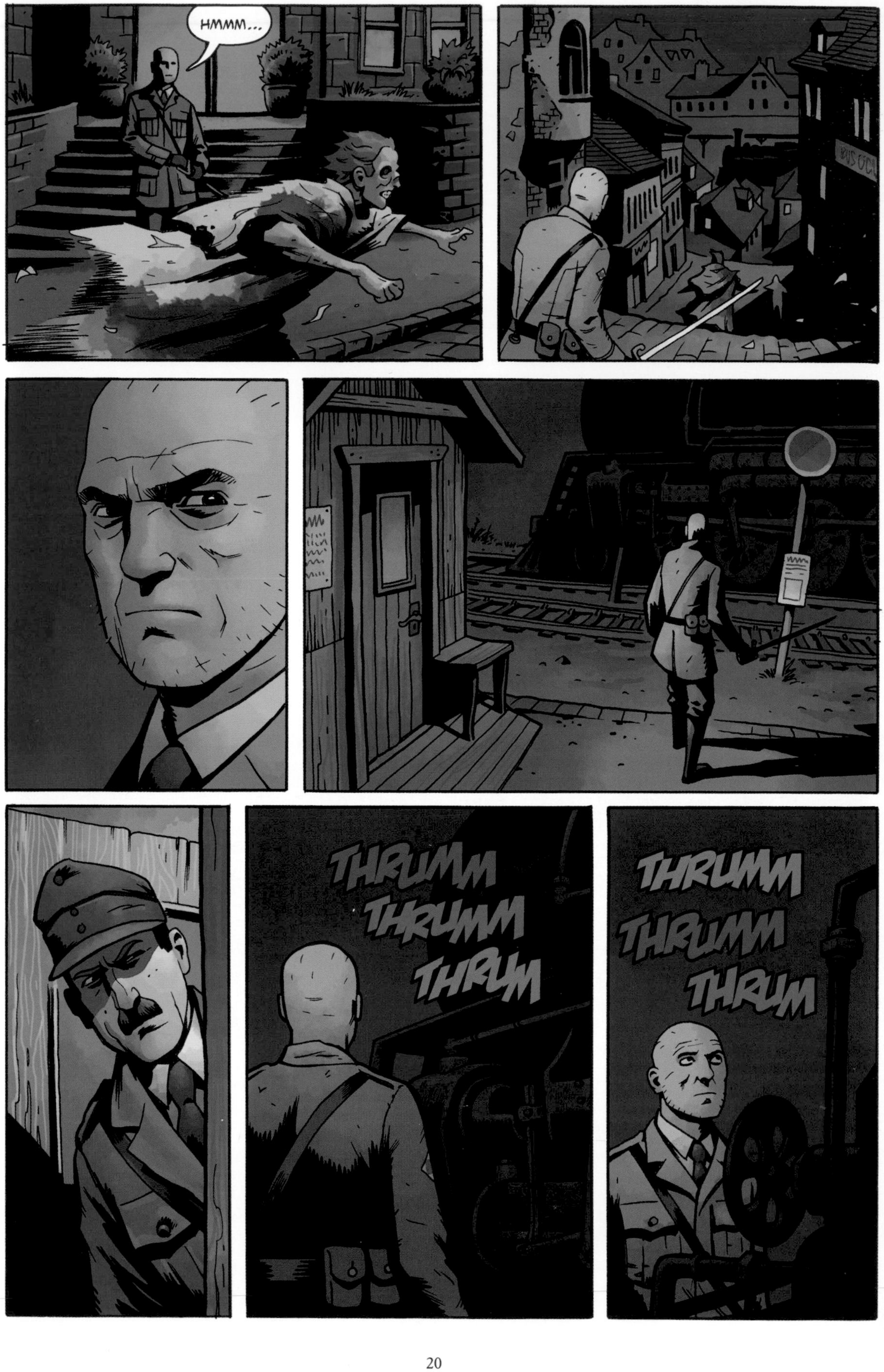
HMMM...
THRUMM
THRUMM
THRUM
THRUMM
THRUMM
THRUM

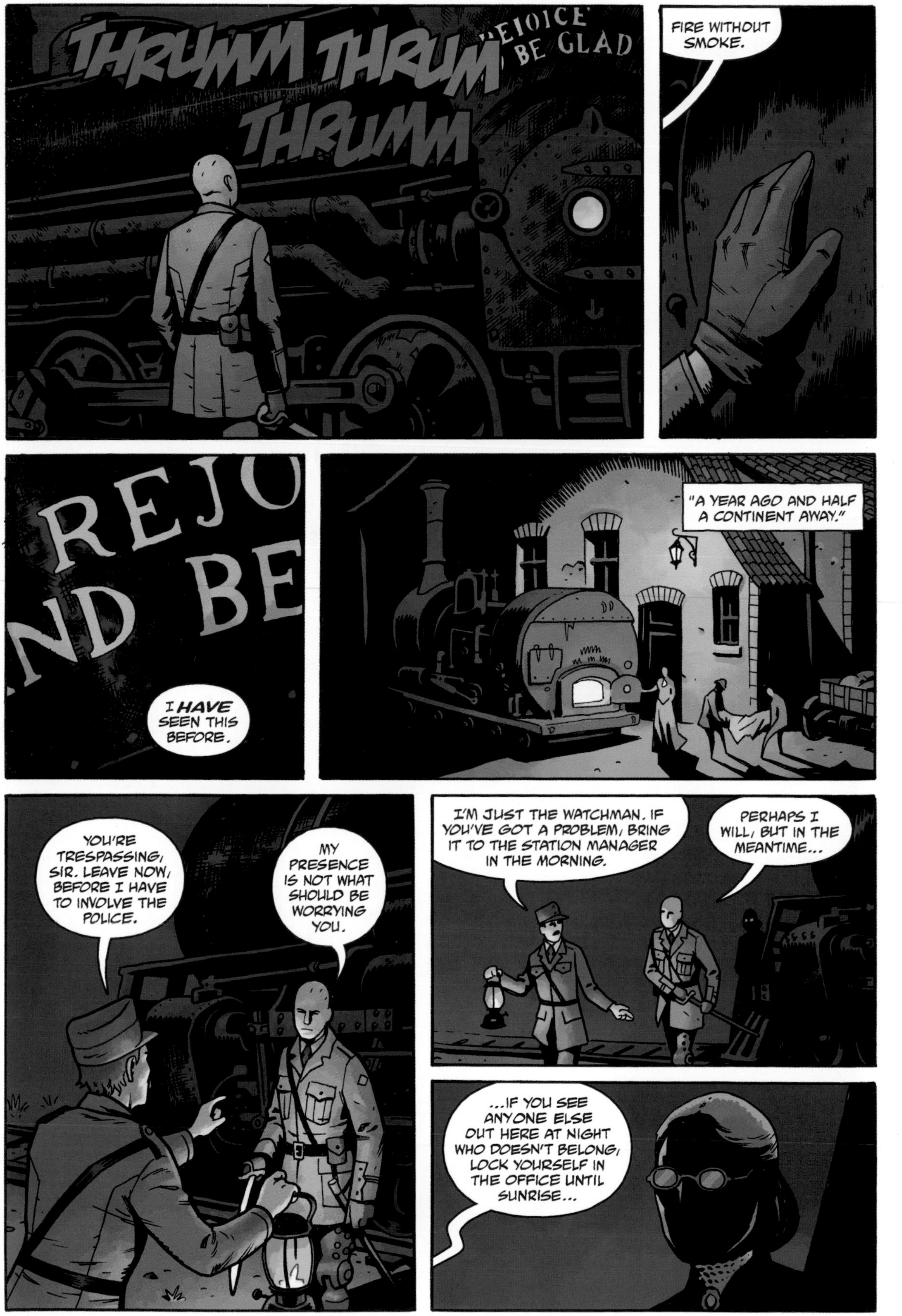

THRUMM THRUM THRUMM
REJOICE BE GLAD
FIRE WITHOUT SMOKE.
REJO ND BE
I HAVE SEEN THIS BEFORE.
"A YEAR AGO AND HALF A CONTINENT AWAY."
YOU'RE TRESPASSING, SIR. LEAVE NOW, BEFORE I HAVE TO INVOLVE THE POLICE.
MY PRESENCE IS NOT WHAT SHOULD BE WORRYING YOU.
I'M JUST THE WATCHMAN. IF YOU'VE GOT A PROBLEM, BRING IT TO THE STATION MANAGER IN THE MORNING.
PERHAPS I WILL, BUT IN THE MEANTIME...
...IF YOU SEE ANYONE ELSE OUT HERE AT NIGHT WHO DOESN'T BELONG, LOCK YOURSELF IN THE OFFICE UNTIL SUNRISE...

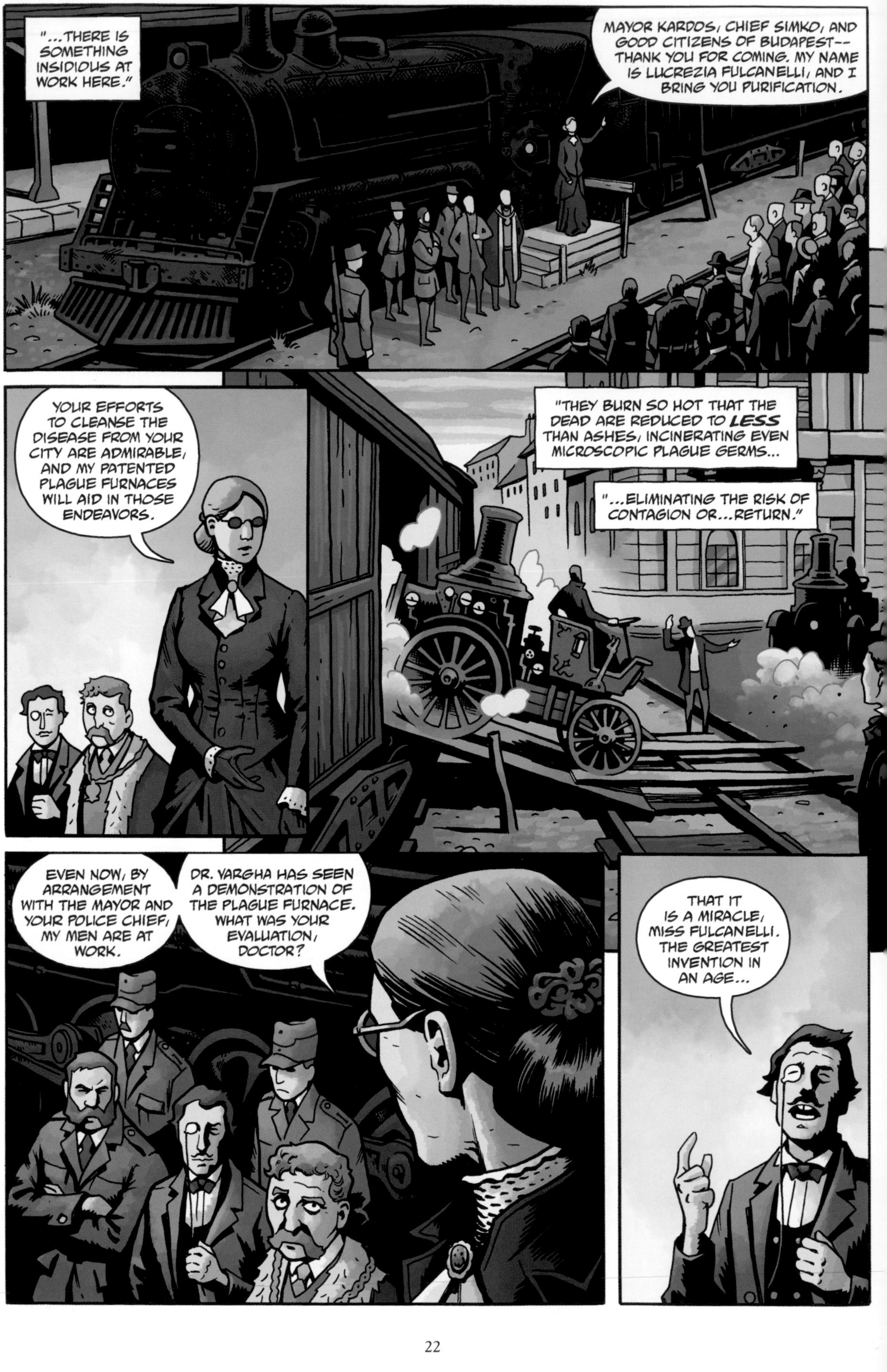
"...THERE IS SOMETHING INSIDIOUS AT WORK HERE."
MAYOR KARDOS, CHIEF SIMKO, AND GOOD CITIZENS OF BUDAPEST-- THANK YOU FOR COMING. MY NAME IS LUCREZIA FULCANELLI, AND I BRING YOU PURIFICATION.
YOUR EFFORTS TO CLEANSE THE DISEASE FROM YOUR CITY ARE ADMIRABLE, AND MY PATENTED PLAGUE FURNACES WILL AID IN THOSE ENDEAVORS.
"THEY BURN SO HOT THAT THE DEAD ARE REDUCED TO LESS THAN ASHES, INCINERATING EVEN MICROSCOPIC PLAGUE GERMS...
"...ELIMINATING THE RISK OF CONTAGION OR...RETURN."
EVEN NOW, BY ARRANGEMENT WITH THE MAYOR AND YOUR POLICE CHIEF, MY MEN ARE AT WORK.
DR. VARGHA HAS SEEN A DEMONSTRATION OF THE PLAGUE FURNACE. WHAT WAS YOUR EVALUATION, DOCTOR?
THAT IT IS A MIRACLE, MISS FULCANELLI. THE GREATEST INVENTION IN AN AGE...

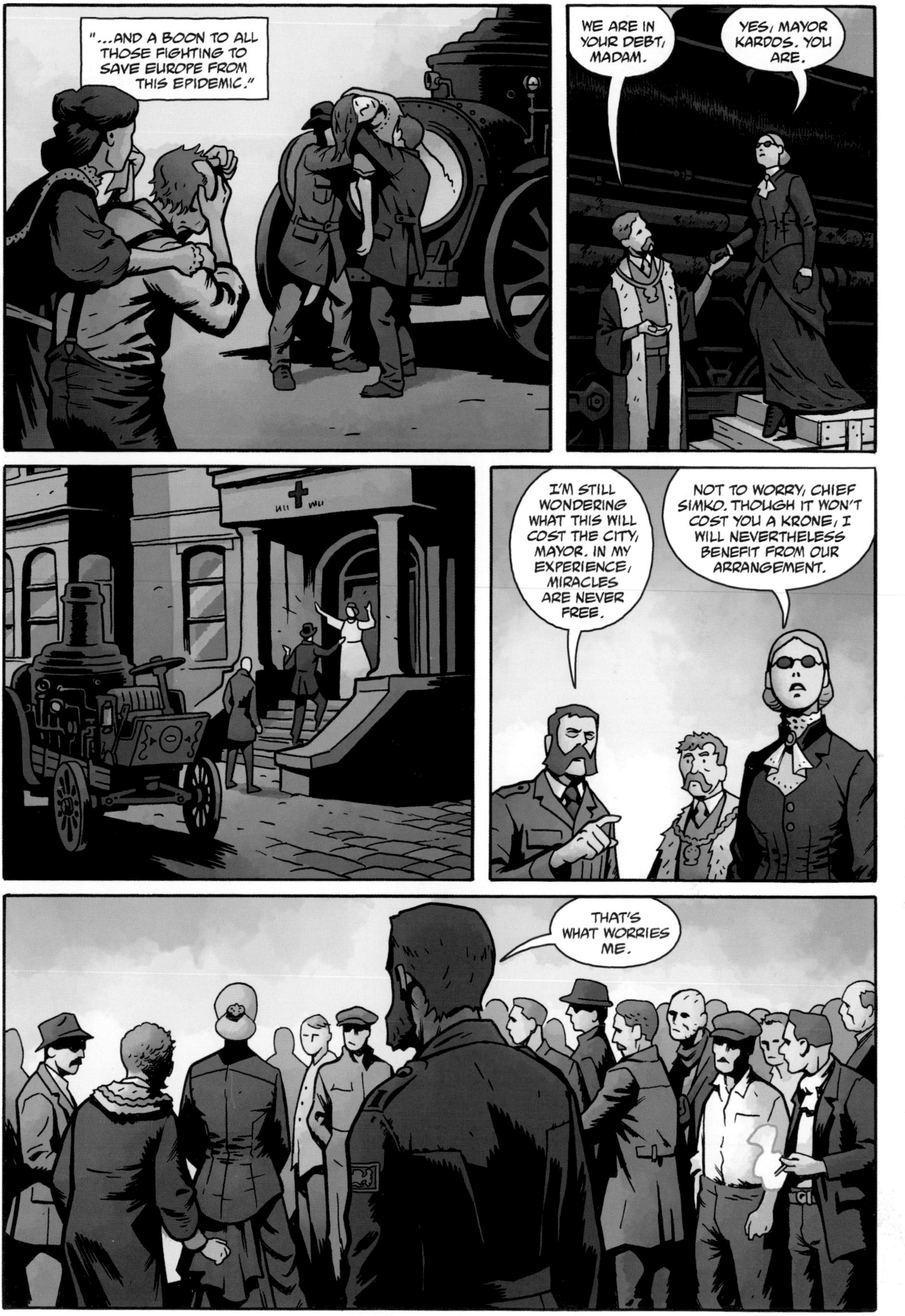
"...AND A BOON TO ALL THOSE FIGHTING TO SAVE EUROPE FROM THIS EPIDEMIC."
WE ARE IN YOUR DEBT, MADAM.
YES, MAYOR KARDOS. YOU ARE.
I'M STILL WONDERING WHAT THIS WILL COST THE CITY, MAYOR. IN MY EXPERIENCE, MIRACLES ARE NEVER FREE.
NOT TO WORRY, CHIEF SIMKO. THOUGH IT WON'T COST YOU A KRONE, I WILL NEVERTHELESS BENEFIT FROM OUR ARRANGEMENT.
THAT'S WHAT WORRIES ME.

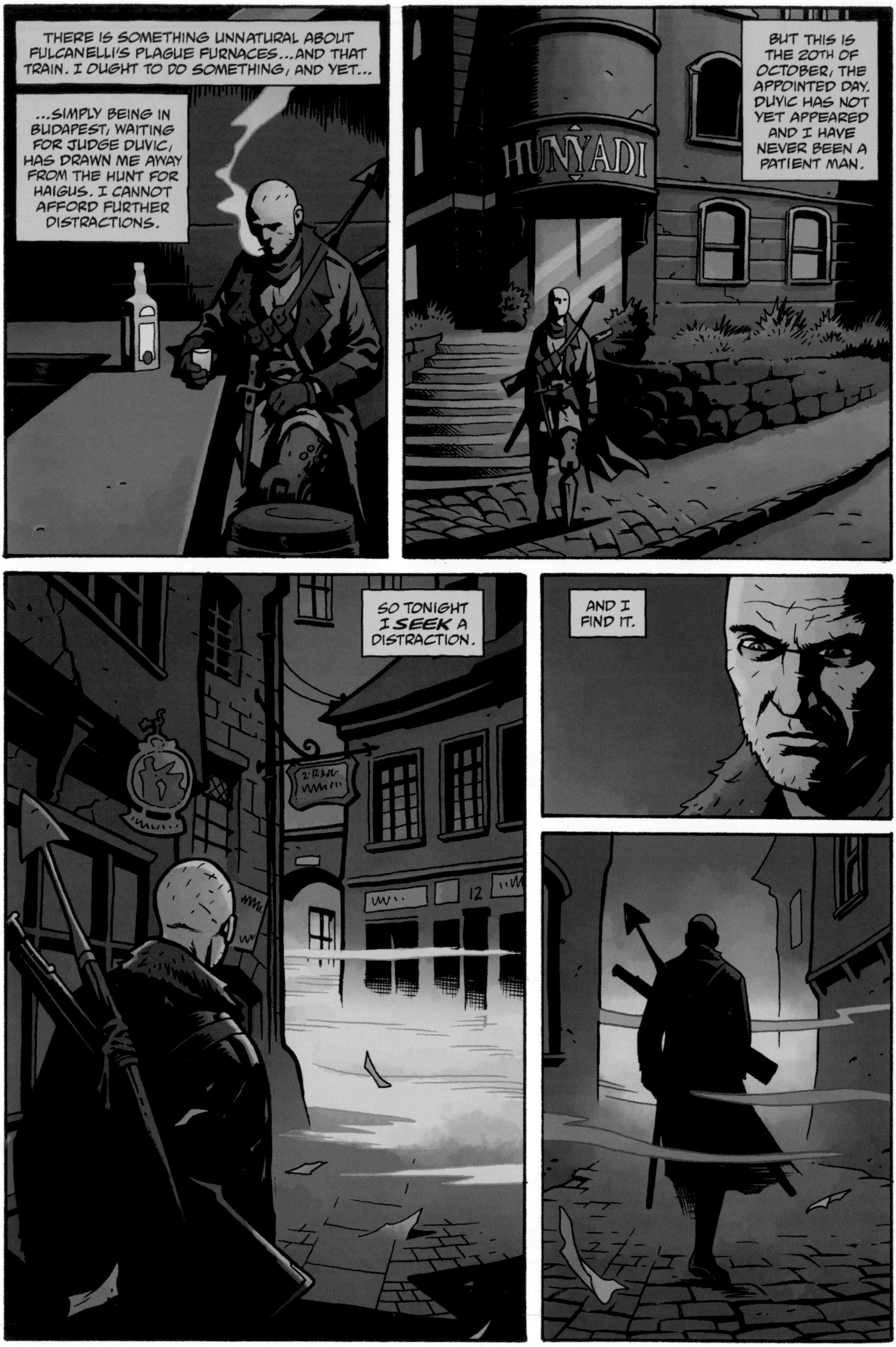
THERE IS SOMETHING UNNATURAL ABOUT FULCANELLI'S PLAGUE FURNACES...AND THAT TRAIN. I OUGHT TO DO SOMETHING, AND YET...
...SIMPLY BEING IN BUDAPEST, WAITING FOR JUDGE DUVIC, HAS DRAWN ME AWAY FROM THE HUNT FOR HAIGUS. I CANNOT AFFORD FURTHER DISTRACTIONS.
HUNYADI
BUT THIS IS THE 20TH OF OCTOBER, THE APPOINTED DAY. DUVIC HAS NOT YET APPEARED AND I HAVE NEVER BEEN A PATIENT MAN.
SO TONIGHT I *SEEK* A DISTRACTION.
AND I FIND IT.

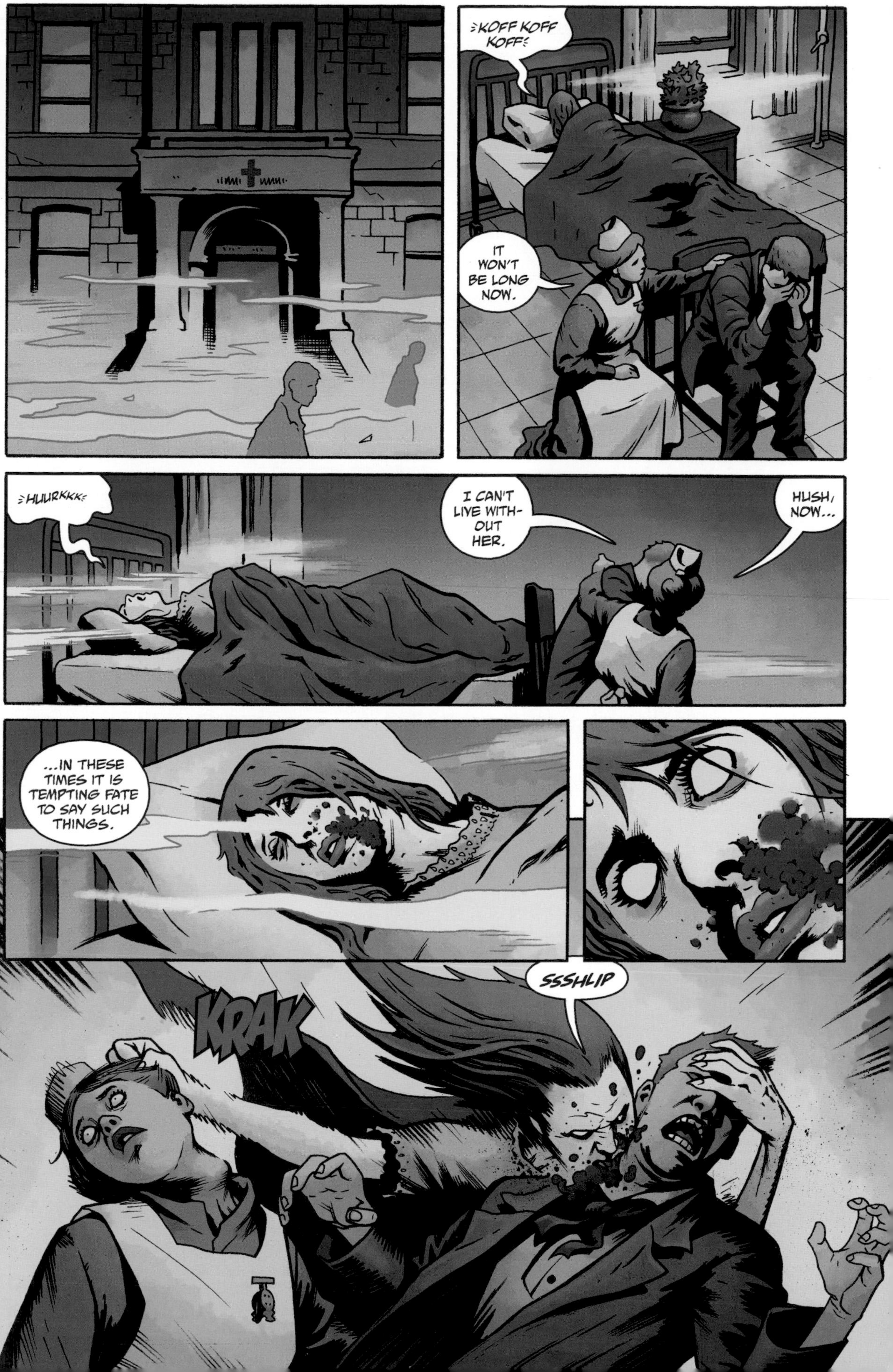

KOFF KOFF KOFF
IT WON'T BE LONG NOW.
HUURKKK
I CAN'T LIVE WITH-OUT HER.
HUSH, NOW...
...IN THESE TIMES IT IS TEMPTING FATE TO SAY SUCH THINGS.
SSSHLIP
KRAK

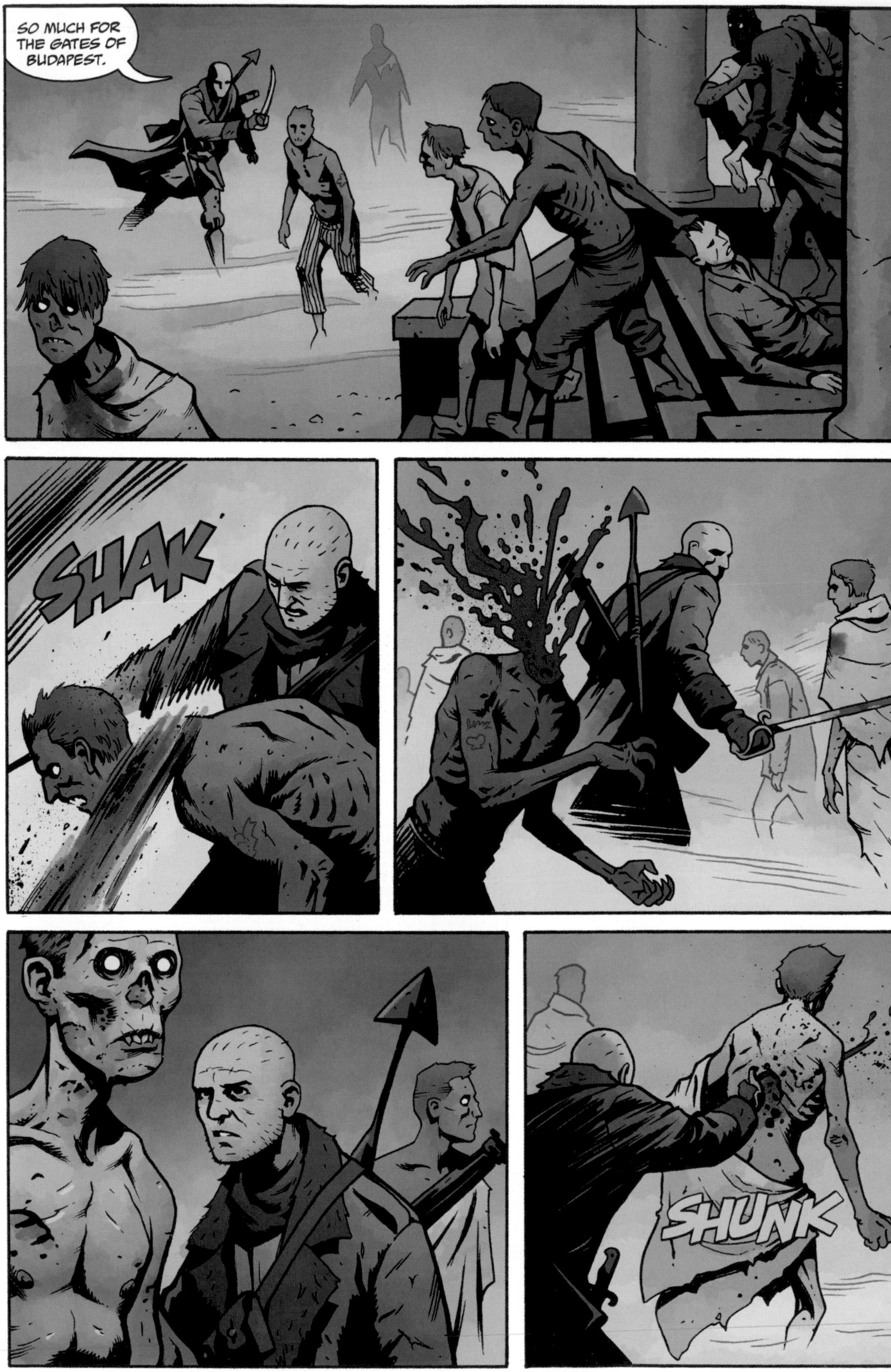
SO MUCH FOR THE GATES OF BUDAPEST.
SHAK
SHUNK

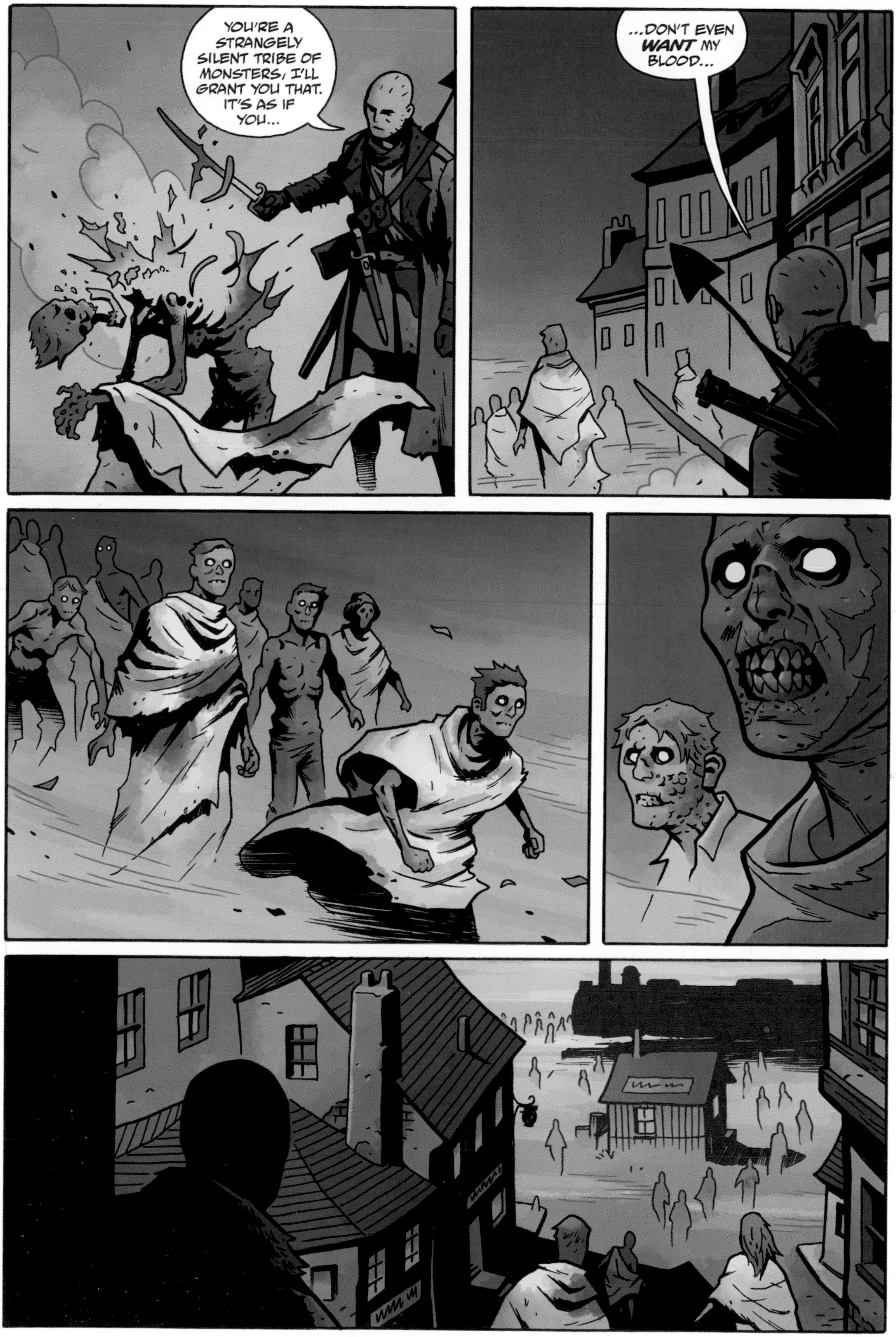
YOU'RE A STRANGELY SILENT TRIBE OF MONSTERS, I'LL GRANT YOU THAT. IT'S AS IF YOU...
...DON'T EVEN *WANT* MY BLOOD...

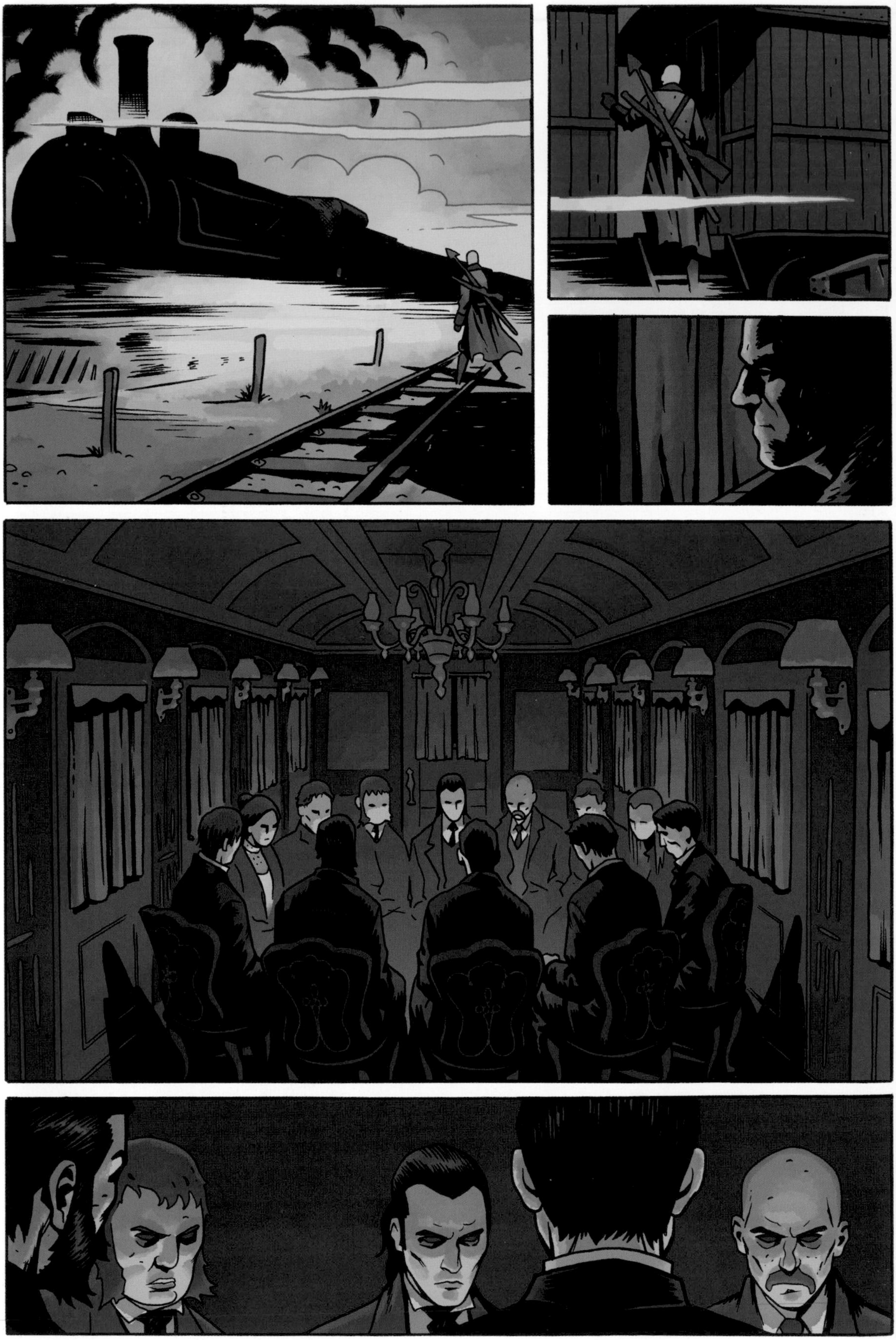

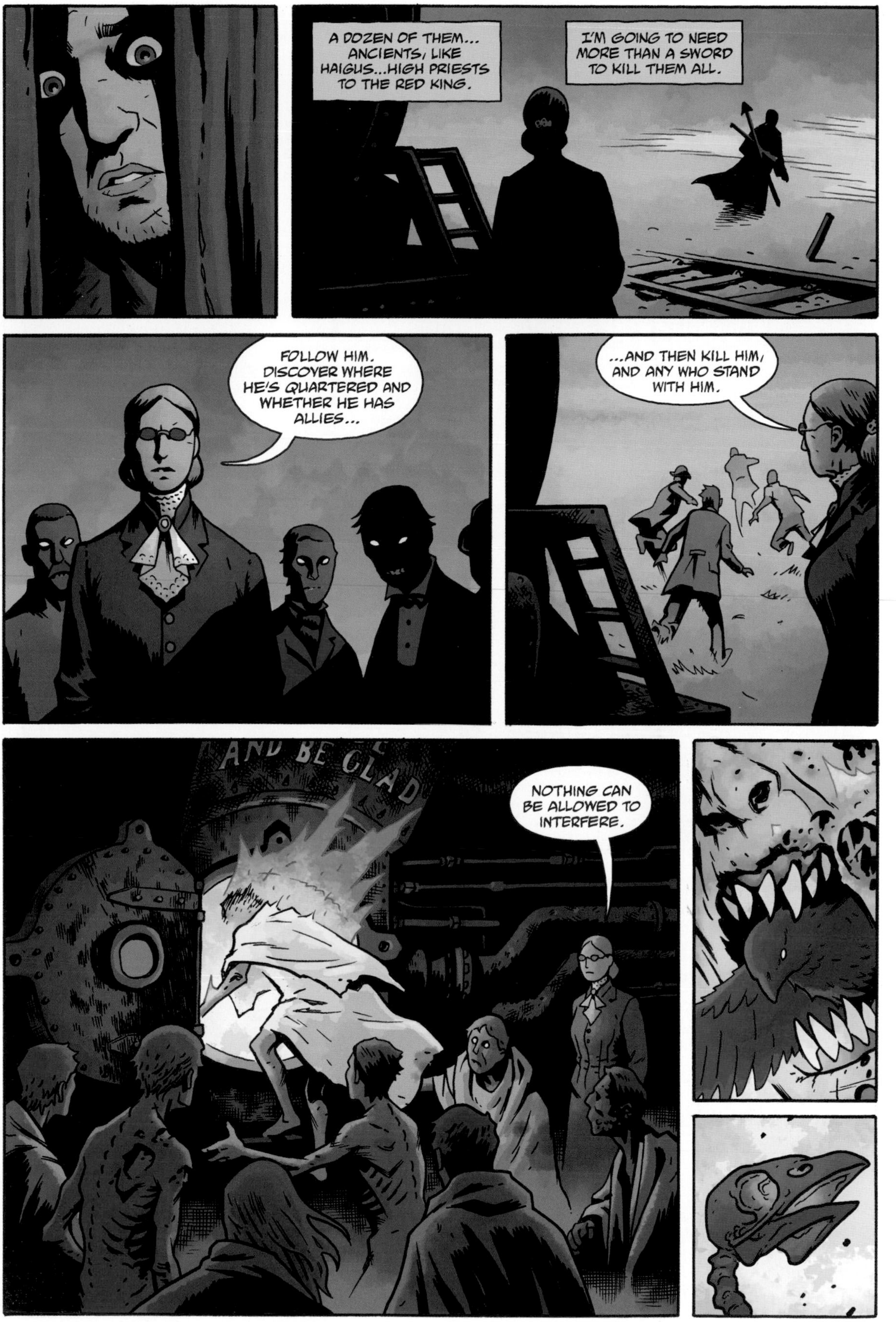
A DOZEN OF THEM... ANCIENTS, LIKE HAIGUS...HIGH PRIESTS TO THE RED KING.
I'M GOING TO NEED MORE THAN A SWORD TO KILL THEM ALL.
FOLLOW HIM. DISCOVER WHERE HE'S QUARTERED AND WHETHER HE HAS ALLIES...
...AND THEN KILL HIM, AND ANY WHO STAND WITH HIM.
AND BE GLAD
NOTHING CAN BE ALLOWED TO INTERFERE.

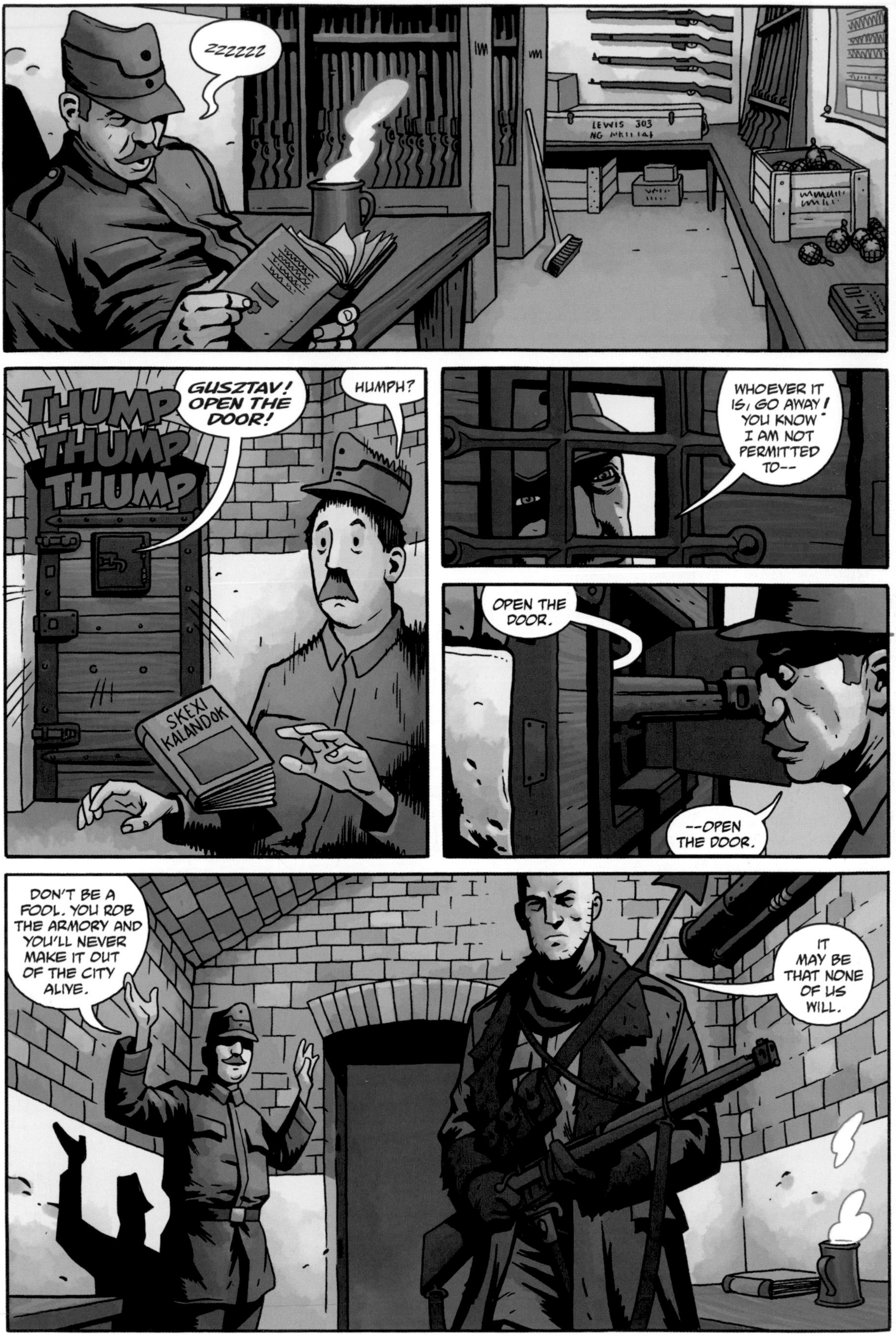
ZZZZZZ
LEWIS 303
THUMP THUMP THUMP
GUSZTAV! OPEN THE DOOR!
HUMPH?
SKEXI KALANDOK
WHOEVER IT IS, GO AWAY! YOU KNOW I AM NOT PERMITTED TO--
OPEN THE DOOR.
--OPEN THE DOOR.
DON'T BE A FOOL. YOU ROB THE ARMORY AND YOU'LL NEVER MAKE IT OUT OF THE CITY ALIVE.
IT MAY BE THAT NONE OF US WILL.

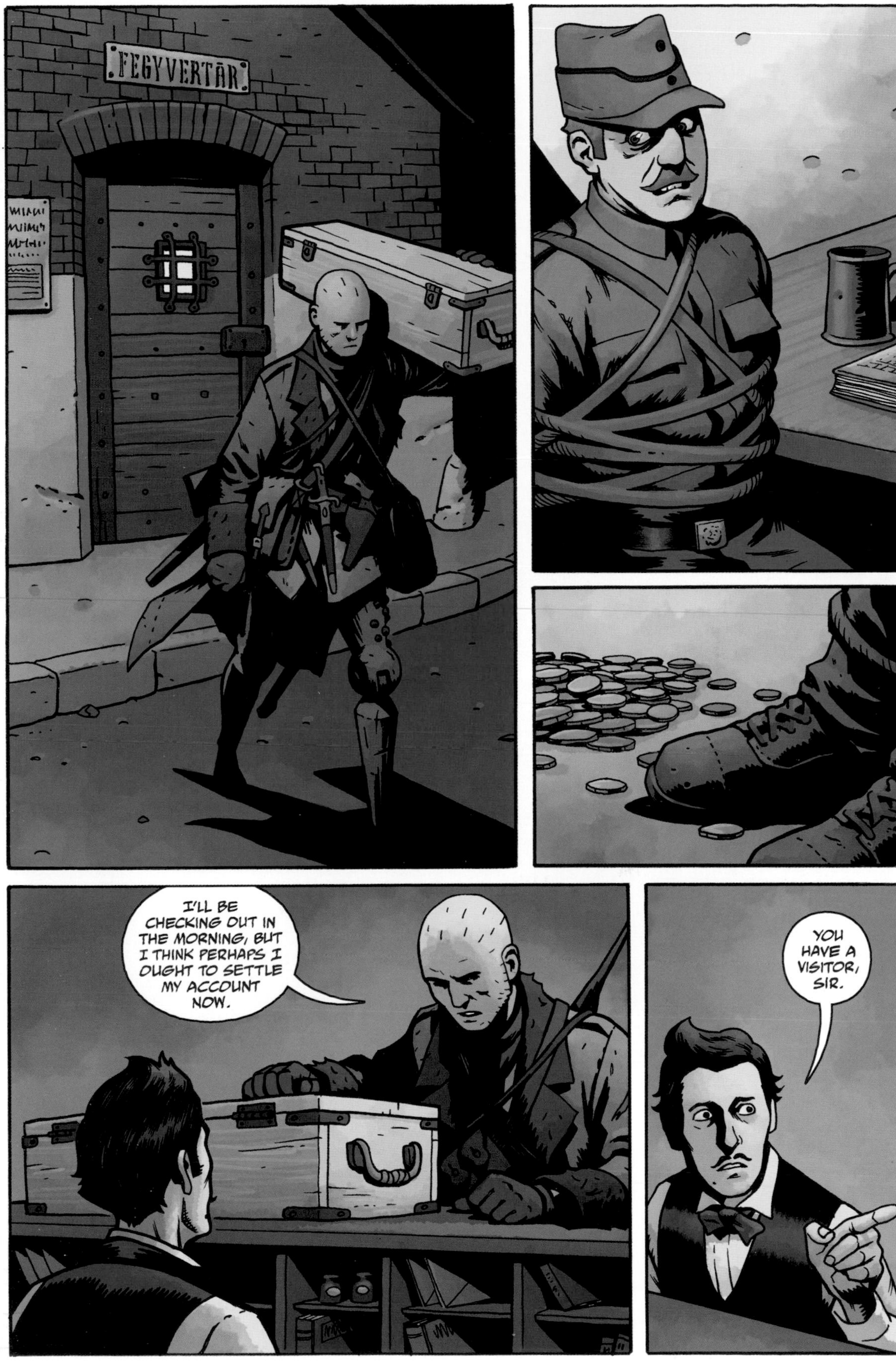
FEGYVERTÁR
I'LL BE CHECKING OUT IN THE MORNING, BUT I THINK PERHAPS I OUGHT TO SETTLE MY ACCOUNT NOW.
YOU HAVE A VISITOR, SIR.

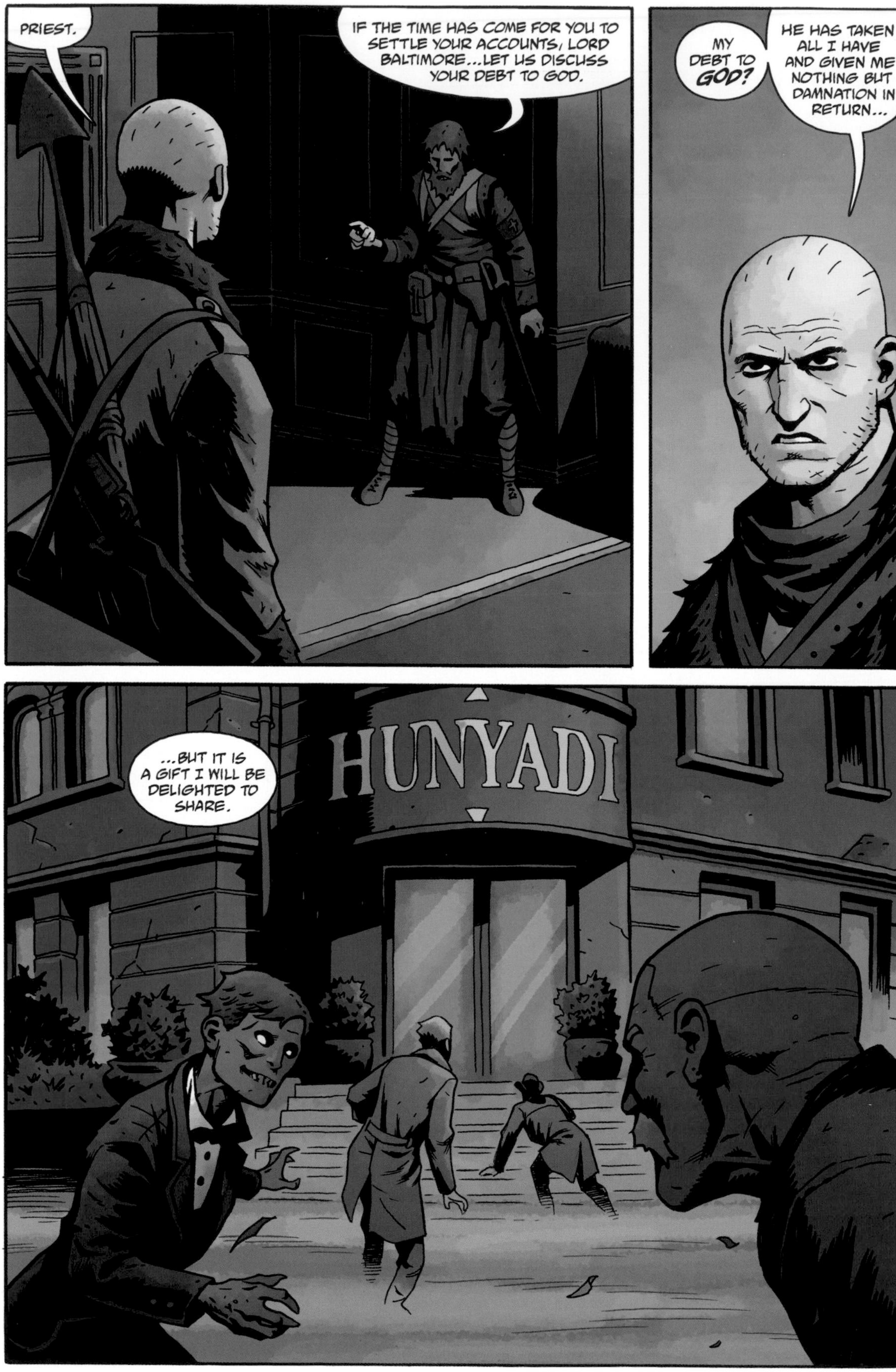
PRIEST.
IF THE TIME HAS COME FOR YOU TO SETTLE YOUR ACCOUNTS, LORD BALTIMORE...LET US DISCUSS YOUR DEBT TO GOD.
MY DEBT TO GOD?
HE HAS TAKEN ALL I HAVE AND GIVEN ME NOTHING BUT DAMNATION IN RETURN...
HUNYADI
...BUT IT IS A GIFT I WILL BE DELIGHTED TO SHARE.

THE INFERNAL TRAIN
Chapter Two

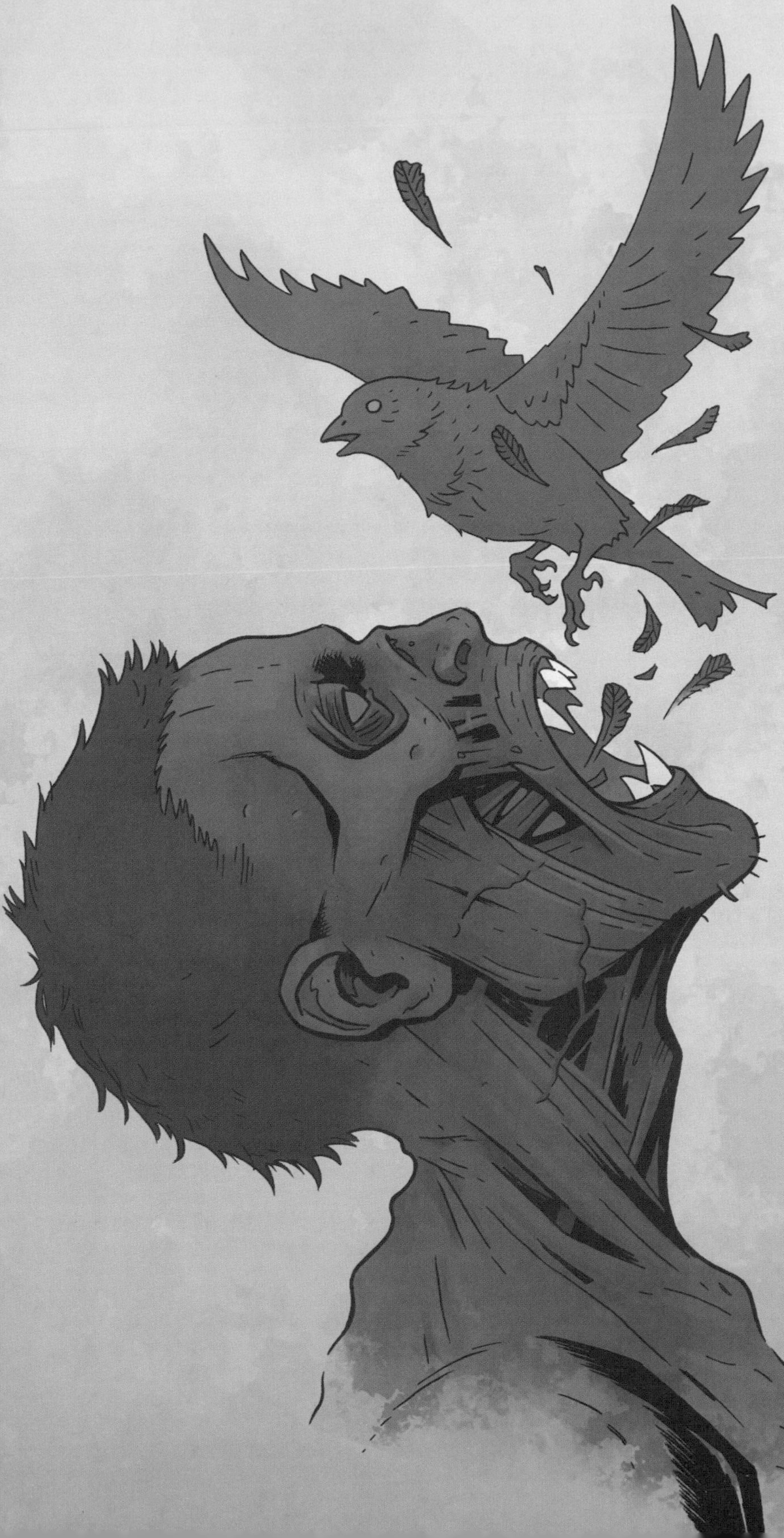

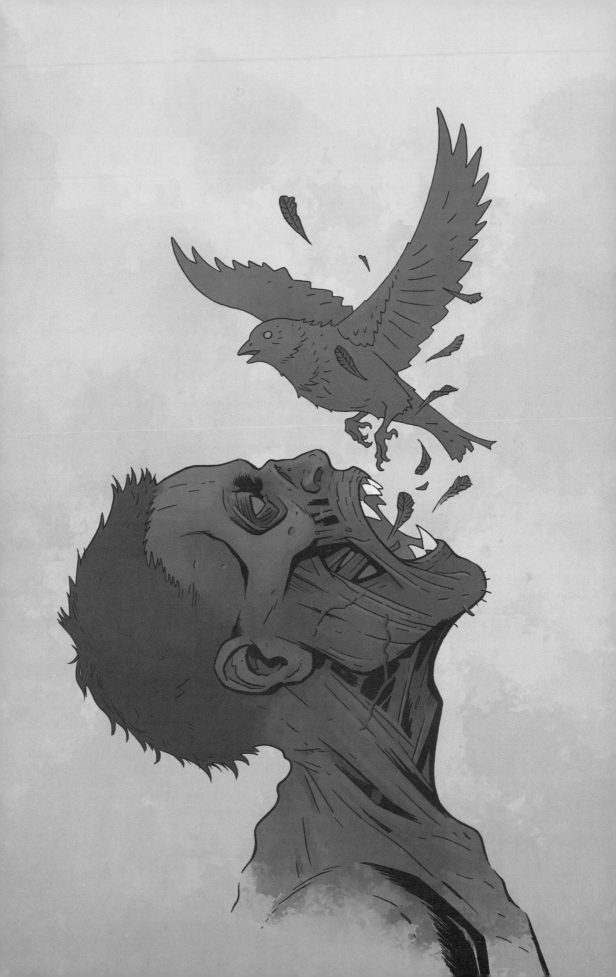

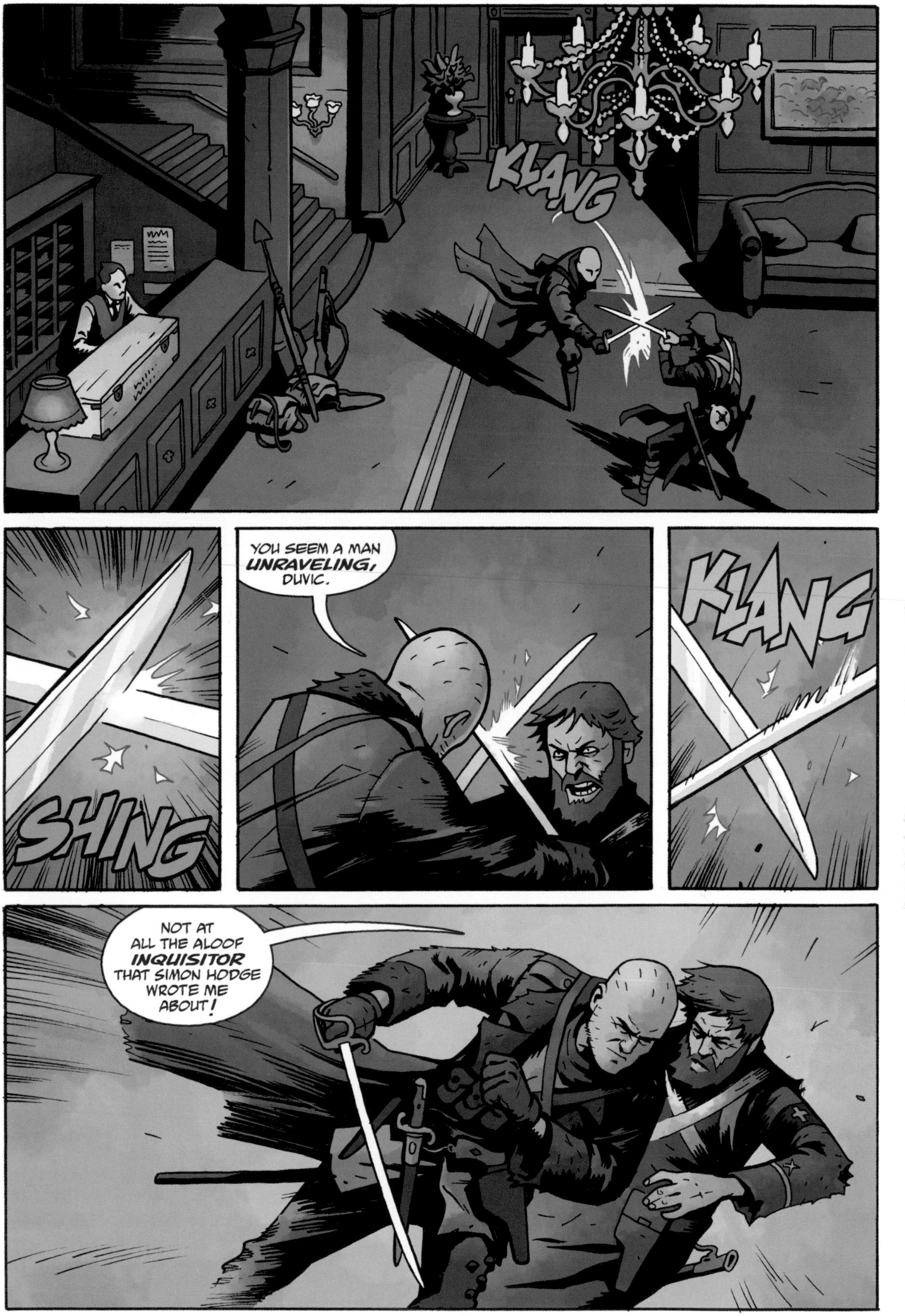
KLANG
SHING
YOU SEEM A MAN UNRAVELING, DUVIC.
KLANG
NOT AT ALL THE ALOOF INQUISITOR THAT SIMON HODGE WROTE ME ABOUT!

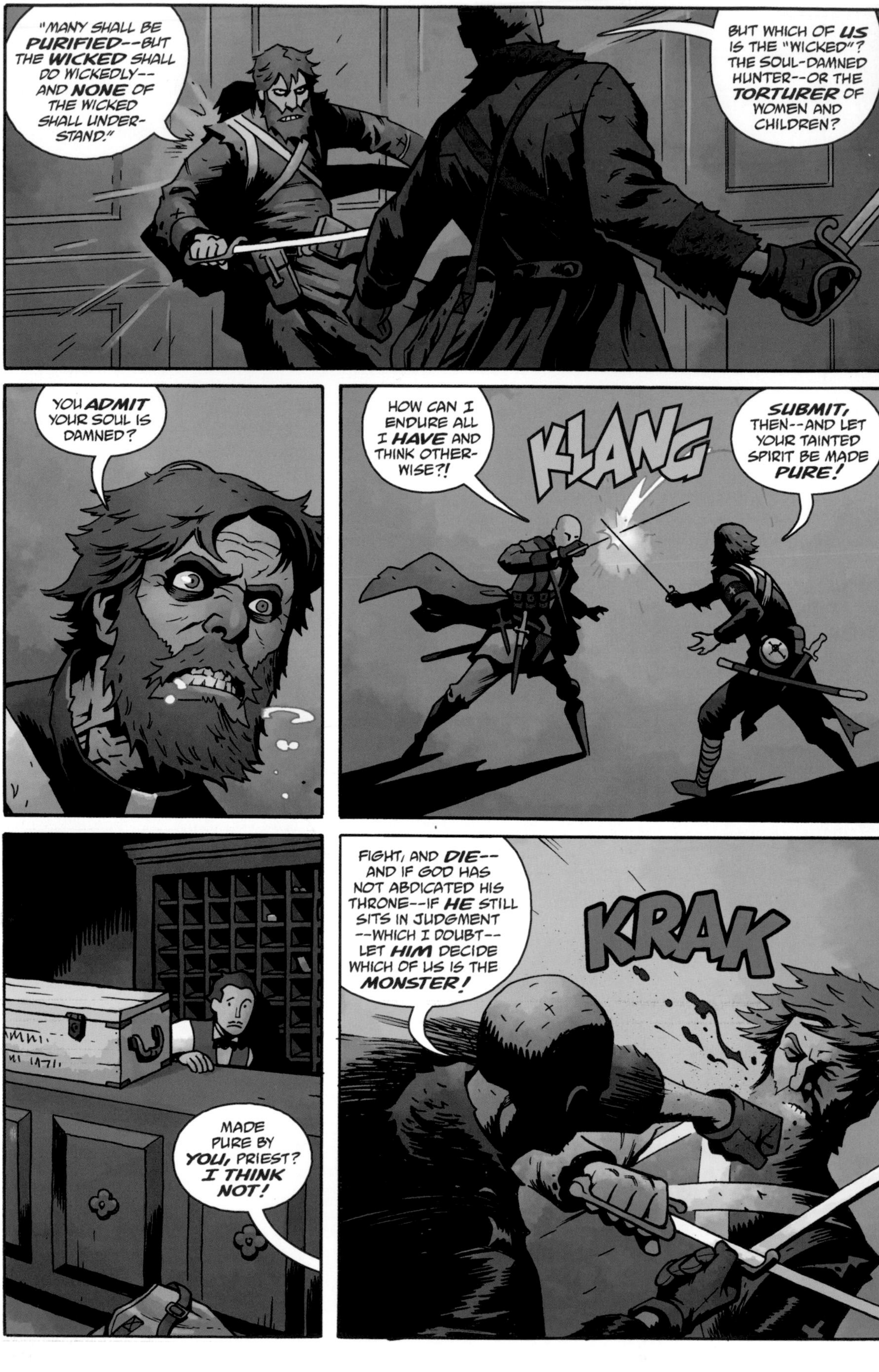
"MANY SHALL BE PURIFIED--BUT THE WICKED SHALL DO WICKEDLY-- AND NONE OF THE WICKED SHALL UNDERSTAND."
BUT WHICH OF US IS THE "WICKED"? THE SOUL-DAMNED HUNTER--OR THE TORTURER OF WOMEN AND CHILDREN?
YOU ADMIT YOUR SOUL IS DAMNED?
HOW CAN I ENDURE ALL I HAVE AND THINK OTHERWISE?!
KLANG
SUBMIT, THEN--AND LET YOUR TAINTED SPIRIT BE MADE PURE!
MADE PURE BY YOU, PRIEST? I THINK NOT!
FIGHT, AND DIE--AND IF GOD HAS NOT ABDICATED HIS THRONE--IF HE STILL SITS IN JUDGMENT --WHICH I DOUBT-- LET HIM DECIDE WHICH OF US IS THE MONSTER!
KRAK

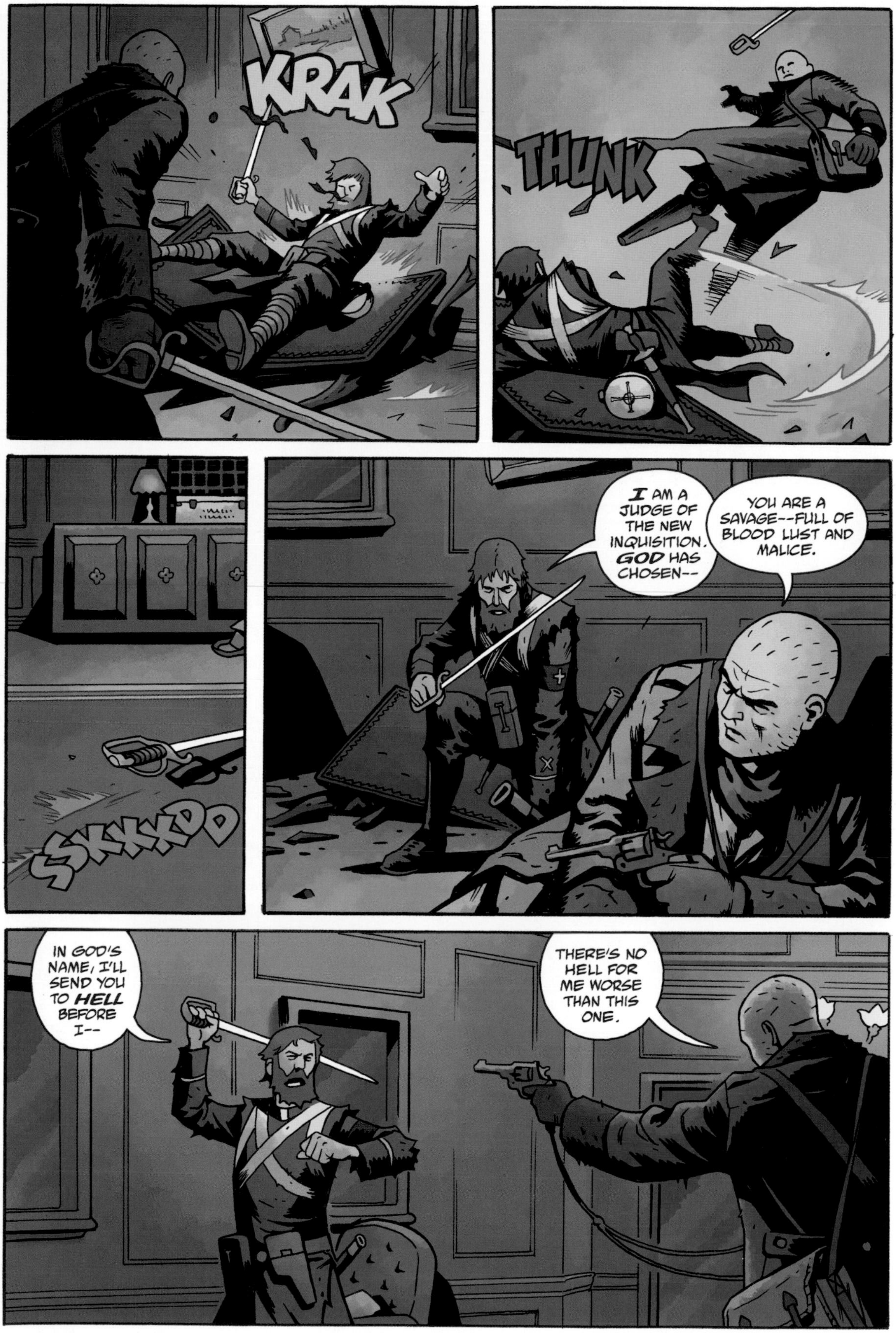
KRAK
THUNK
SSKKKDD
I AM A JUDGE OF THE NEW INQUISITION. GOD HAS CHOSEN--
YOU ARE A SAVAGE--FULL OF BLOOD LUST AND MALICE.
IN GOD'S NAME, I'LL SEND YOU TO HELL BEFORE I--
THERE'S NO HELL FOR ME WORSE THAN THIS ONE.

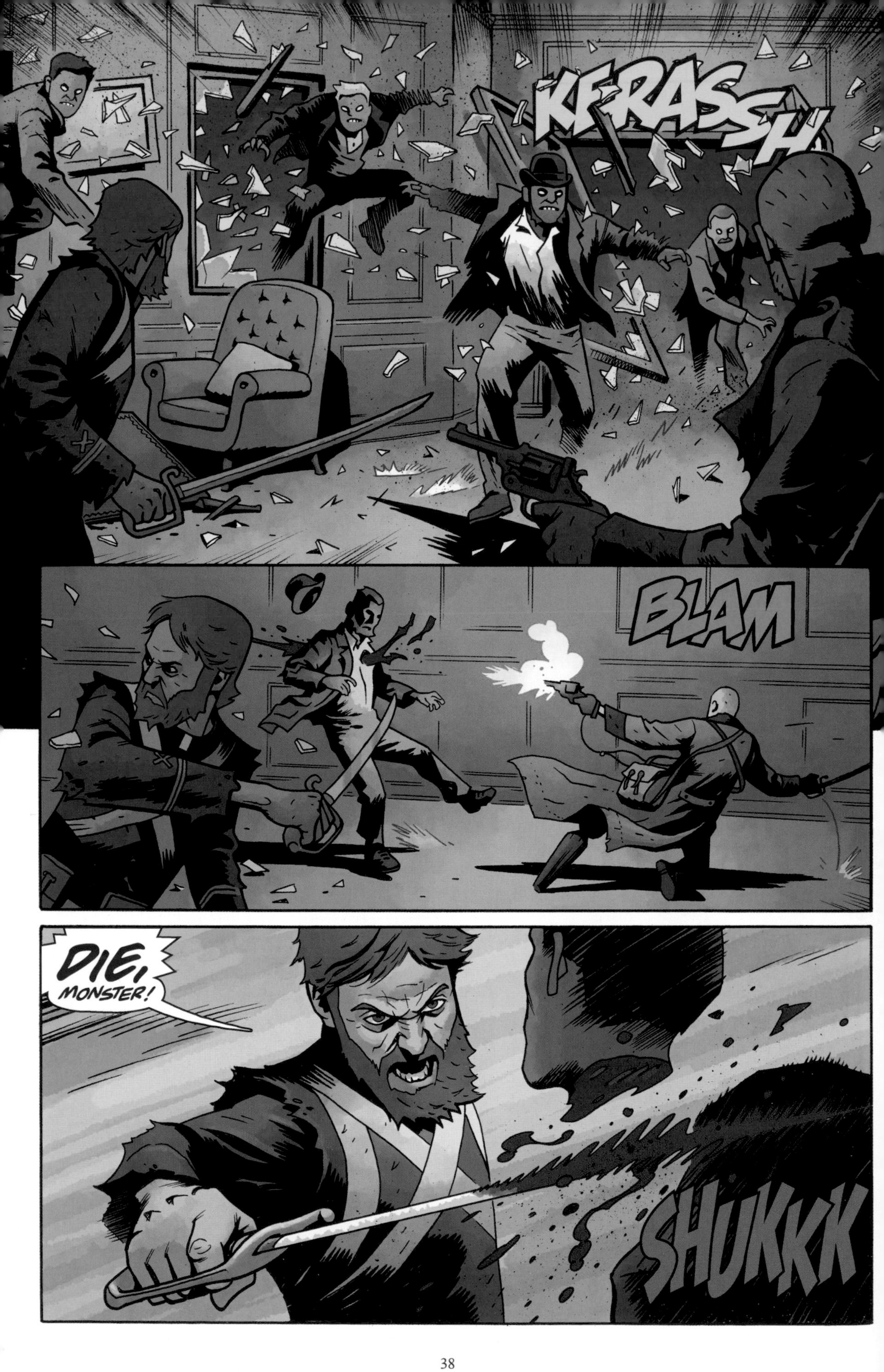
KERASSH
BLAM
DIE, MONSTER!
SHUKKK

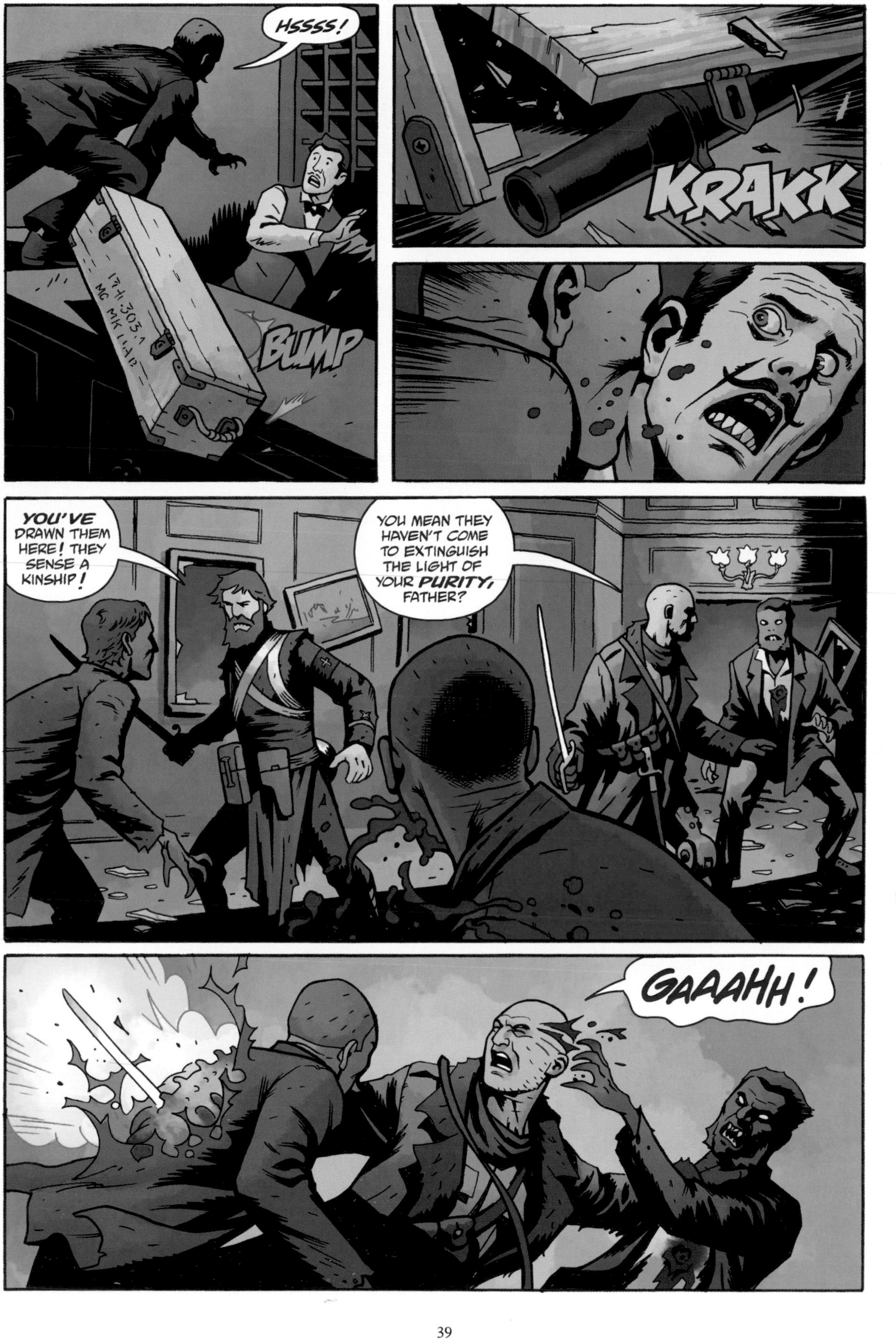
HSSSS!
BUMP
KRAKK
YOU'VE DRAWN THEM HERE! THEY SENSE A KINSHIP!
YOU MEAN THEY HAVEN'T COME TO EXTINGUISH THE LIGHT OF YOUR PURITY, FATHER?
GAAAHH!

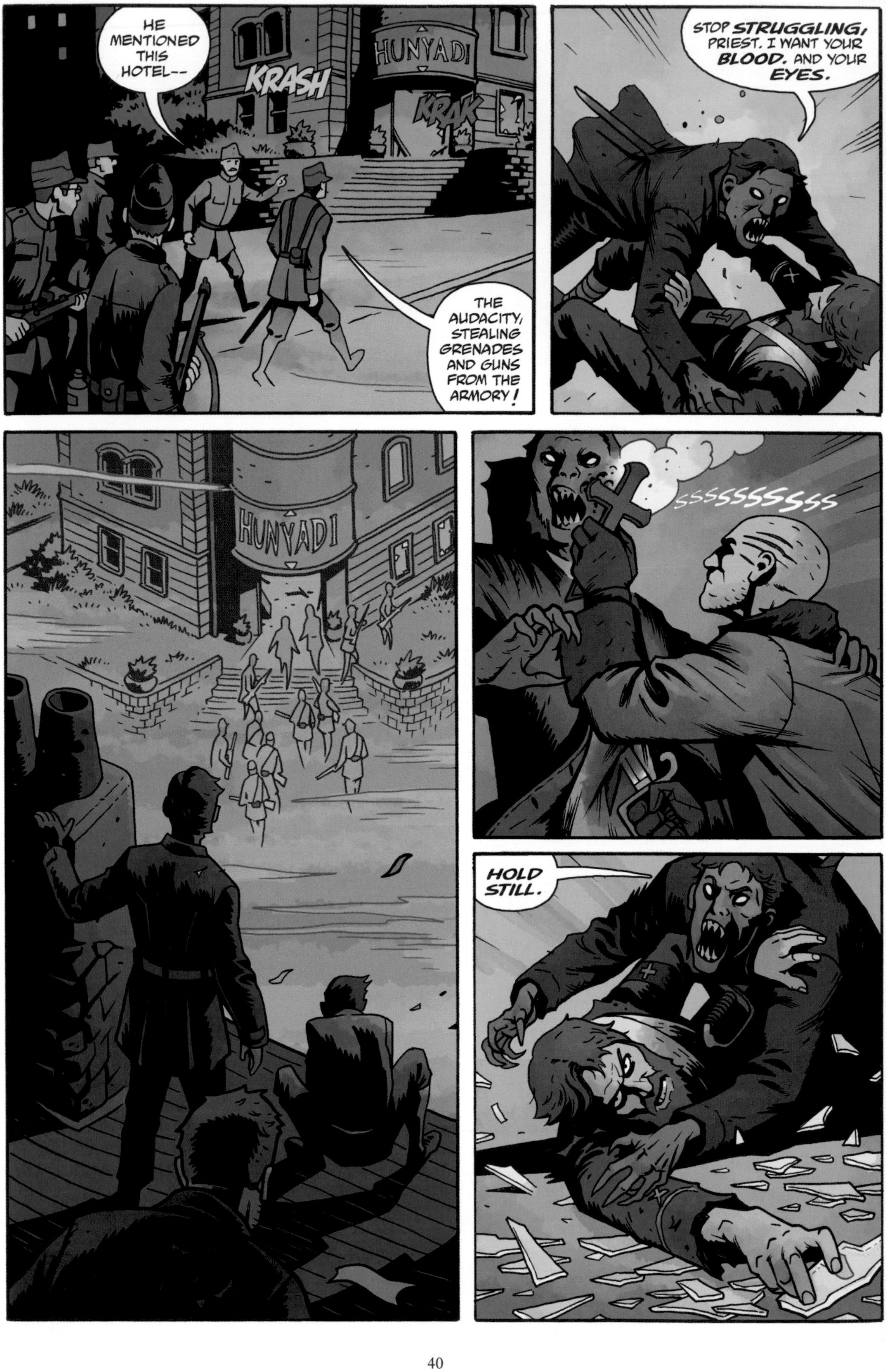

HE MENTIONED THIS HOTEL--
HUNYADI
KRASH
KRAK
THE AUDACITY, STEALING GRENADES AND GUNS FROM THE ARMORY!
STOP STRUGGLING, PRIEST. I WANT YOUR BLOOD. AND YOUR EYES.
HUNYADI
SSSSSSSSSSS
HOLD STILL.

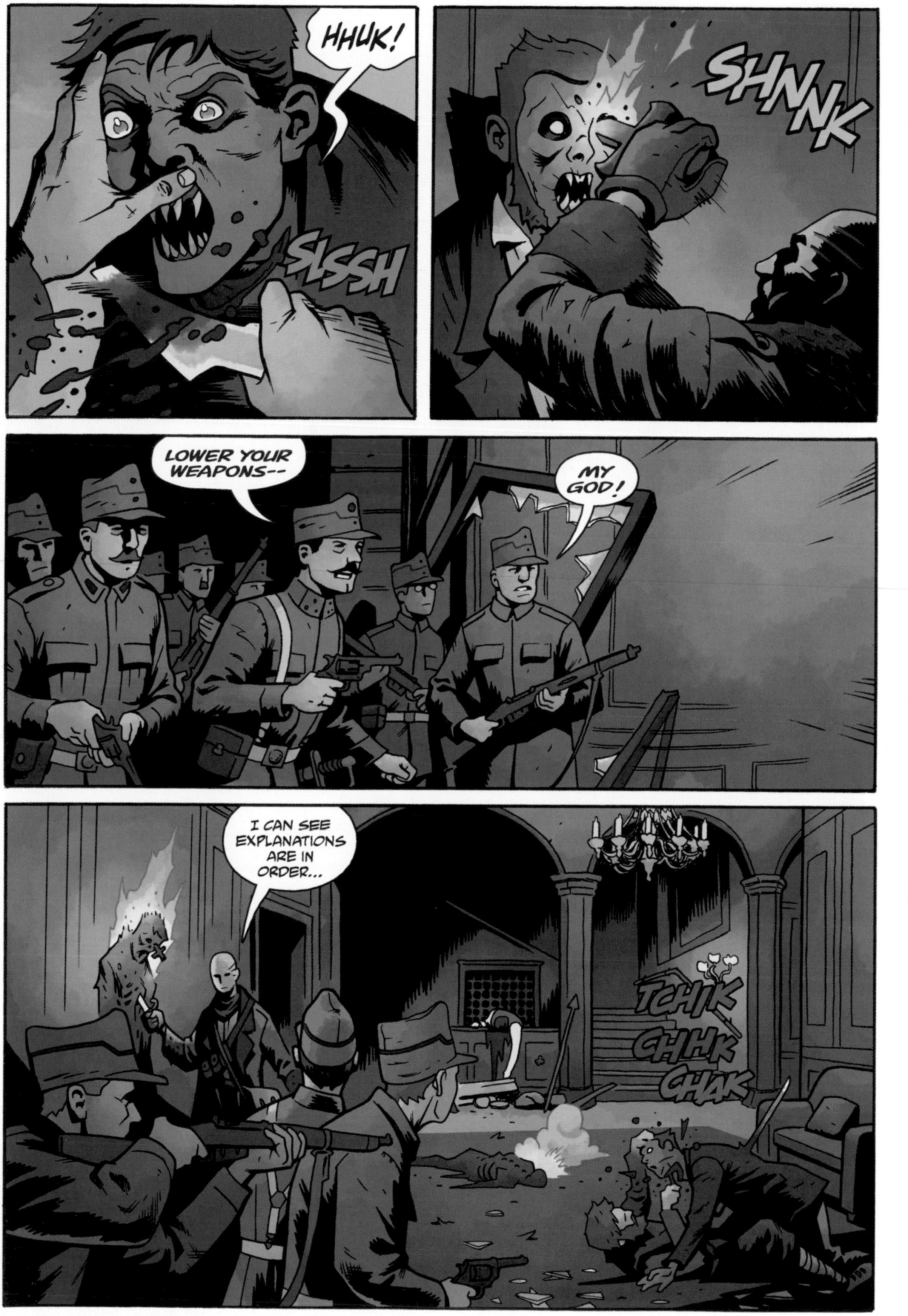
HHUK!
SISSH
SHNNK
LOWER YOUR WEAPONS--
MY GOD!
I CAN SEE EXPLANATIONS ARE IN ORDER...
TCHIK
CHHK
CHAK

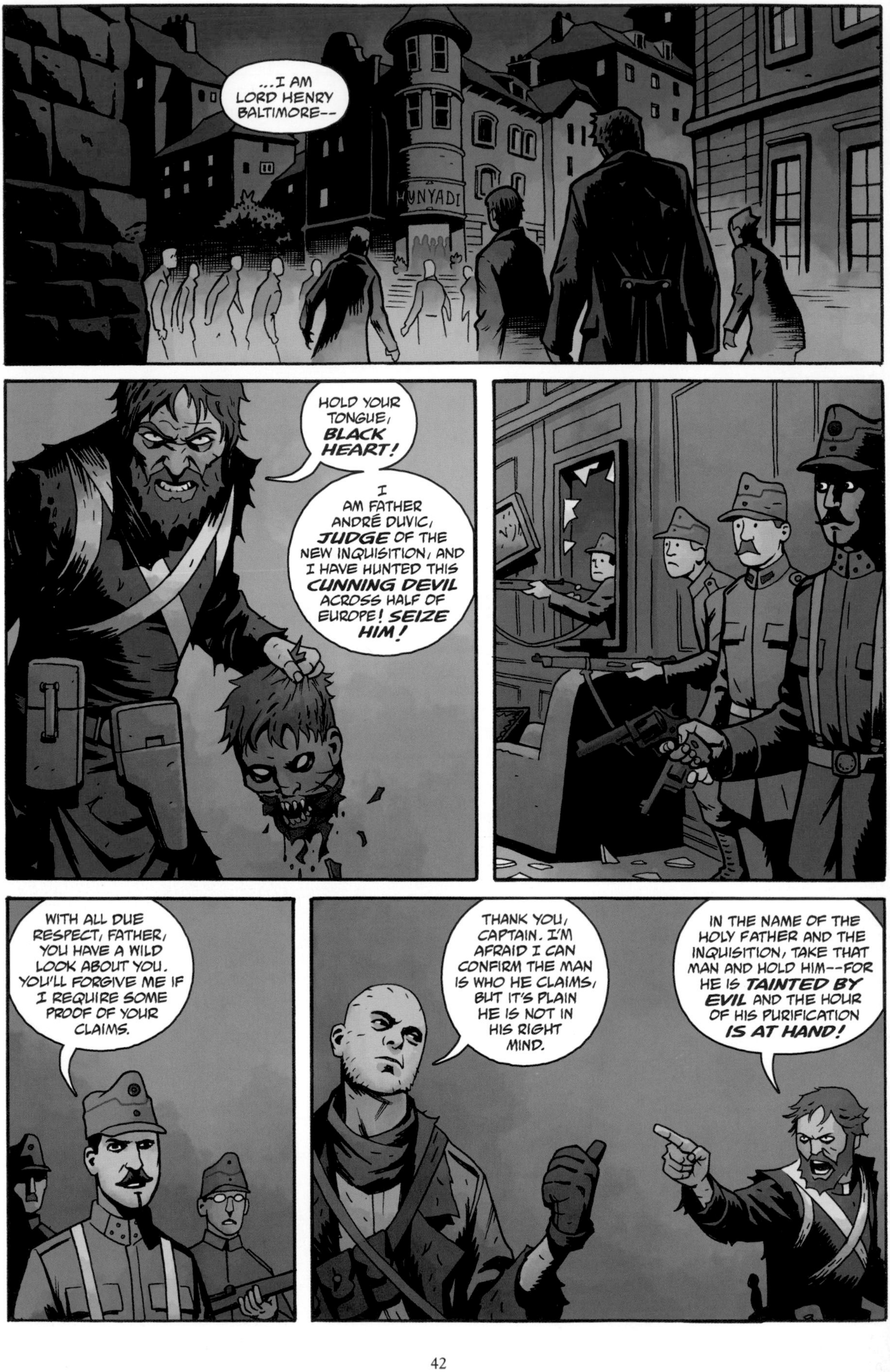
...I AM LORD HENRY BALTIMORE--
HUNYADI
HOLD YOUR TONGUE, BLACK HEART!
I AM FATHER ANDRÉ DUVIC, JUDGE OF THE NEW INQUISITION, AND I HAVE HUNTED THIS CUNNING DEVIL ACROSS HALF OF EUROPE! SEIZE HIM!
WITH ALL DUE RESPECT, FATHER, YOU HAVE A WILD LOOK ABOUT YOU. YOU'LL FORGIVE ME IF I REQUIRE SOME PROOF OF YOUR CLAIMS.
THANK YOU, CAPTAIN. I'M AFRAID I CAN CONFIRM THE MAN IS WHO HE CLAIMS, BUT IT'S PLAIN HE IS NOT IN HIS RIGHT MIND.
IN THE NAME OF THE HOLY FATHER AND THE INQUISITION, TAKE THAT MAN AND HOLD HIM--FOR HE IS TAINTED BY EVIL AND THE HOUR OF HIS PURIFICATION IS AT HAND!

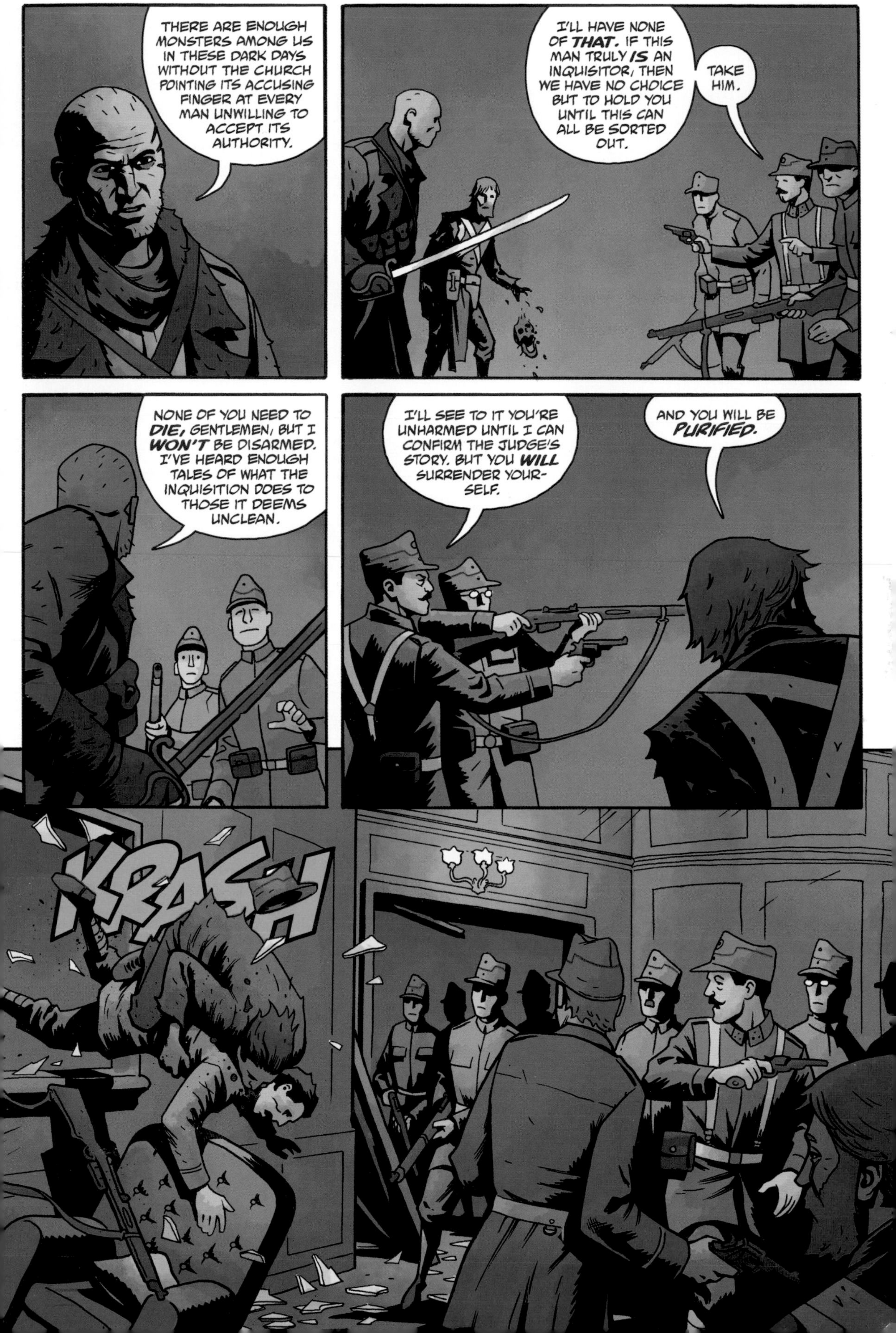
THERE ARE ENOUGH MONSTERS AMONG US IN THESE DARK DAYS WITHOUT THE CHURCH POINTING ITS ACCUSING FINGER AT EVERY MAN UNWILLING TO ACCEPT ITS AUTHORITY.
I'LL HAVE NONE OF THAT. IF THIS MAN TRULY IS AN INQUISITOR, THEN WE HAVE NO CHOICE BUT TO HOLD YOU UNTIL THIS CAN ALL BE SORTED OUT.
TAKE HIM.
NONE OF YOU NEED TO DIE, GENTLEMEN, BUT I WON'T BE DISARMED. I'VE HEARD ENOUGH TALES OF WHAT THE INQUISITION DOES TO THOSE IT DEEMS UNCLEAN.
I'LL SEE TO IT YOU'RE UNHARMED UNTIL I CAN CONFIRM THE JUDGE'S STORY. BUT YOU WILL SURRENDER YOURSELF.
AND YOU WILL BE PURIFIED.
KRASH

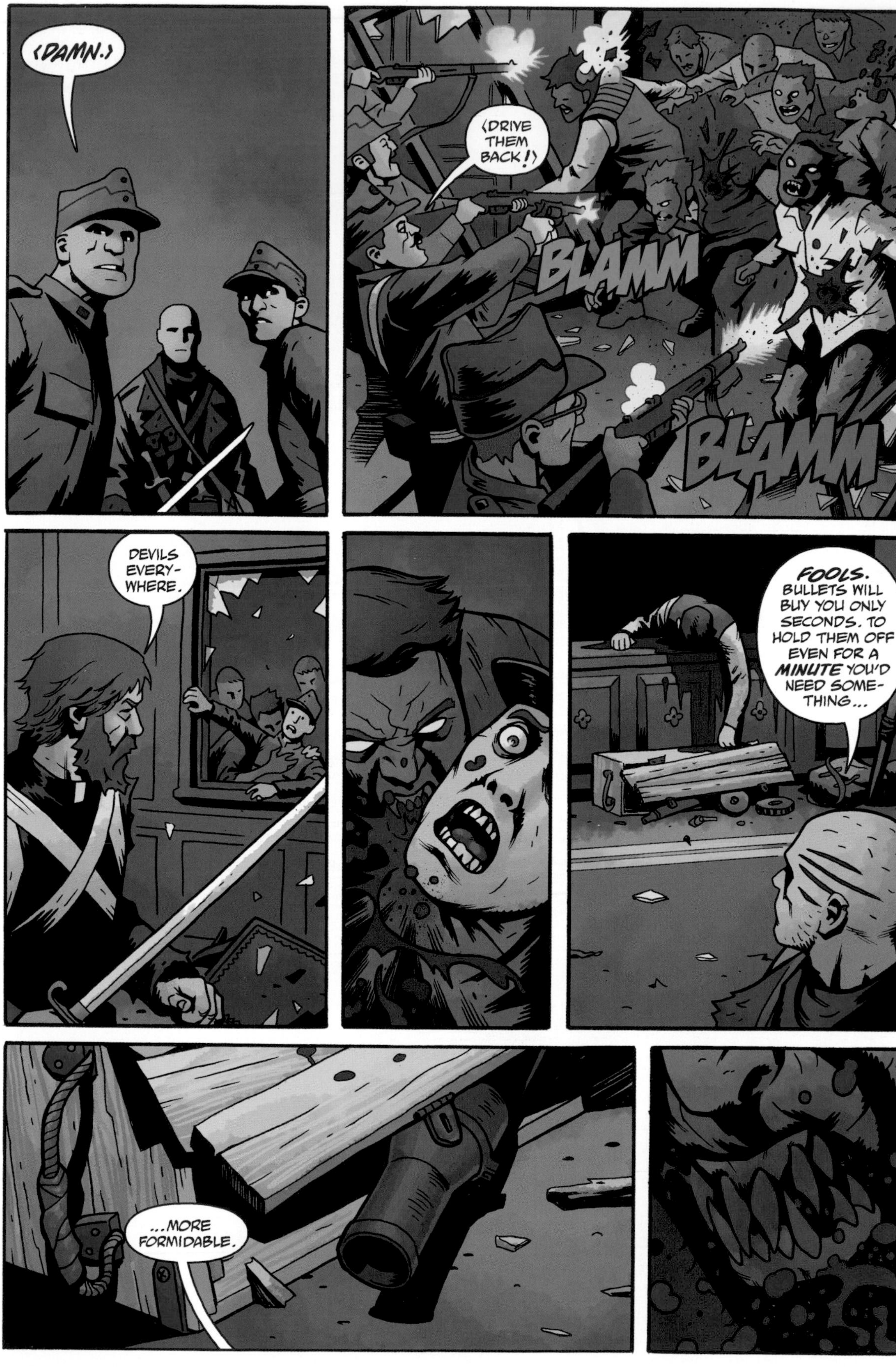
‹DAMN.›
‹DRIVE THEM BACK!›
BLAMM
BLAMM
DEVILS EVERY-WHERE.
FOOLS. BULLETS WILL BUY YOU ONLY SECONDS. TO HOLD THEM OFF EVEN FOR A MINUTE YOU'D NEED SOME-THING...
...MORE FORMIDABLE.

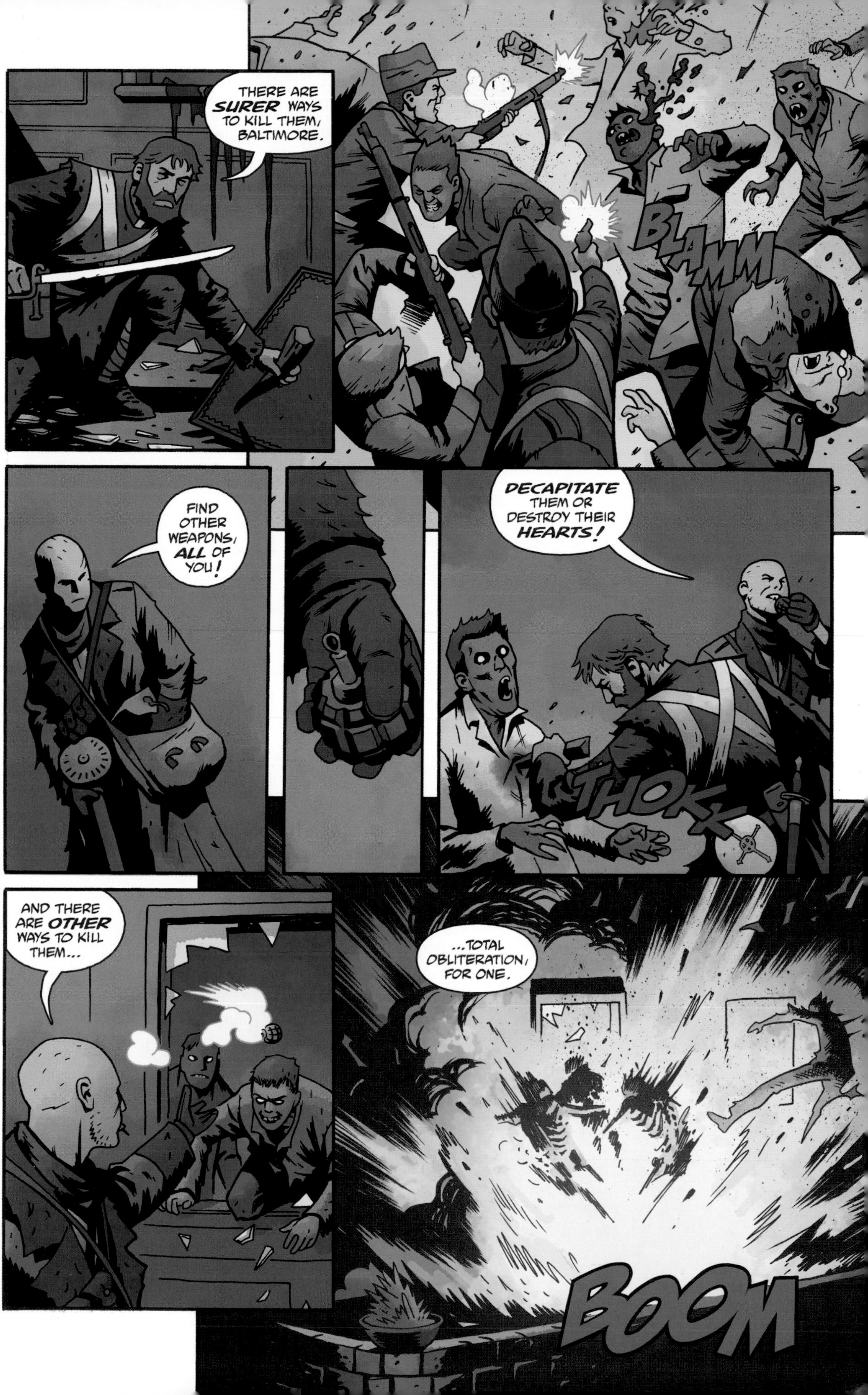
THERE ARE SURER WAYS TO KILL THEM, BALTIMORE.
BLAMM
FIND OTHER WEAPONS, ALL OF YOU!
DECAPITATE THEM OR DESTROY THEIR HEARTS!
THOKK
AND THERE ARE OTHER WAYS TO KILL THEM...
...TOTAL OBLITERATION, FOR ONE.
BOOM

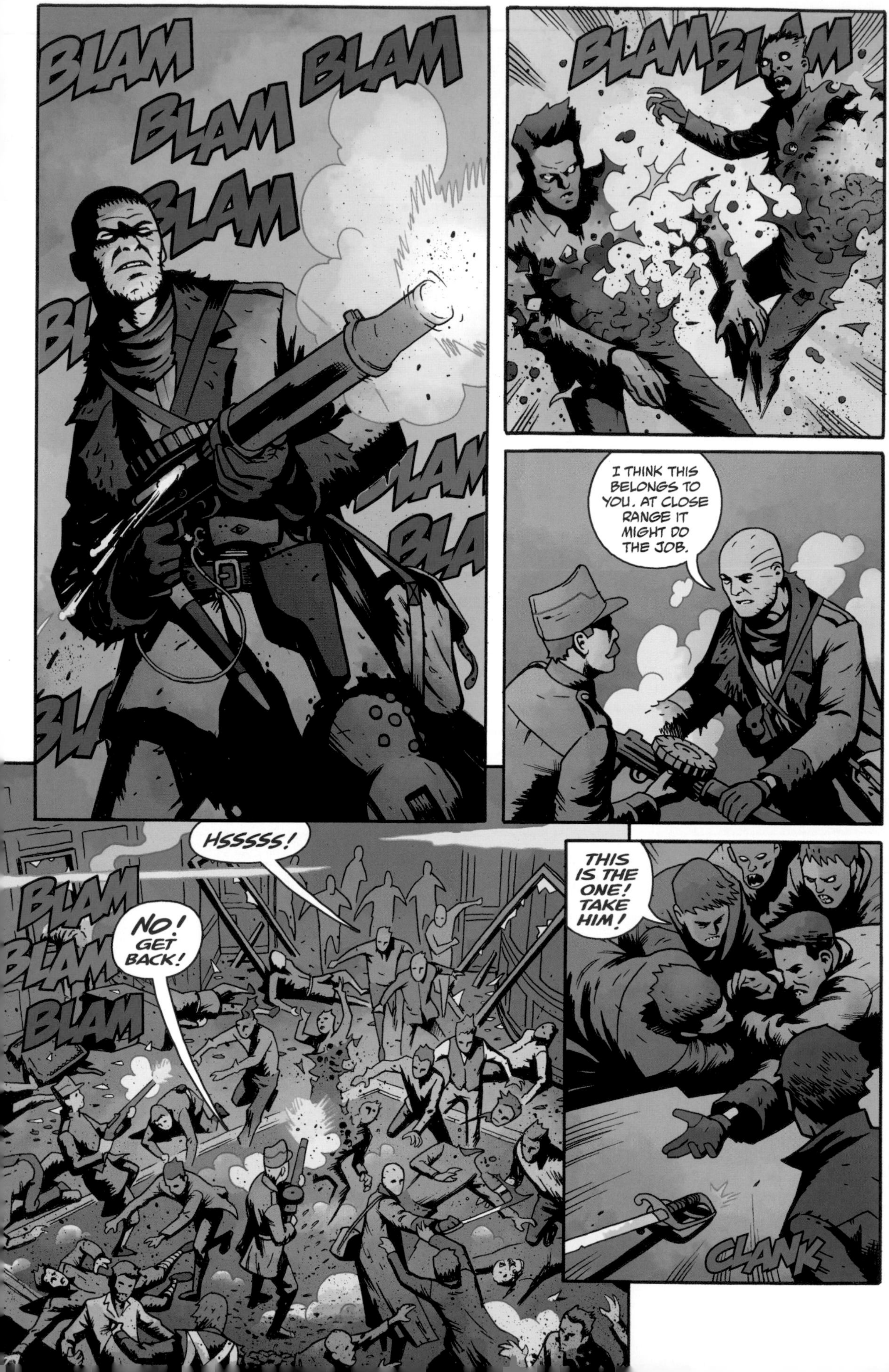
BLAM
BLAM
BLAM
BLAM
BLAM
BLAM
BLAM
BLAM
BLAMBLAM
I THINK THIS BELONGS TO YOU. AT CLOSE RANGE IT MIGHT DO THE JOB.
HSSSSS!
BLAM
BLAM
BLAM
NO! GET BACK!
THIS IS THE ONE! TAKE HIM!
CLANK

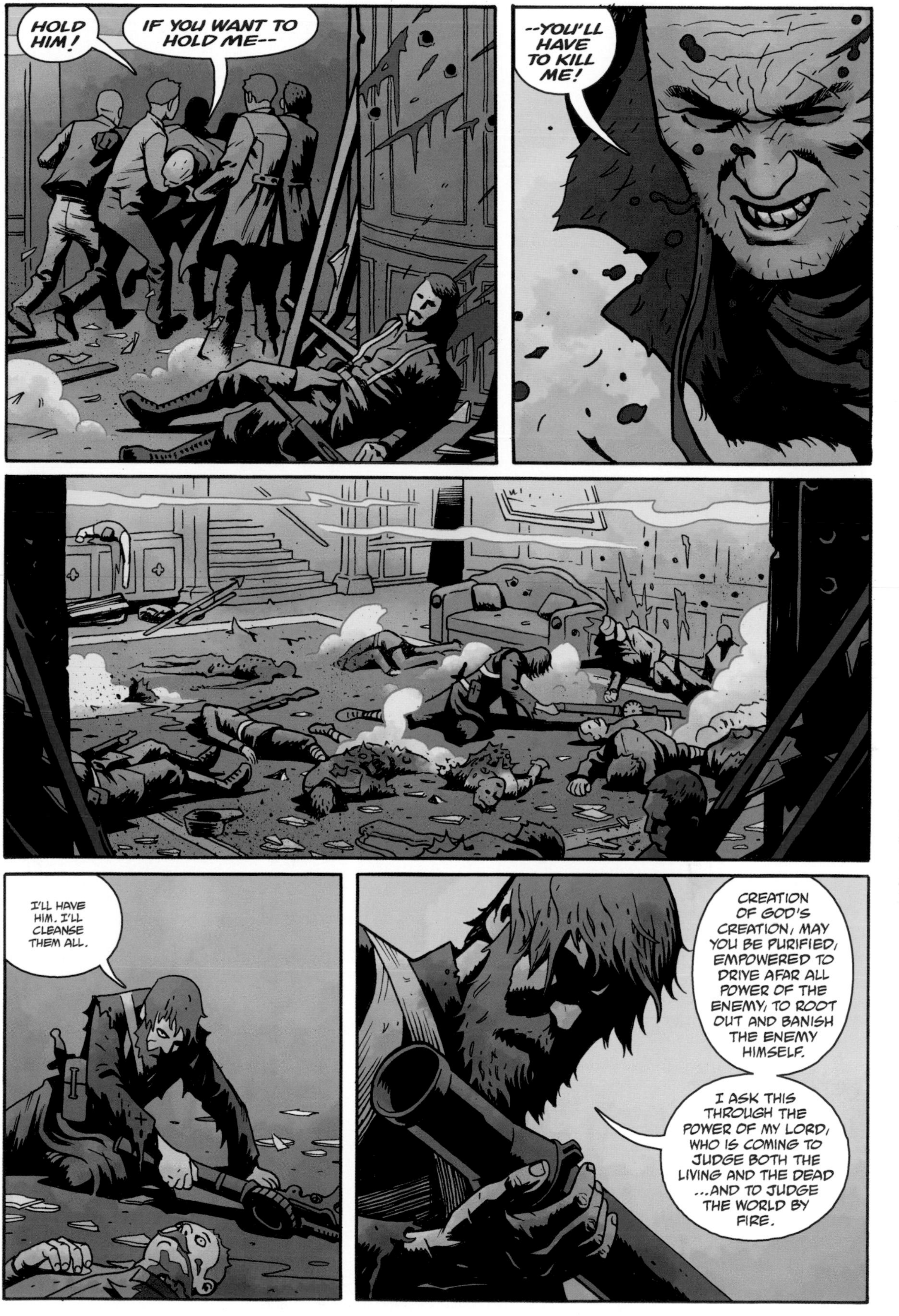
HOLD HIM!
IF YOU WANT TO HOLD ME--
--YOU'LL HAVE TO KILL ME!
I'LL HAVE HIM. I'LL CLEANSE THEM ALL.
CREATION OF GOD'S CREATION, MAY YOU BE PURIFIED, EMPOWERED TO DRIVE AFAR ALL POWER OF THE ENEMY, TO ROOT OUT AND BANISH THE ENEMY HIMSELF.
I ASK THIS THROUGH THE POWER OF MY LORD, WHO IS COMING TO JUDGE BOTH THE LIVING AND THE DEAD ...AND TO JUDGE THE WORLD BY FIRE.

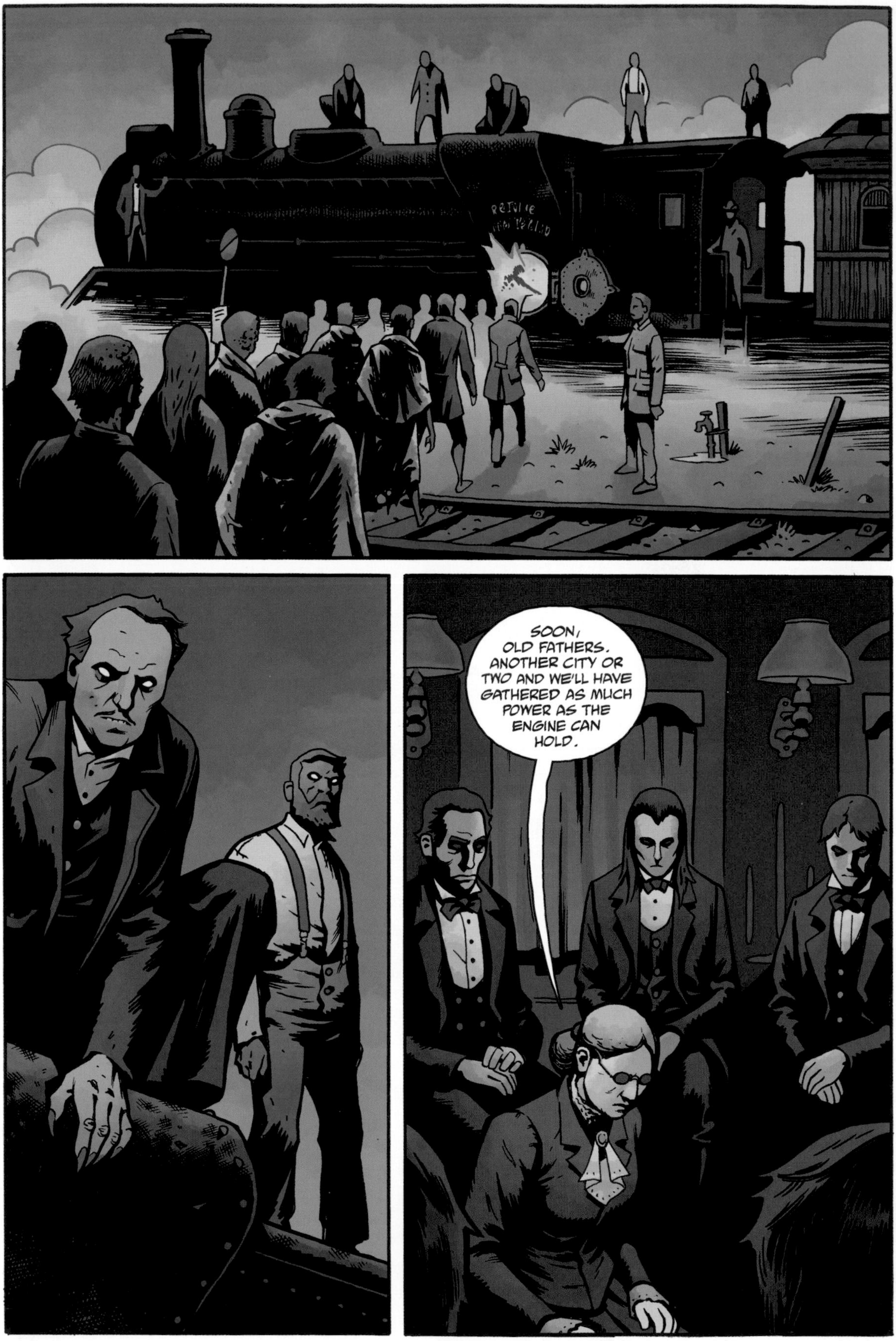
SOON, OLD FATHERS. ANOTHER CITY OR TWO AND WE'LL HAVE GATHERED AS MUCH POWER AS THE ENGINE CAN HOLD.

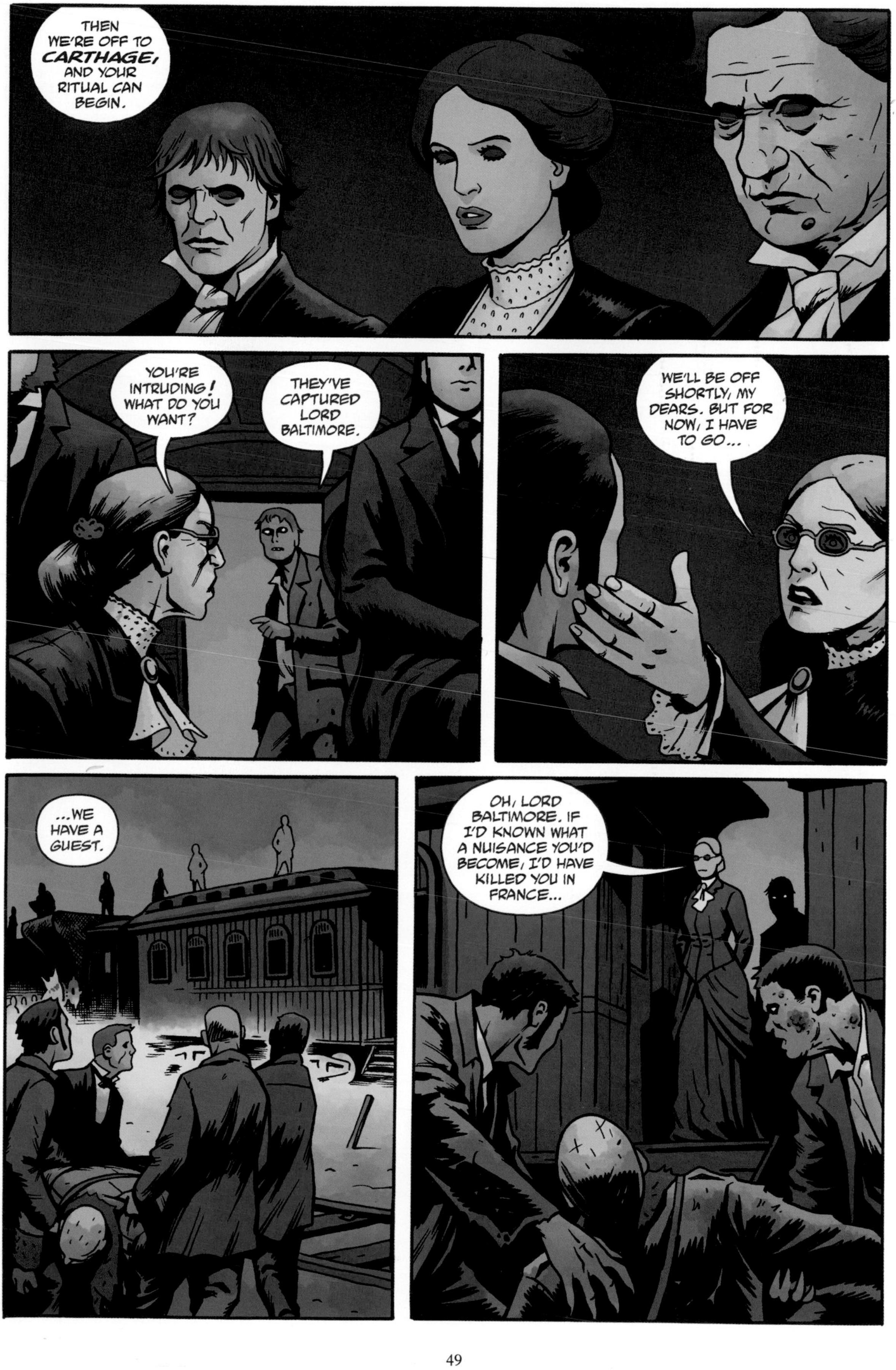
THEN WE'RE OFF TO CARTHAGE, AND YOUR RITUAL CAN BEGIN.
YOU'RE INTRUDING! WHAT DO YOU WANT?
THEY'VE CAPTURED LORD BALTIMORE.
WE'LL BE OFF SHORTLY, MY DEARS. BUT FOR NOW, I HAVE TO GO...
...WE HAVE A GUEST.
OH, LORD BALTIMORE. IF I'D KNOWN WHAT A NUISANCE YOU'D BECOME, I'D HAVE KILLED YOU IN FRANCE...

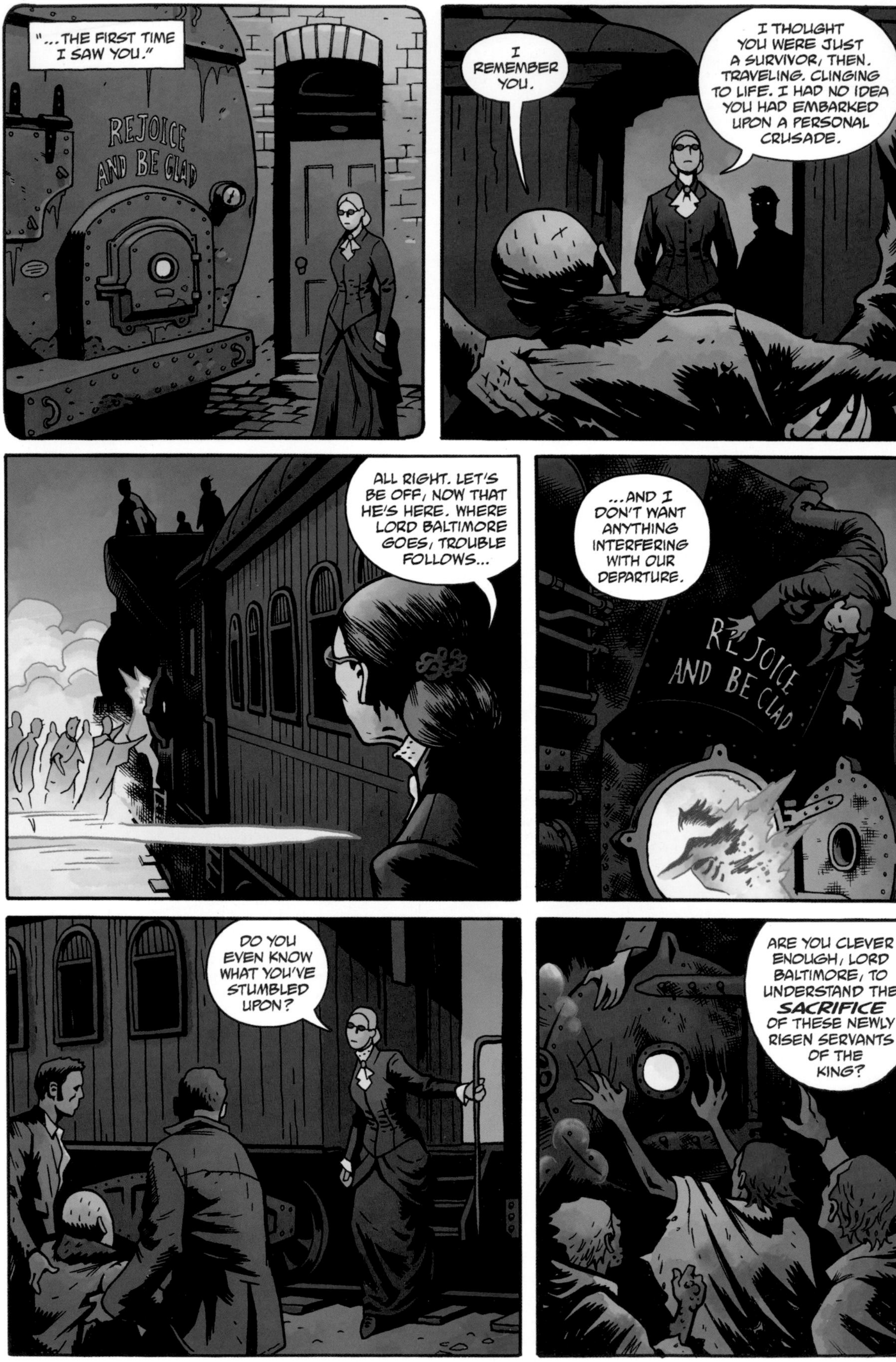
"...THE FIRST TIME I SAW YOU."
REJOICE AND BE GLAD
I REMEMBER YOU.
I THOUGHT YOU WERE JUST A SURVIVOR, THEN. TRAVELING. CLINGING TO LIFE. I HAD NO IDEA YOU HAD EMBARKED UPON A PERSONAL CRUSADE.
ALL RIGHT. LET'S BE OFF, NOW THAT HE'S HERE. WHERE LORD BALTIMORE GOES, TROUBLE FOLLOWS...
...AND I DON'T WANT ANYTHING INTERFERING WITH OUR DEPARTURE.
REJOICE AND BE GLAD
DO YOU EVEN KNOW WHAT YOU'VE STUMBLED UPON?
ARE YOU CLEVER ENOUGH, LORD BALTIMORE, TO UNDERSTAND THE ***SACRIFICE*** OF THESE NEWLY RISEN SERVANTS OF THE KING?

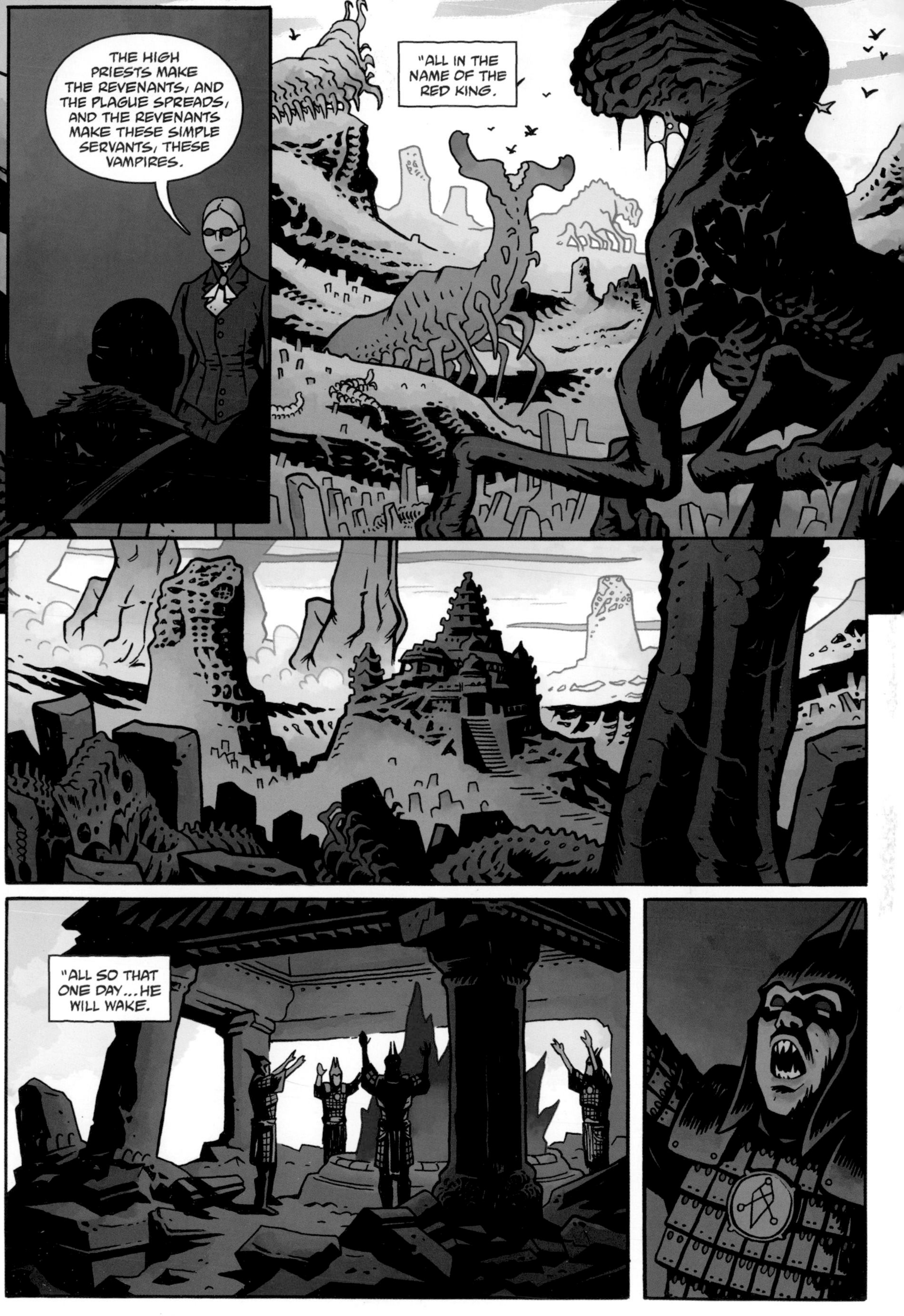
THE HIGH PRIESTS MAKE THE REVENANTS, AND THE PLAGUE SPREADS, AND THE REVENANTS MAKE THESE SIMPLE SERVANTS, THESE VAMPIRES.
"ALL IN THE NAME OF THE RED KING.
"ALL SO THAT ONE DAY... HE WILL WAKE.

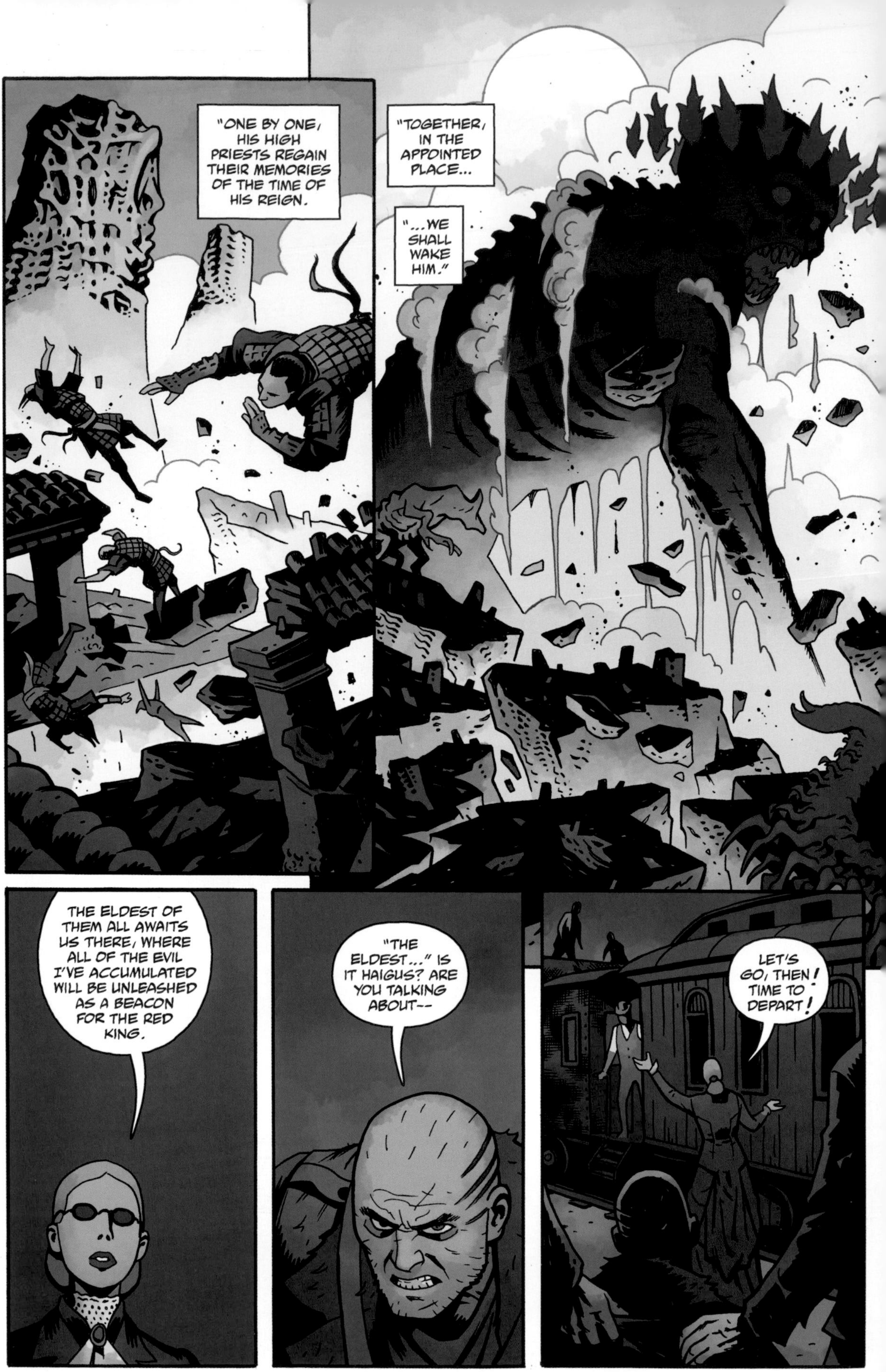
"ONE BY ONE, HIS HIGH PRIESTS REGAIN THEIR MEMORIES OF THE TIME OF HIS REIGN.
"TOGETHER, IN THE APPOINTED PLACE...
"...WE SHALL WAKE HIM."
THE ELDEST OF THEM ALL AWAITS US THERE, WHERE ALL OF THE EVIL I'VE ACCUMULATED WILL BE UNLEASHED AS A BEACON FOR THE RED KING.
"THE ELDEST..." IS IT HAIGUS? ARE YOU TALKING ABOUT--
LET'S GO, THEN! TIME TO DEPART!

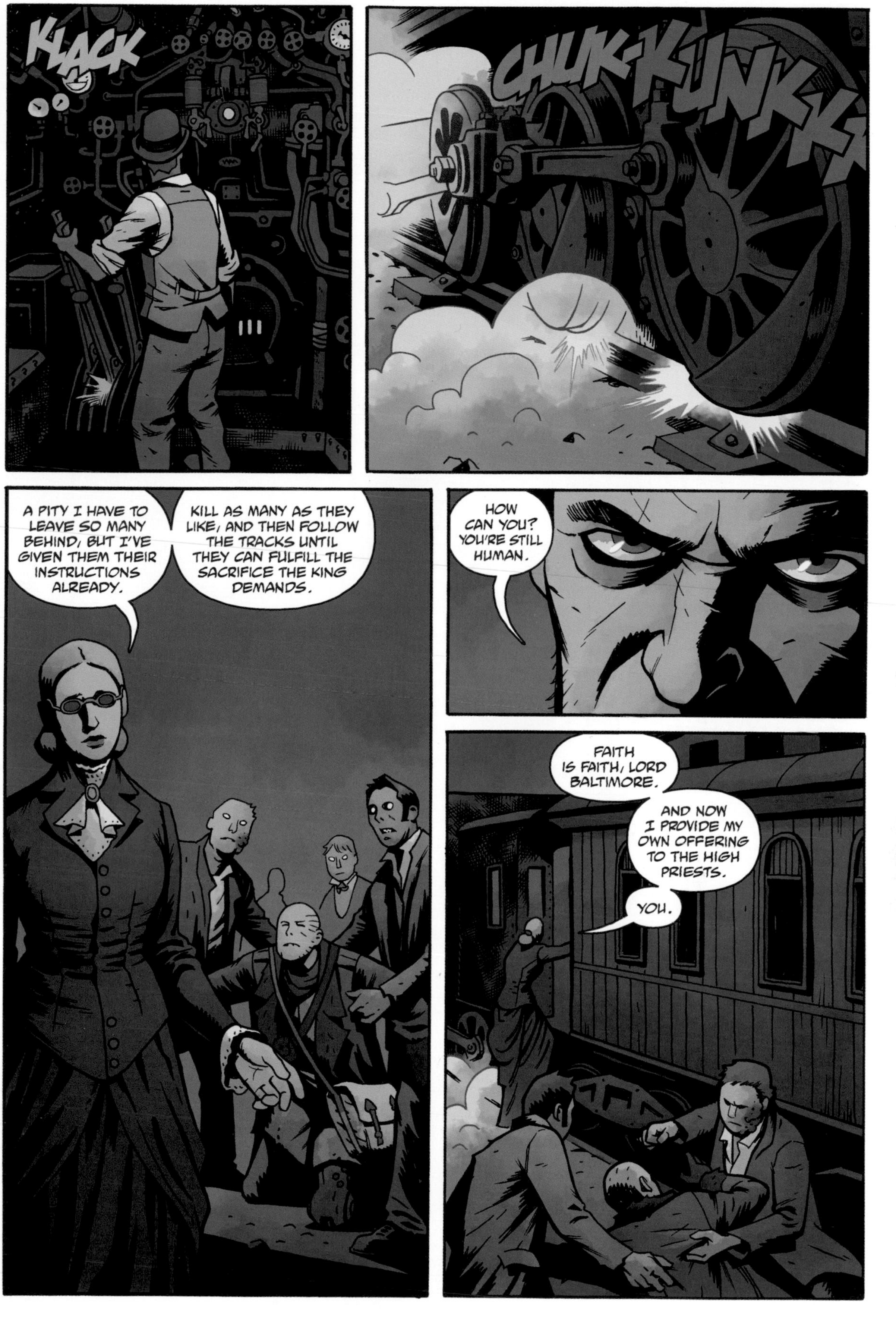
KLACK
CHUK-KUNKK
A PITY I HAVE TO LEAVE SO MANY BEHIND, BUT I'VE GIVEN THEM THEIR INSTRUCTIONS ALREADY.
KILL AS MANY AS THEY LIKE, AND THEN FOLLOW THE TRACKS UNTIL THEY CAN FULFILL THE SACRIFICE THE KING DEMANDS.
HOW CAN YOU? YOU'RE STILL HUMAN.
FAITH IS FAITH, LORD BALTIMORE.
AND NOW I PROVIDE MY OWN OFFERING TO THE HIGH PRIESTS.
YOU.

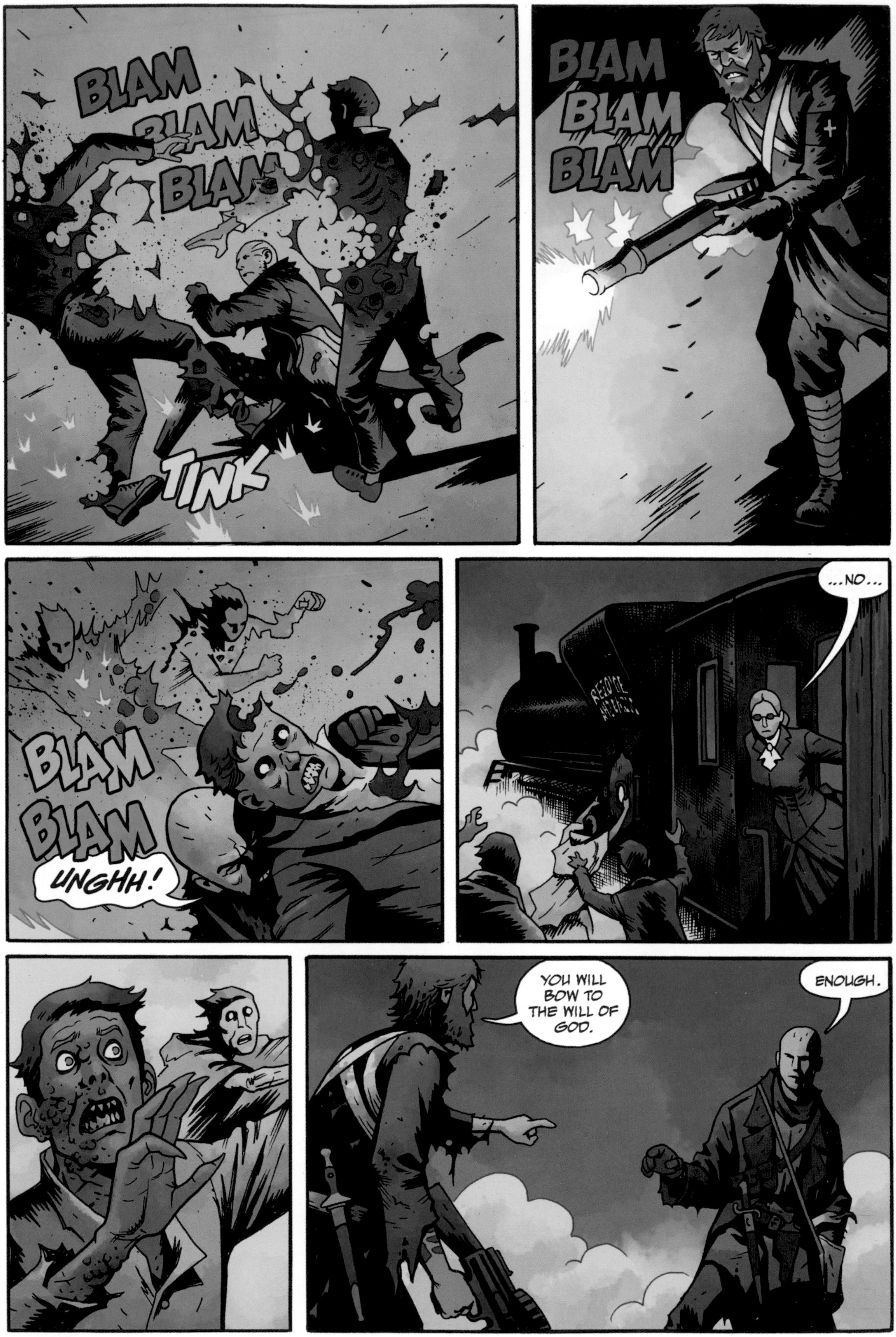
BLAM
BLAM
BLAM
TINK
BLAM
BLAM
BLAM
BLAM
BLAM
UNGHH!
...NO...
YOU WILL BOW TO THE WILL OF GOD.
ENOUGH.

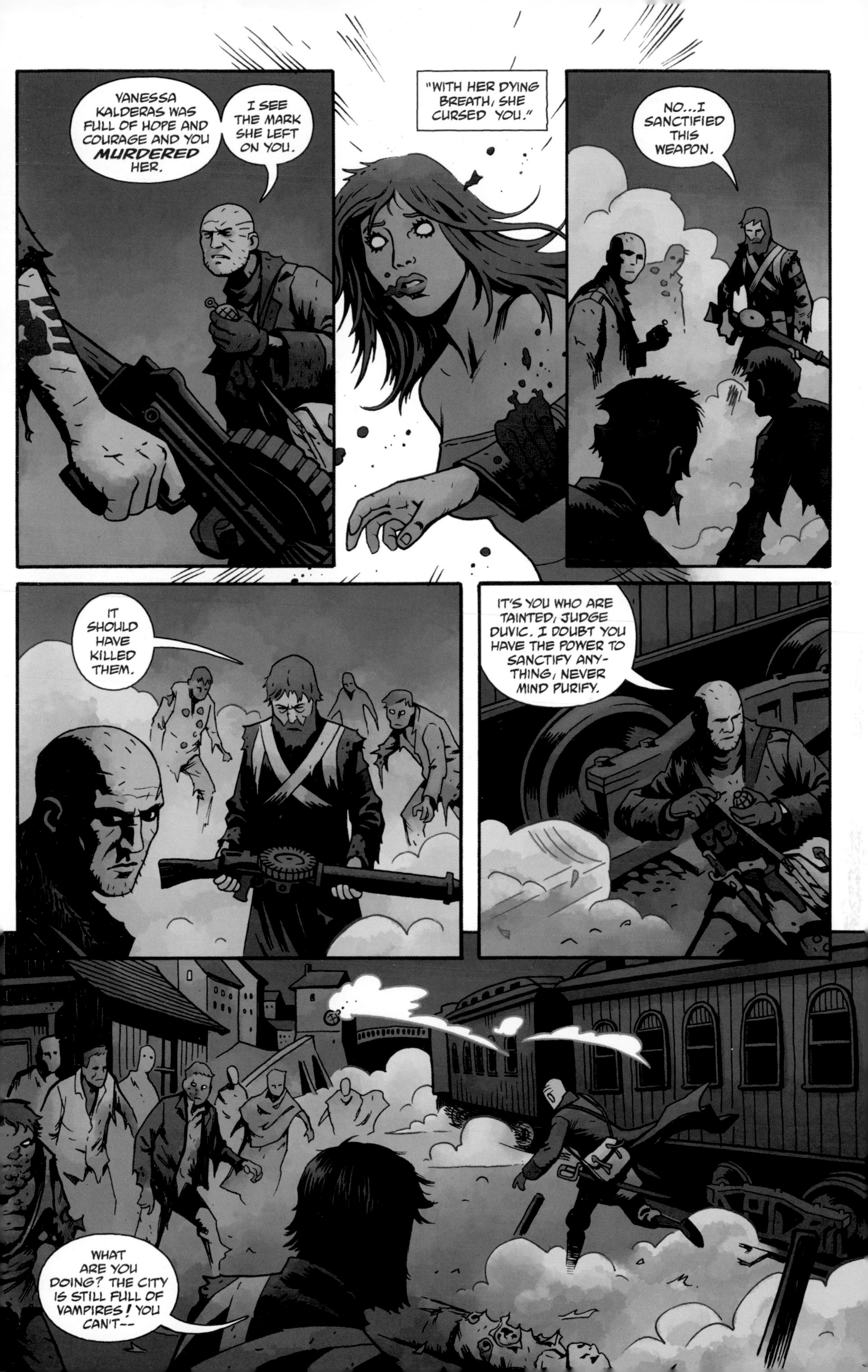
VANESSA KALDERAS WAS FULL OF HOPE AND COURAGE AND YOU MURDERED HER.
I SEE THE MARK SHE LEFT ON YOU.
"WITH HER DYING BREATH, SHE CURSED YOU."
NO...I SANCTIFIED THIS WEAPON.
IT SHOULD HAVE KILLED THEM.
IT'S YOU WHO ARE TAINTED, JUDGE DUVIC. I DOUBT YOU HAVE THE POWER TO SANCTIFY ANY-THING, NEVER MIND PURIFY.
WHAT ARE YOU DOING? THE CITY IS STILL FULL OF VAMPIRES! YOU CAN'T--

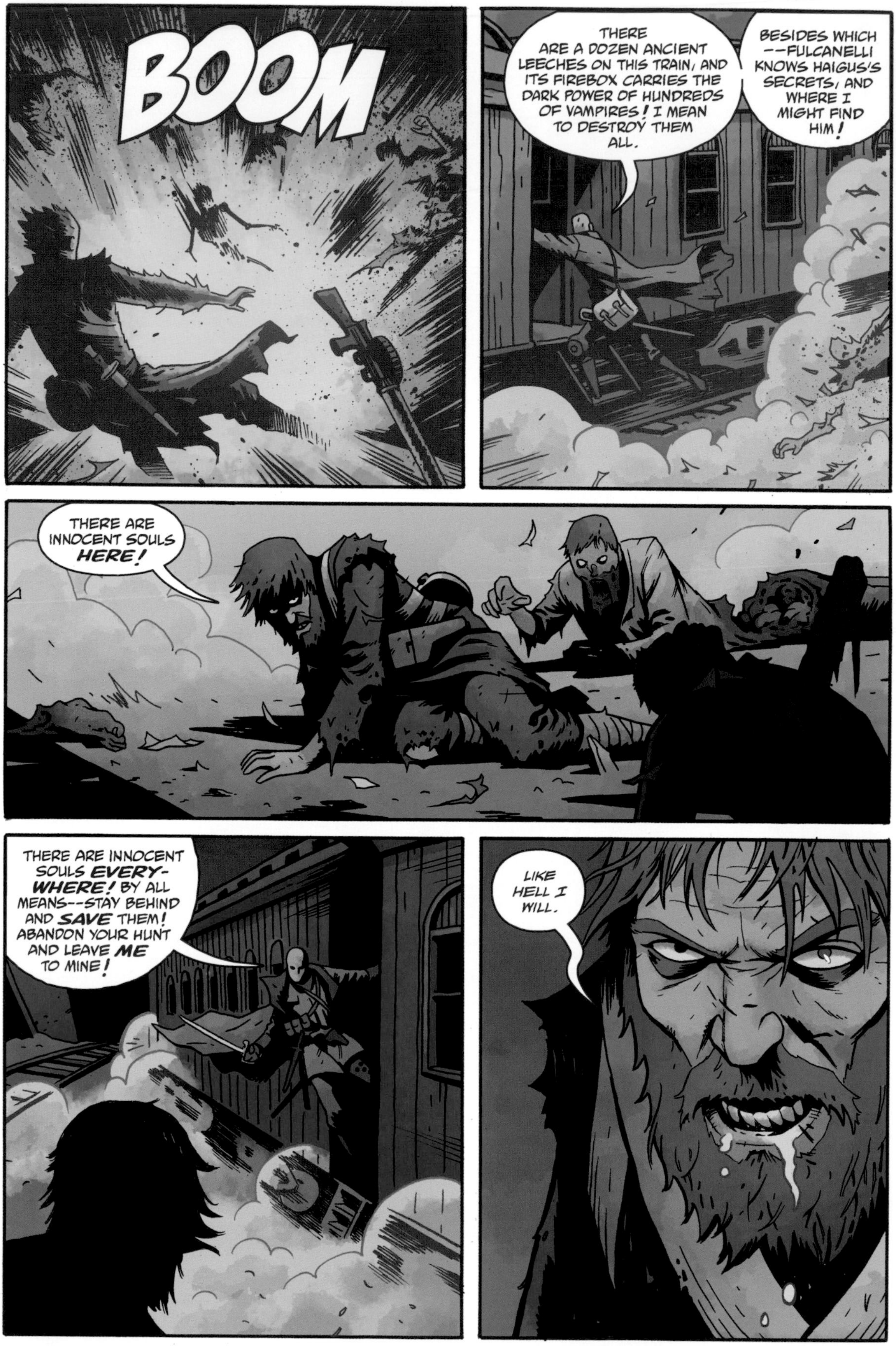
BOOM
THERE ARE A DOZEN ANCIENT LEECHES ON THIS TRAIN, AND ITS FIREBOX CARRIES THE DARK POWER OF HUNDREDS OF VAMPIRES! I MEAN TO DESTROY THEM ALL.
BESIDES WHICH --FULCANELLI KNOWS HAIGUS'S SECRETS, AND WHERE I MIGHT FIND HIM!
THERE ARE INNOCENT SOULS HERE!
THERE ARE INNOCENT SOULS EVERY-WHERE! BY ALL MEANS--STAY BEHIND AND SAVE THEM! ABANDON YOUR HUNT AND LEAVE ME TO MINE!
LIKE HELL I WILL.

THE INFERNAL TRAIN
Chapter Three

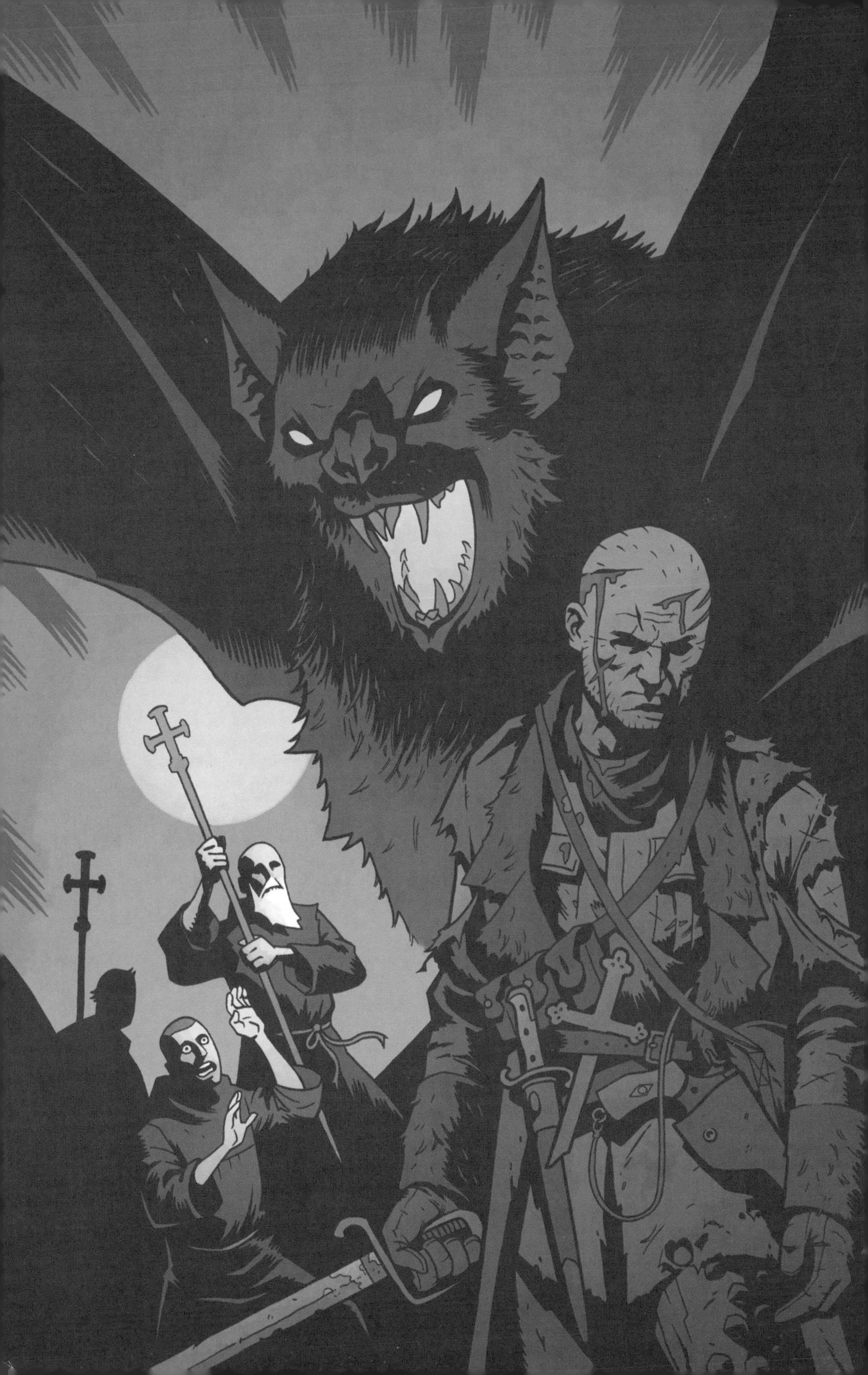

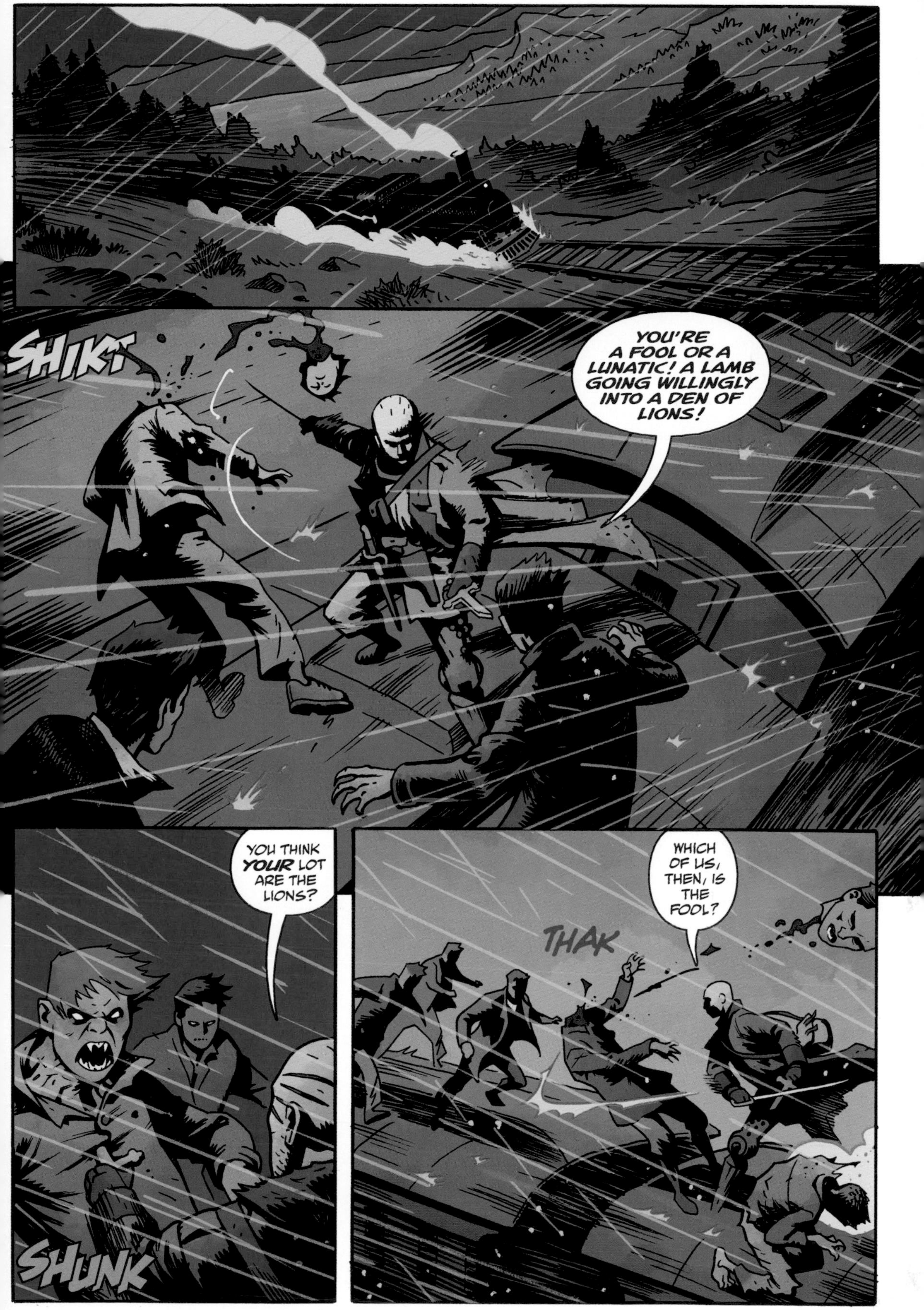
SHIKT
YOU'RE A FOOL OR A LUNATIC! A LAMB GOING WILLINGLY INTO A DEN OF LIONS!
YOU THINK YOUR LOT ARE THE LIONS?
SHUNK
WHICH OF US, THEN, IS THE FOOL?
THAK

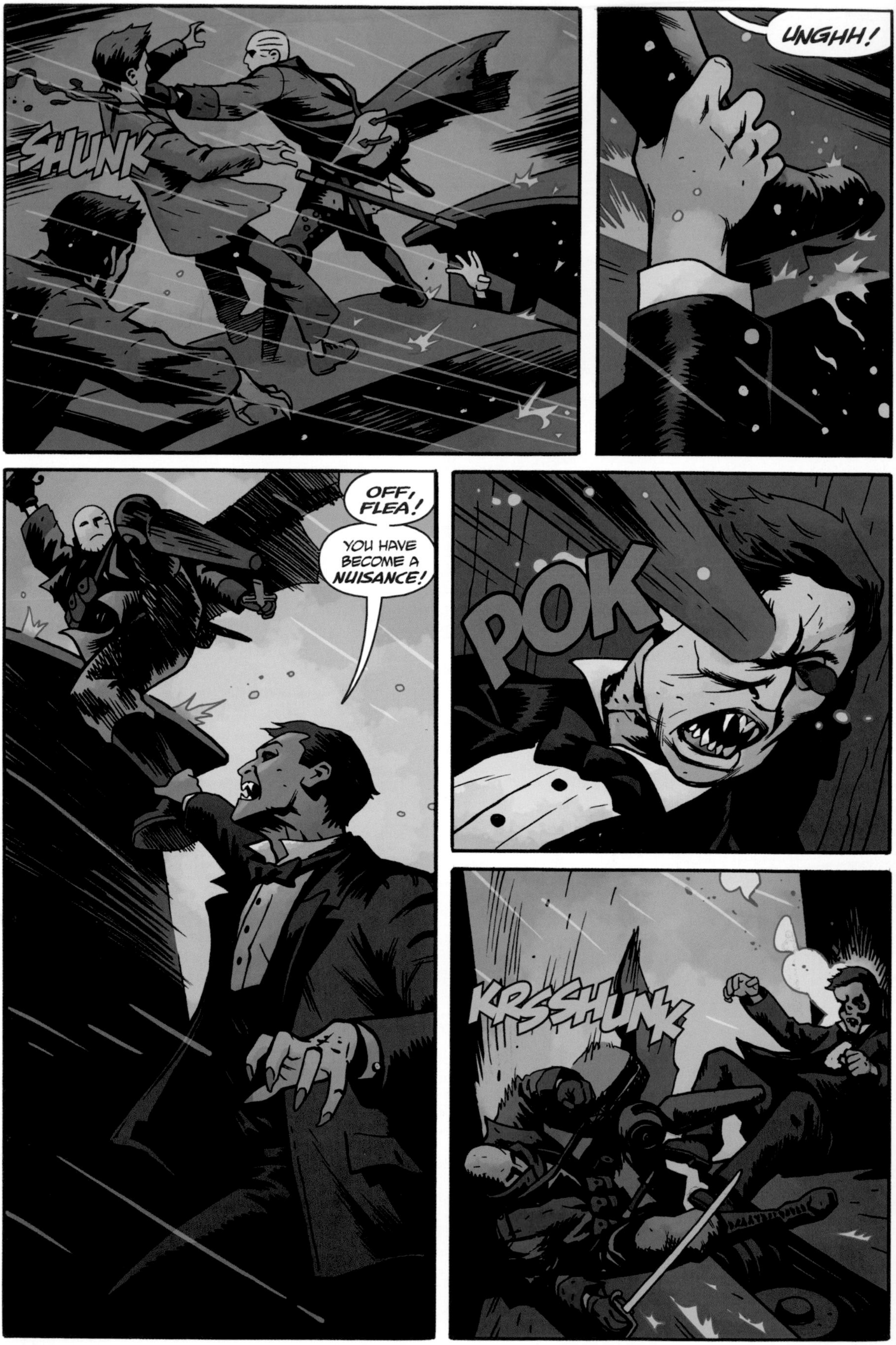
SHUNK
UNGHH!
OFF, FLEA!
YOU HAVE BECOME A NUISANCE!
POK
KRSSHUNK

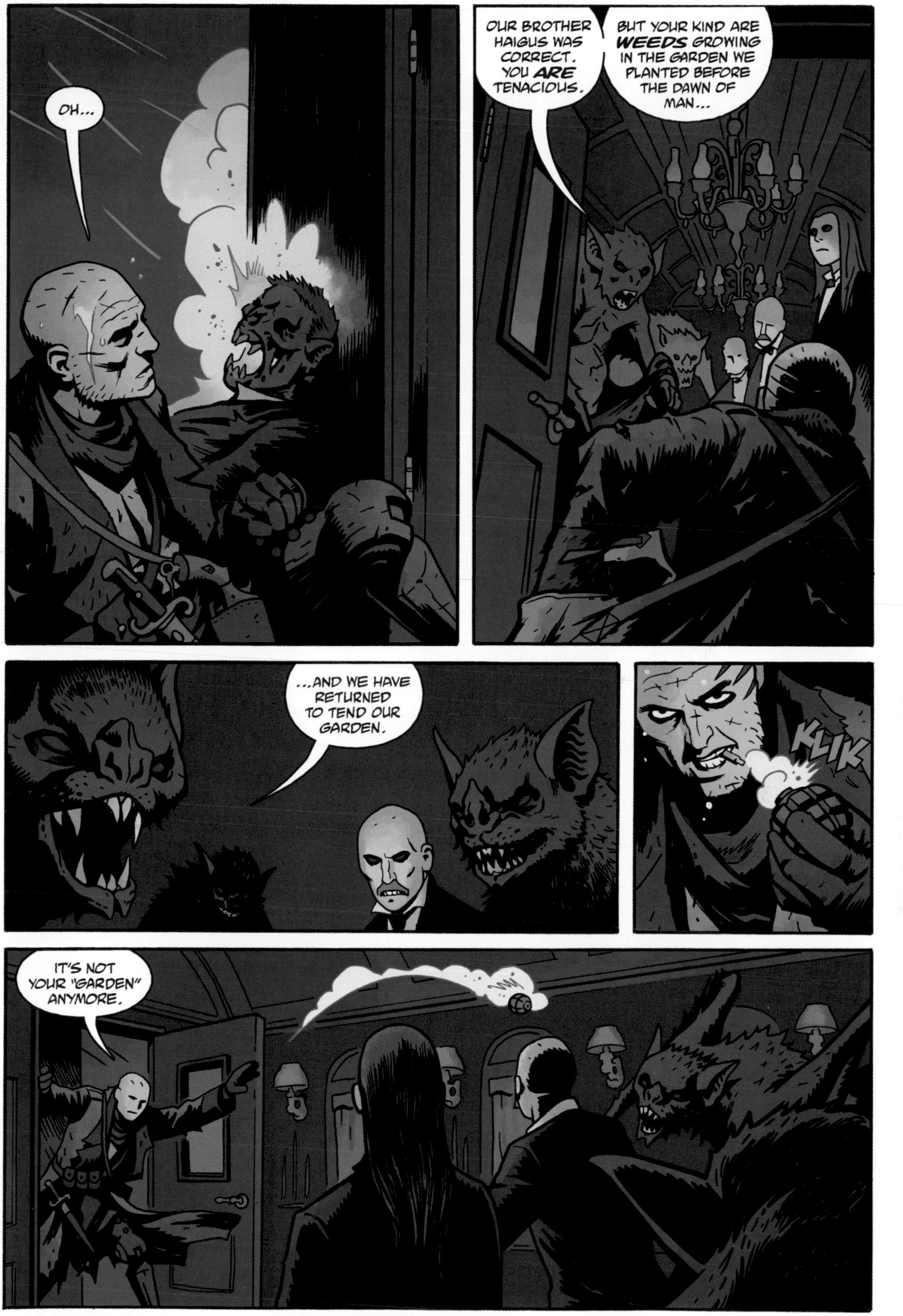
OH...
OUR BROTHER HAIGUS WAS CORRECT. YOU ARE TENACIOUS.
BUT YOUR KIND ARE WEEDS GROWING IN THE GARDEN WE PLANTED BEFORE THE DAWN OF MAN...
...AND WE HAVE RETURNED TO TEND OUR GARDEN.
KLIK
IT'S NOT YOUR "GARDEN" ANYMORE.

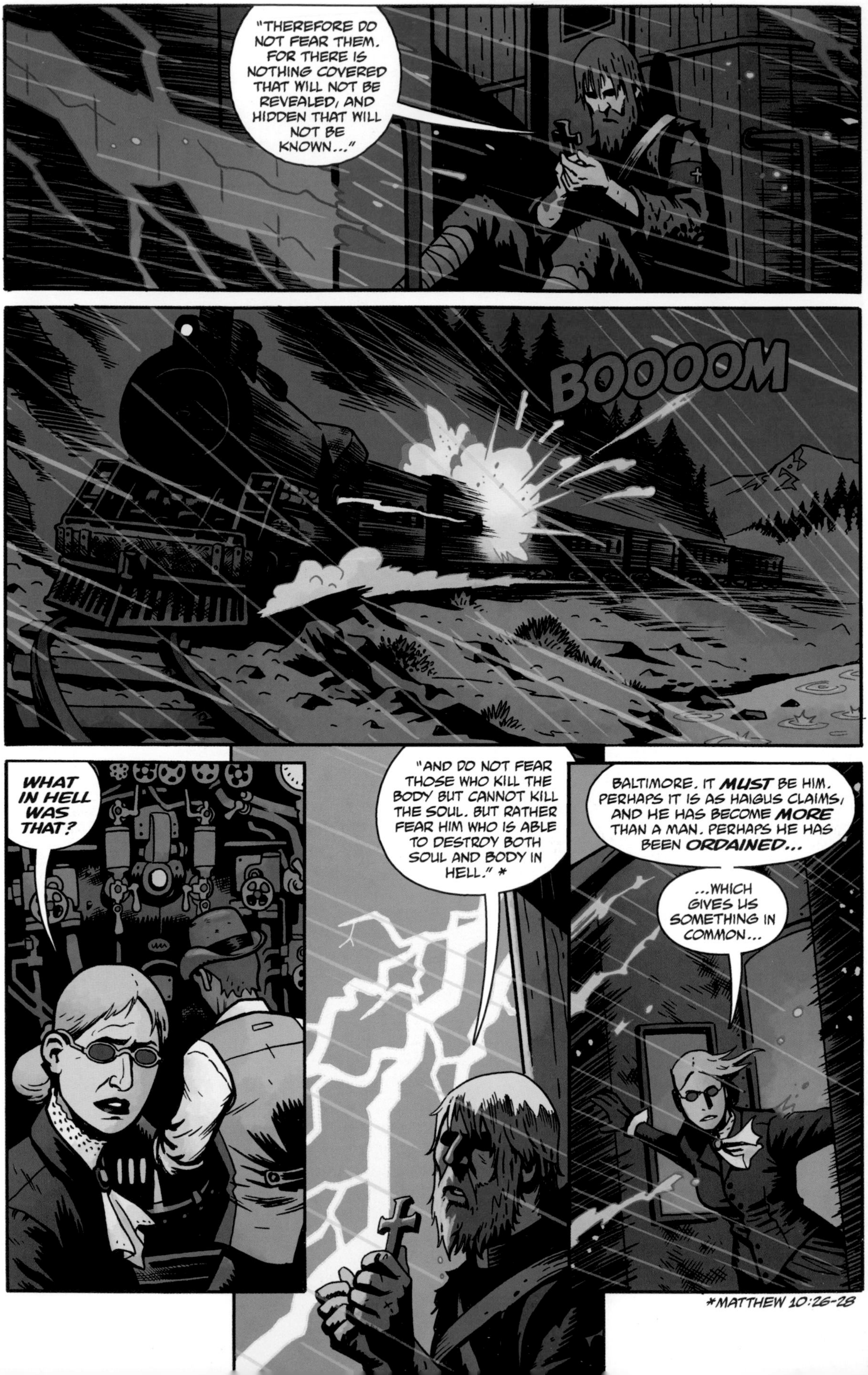
"THEREFORE DO NOT FEAR THEM. FOR THERE IS NOTHING COVERED THAT WILL NOT BE REVEALED, AND HIDDEN THAT WILL NOT BE KNOWN..."
BOOOOM
WHAT IN HELL WAS THAT?
"AND DO NOT FEAR THOSE WHO KILL THE BODY BUT CANNOT KILL THE SOUL. BUT RATHER FEAR HIM WHO IS ABLE TO DESTROY BOTH SOUL AND BODY IN HELL." *
BALTIMORE. IT MUST BE HIM. PERHAPS IT IS AS HAIGUS CLAIMS, AND HE HAS BECOME MORE THAN A MAN. PERHAPS HE HAS BEEN ORDAINED...
...WHICH GIVES US SOMETHING IN COMMON...
*MATTHEW 10:26-28

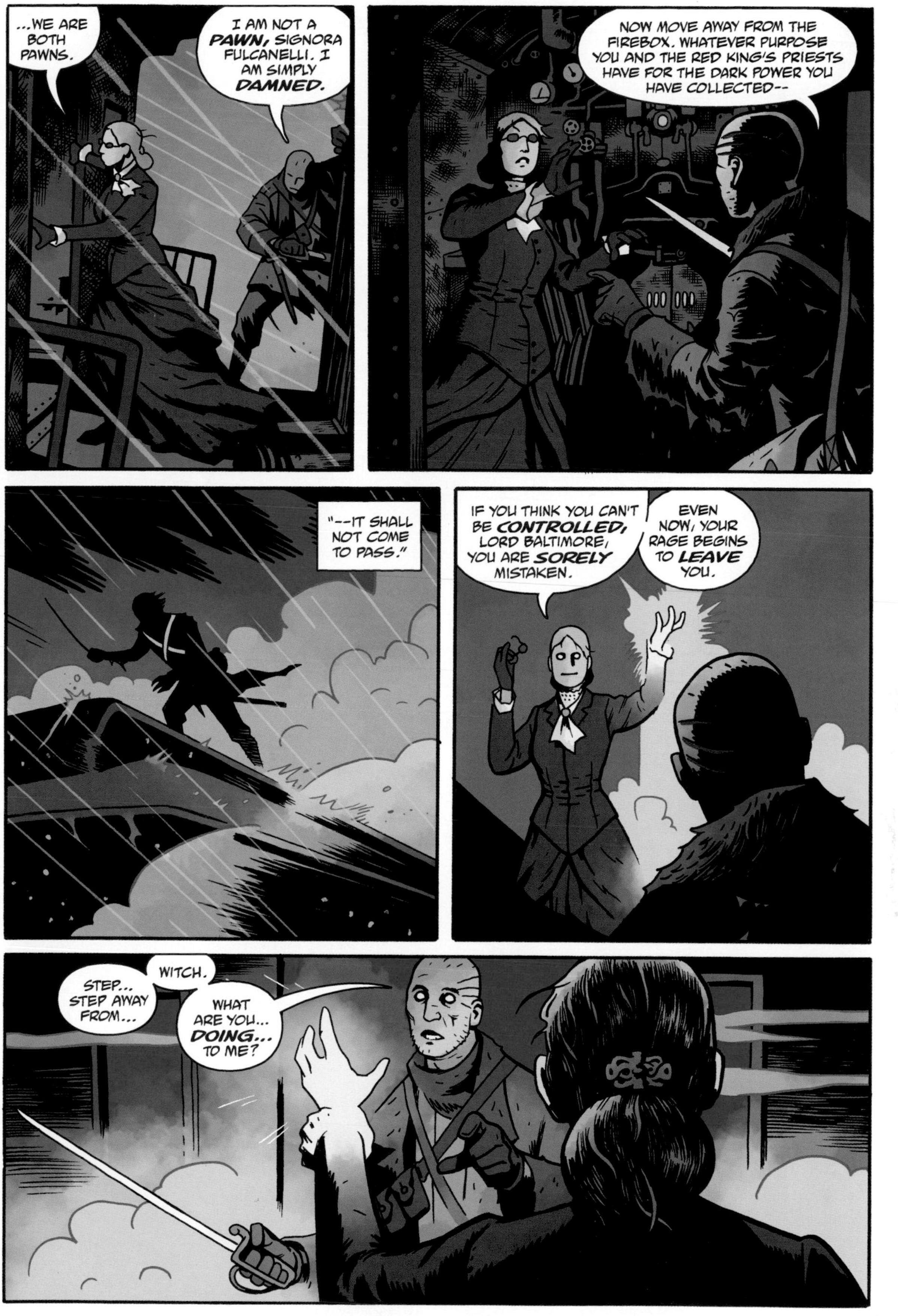
...WE ARE BOTH PAWNS.
I AM NOT A PAWN, SIGNORA FULCANELLI. I AM SIMPLY DAMNED.
NOW MOVE AWAY FROM THE FIREBOX. WHATEVER PURPOSE YOU AND THE RED KING'S PRIESTS HAVE FOR THE DARK POWER YOU HAVE COLLECTED--
"--IT SHALL NOT COME TO PASS."
IF YOU THINK YOU CAN'T BE CONTROLLED, LORD BALTIMORE, YOU ARE SORELY MISTAKEN.
EVEN NOW, YOUR RAGE BEGINS TO LEAVE YOU.
STEP... STEP AWAY FROM...
WITCH.
WHAT ARE YOU... DOING... TO ME?

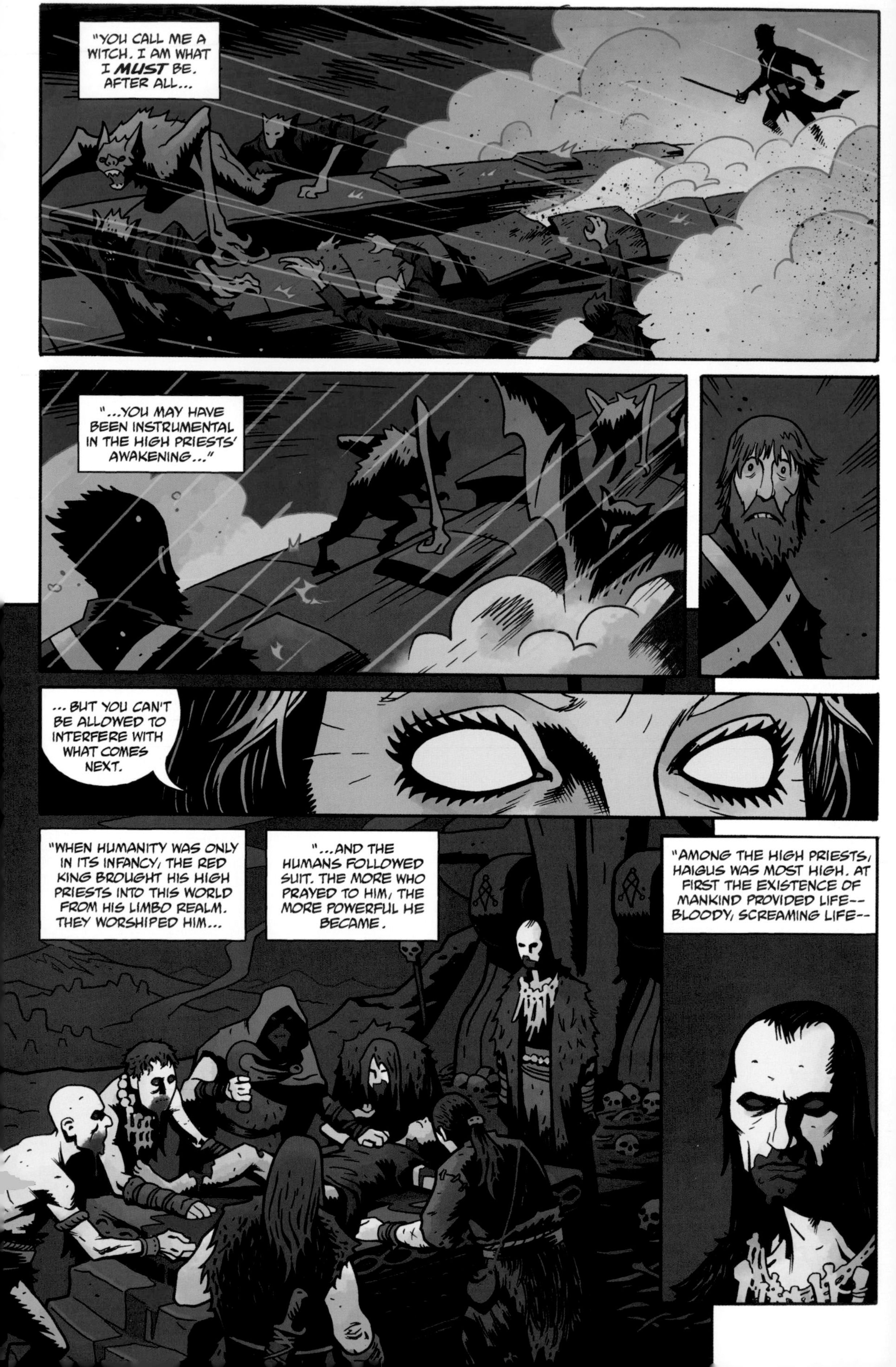
"YOU CALL ME A WITCH. I AM WHAT I **MUST** BE. AFTER ALL...
"...YOU MAY HAVE BEEN INSTRUMENTAL IN THE HIGH PRIESTS' AWAKENING..."
...BUT YOU CAN'T BE ALLOWED TO INTERFERE WITH WHAT COMES NEXT.
"WHEN HUMANITY WAS ONLY IN ITS INFANCY, THE RED KING BROUGHT HIS HIGH PRIESTS INTO THIS WORLD FROM HIS LIMBO REALM. THEY WORSHIPED HIM...
"...AND THE HUMANS FOLLOWED SUIT. THE MORE WHO PRAYED TO HIM, THE MORE POWERFUL HE BECAME.
"AMONG THE HIGH PRIESTS, HAIGUS WAS MOST HIGH. AT FIRST THE EXISTENCE OF MANKIND PROVIDED LIFE-- BLOODY, SCREAMING LIFE--

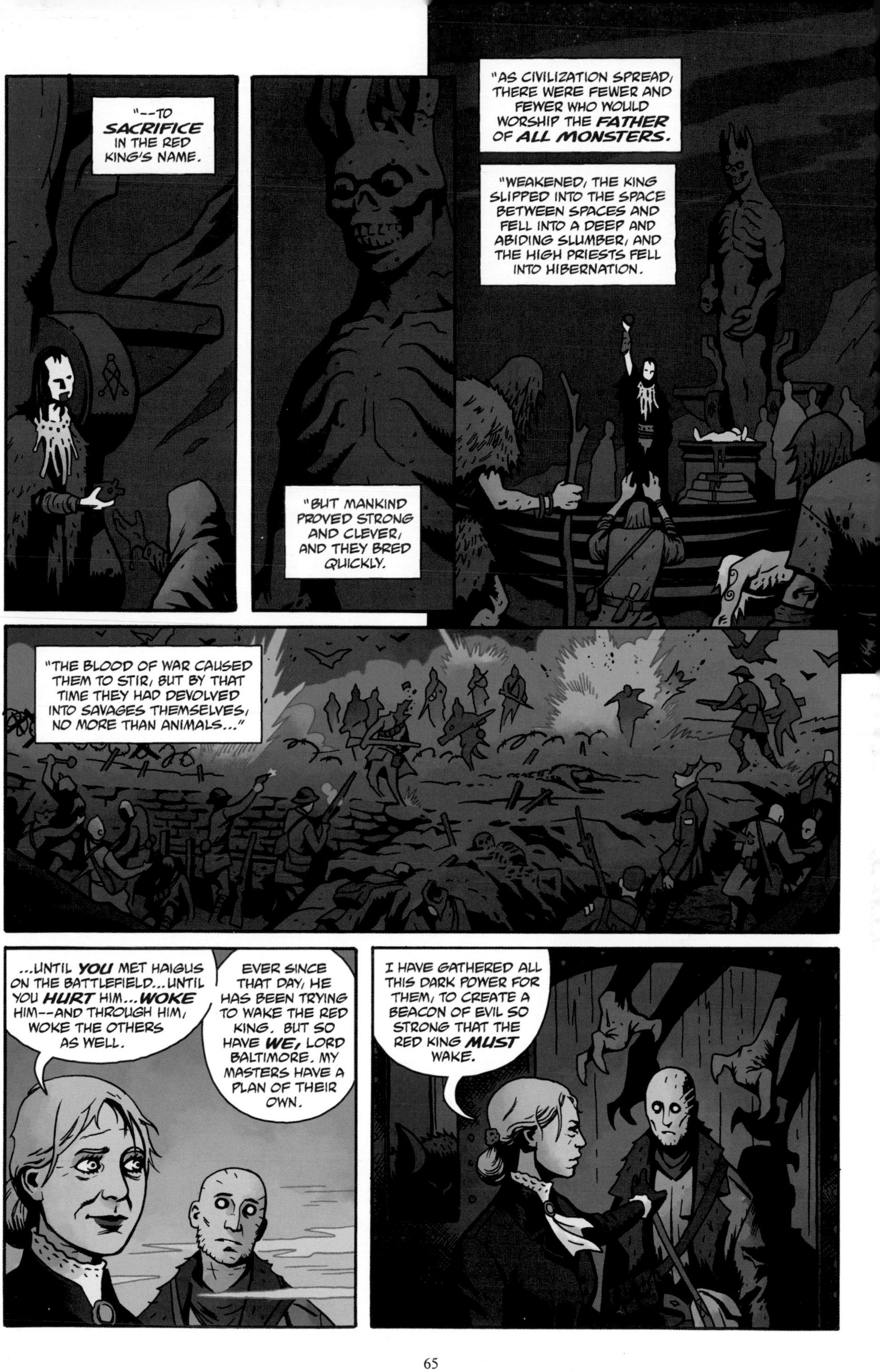
"--TO SACRIFICE IN THE RED KING'S NAME.
"BUT MANKIND PROVED STRONG AND CLEVER, AND THEY BRED QUICKLY.
"AS CIVILIZATION SPREAD, THERE WERE FEWER AND FEWER WHO WOULD WORSHIP THE FATHER OF ALL MONSTERS.
"WEAKENED, THE KING SLIPPED INTO THE SPACE BETWEEN SPACES AND FELL INTO A DEEP AND ABIDING SLUMBER, AND THE HIGH PRIESTS FELL INTO HIBERNATION.
"THE BLOOD OF WAR CAUSED THEM TO STIR, BUT BY THAT TIME THEY HAD DEVOLVED INTO SAVAGES THEMSELVES, NO MORE THAN ANIMALS..."
...UNTIL YOU MET HAIGUS ON THE BATTLEFIELD...UNTIL YOU HURT HIM...WOKE HIM--AND THROUGH HIM, WOKE THE OTHERS AS WELL.
EVER SINCE THAT DAY, HE HAS BEEN TRYING TO WAKE THE RED KING. BUT SO HAVE WE, LORD BALTIMORE. MY MASTERS HAVE A PLAN OF THEIR OWN.
I HAVE GATHERED ALL THIS DARK POWER FOR THEM, TO CREATE A BEACON OF EVIL SO STRONG THAT THE RED KING MUST WAKE.

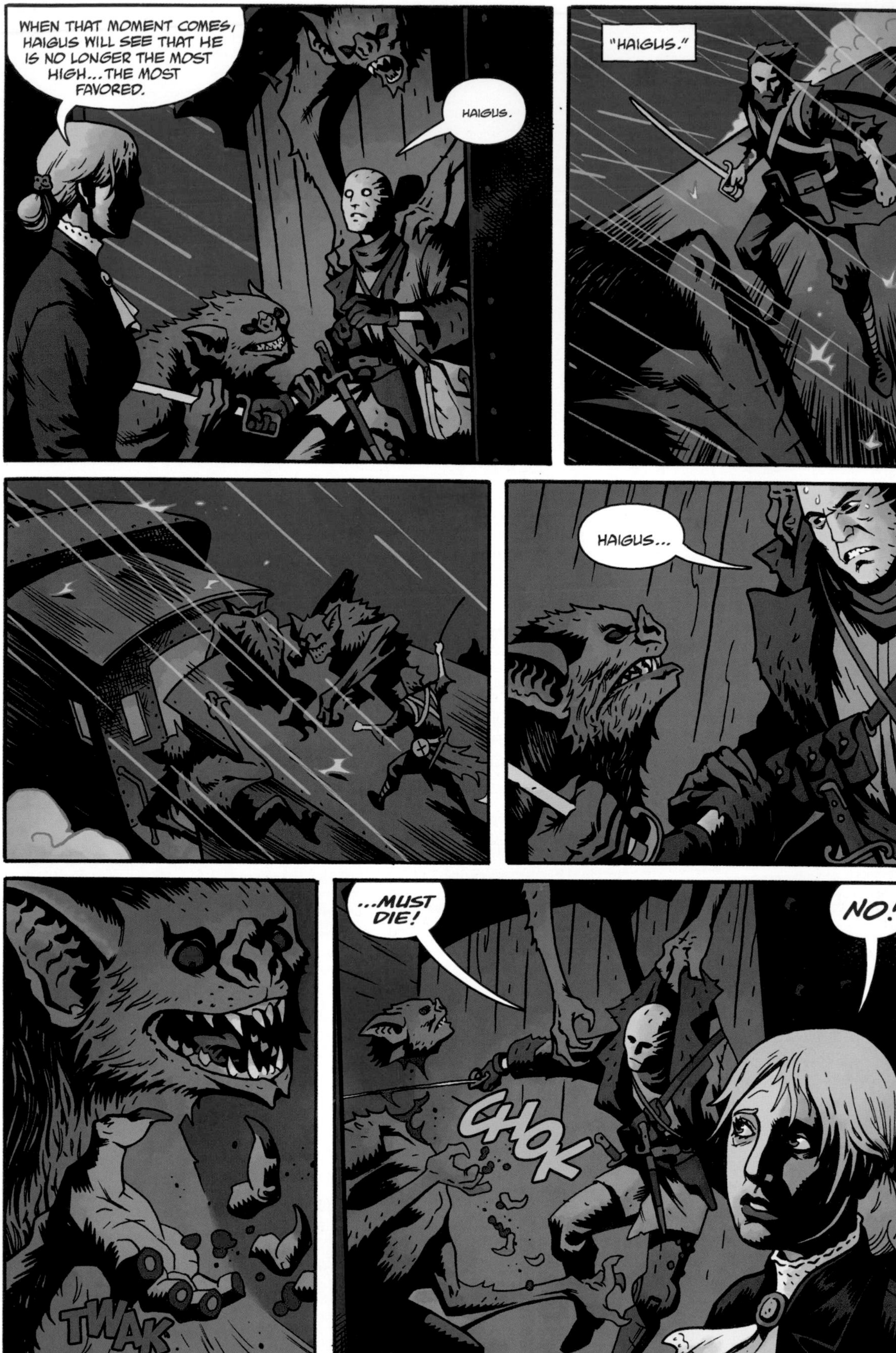
WHEN THAT MOMENT COMES, HAIGUS WILL SEE THAT HE IS NO LONGER THE MOST HIGH... THE MOST FAVORED.
HAIGUS.
"HAIGUS."
HAIGUS...
TWAK
...MUST DIE!
CHOK
NO!

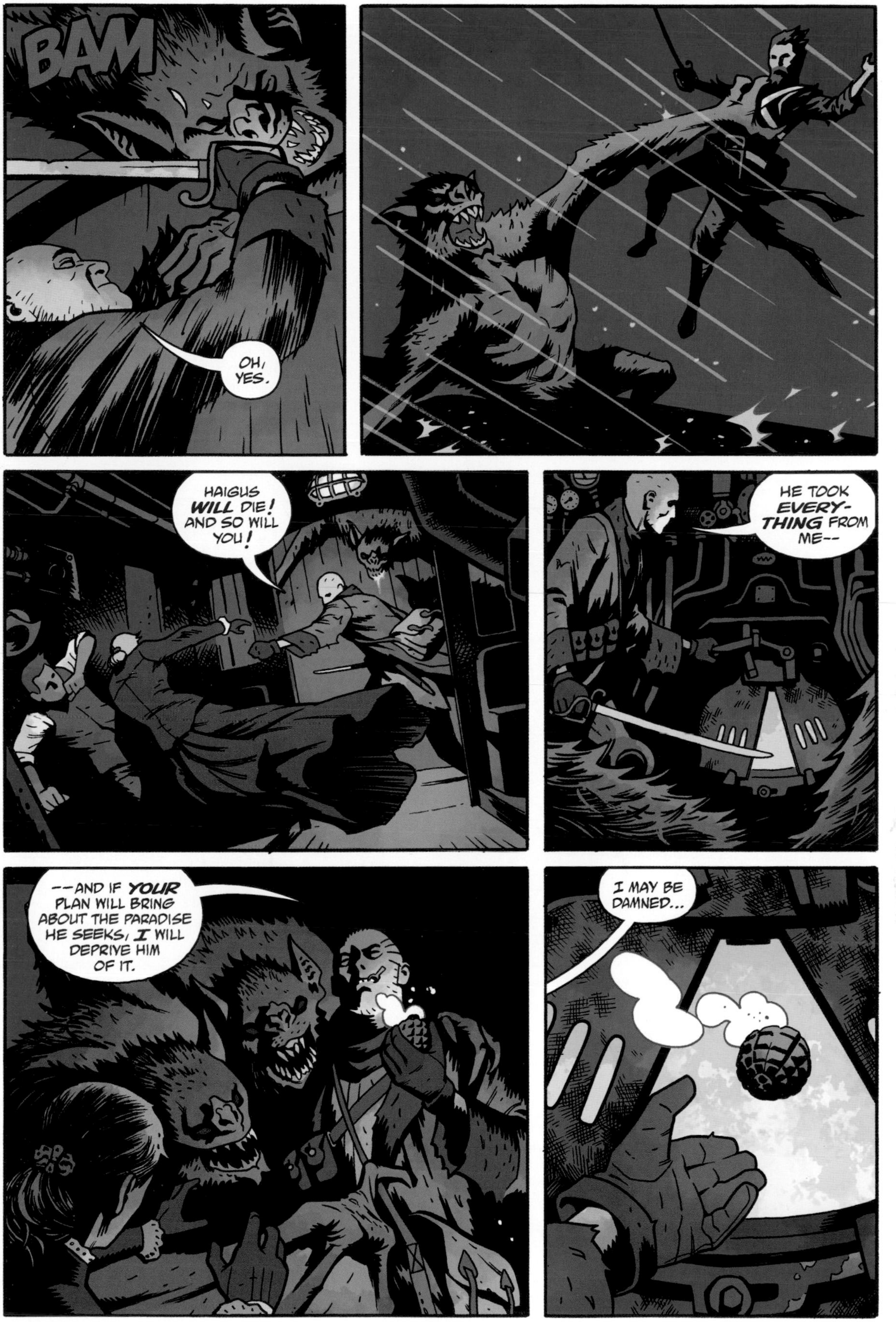
BAM
OH, YES.
HAIGUS WILL DIE! AND SO WILL YOU!
HE TOOK EVERYTHING FROM ME--
--AND IF YOUR PLAN WILL BRING ABOUT THE PARADISE HE SEEKS, I WILL DEPRIVE HIM OF IT.
I MAY BE DAMNED...

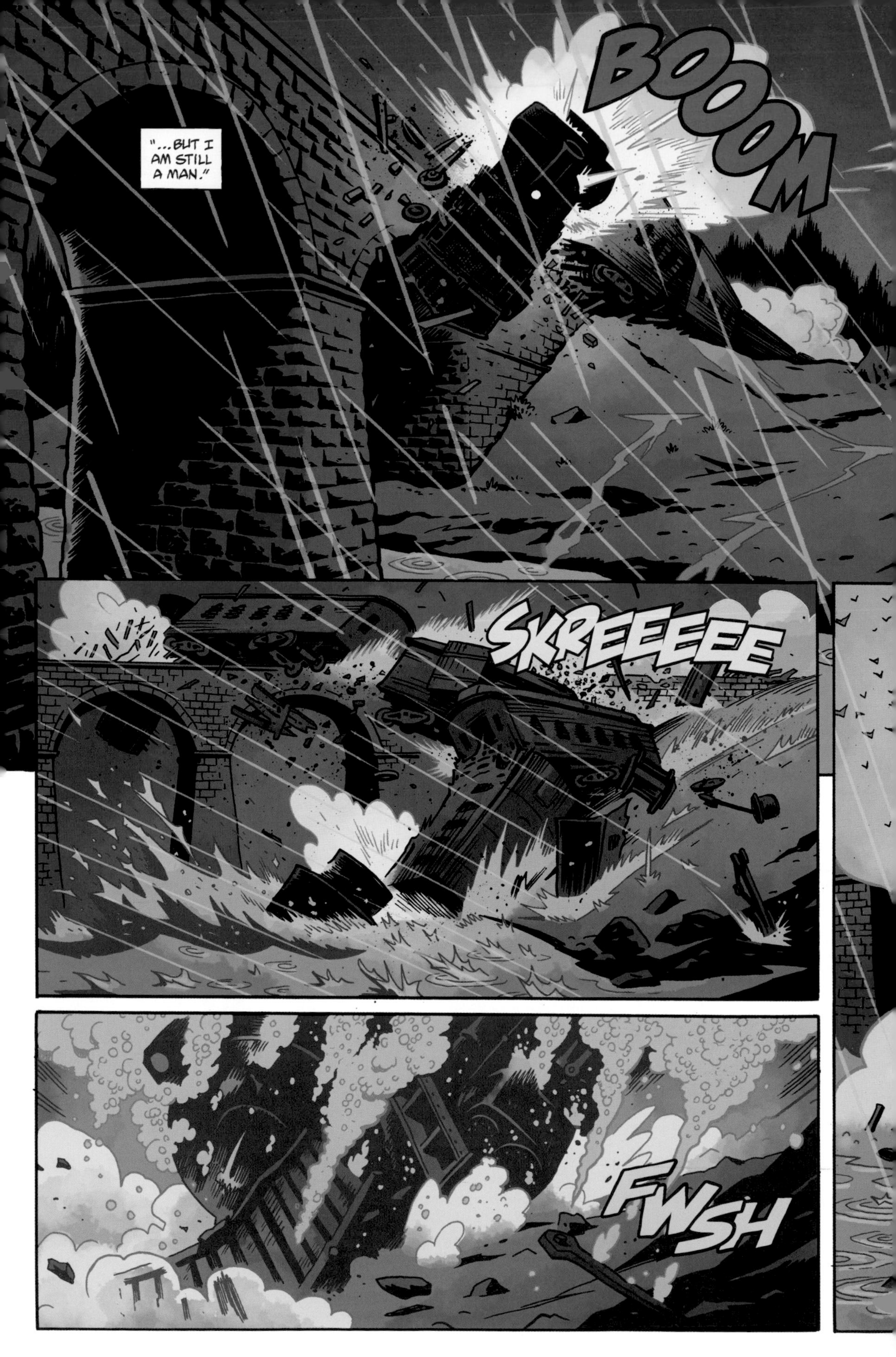
"...BUT I AM STILL A MAN."
BOOOM
SKREEEEEE
FWSH

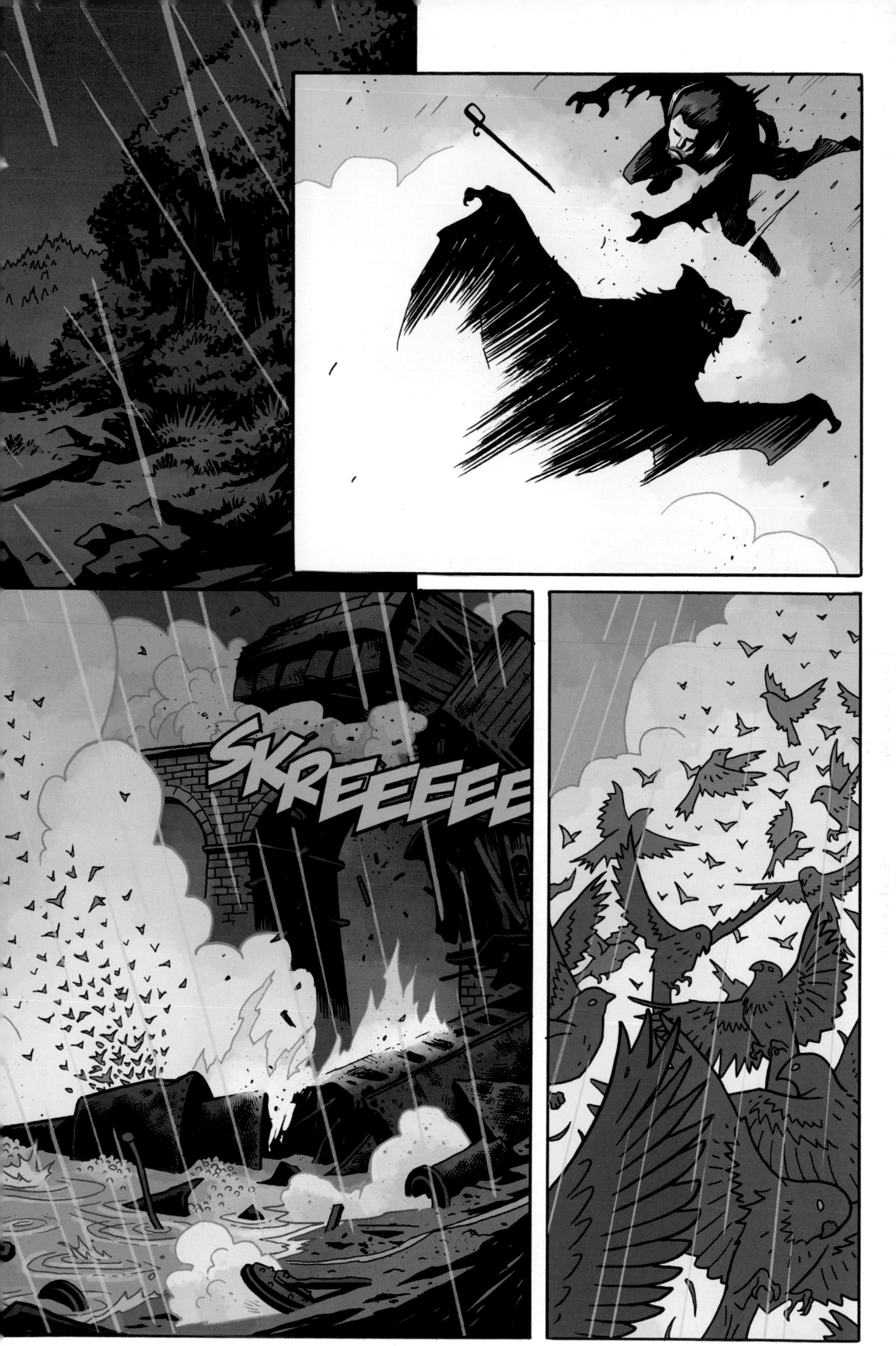
SKREEEEEE

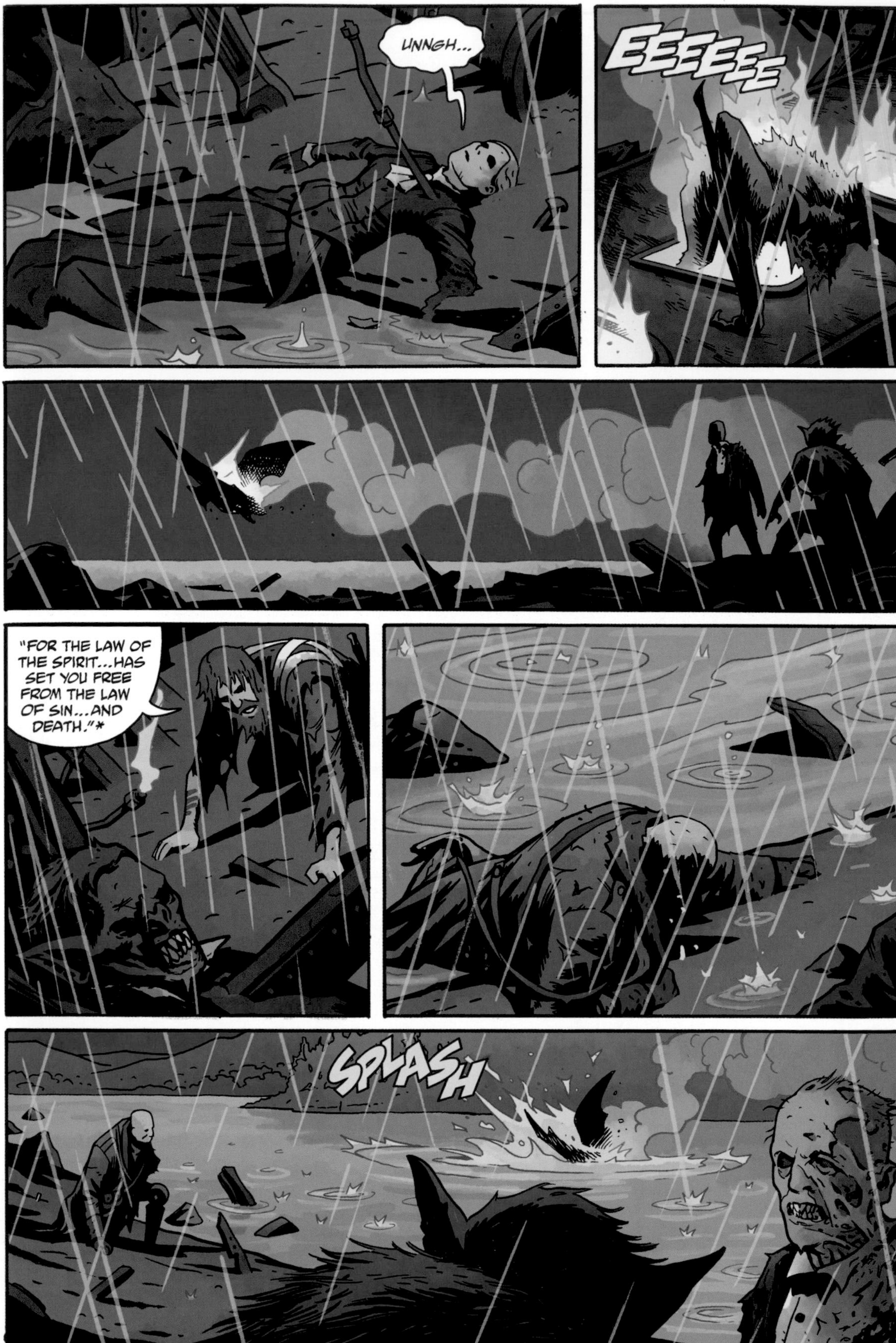
UNNGH...
EEEEEE
"FOR THE LAW OF THE SPIRIT...HAS SET YOU FREE FROM THE LAW OF SIN...AND DEATH."*
SPLASH

*ROMANS 8:2

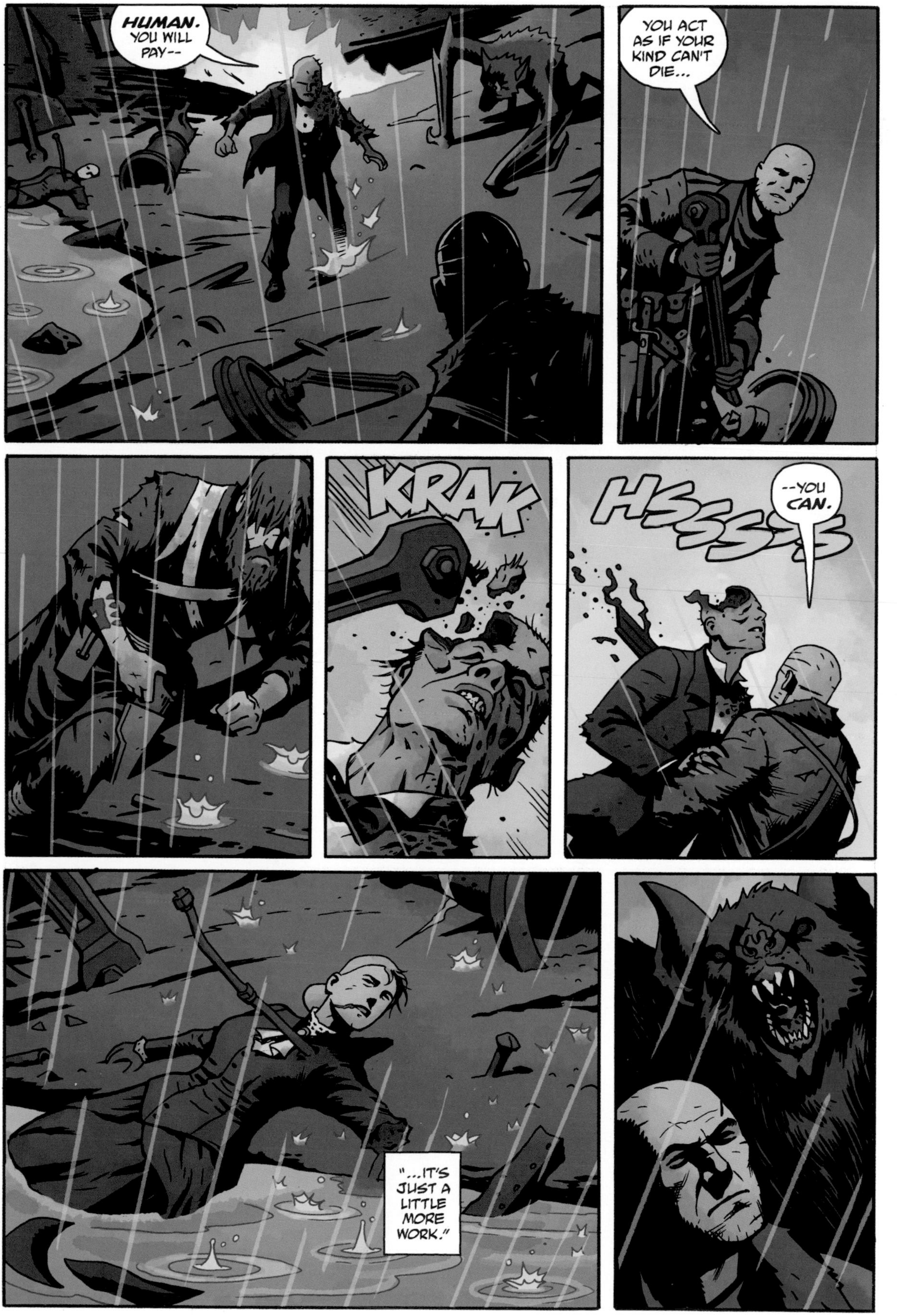
HUMAN. YOU WILL PAY--
YOU ACT AS IF YOUR KIND CAN'T DIE...
KRAK
HSSSSS
--YOU CAN.
"...IT'S JUST A LITTLE MORE WORK."

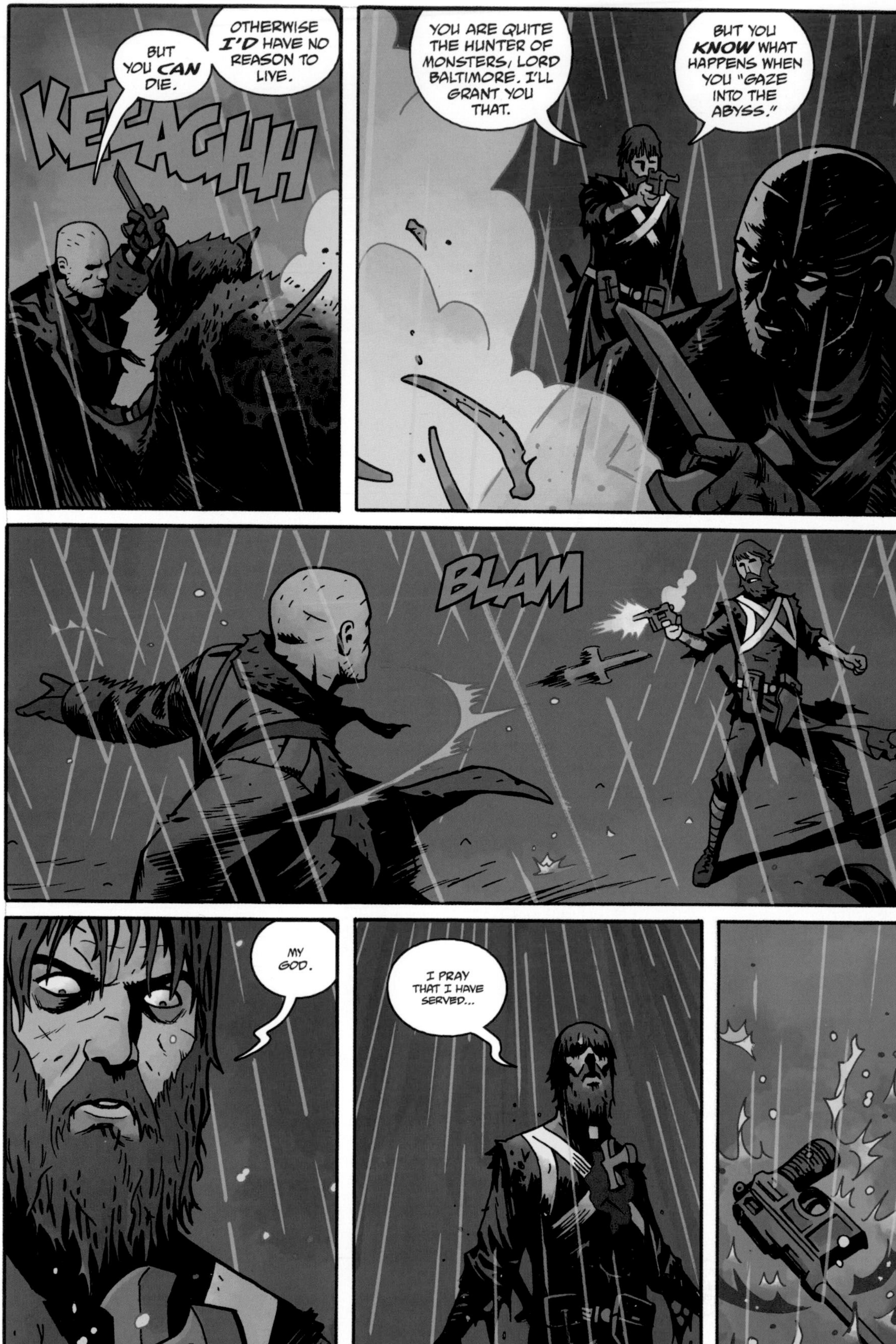

BUT YOU CAN DIE.
OTHERWISE I'D HAVE NO REASON TO LIVE.
KEEAGHH
YOU ARE QUITE THE HUNTER OF MONSTERS, LORD BALTIMORE. I'LL GRANT YOU THAT.
BUT YOU KNOW WHAT HAPPENS WHEN YOU "GAZE INTO THE ABYSS."
BLAM
MY GOD.
I PRAY THAT I HAVE SERVED...

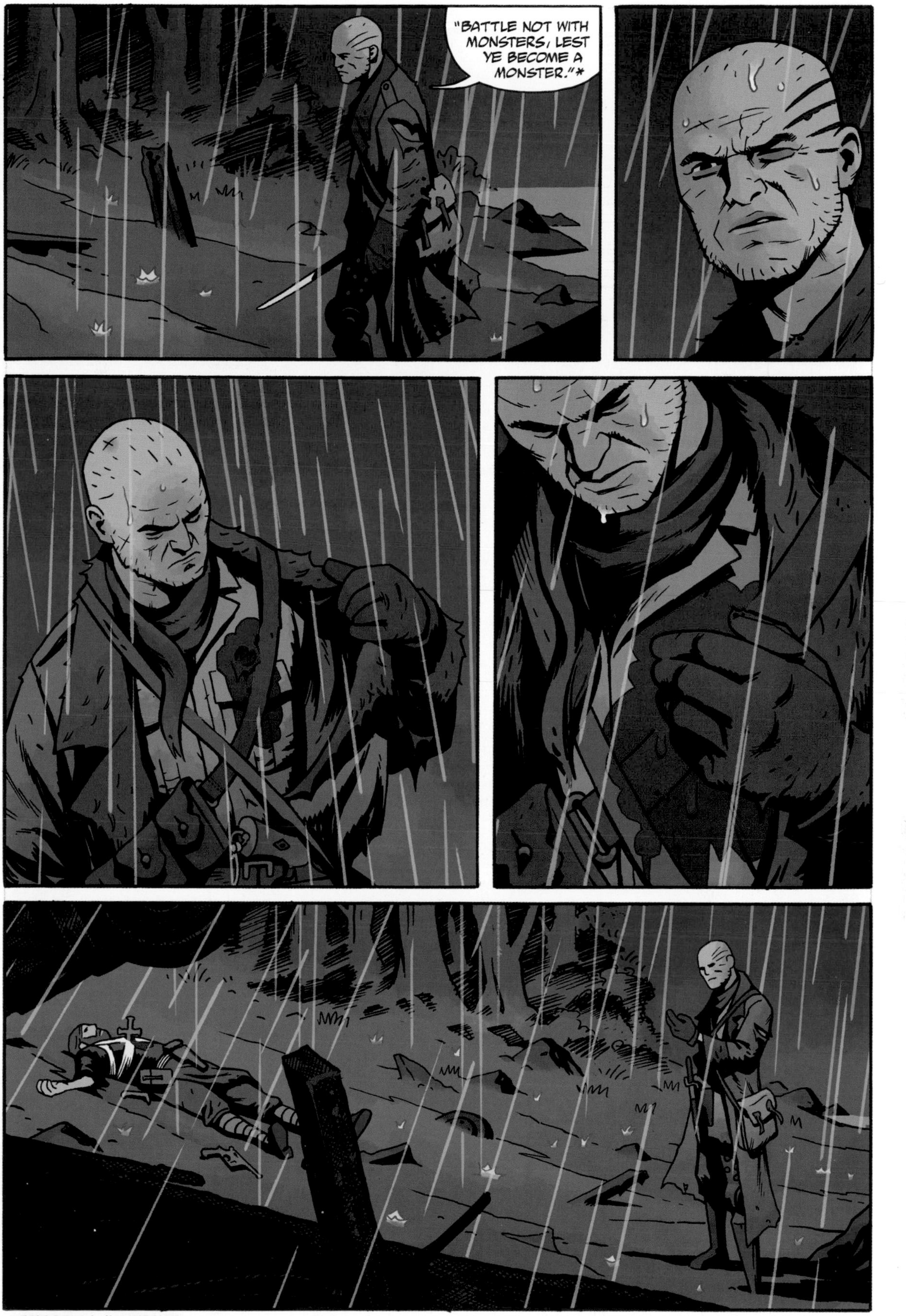
"BATTLE NOT WITH MONSTERS, LEST YE BECOME A MONSTER."*

*FRIEDRICH NIETZSCHE

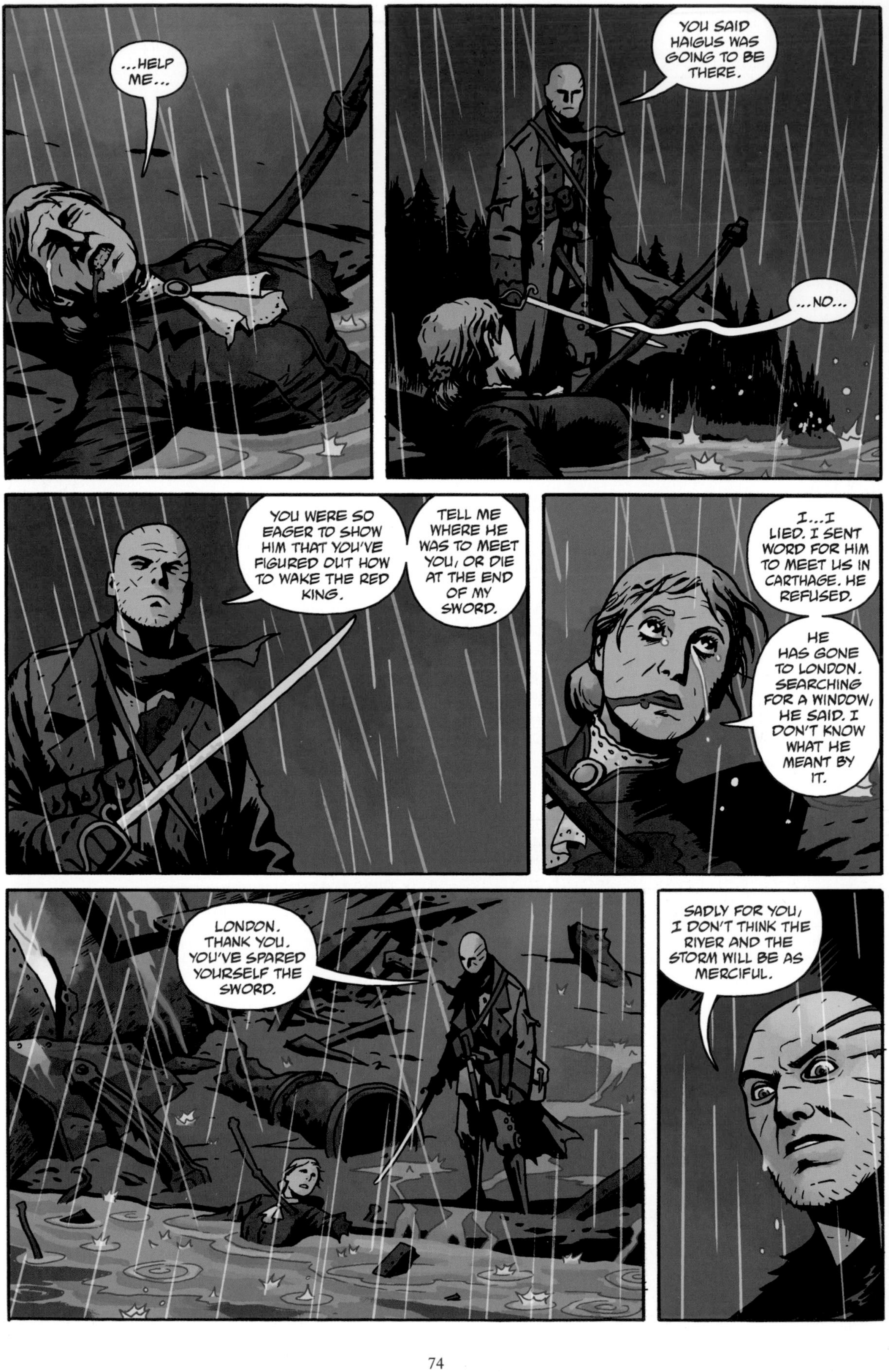
...HELP ME...
YOU SAID HAIGUS WAS GOING TO BE THERE.
...NO...
YOU WERE SO EAGER TO SHOW HIM THAT YOU'VE FIGURED OUT HOW TO WAKE THE RED KING.
TELL ME WHERE HE WAS TO MEET YOU, OR DIE AT THE END OF MY SWORD.
I...I LIED. I SENT WORD FOR HIM TO MEET US IN CARTHAGE. HE REFUSED.
HE HAS GONE TO LONDON. SEARCHING FOR A WINDOW, HE SAID. I DON'T KNOW WHAT HE MEANT BY IT.
LONDON. THANK YOU. YOU'VE SPARED YOURSELF THE SWORD.
SADLY FOR YOU, I DON'T THINK THE RIVER AND THE STORM WILL BE AS MERCIFUL.

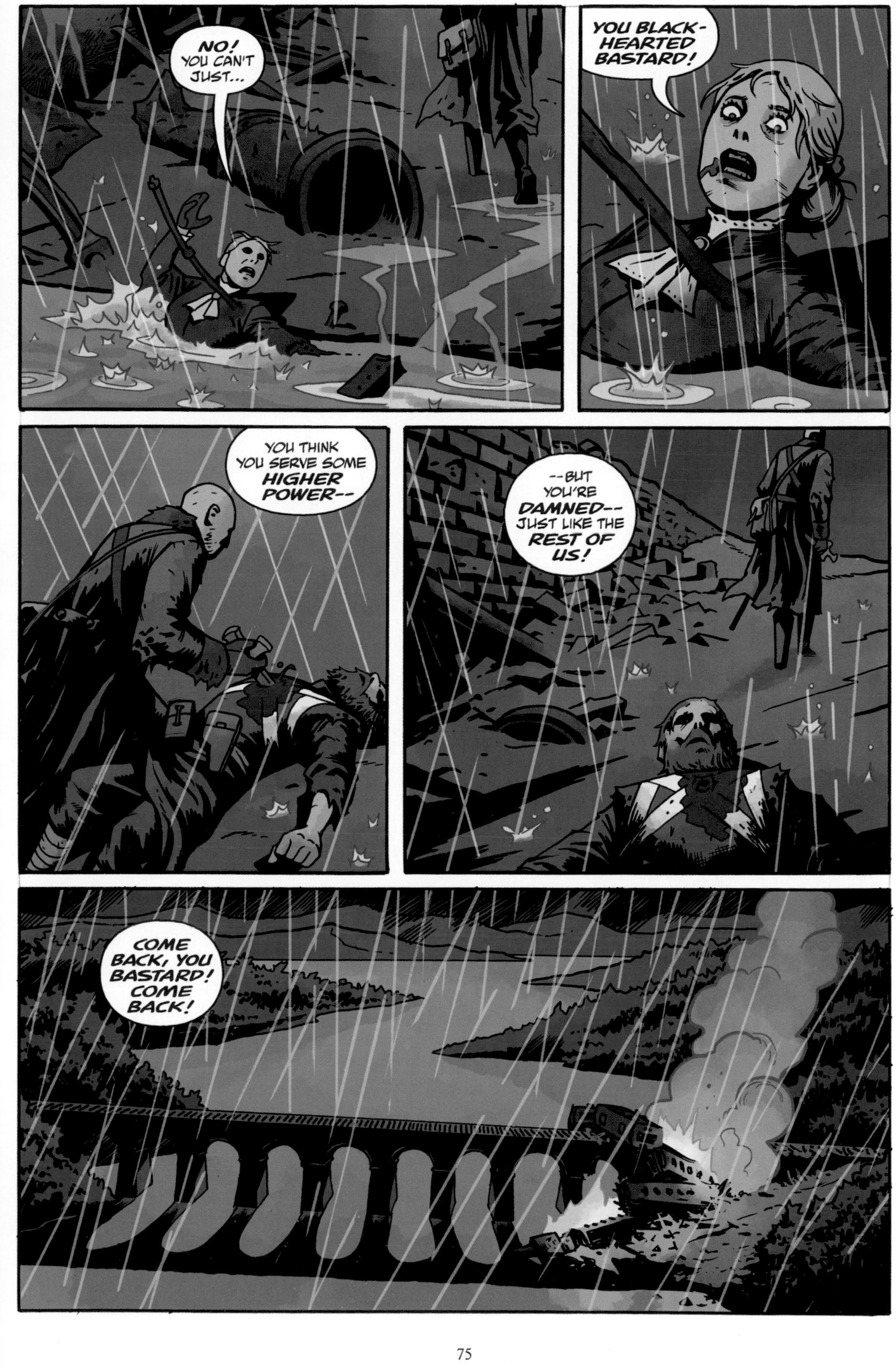
NO! YOU CAN'T JUST...
YOU BLACK-HEARTED BASTARD!
YOU THINK YOU SERVE SOME HIGHER POWER--
--BUT YOU'RE DAMNED-- JUST LIKE THE REST OF US!
COME BACK, YOU BASTARD! COME BACK!

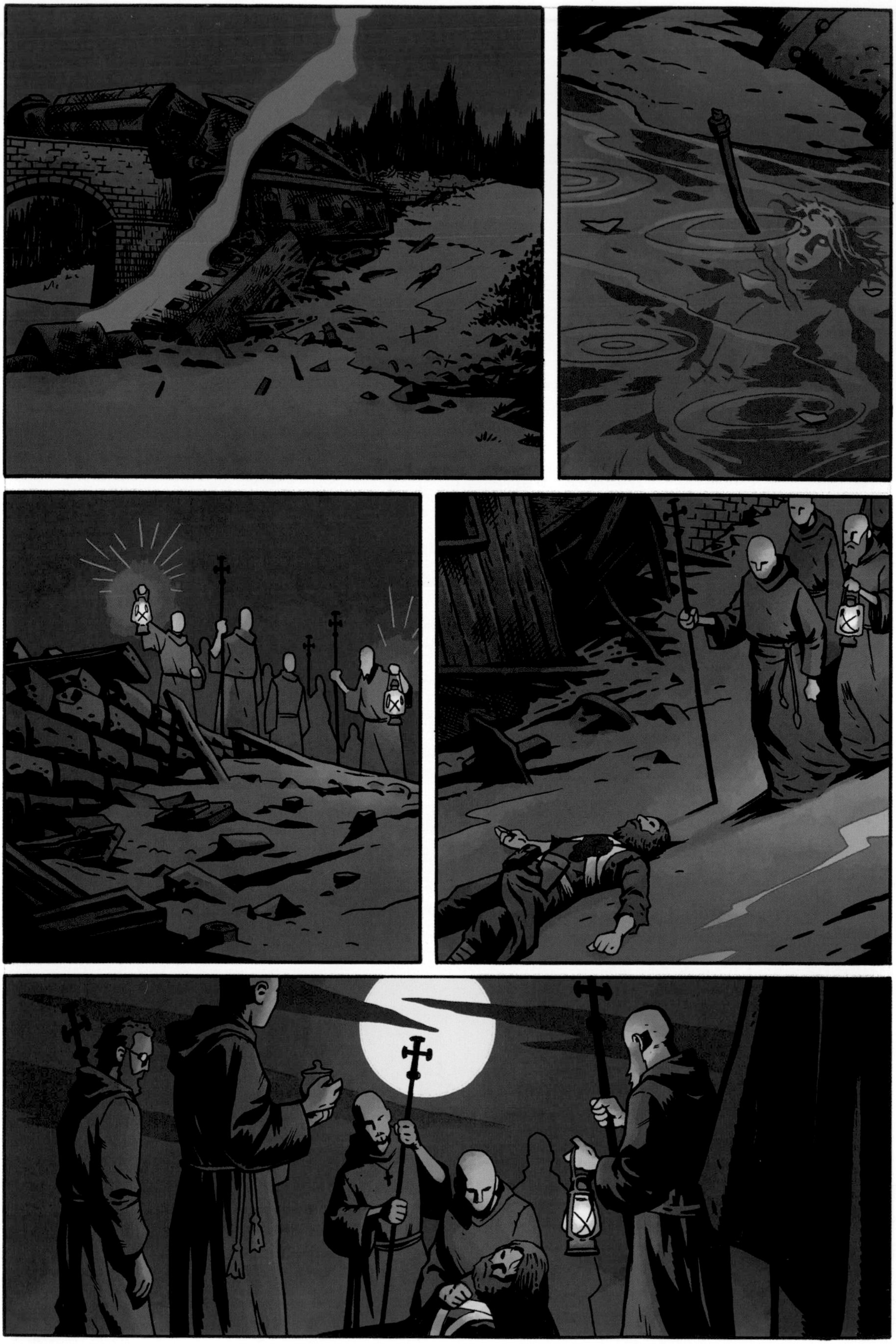

MAN THAT IS BORN OF WOMAN HAS BUT A SHORT TIME TO LIVE, AND IS FULL OF MISERY.

MAY GOD HAVE MERCY ON YOUR SOUL.

SUBVENITE SANCTI DEI, OCCURRITE ANGELI DOMINI--SUSCIPIENTES ANIMAM EJUS, OFFERENTES EAM IN CONSPECTU ALTISSIMI.

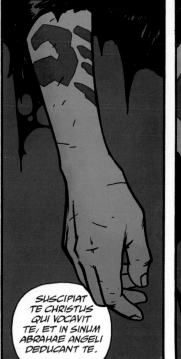

SUSCIPIAT TE CHRISTUS QUI VOCAVIT TE, ET IN SINUM ABRAHAE ANGELI DEDUCANT TE.

SUSCIPIENTES ANIMAM EJUS, OFFERENTES EAM IN CONSPECTU ALTISSIMI.

REQUIEM AETERNAM DONA EI, DOMINE--ET LUX PERPETUA LUCEAT EI.

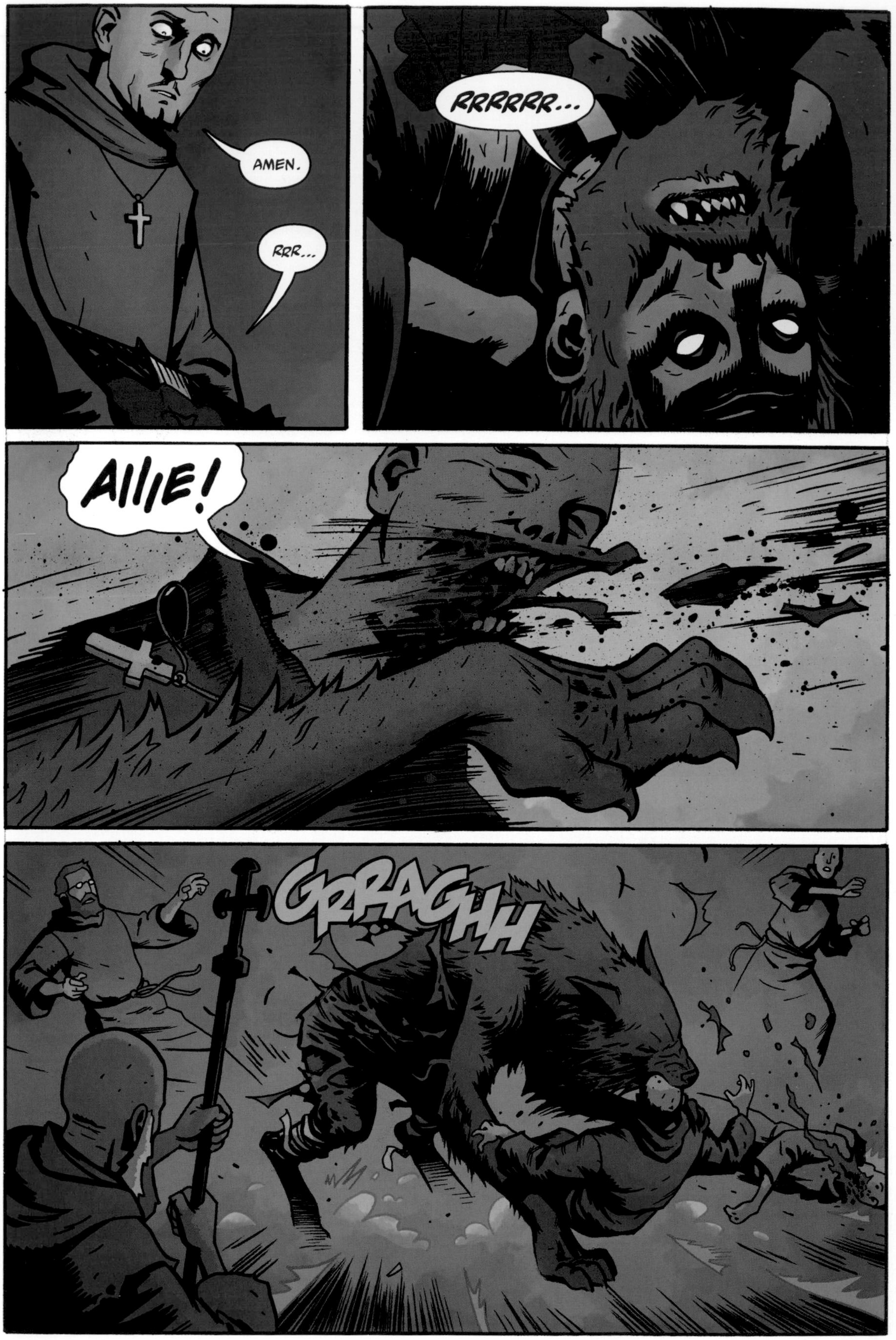
AMEN.
RRR...
RRRRRR...
AIIIE!
GRRAGHH

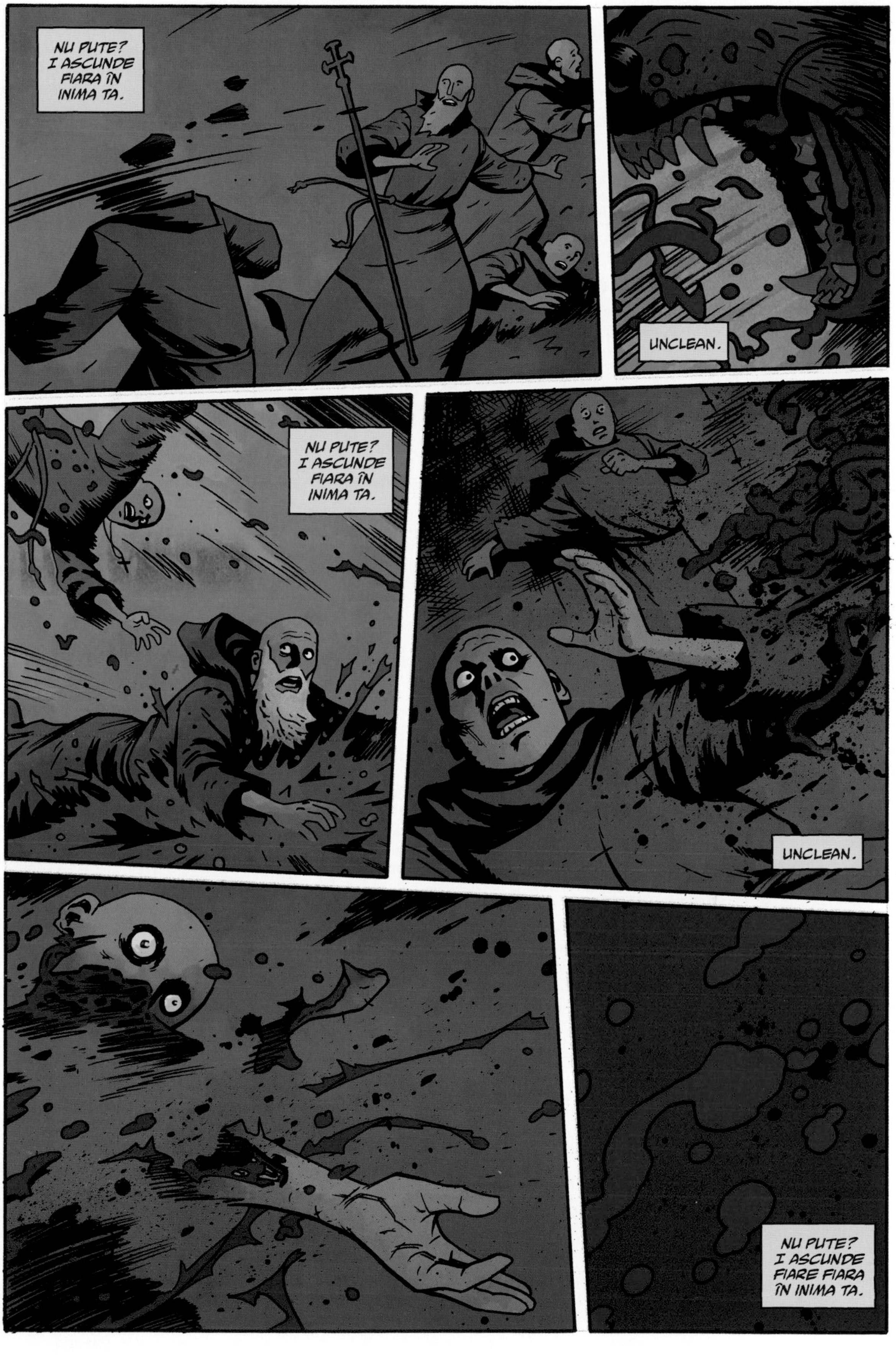
NU PUTE? I ASCUNDE FIARA ÎN INIMA TA.
UNCLEAN.
NU PUTE? I ASCUNDE FIARA ÎN INIMA TA.
UNCLEAN.
NU PUTE? I ASCUNDE FIARE FIARA ÎN INIMA TA.

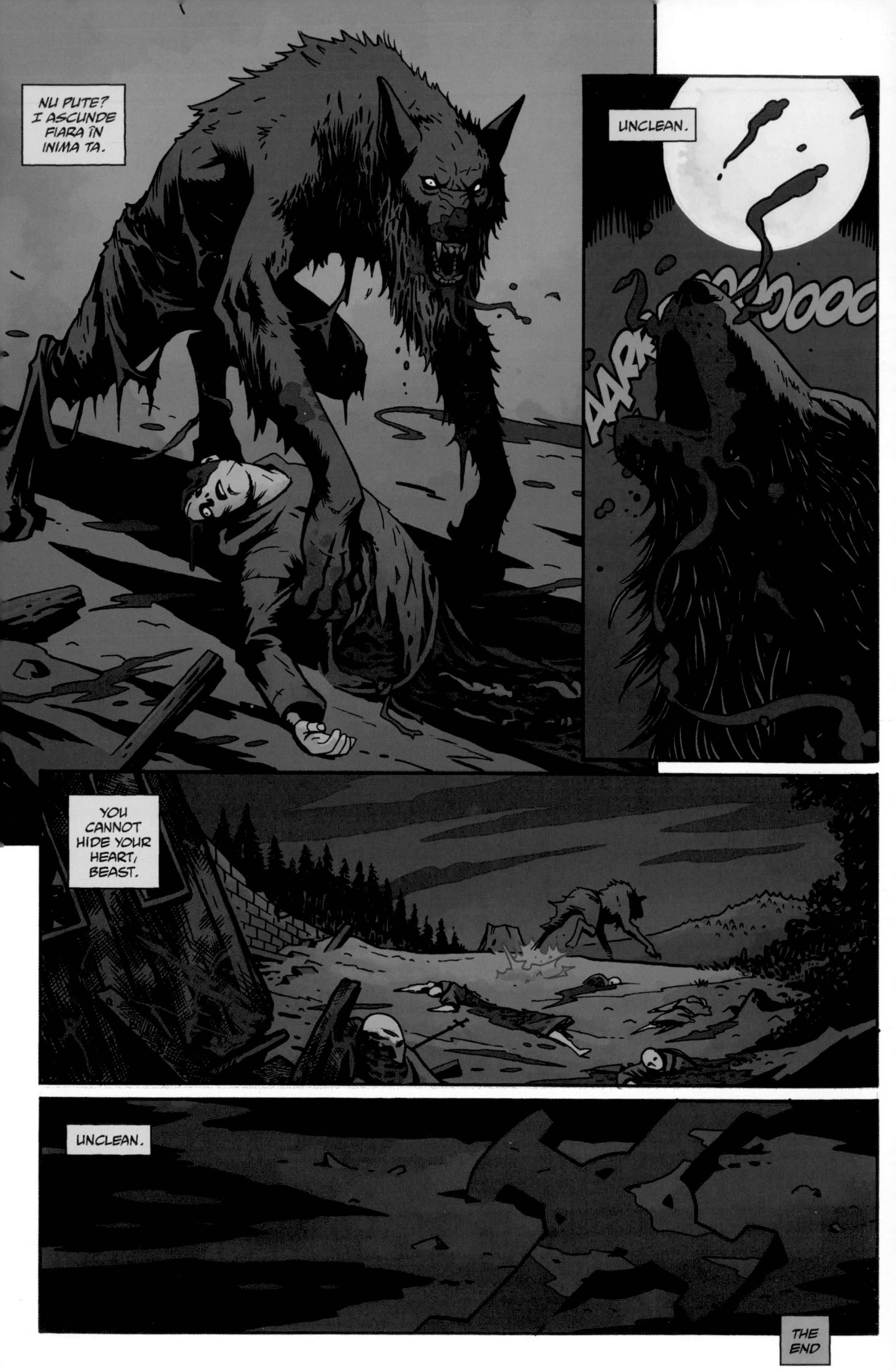
NU PUTE? I ASCUNDE FIARA ÎN INIMA TA.
UNCLEAN.
AARR
OOOO
YOU CANNOT HIDE YOUR HEART, BEAST.
UNCLEAN.
THE END

CHAPEL OF BONES
Chapter One

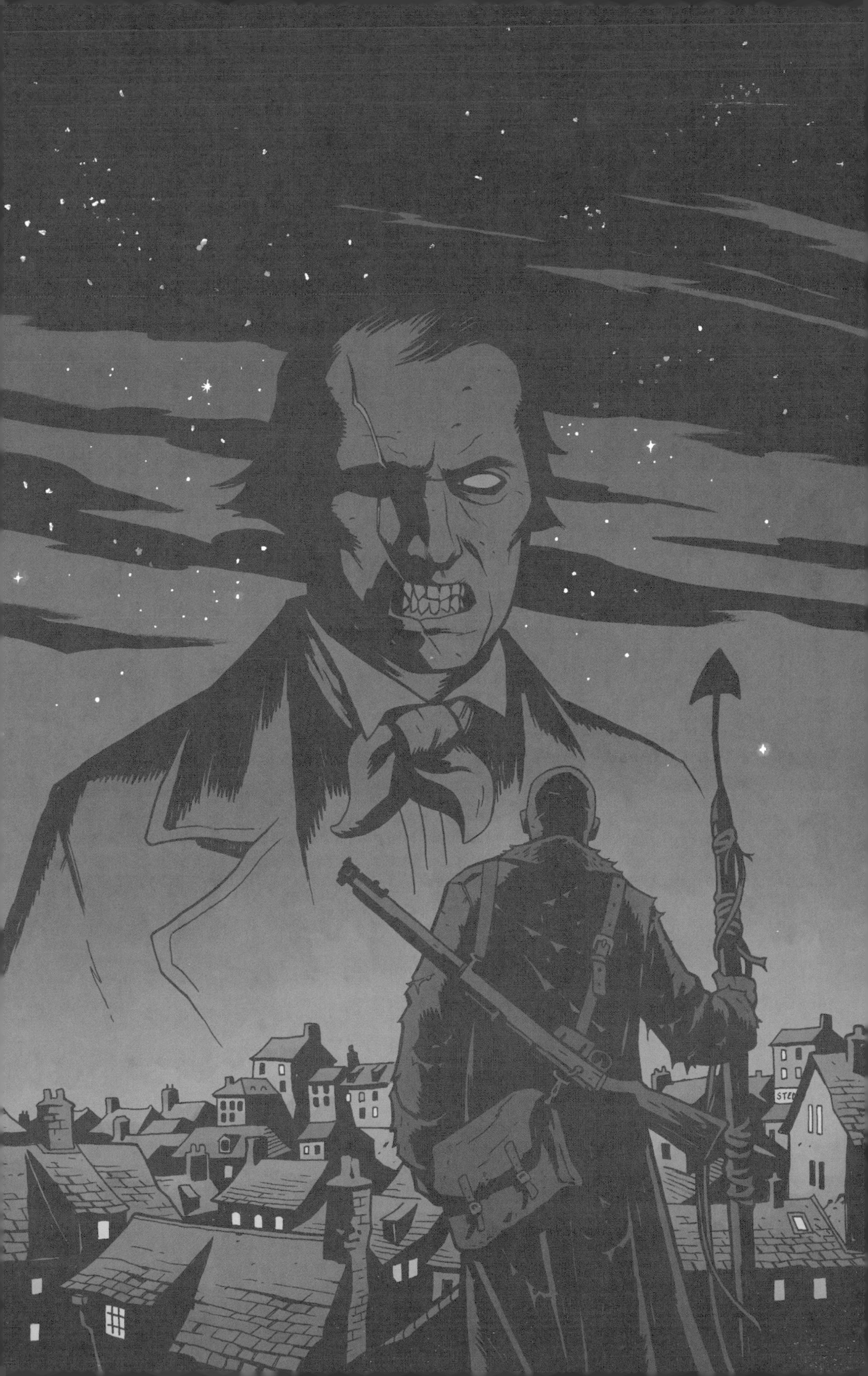

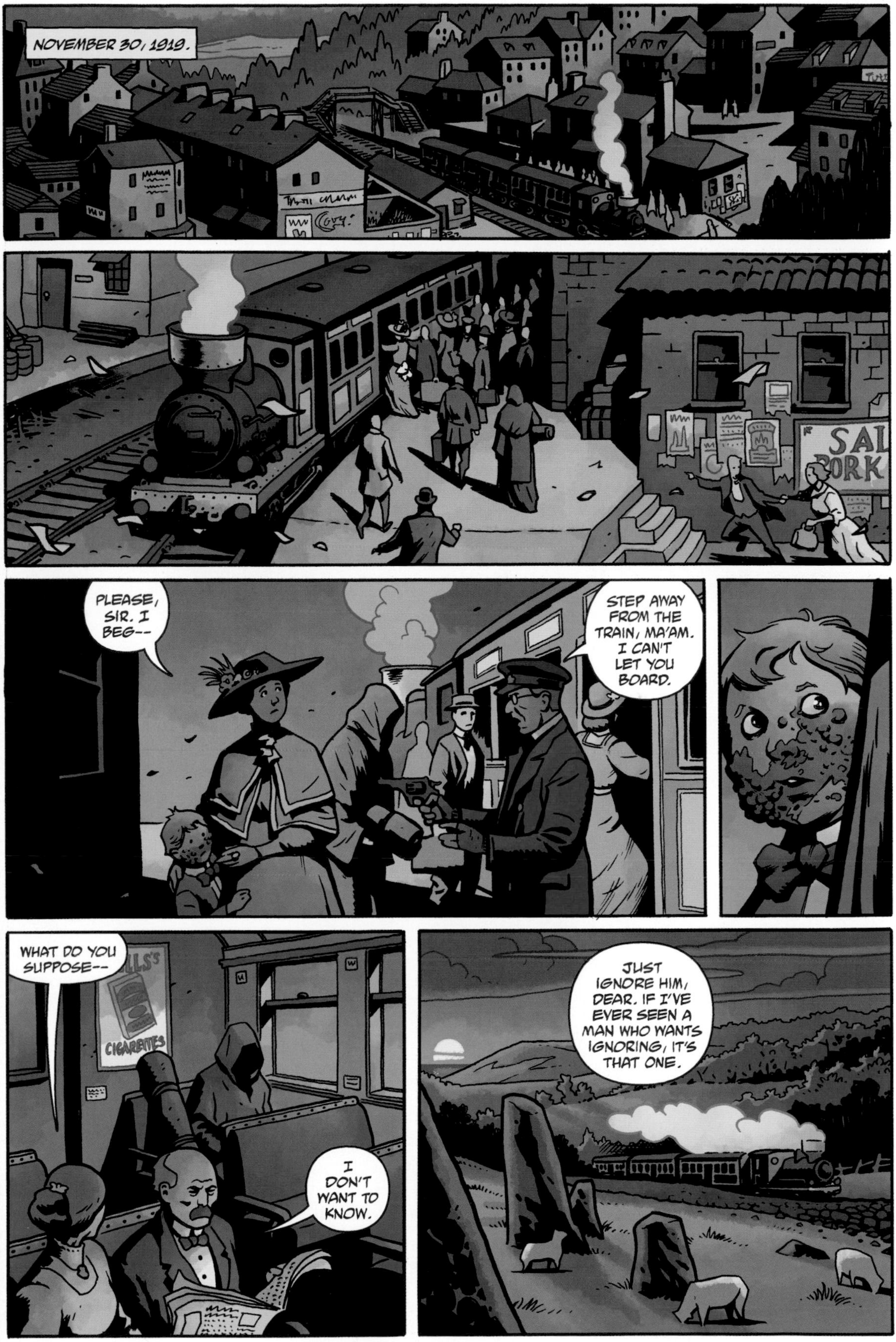
NOVEMBER 30, 1919.
PLEASE, SIR. I BEG--
STEP AWAY FROM THE TRAIN, MA'AM. I CAN'T LET YOU BOARD.
WHAT DO YOU SUPPOSE--
CIGARETTES
I DON'T WANT TO KNOW.
JUST IGNORE HIM, DEAR. IF I'VE EVER SEEN A MAN WHO WANTS IGNORING, IT'S THAT ONE.

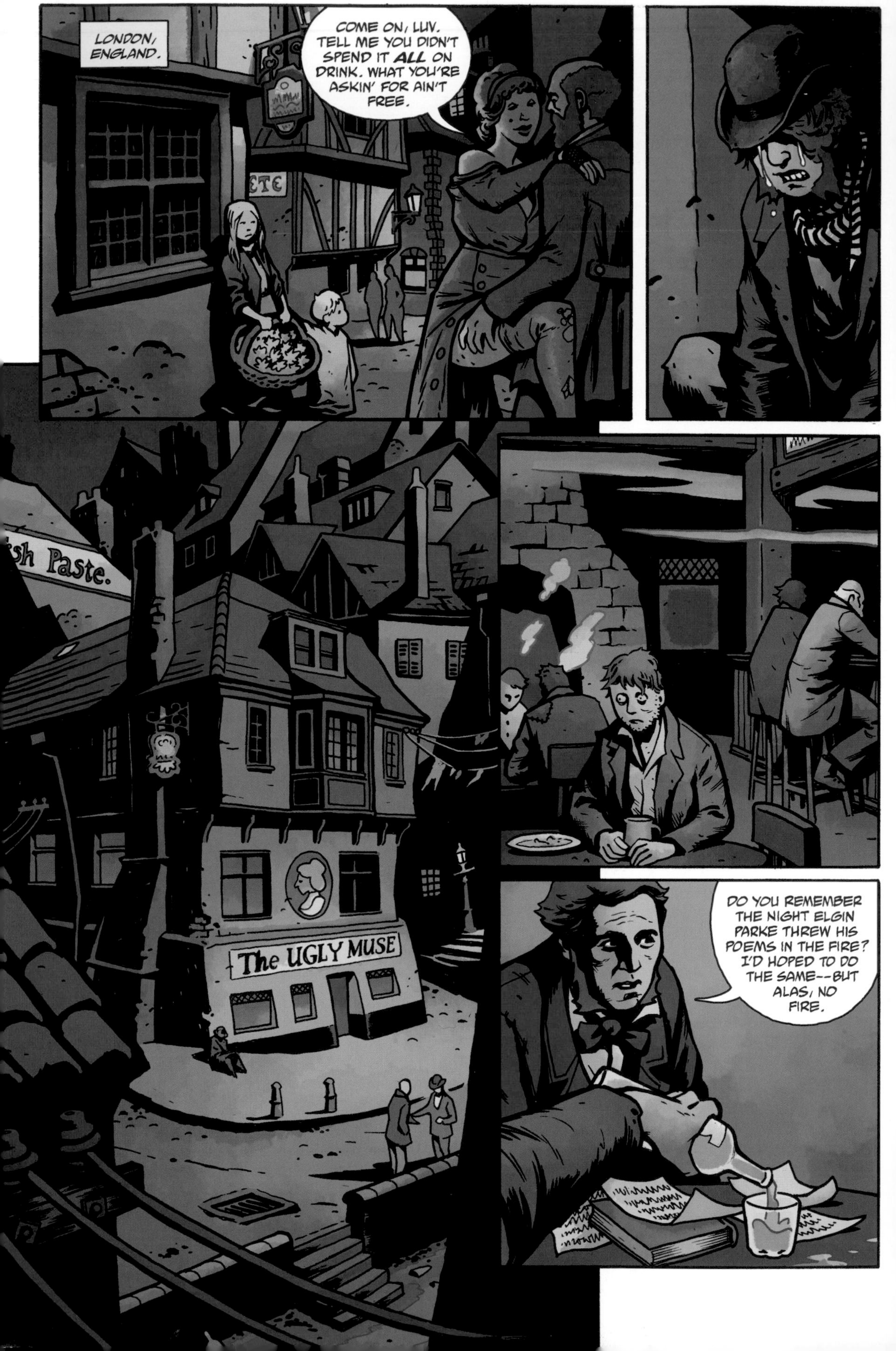
LONDON, ENGLAND.
COME ON, LUV. TELL ME YOU DIDN'T SPEND IT ALL ON DRINK. WHAT YOU'RE ASKIN' FOR AIN'T FREE.
sh Paste.
The UGLY MUSE
DO YOU REMEMBER THE NIGHT ELGIN PARKE THREW HIS POEMS IN THE FIRE? I'D HOPED TO DO THE SAME--BUT ALAS, NO FIRE.

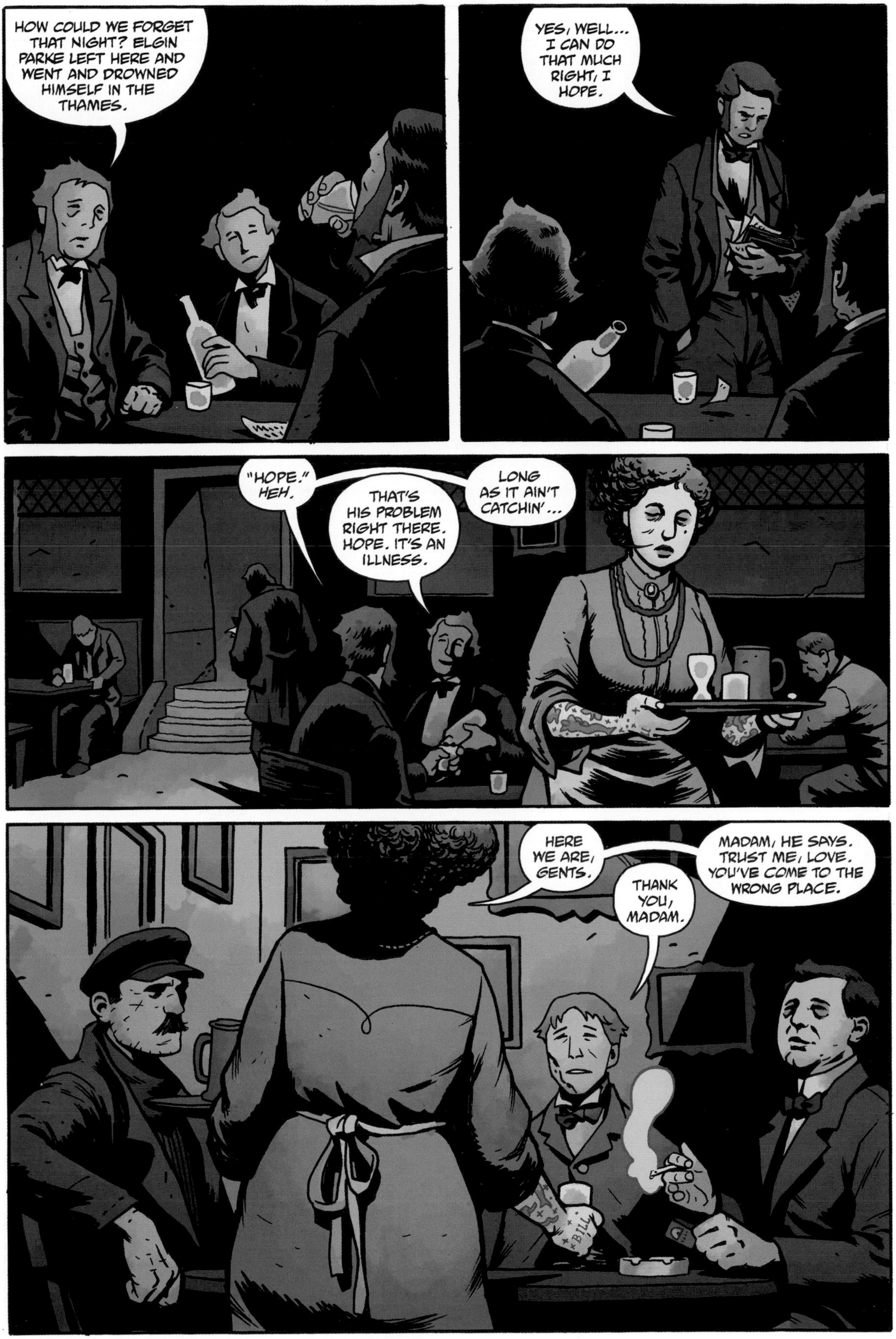
HOW COULD WE FORGET THAT NIGHT? ELGIN PARKE LEFT HERE AND WENT AND DROWNED HIMSELF IN THE THAMES.
YES, WELL... I CAN DO THAT MUCH RIGHT, I HOPE.
"HOPE." HEH.
THAT'S HIS PROBLEM RIGHT THERE. HOPE. IT'S AN ILLNESS.
LONG AS IT AIN'T CATCHIN'...
HERE WE ARE, GENTS.
THANK YOU, MADAM.
MADAM, HE SAYS. TRUST ME, LOVE. YOU'VE COME TO THE WRONG PLACE.
BILL

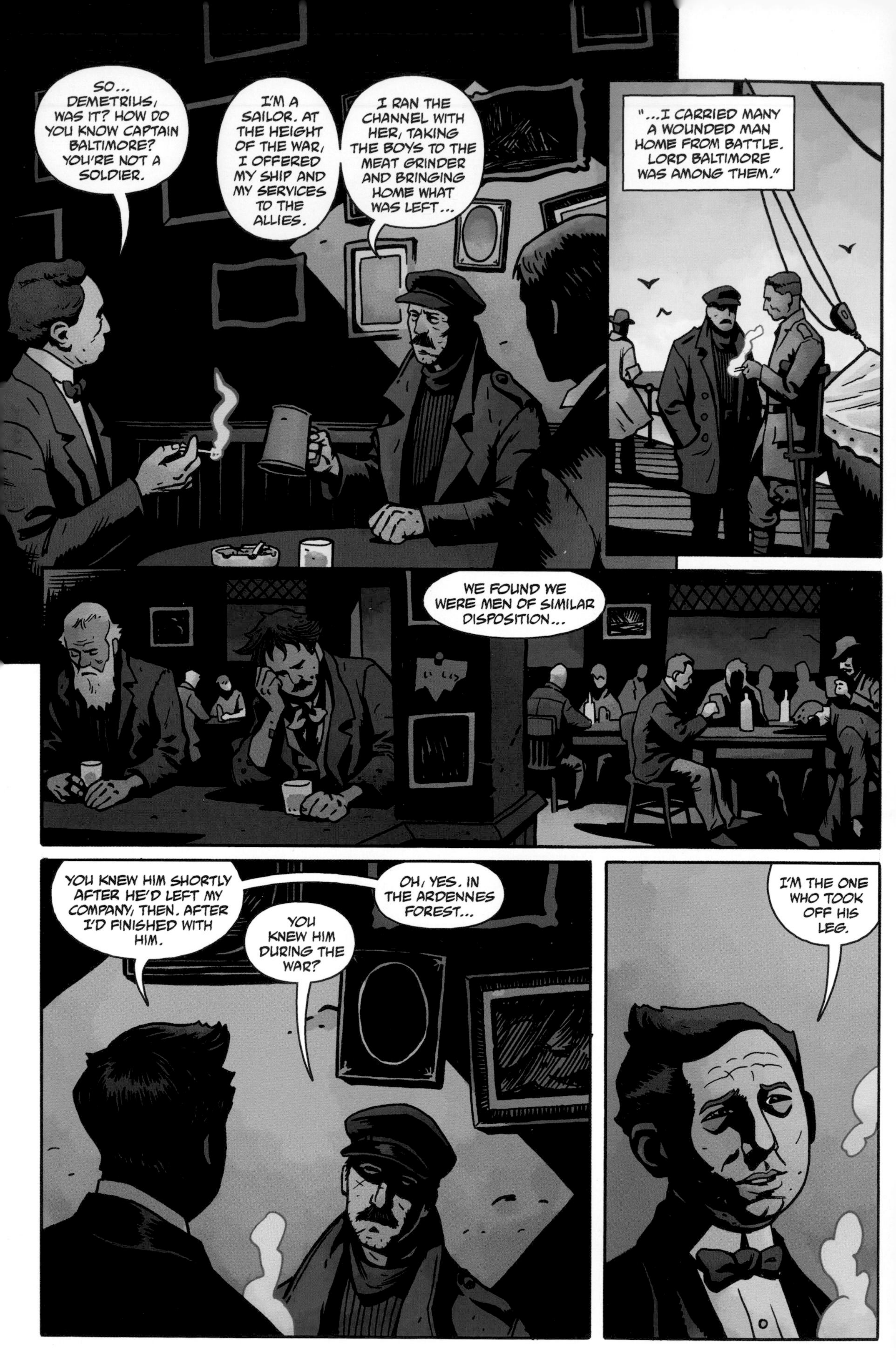
SO... DEMETRIUS, WAS IT? HOW DO YOU KNOW CAPTAIN BALTIMORE? YOU'RE NOT A SOLDIER.
I'M A SAILOR. AT THE HEIGHT OF THE WAR, I OFFERED MY SHIP AND MY SERVICES TO THE ALLIES.
I RAN THE CHANNEL WITH HER, TAKING THE BOYS TO THE MEAT GRINDER AND BRINGING HOME WHAT WAS LEFT...
"...I CARRIED MANY A WOUNDED MAN HOME FROM BATTLE. LORD BALTIMORE WAS AMONG THEM."
WE FOUND WE WERE MEN OF SIMILAR DISPOSITION...
YOU KNEW HIM DURING THE WAR?
OH, YES. IN THE ARDENNES FOREST...
YOU KNEW HIM SHORTLY AFTER HE'D LEFT MY COMPANY, THEN. AFTER I'D FINISHED WITH HIM.
I'M THE ONE WHO TOOK OFF HIS LEG.

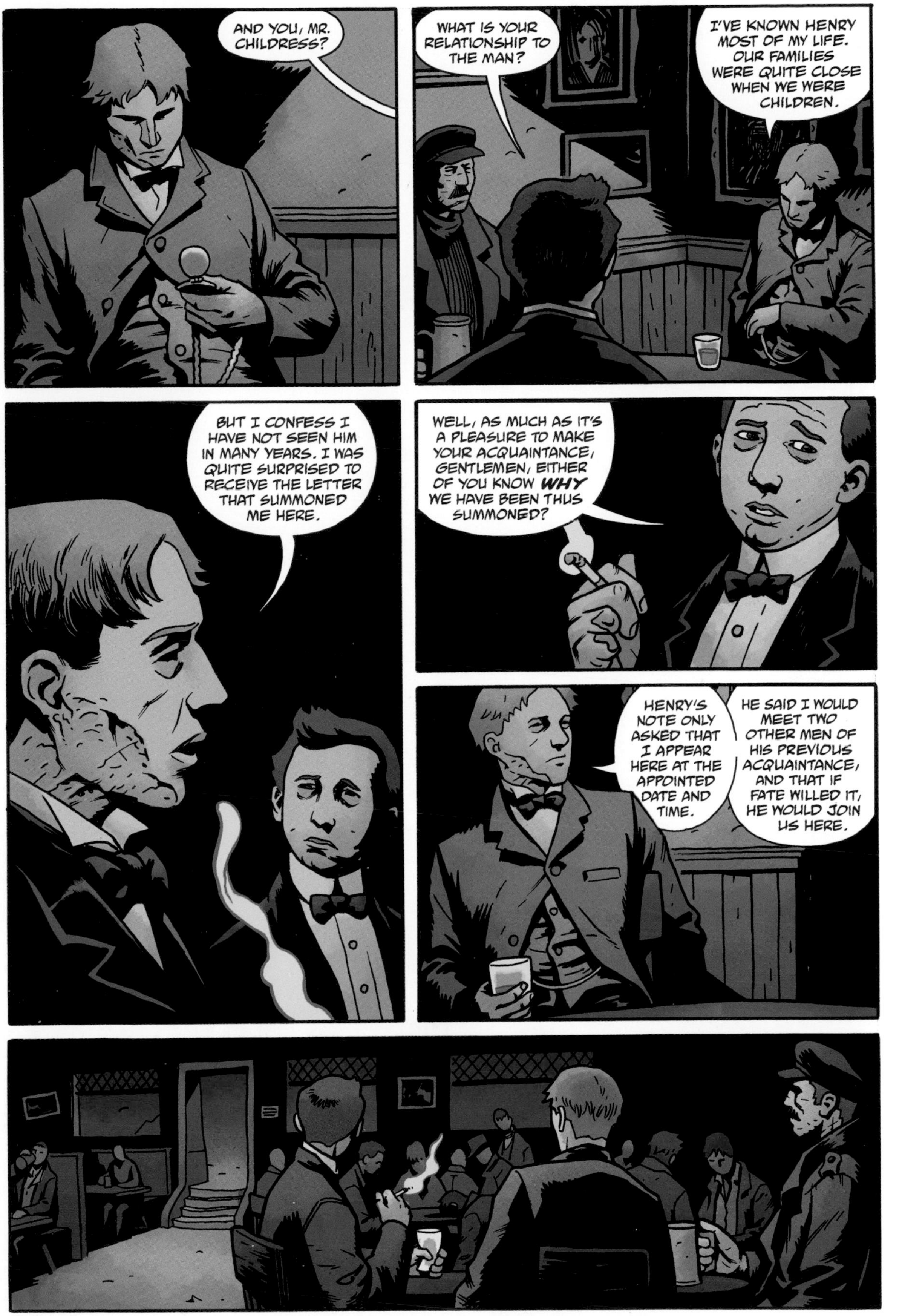
AND YOU, MR. CHILDRESS?
WHAT IS YOUR RELATIONSHIP TO THE MAN?
I'VE KNOWN HENRY MOST OF MY LIFE. OUR FAMILIES WERE QUITE CLOSE WHEN WE WERE CHILDREN.
BUT I CONFESS I HAVE NOT SEEN HIM IN MANY YEARS. I WAS QUITE SURPRISED TO RECEIVE THE LETTER THAT SUMMONED ME HERE.
WELL, AS MUCH AS IT'S A PLEASURE TO MAKE YOUR ACQUAINTANCE, GENTLEMEN, EITHER OF YOU KNOW WHY WE HAVE BEEN THUS SUMMONED?
HENRY'S NOTE ONLY ASKED THAT I APPEAR HERE AT THE APPOINTED DATE AND TIME.
HE SAID I WOULD MEET TWO OTHER MEN OF HIS PREVIOUS ACQUAINTANCE, AND THAT IF FATE WILLED IT, HE WOULD JOIN US HERE.

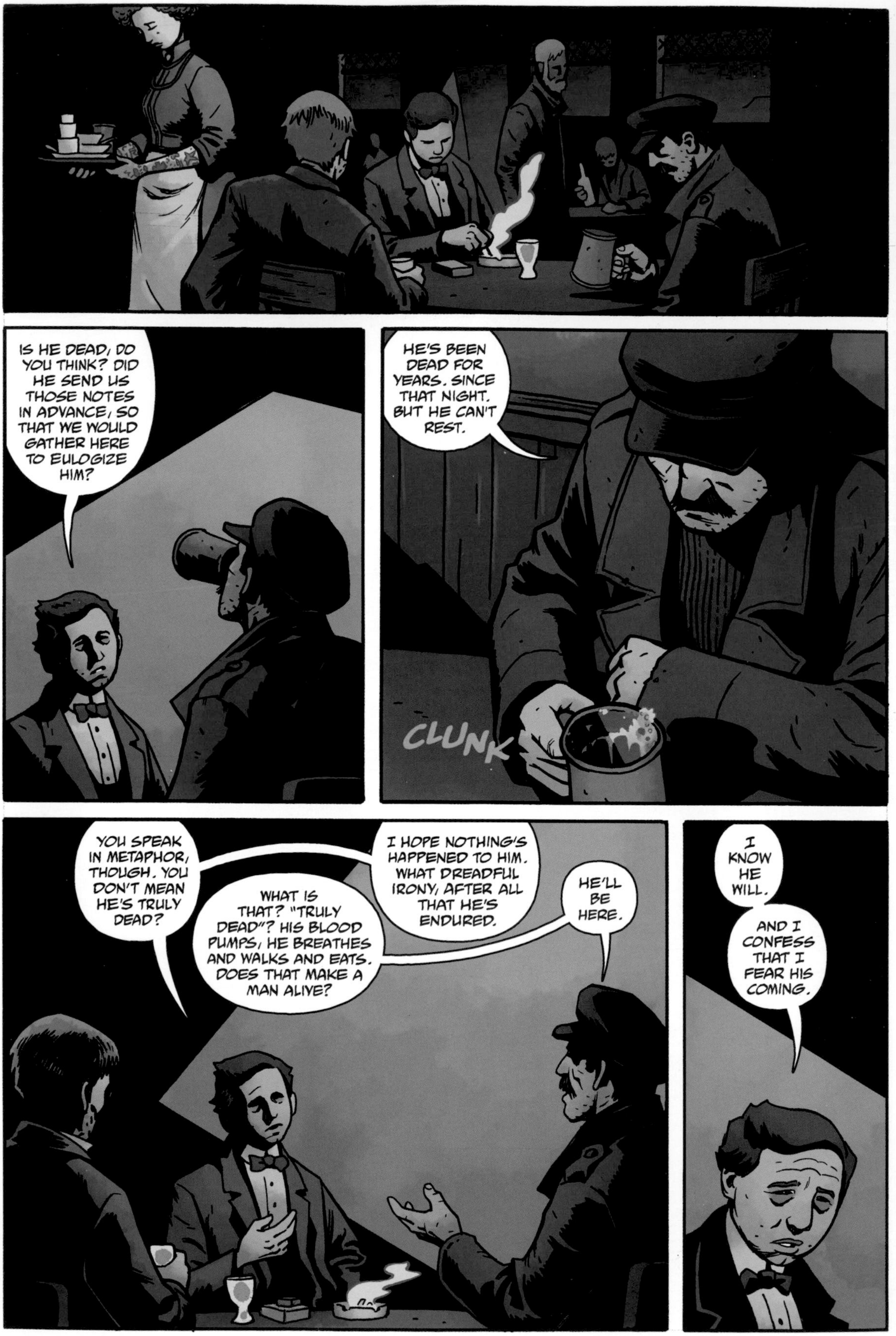
IS HE DEAD, DO YOU THINK? DID HE SEND US THOSE NOTES IN ADVANCE, SO THAT WE WOULD GATHER HERE TO EULOGIZE HIM?
HE'S BEEN DEAD FOR YEARS. SINCE THAT NIGHT. BUT HE CAN'T REST.
CLUNK
YOU SPEAK IN METAPHOR, THOUGH. YOU DON'T MEAN HE'S TRULY DEAD?
WHAT IS THAT? "TRULY DEAD"? HIS BLOOD PUMPS, HE BREATHES AND WALKS AND EATS. DOES THAT MAKE A MAN ALIVE?
I HOPE NOTHING'S HAPPENED TO HIM. WHAT DREADFUL IRONY, AFTER ALL THAT HE'S ENDURED.
HE'LL BE HERE.
I KNOW HE WILL.
AND I CONFESS THAT I FEAR HIS COMING.

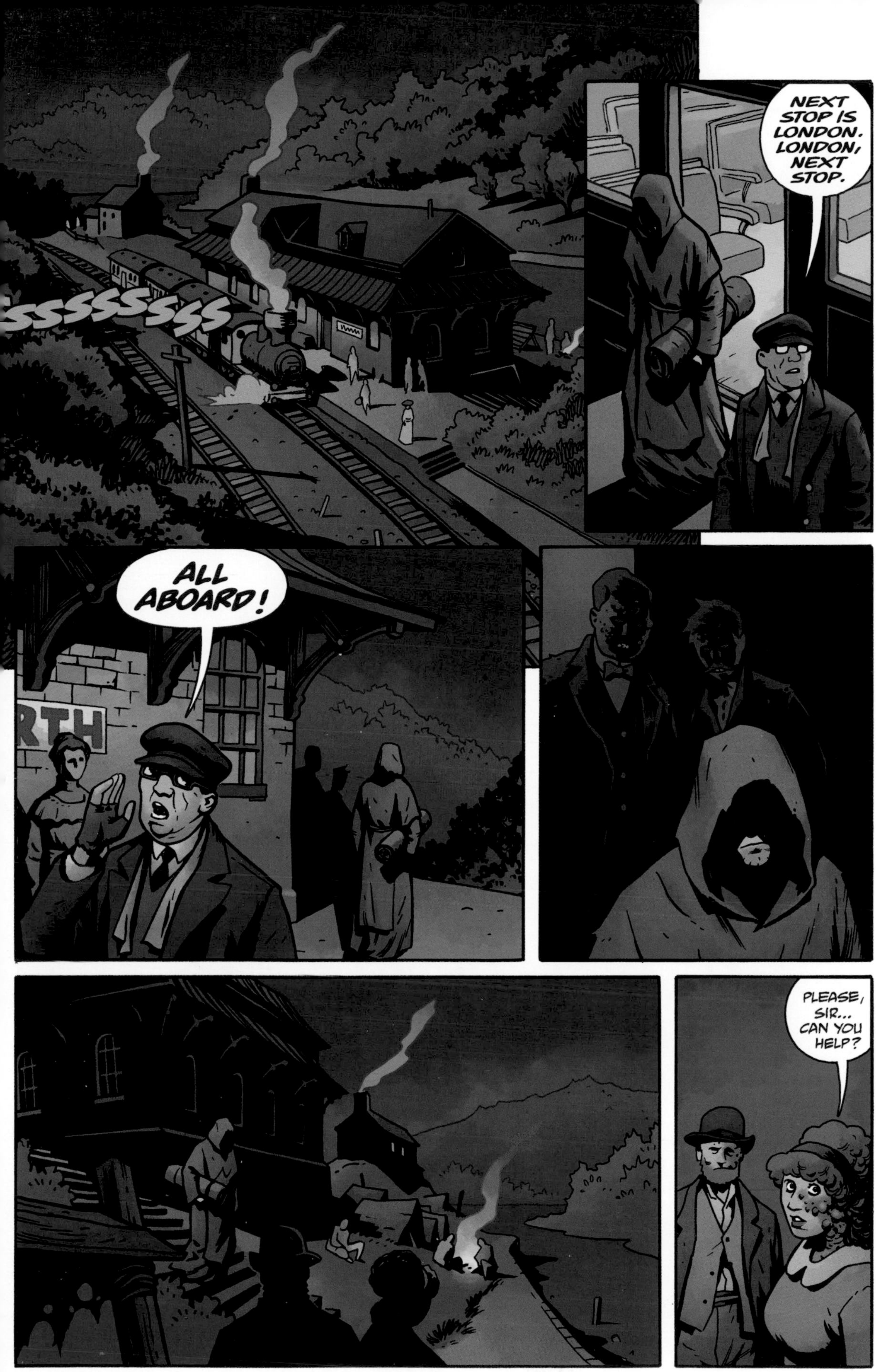
SSSSSSSSS
NEXT STOP IS LONDON. LONDON, NEXT STOP.
ALL ABOARD!
RTH
PLEASE, SIR... CAN YOU HELP?

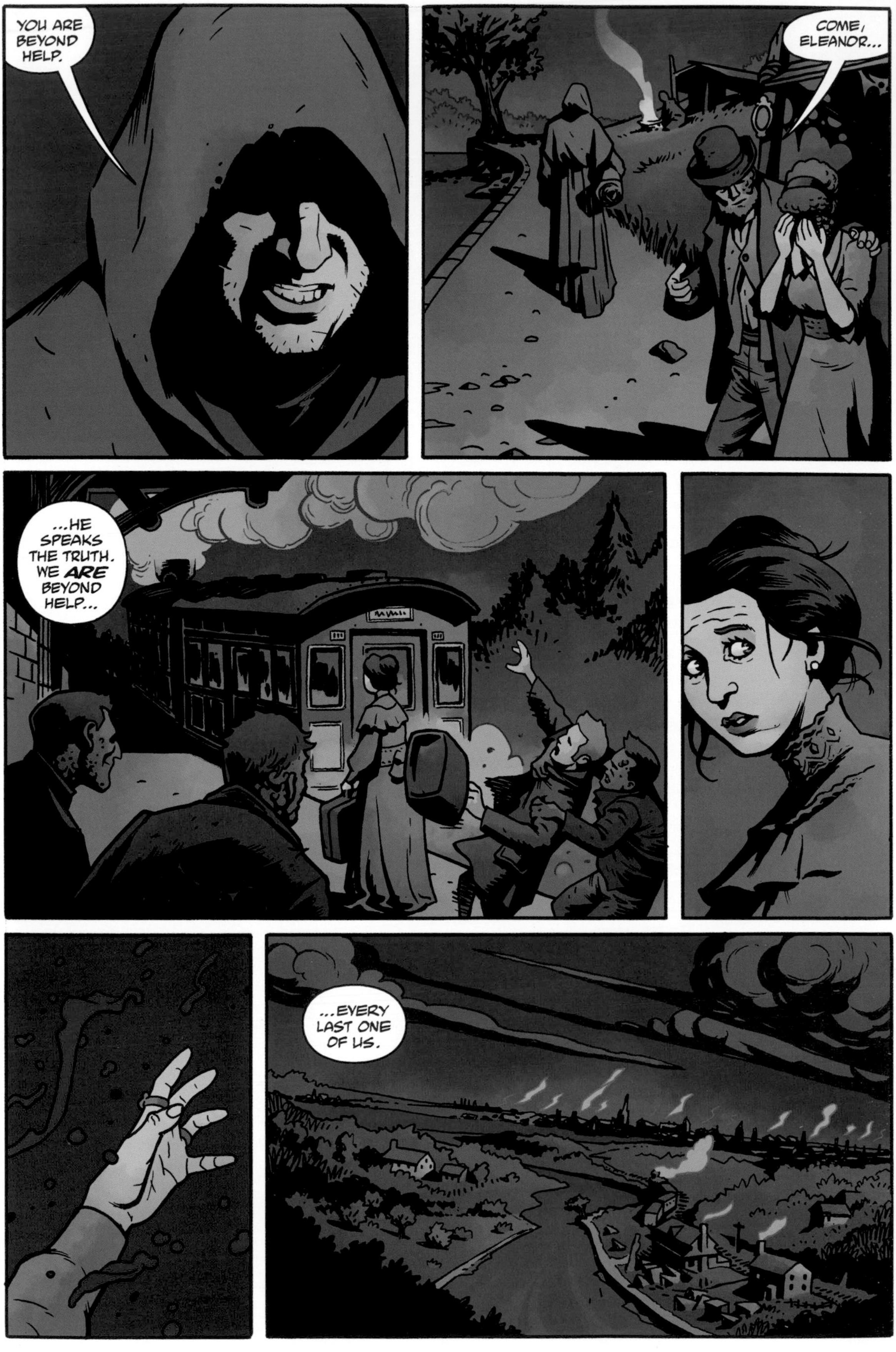
YOU ARE BEYOND HELP.
COME, ELEANOR...
...HE SPEAKS THE TRUTH. WE ARE BEYOND HELP...
...EVERY LAST ONE OF US.

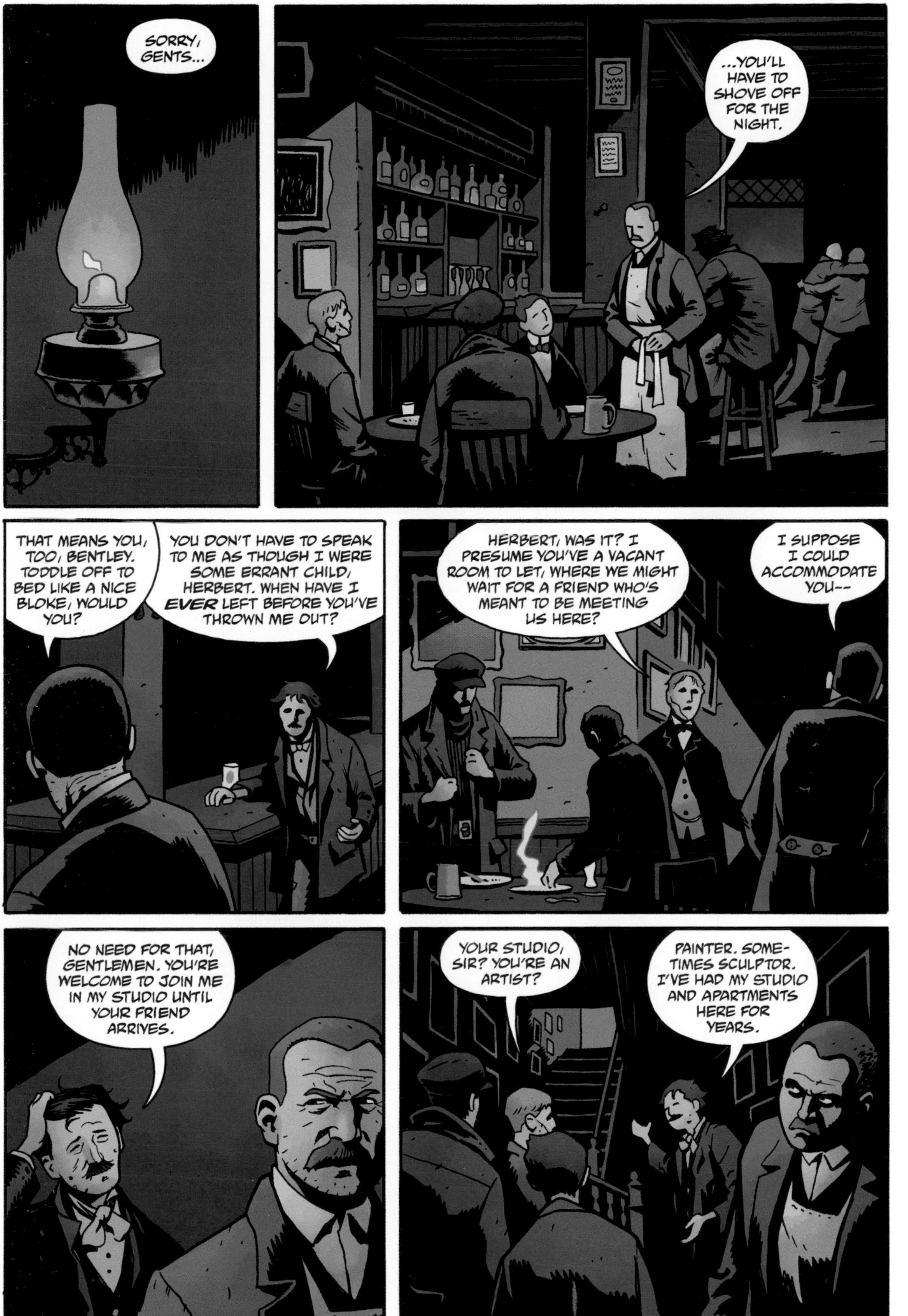
SORRY, GENTS...
...YOU'LL HAVE TO SHOVE OFF FOR THE NIGHT.
THAT MEANS YOU, TOO, BENTLEY. TODDLE OFF TO BED LIKE A NICE BLOKE, WOULD YOU?
YOU DON'T HAVE TO SPEAK TO ME AS THOUGH I WERE SOME ERRANT CHILD, HERBERT. WHEN HAVE I EVER LEFT BEFORE YOU'VE THROWN ME OUT?
HERBERT, WAS IT? I PRESUME YOU'VE A VACANT ROOM TO LET, WHERE WE MIGHT WAIT FOR A FRIEND WHO'S MEANT TO BE MEETING US HERE?
I SUPPOSE I COULD ACCOMMODATE YOU--
NO NEED FOR THAT, GENTLEMEN. YOU'RE WELCOME TO JOIN ME IN MY STUDIO UNTIL YOUR FRIEND ARRIVES.
YOUR STUDIO, SIR? YOU'RE AN ARTIST?
PAINTER. SOMETIMES SCULPTOR. I'VE HAD MY STUDIO AND APARTMENTS HERE FOR YEARS.

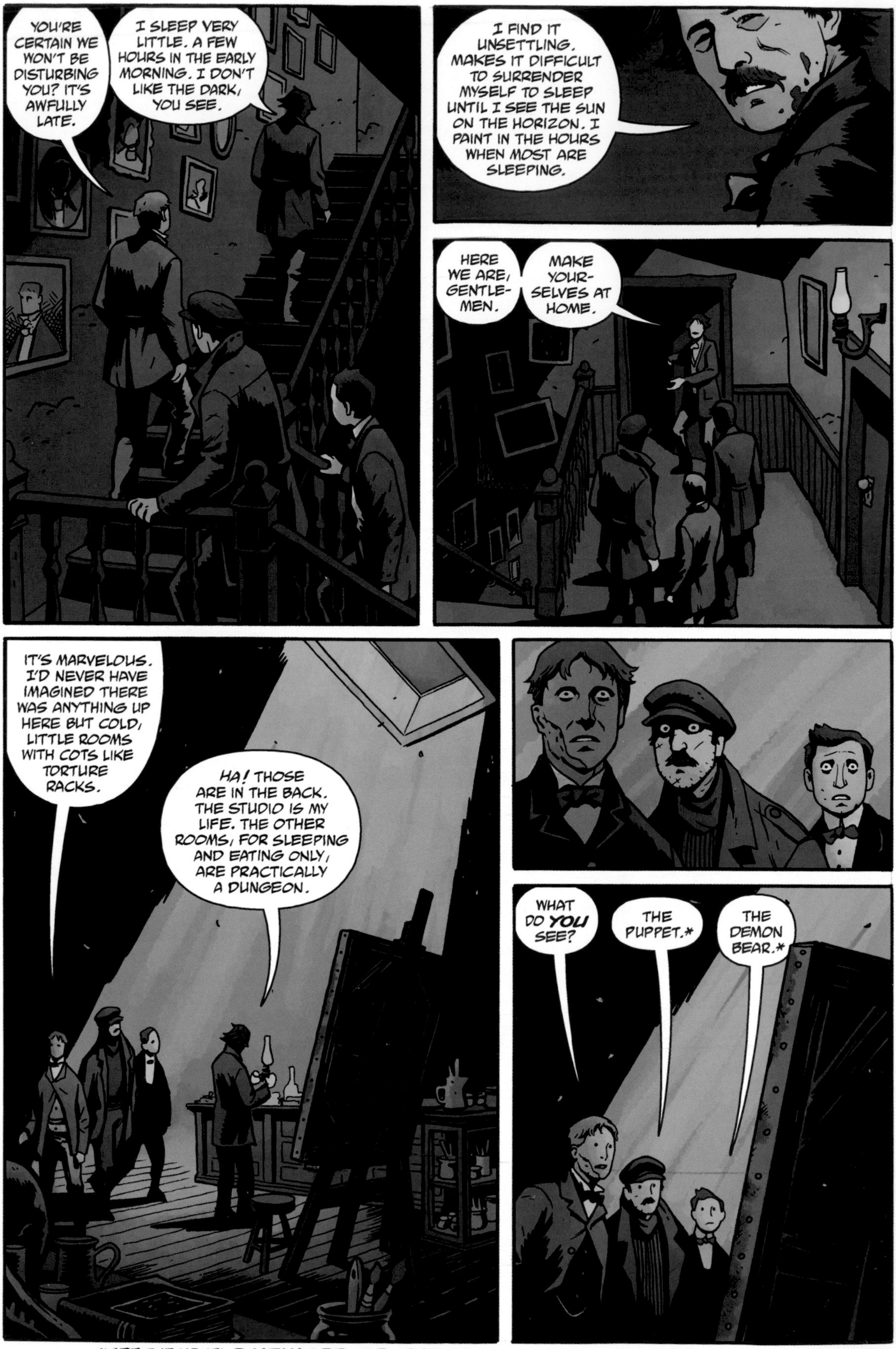
YOU'RE CERTAIN WE WON'T BE DISTURBING YOU? IT'S AWFULLY LATE.
I SLEEP VERY LITTLE. A FEW HOURS IN THE EARLY MORNING. I DON'T LIKE THE DARK, YOU SEE.
I FIND IT UNSETTLING. MAKES IT DIFFICULT TO SURRENDER MYSELF TO SLEEP UNTIL I SEE THE SUN ON THE HORIZON. I PAINT IN THE HOURS WHEN MOST ARE SLEEPING.
HERE WE ARE, GENTLEMEN.
MAKE YOURSELVES AT HOME.
IT'S MARVELOUS. I'D NEVER HAVE IMAGINED THERE WAS ANYTHING UP HERE BUT COLD, LITTLE ROOMS WITH COTS LIKE TORTURE RACKS.
HA! THOSE ARE IN THE BACK. THE STUDIO IS MY LIFE. THE OTHER ROOMS, FOR SLEEPING AND EATING ONLY, ARE PRACTICALLY A DUNGEON.
WHAT DO YOU SEE?
THE PUPPET.*
THE DEMON BEAR.*

*SEE THE NOVEL **BALTIMORE, OR, THE STEADFAST TIN SOLDIER AND THE VAMPIRE**

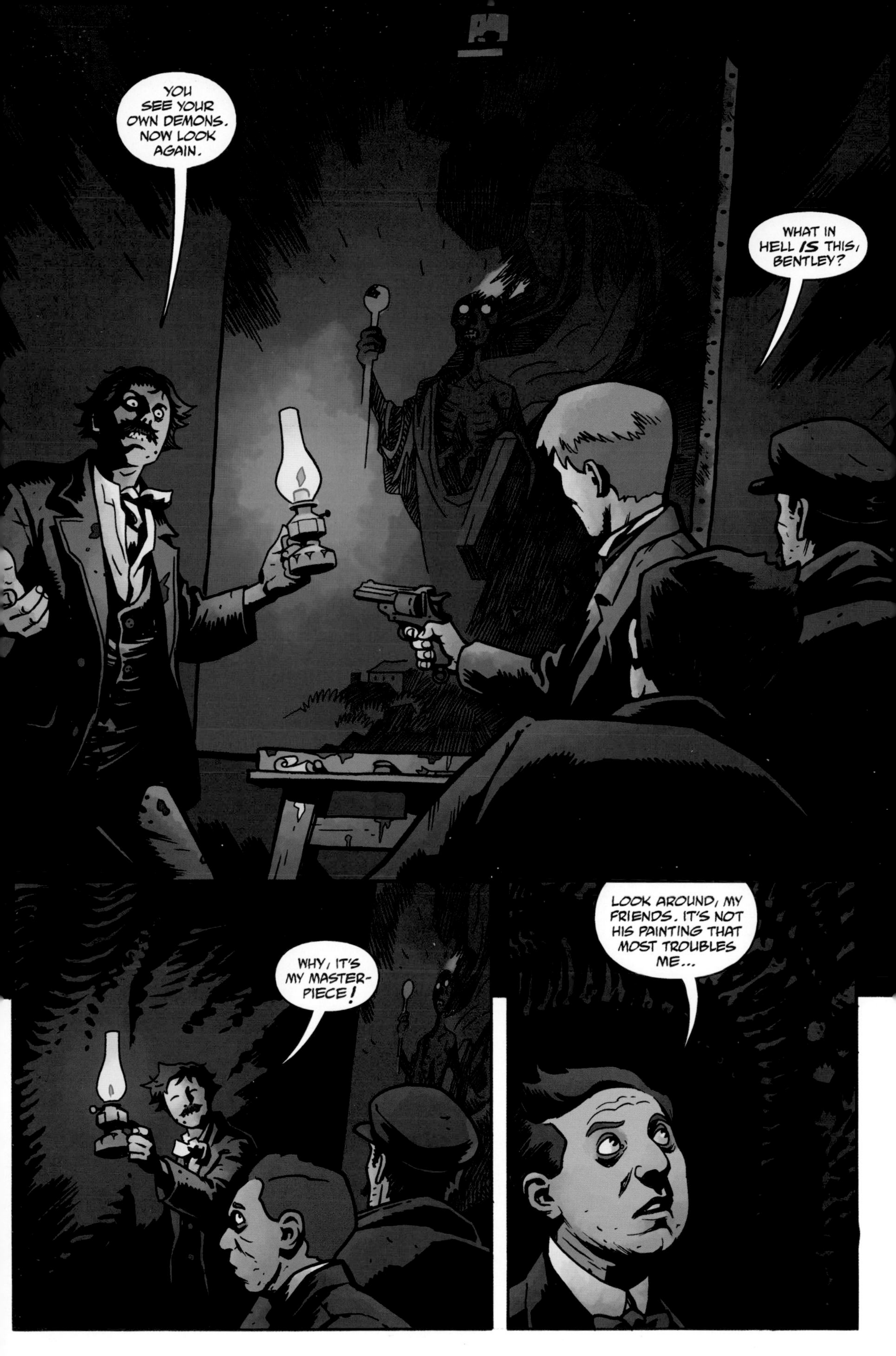
YOU SEE YOUR OWN DEMONS. NOW LOOK AGAIN.
WHAT IN HELL *IS* THIS, BENTLEY?
WHY, IT'S MY MASTER-PIECE!
LOOK AROUND, MY FRIENDS. IT'S NOT HIS PAINTING THAT MOST TROUBLES ME...

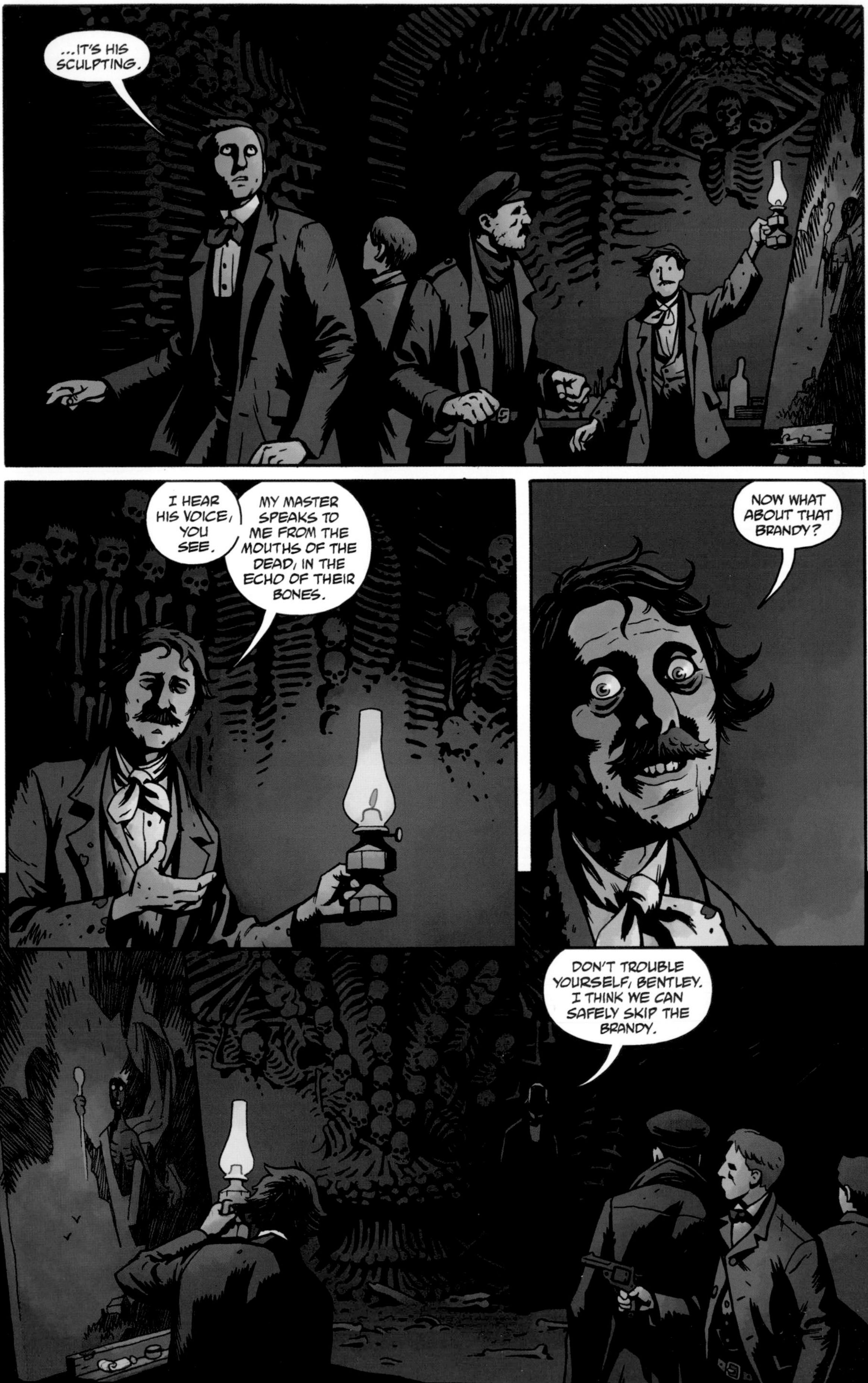
...IT'S HIS SCULPTING.
I HEAR HIS VOICE, YOU SEE.
MY MASTER SPEAKS TO ME FROM THE MOUTHS OF THE DEAD, IN THE ECHO OF THEIR BONES.
NOW WHAT ABOUT THAT BRANDY?
DON'T TROUBLE YOURSELF, BENTLEY. I THINK WE CAN SAFELY SKIP THE BRANDY.

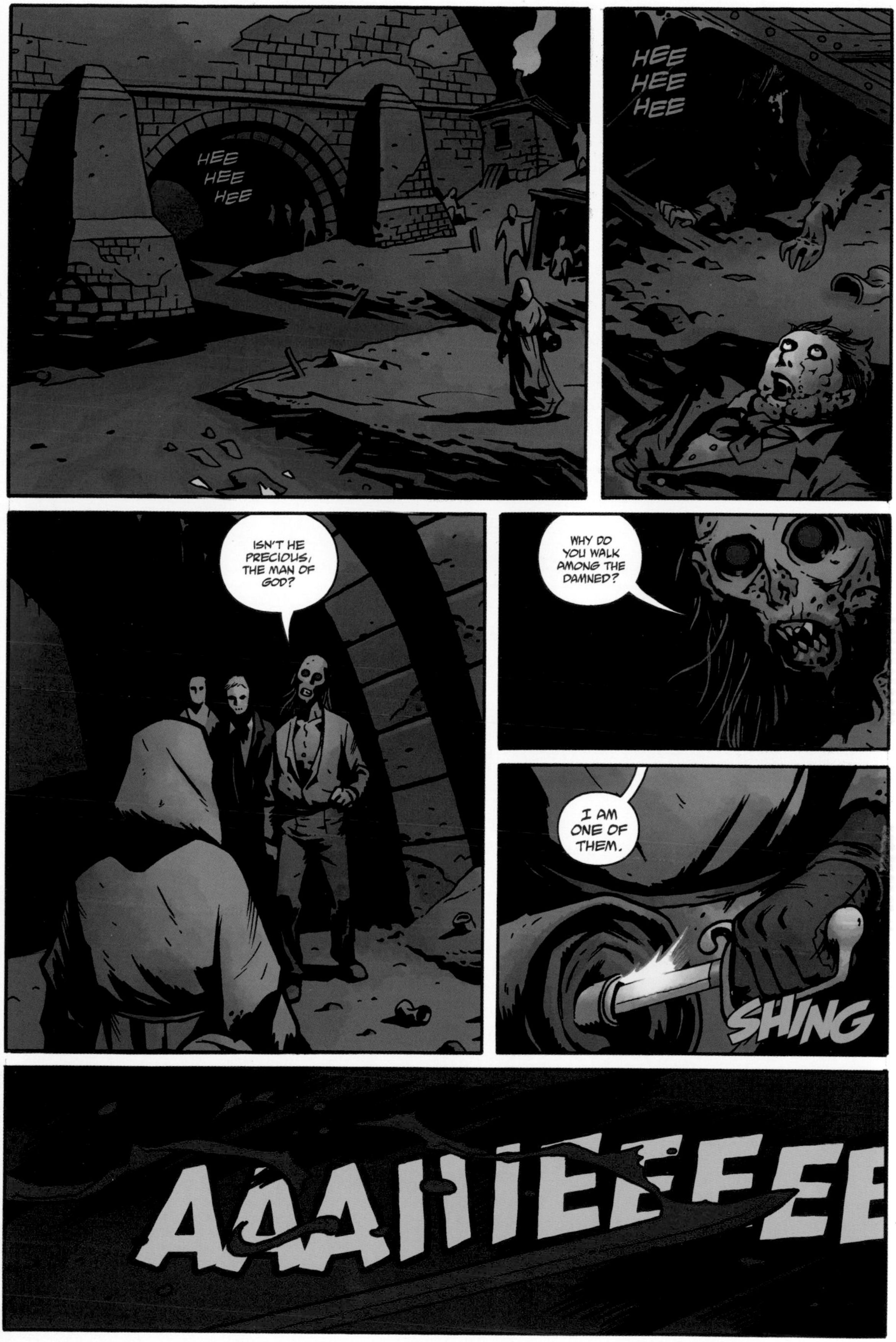
HEE
HEE
HEE
HEE
HEE
HEE
ISN'T HE PRECIOUS, THE MAN OF GOD?
WHY DO YOU WALK AMONG THE DAMNED?
I AM ONE OF THEM.
SHING
AAAHIEEEEE

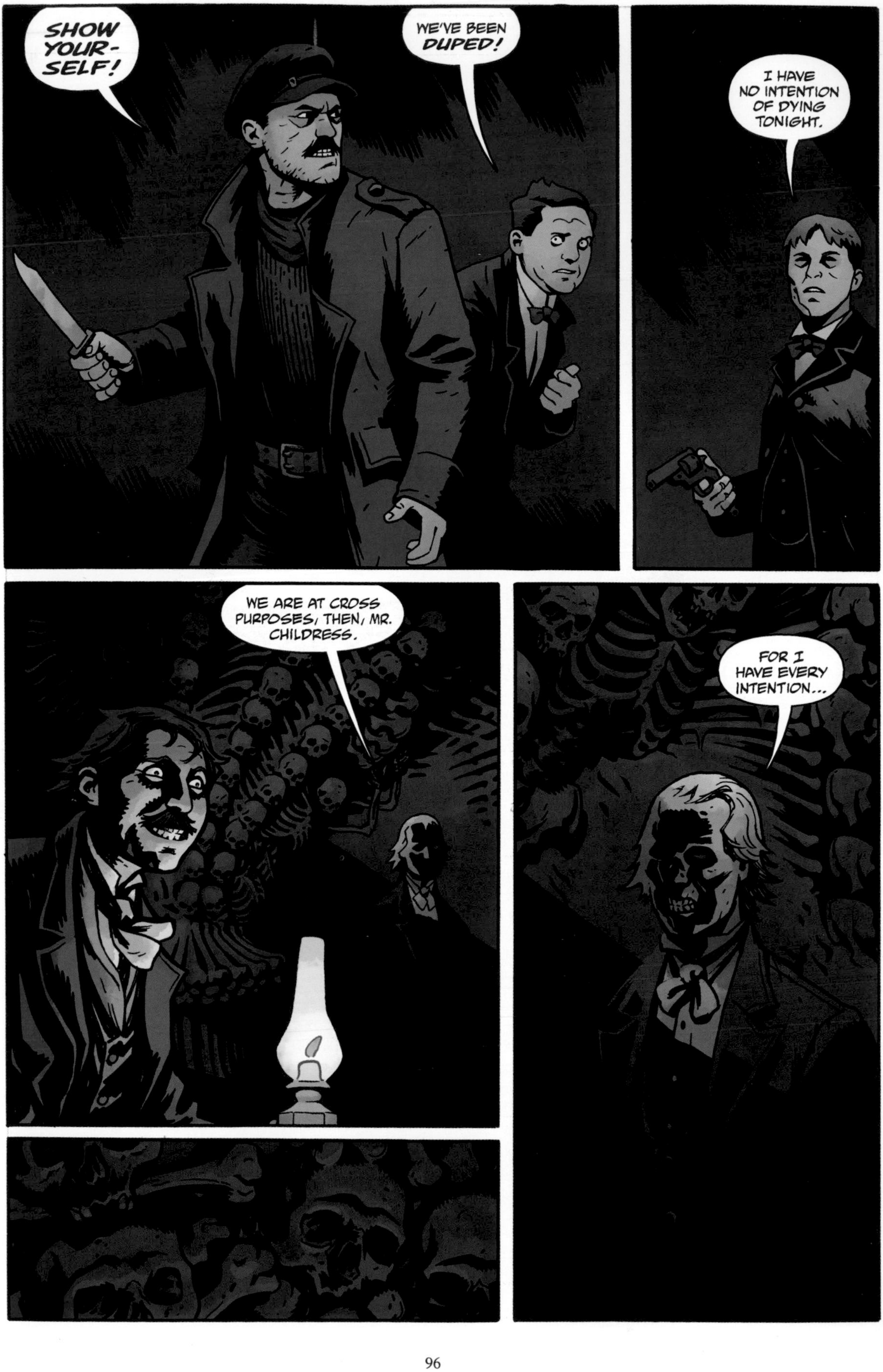
SHOW YOUR-SELF!
WE'VE BEEN DUPED!
I HAVE NO INTENTION OF DYING TONIGHT.
WE ARE AT CROSS PURPOSES, THEN, MR. CHILDRESS.
FOR I HAVE EVERY INTENTION...

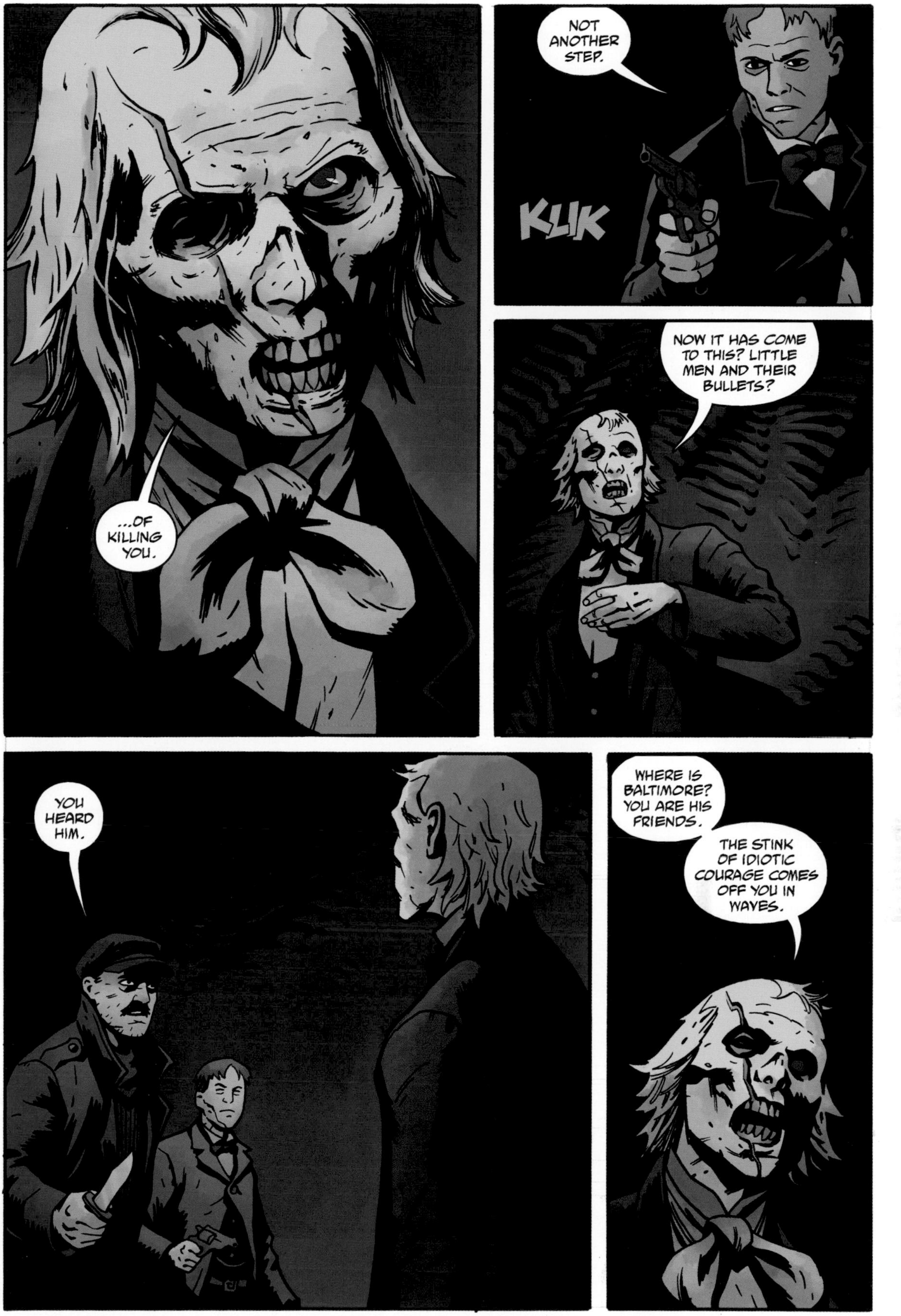
...OF KILLING YOU.
NOT ANOTHER STEP.
KLIK
NOW IT HAS COME TO THIS? LITTLE MEN AND THEIR BULLETS?
YOU HEARD HIM.
WHERE IS BALTIMORE? YOU ARE HIS FRIENDS.
THE STINK OF IDIOTIC COURAGE COMES OFF YOU IN WAVES.

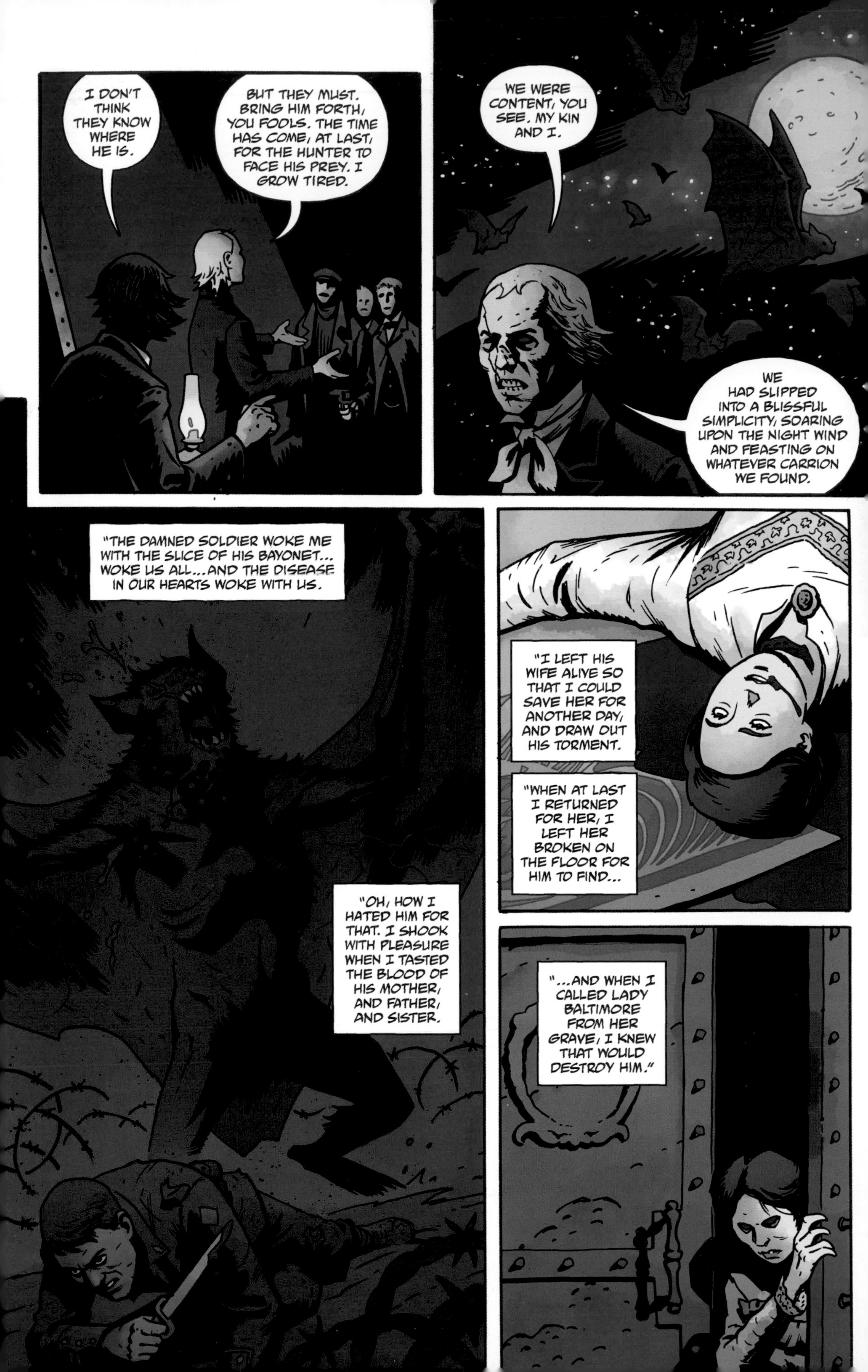
I DON'T THINK THEY KNOW WHERE HE IS.
BUT THEY MUST. BRING HIM FORTH, YOU FOOLS. THE TIME HAS COME, AT LAST, FOR THE HUNTER TO FACE HIS PREY. I GROW TIRED.
WE WERE CONTENT, YOU SEE. MY KIN AND I.
WE HAD SLIPPED INTO A BLISSFUL SIMPLICITY, SOARING UPON THE NIGHT WIND AND FEASTING ON WHATEVER CARRION WE FOUND.
"THE DAMNED SOLDIER WOKE ME WITH THE SLICE OF HIS BAYONET... WOKE US ALL...AND THE DISEASE IN OUR HEARTS WOKE WITH US.
"OH, HOW I HATED HIM FOR THAT. I SHOOK WITH PLEASURE WHEN I TASTED THE BLOOD OF HIS MOTHER, AND FATHER, AND SISTER.
"I LEFT HIS WIFE ALIVE SO THAT I COULD SAVE HER FOR ANOTHER DAY, AND DRAW OUT HIS TORMENT.
"WHEN AT LAST I RETURNED FOR HER, I LEFT HER BROKEN ON THE FLOOR FOR HIM TO FIND...
"...AND WHEN I CALLED LADY BALTIMORE FROM HER GRAVE, I KNEW THAT WOULD DESTROY HIM."

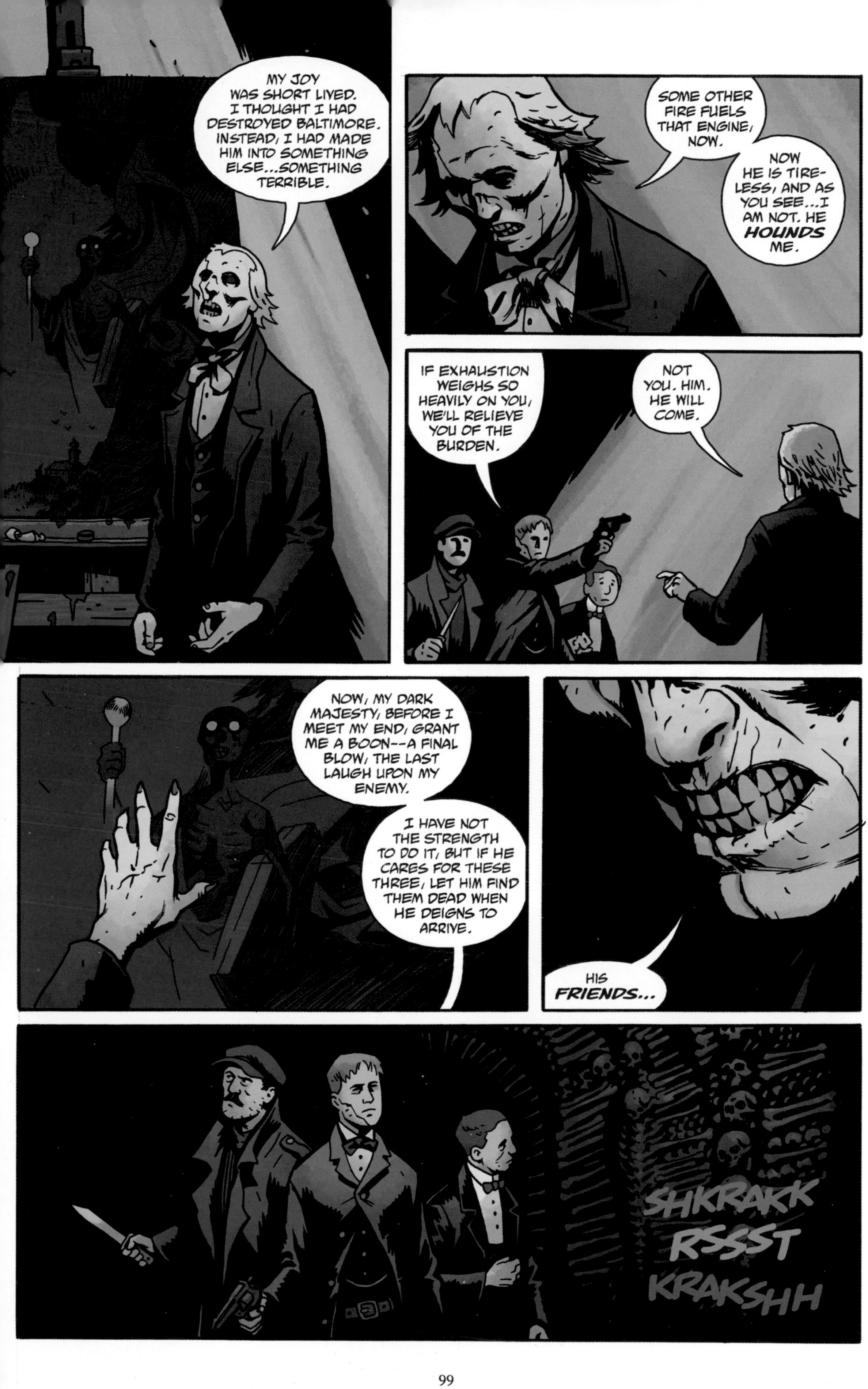
MY JOY WAS SHORT LIVED. I THOUGHT I HAD DESTROYED BALTIMORE. INSTEAD, I HAD MADE HIM INTO SOMETHING ELSE...SOMETHING TERRIBLE.
SOME OTHER FIRE FUELS THAT ENGINE, NOW.
NOW HE IS TIRE-LESS, AND AS YOU SEE...I AM NOT. HE **HOUNDS** ME.
IF EXHAUSTION WEIGHS SO HEAVILY ON YOU, WE'LL RELIEVE YOU OF THE BURDEN.
NOT YOU. HIM. HE WILL COME.
NOW, MY DARK MAJESTY, BEFORE I MEET MY END, GRANT ME A BOON--A FINAL BLOW, THE LAST LAUGH UPON MY ENEMY.
I HAVE NOT THE STRENGTH TO DO IT, BUT IF HE CARES FOR THESE THREE, LET HIM FIND THEM DEAD WHEN HE DEIGNS TO ARRIVE.
HIS ***FRIENDS...***
SHKRAKK
RSSST
KRAKSHH

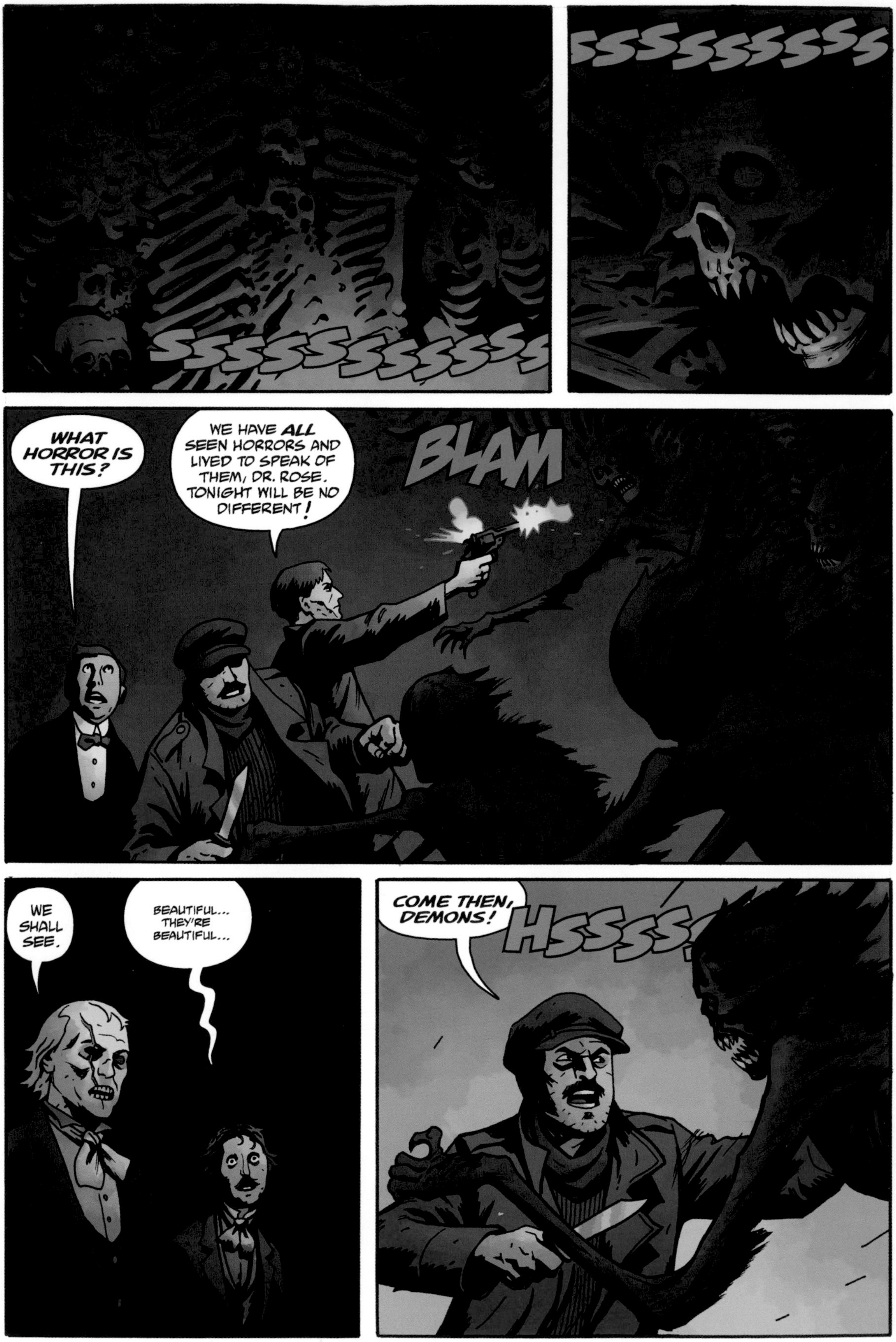
SSSSSSSSSSSSS
SSSSSSSSSS
WHAT HORROR IS THIS?
WE HAVE ALL SEEN HORRORS AND LIVED TO SPEAK OF THEM, DR. ROSE. TONIGHT WILL BE NO DIFFERENT!
BLAM
WE SHALL SEE.
BEAUTIFUL... THEY'RE BEAUTIFUL...
COME THEN, DEMONS!
HSSSS

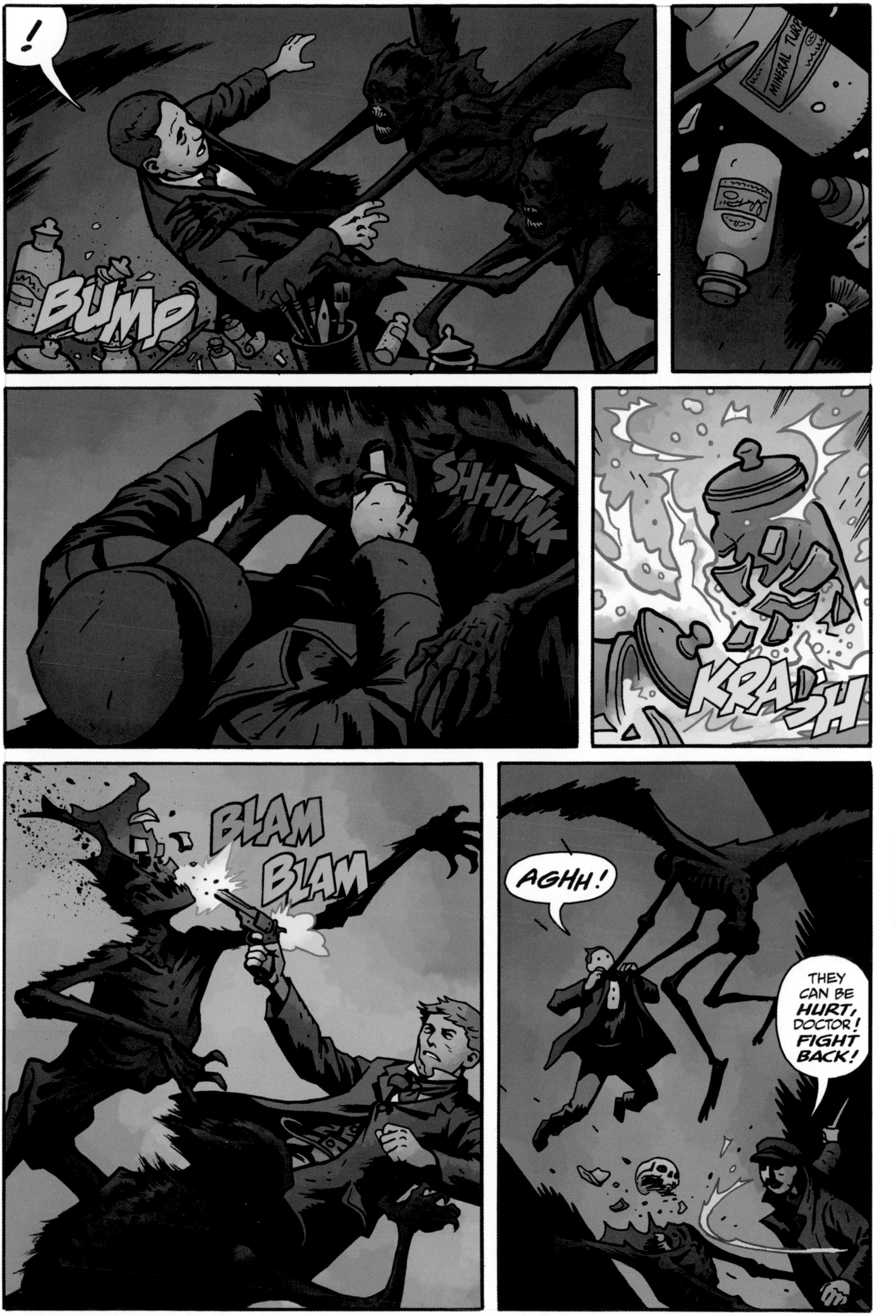
!
BUMP
MINERAL TURP
SHHUNK
KRASH
BLAM
BLAM
AGHH!
THEY CAN BE HURT, DOCTOR! FIGHT BACK!

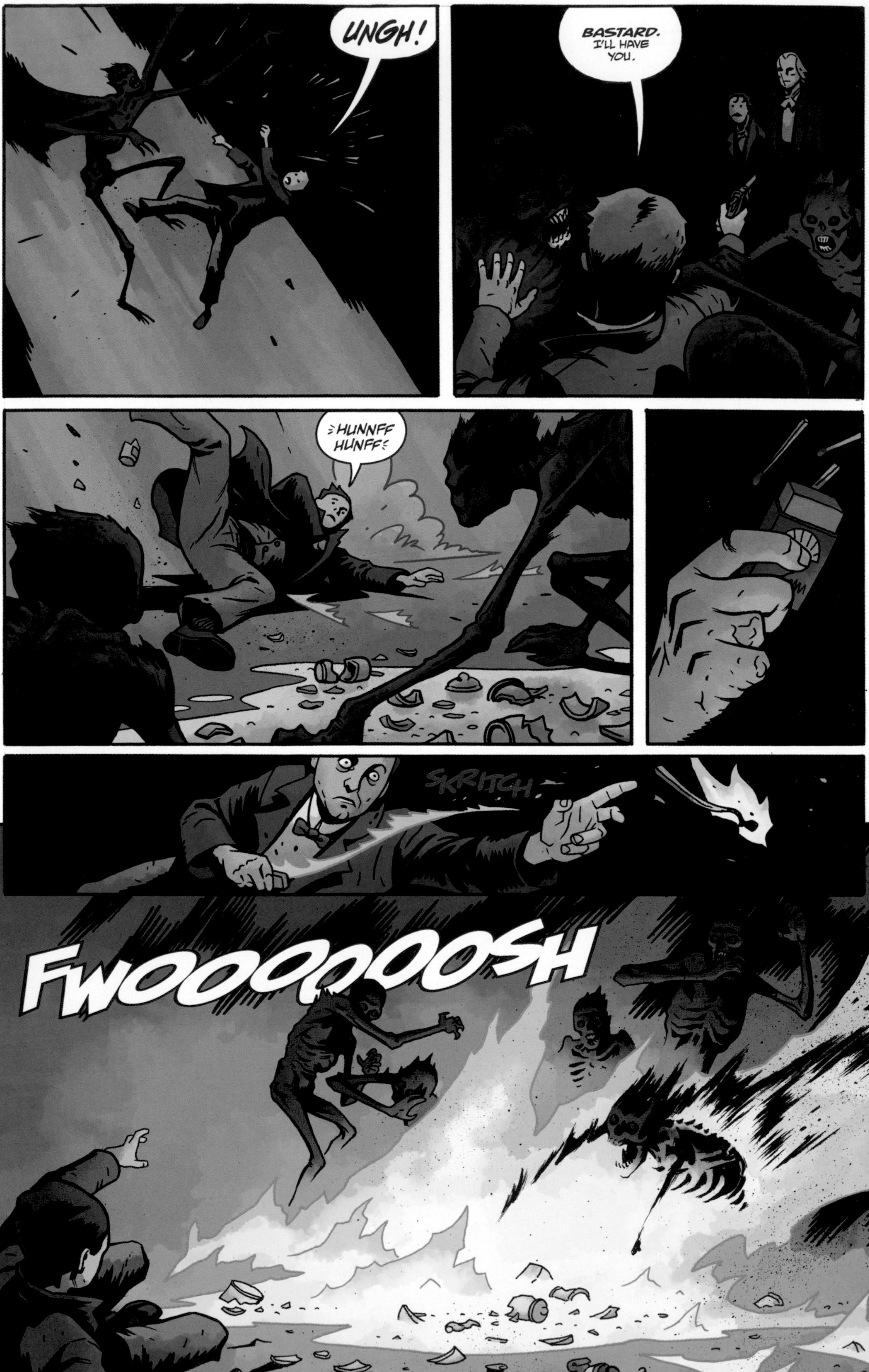
UNGH!
BASTARD. I'LL HAVE YOU.
HUNNFF HUNFF
SKRITCH
FWOOOOOOSH

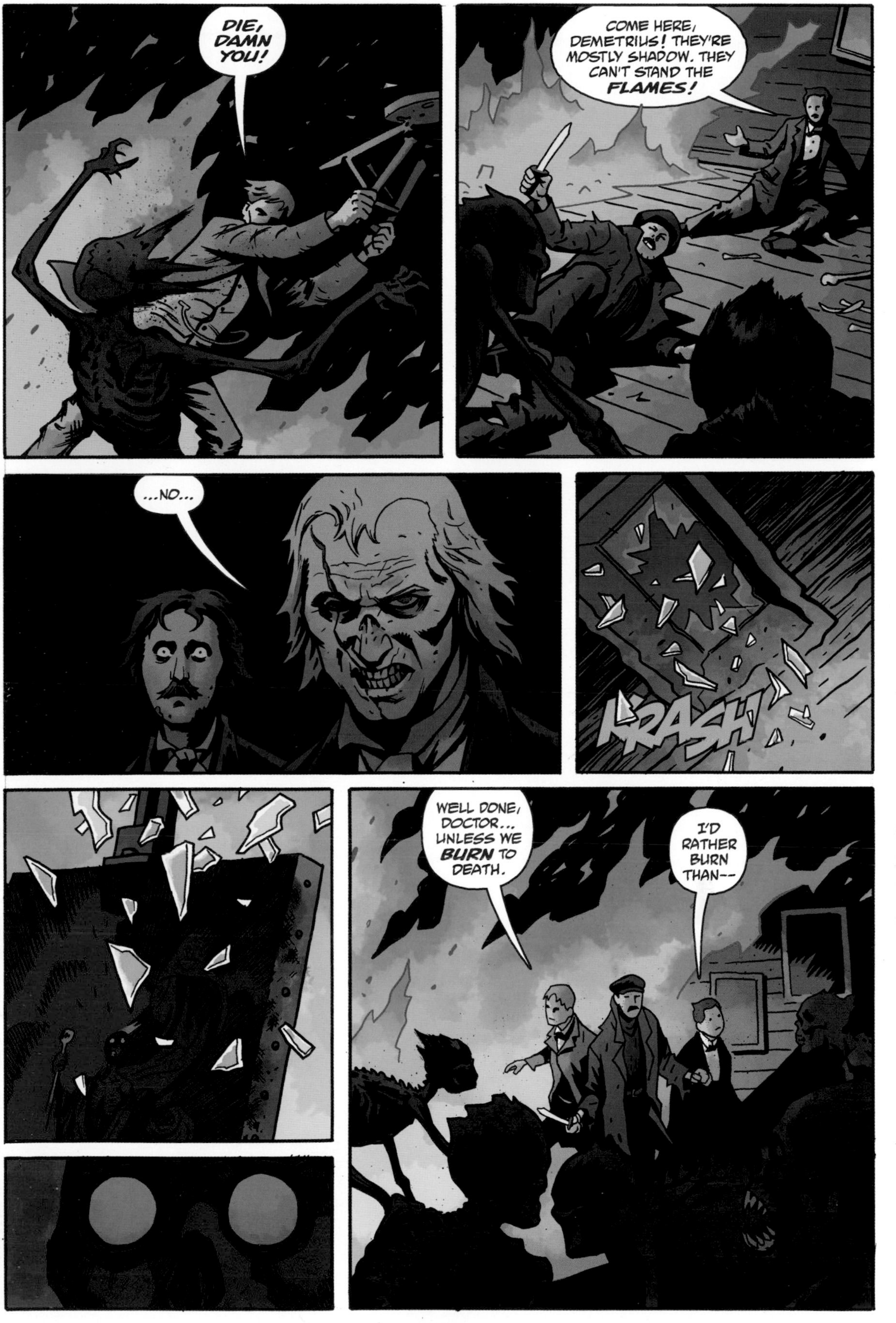
DIE, DAMN YOU!
COME HERE, DEMETRIUS! THEY'RE MOSTLY SHADOW. THEY CAN'T STAND THE FLAMES!
...NO...
KRASH!
WELL DONE, DOCTOR... UNLESS WE BURN TO DEATH.
I'D RATHER BURN THAN--

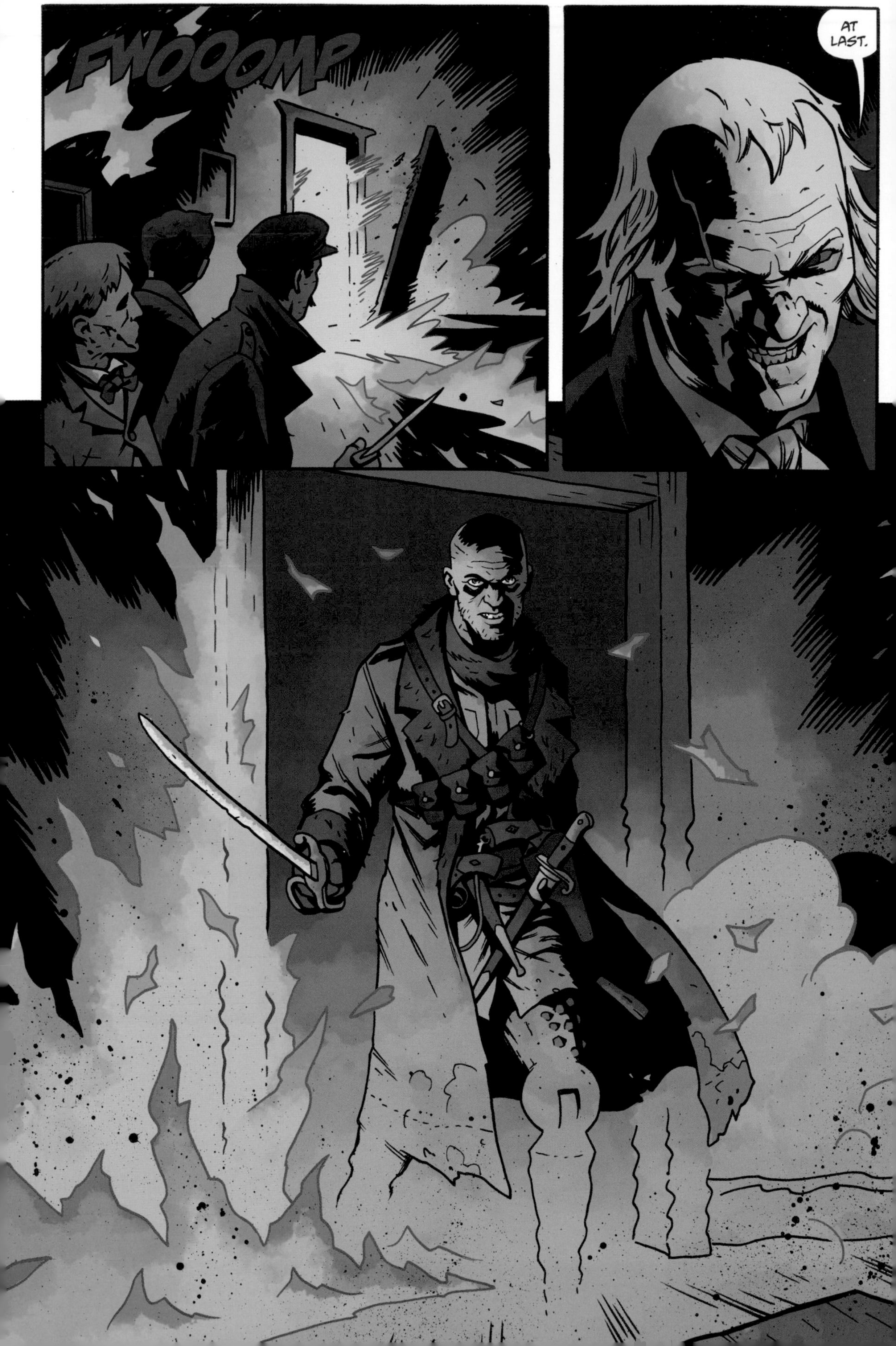
FWOOOMP
AT LAST.

CHAPEL OF BONES
Chapter Two

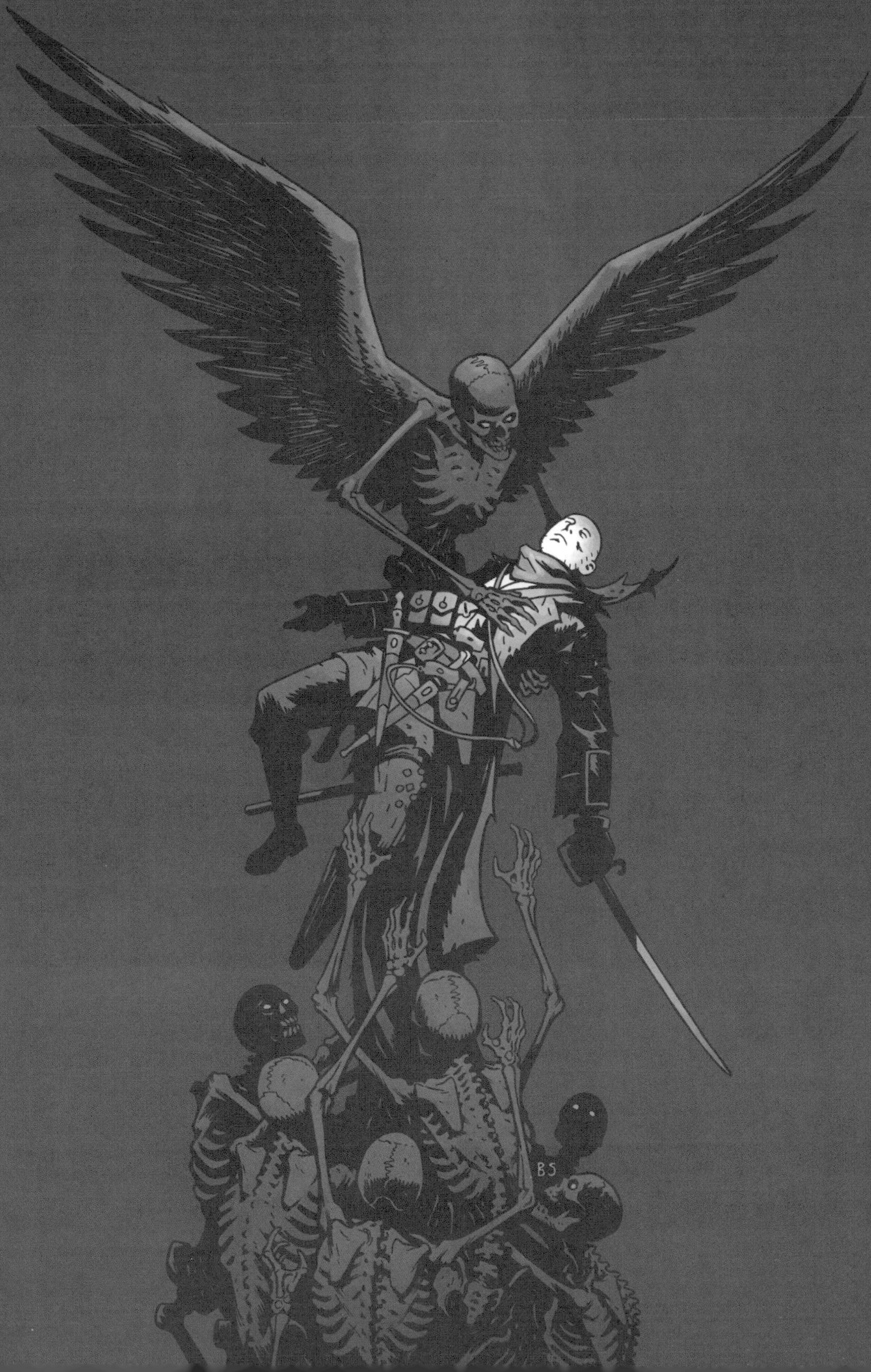

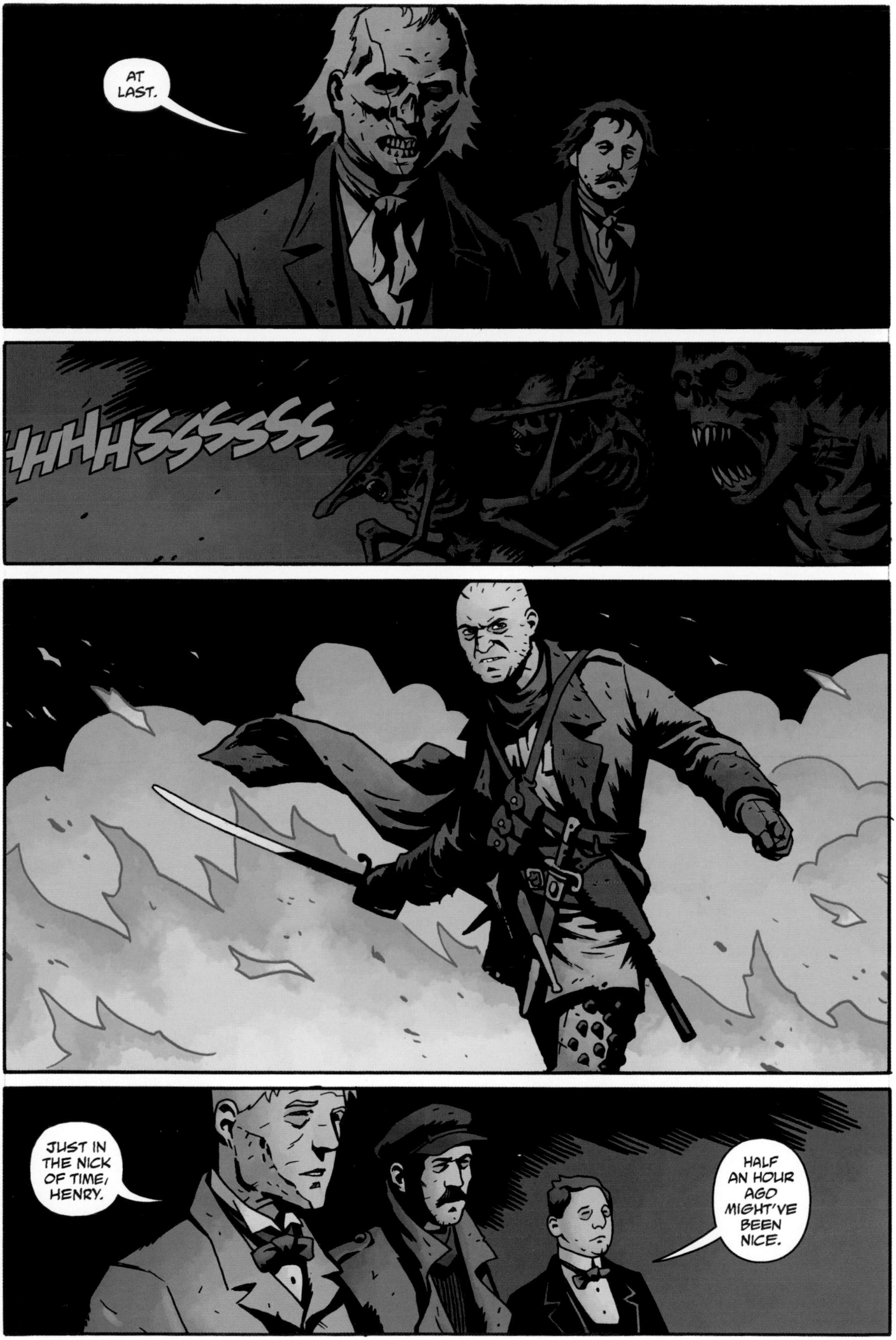
AT LAST.
HHHHSSSSSS
JUST IN THE NICK OF TIME, HENRY.
HALF AN HOUR AGO MIGHT'VE BEEN NICE.

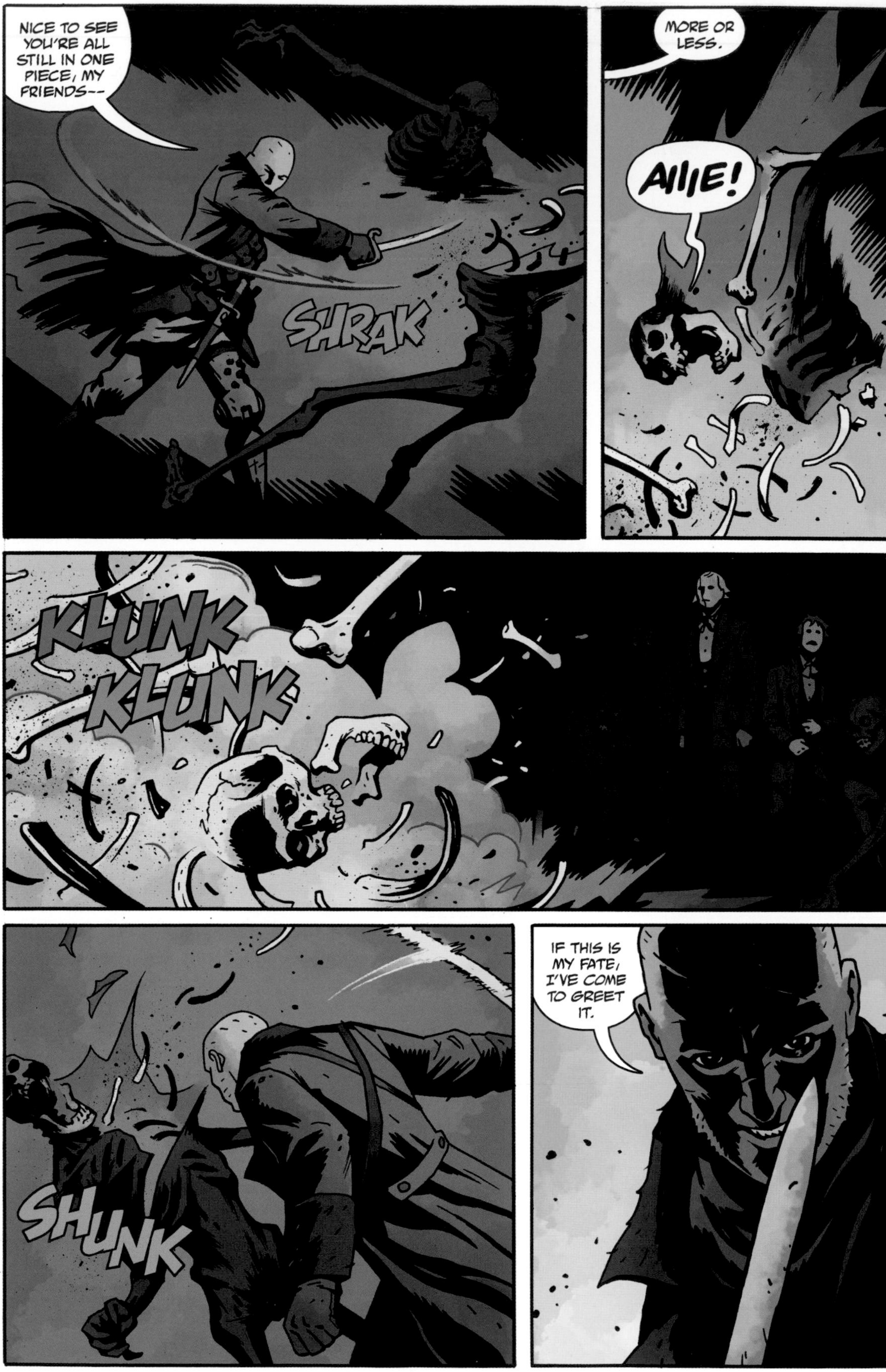
NICE TO SEE YOU'RE ALL STILL IN ONE PIECE, MY FRIENDS--
SHRAK
MORE OR LESS.
AIIIE!
KLUNK KLUNK
SHUNK
IF THIS IS MY FATE, I'VE COME TO GREET IT.

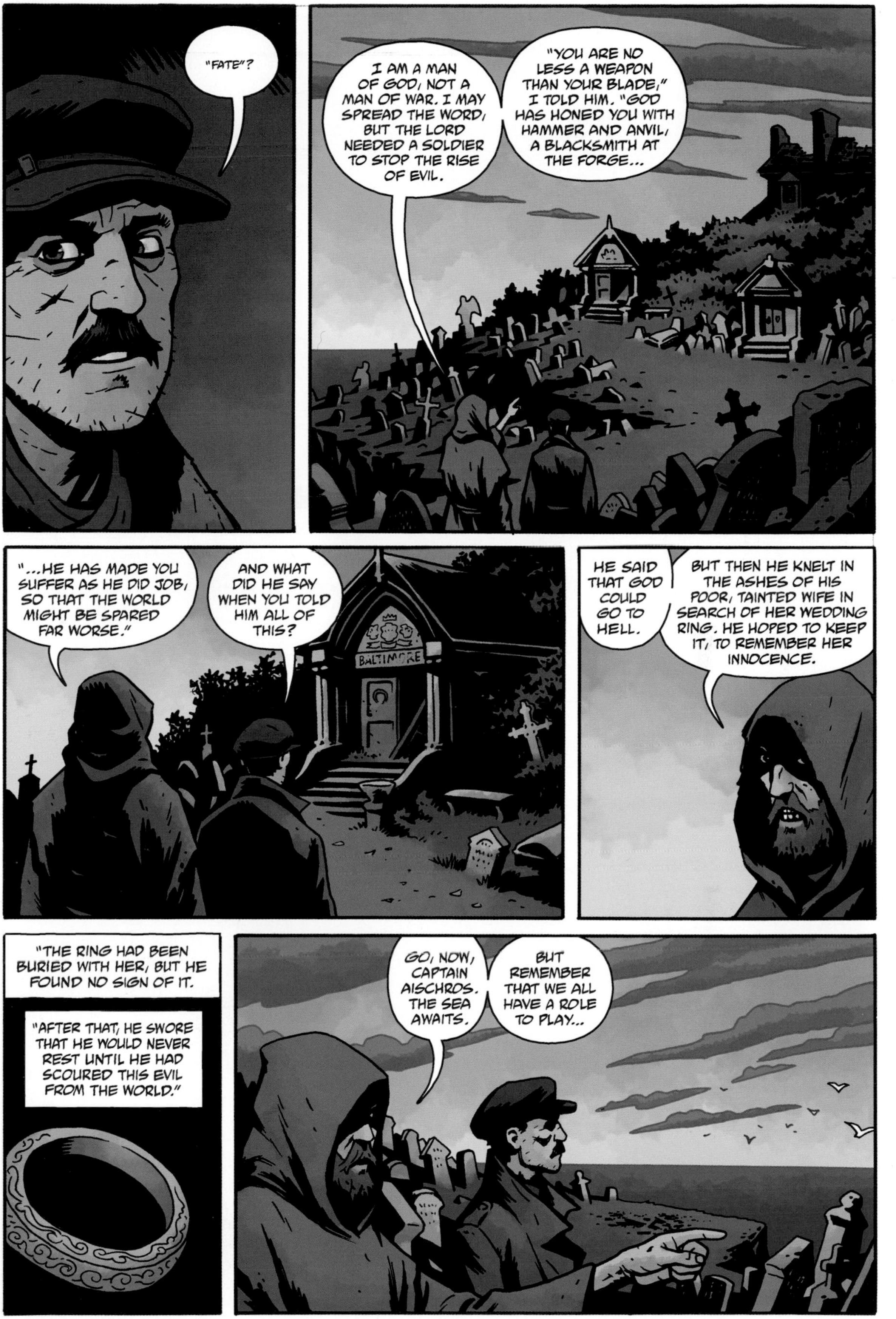
"FATE"?
I AM A MAN OF GOD, NOT A MAN OF WAR. I MAY SPREAD THE WORD, BUT THE LORD NEEDED A SOLDIER TO STOP THE RISE OF EVIL.
"YOU ARE NO LESS A WEAPON THAN YOUR BLADE," I TOLD HIM. "GOD HAS HONED YOU WITH HAMMER AND ANVIL, A BLACKSMITH AT THE FORGE...
"...HE HAS MADE YOU SUFFER AS HE DID JOB, SO THAT THE WORLD MIGHT BE SPARED FAR WORSE."
AND WHAT DID HE SAY WHEN YOU TOLD HIM ALL OF THIS?
BALTIMORE
HE SAID THAT GOD COULD GO TO HELL.
BUT THEN HE KNELT IN THE ASHES OF HIS POOR, TAINTED WIFE IN SEARCH OF HER WEDDING RING. HE HOPED TO KEEP IT, TO REMEMBER HER INNOCENCE.
"THE RING HAD BEEN BURIED WITH HER, BUT HE FOUND NO SIGN OF IT.
"AFTER THAT, HE SWORE THAT HE WOULD NEVER REST UNTIL HE HAD SCOURED THIS EVIL FROM THE WORLD."
GO, NOW, CAPTAIN AISCHROS. THE SEA AWAITS.
BUT REMEMBER THAT WE ALL HAVE A ROLE TO PLAY...

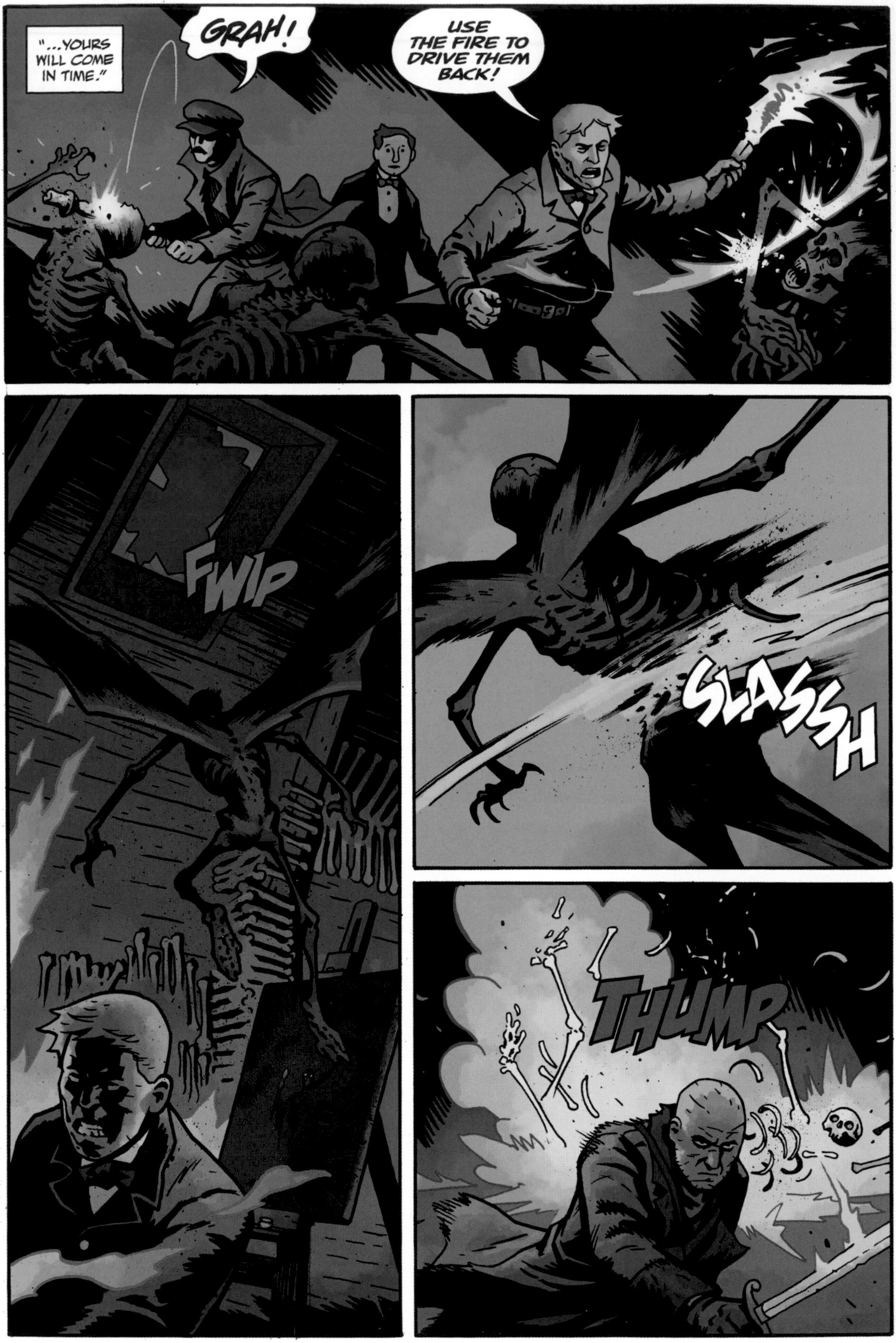
"...YOURS WILL COME IN TIME."
GRAH!
USE THE FIRE TO DRIVE THEM BACK!
FWIP
SLASSSH
THUMP

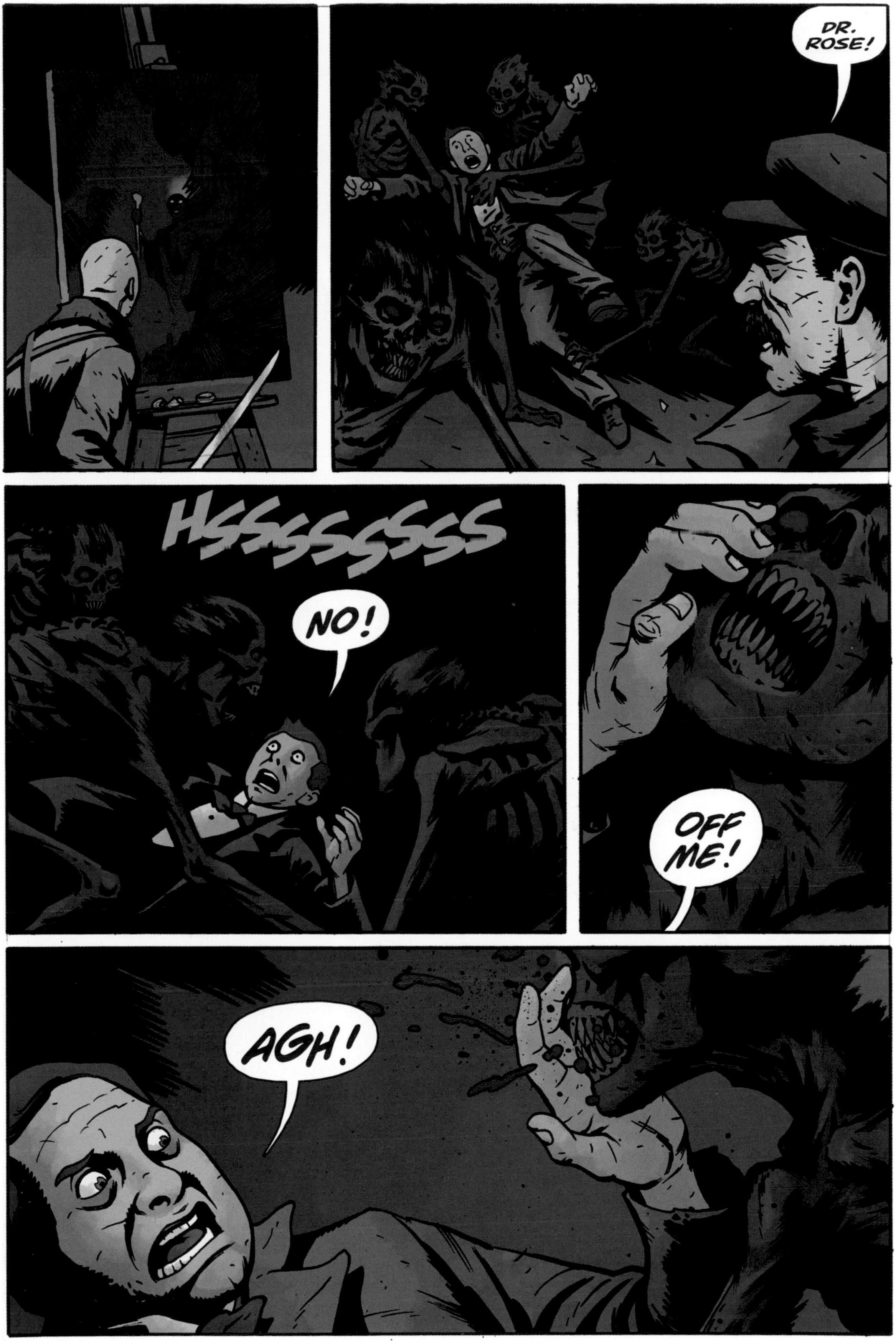
DR. ROSE!
HSSSSSSSS
NO!
OFF ME!
AGH!

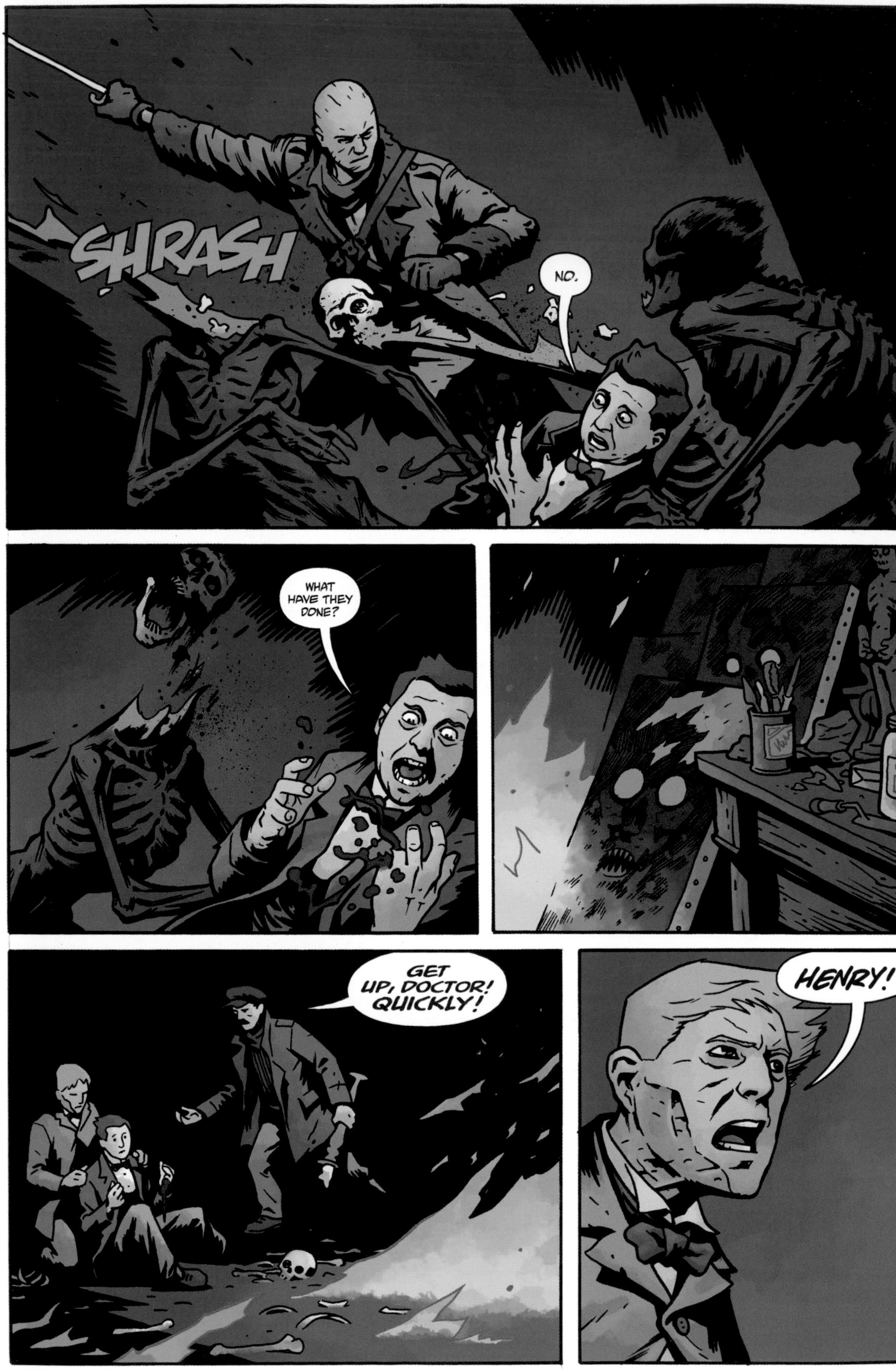
SHRASH
NO.
WHAT HAVE THEY DONE?
GET UP, DOCTOR! QUICKLY!
HENRY!

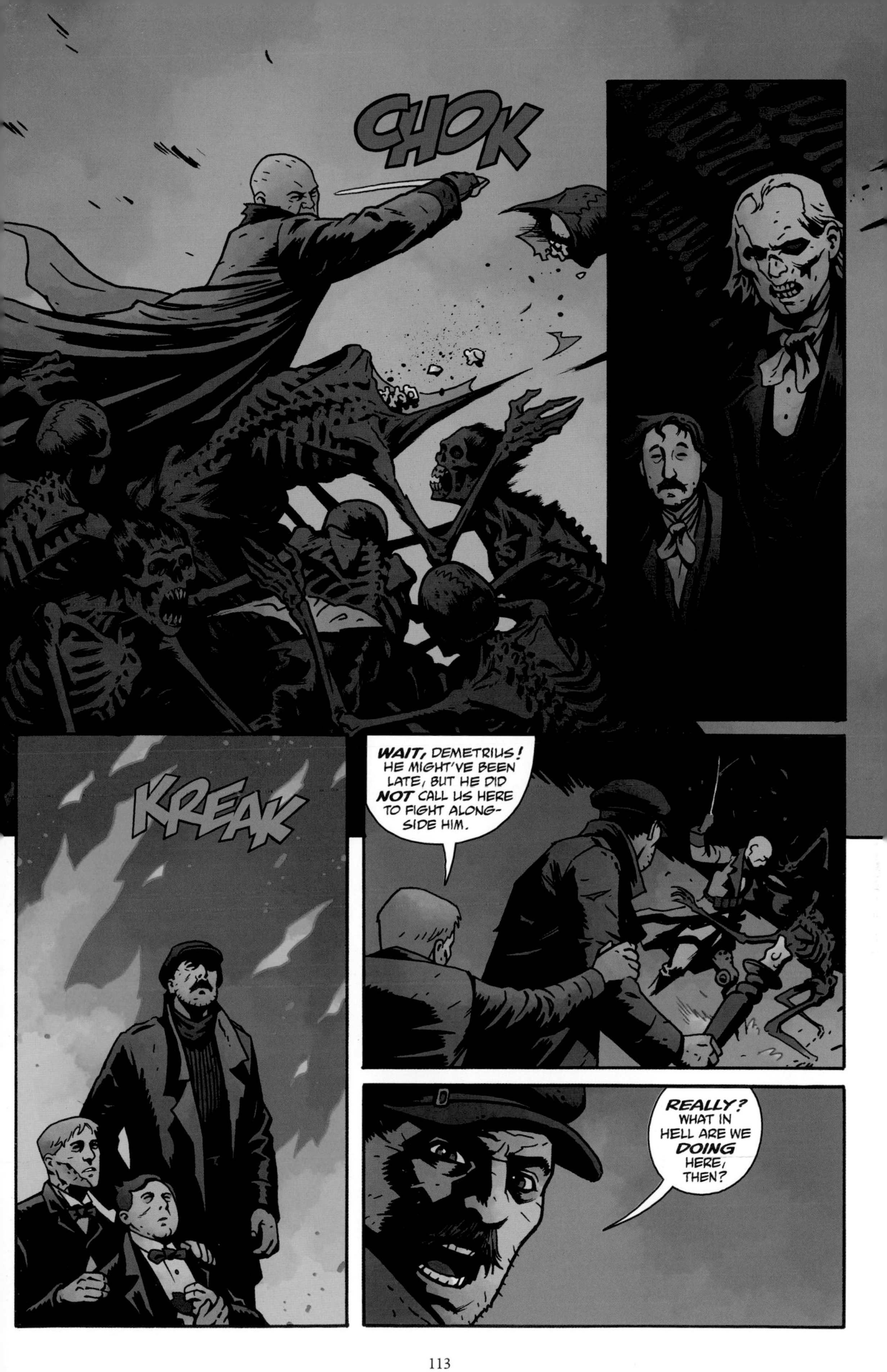
CHOK
KREAK
WAIT, DEMETRIUS! HE MIGHT'VE BEEN LATE, BUT HE DID NOT CALL US HERE TO FIGHT ALONGSIDE HIM.
REALLY? WHAT IN HELL ARE WE DOING HERE, THEN?

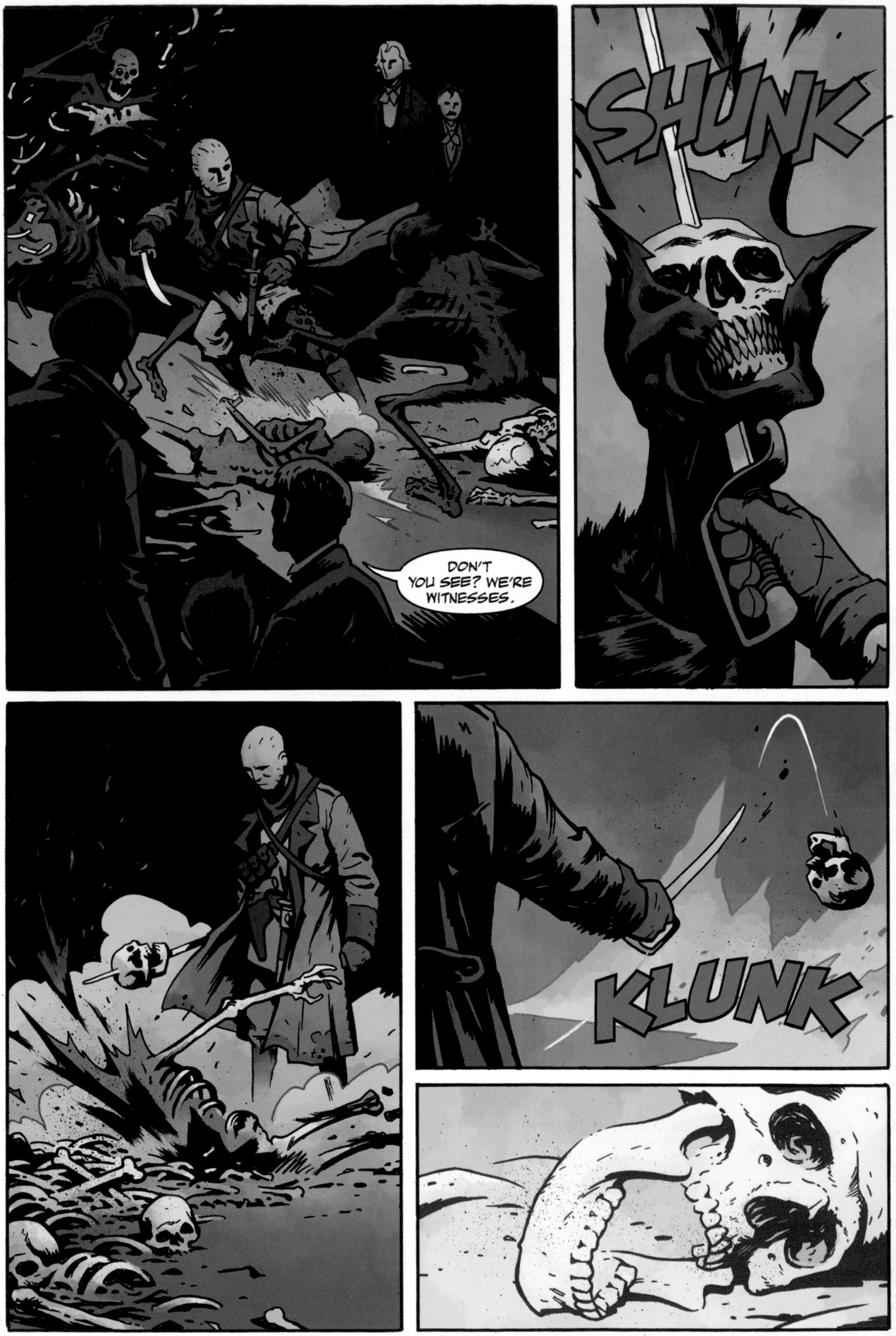
DON'T YOU SEE? WE'RE WITNESSES.
SHUNK
KLUNK

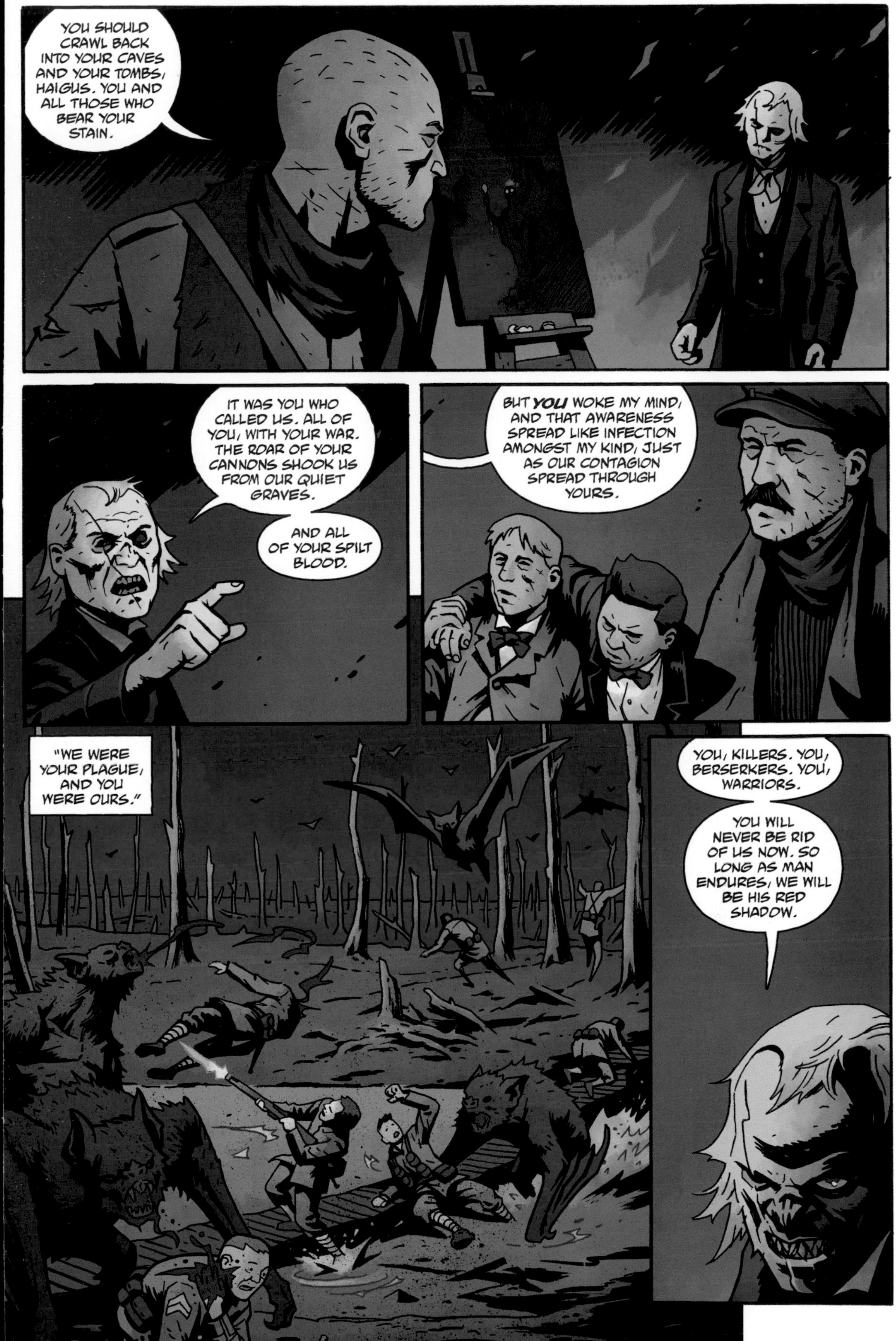
YOU SHOULD CRAWL BACK INTO YOUR CAVES AND YOUR TOMBS, HAIGUS. YOU AND ALL THOSE WHO BEAR YOUR STAIN.
IT WAS YOU WHO CALLED US. ALL OF YOU, WITH YOUR WAR. THE ROAR OF YOUR CANNONS SHOOK US FROM OUR QUIET GRAVES.
AND ALL OF YOUR SPILT BLOOD.
BUT YOU WOKE MY MIND, AND THAT AWARENESS SPREAD LIKE INFECTION AMONGST MY KIND, JUST AS OUR CONTAGION SPREAD THROUGH YOURS.
"WE WERE YOUR PLAGUE, AND YOU WERE OURS."
YOU, KILLERS. YOU, BERSERKERS. YOU, WARRIORS.
YOU WILL NEVER BE RID OF US NOW. SO LONG AS MAN ENDURES, WE WILL BE HIS RED SHADOW.

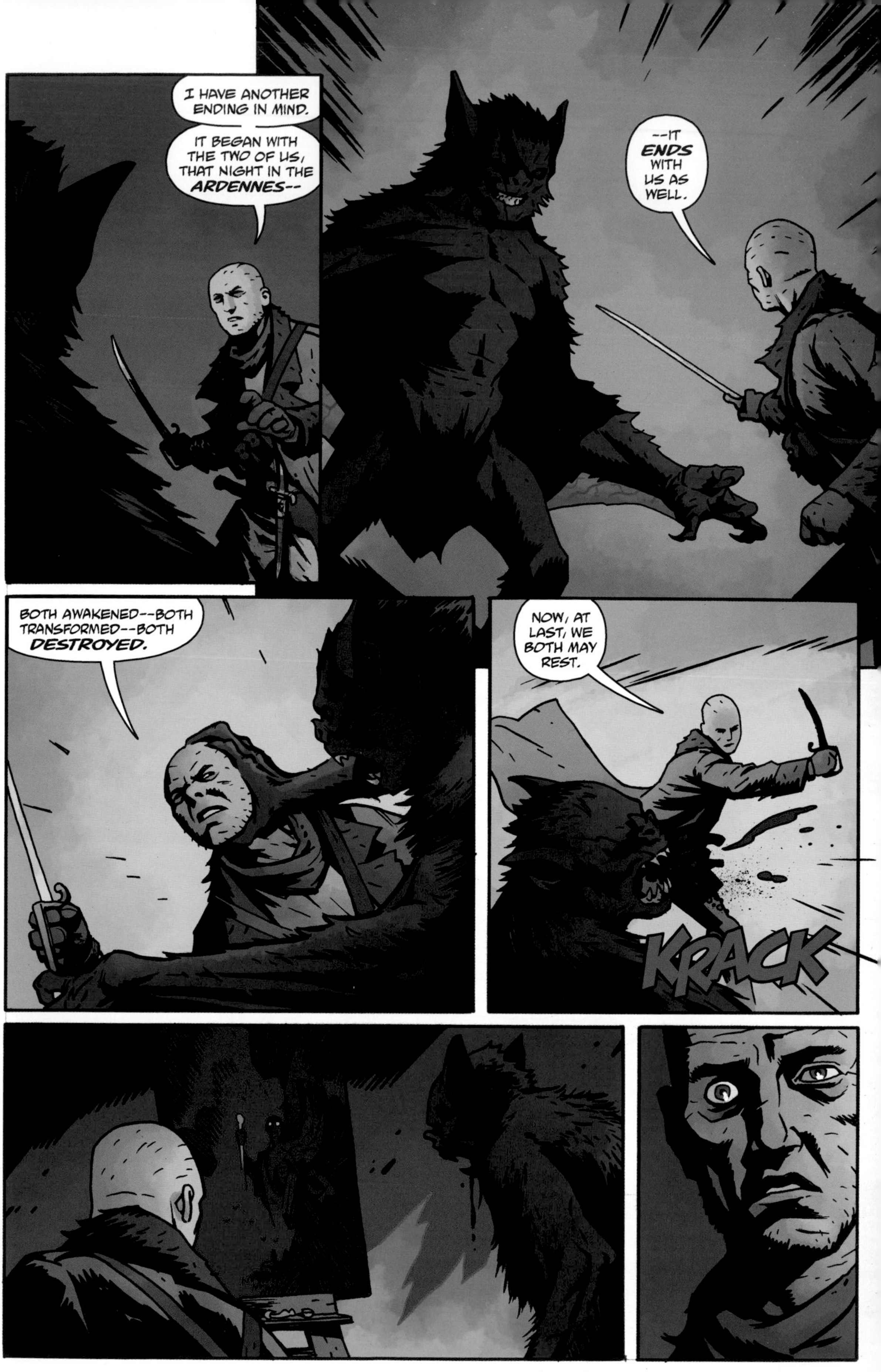
I HAVE ANOTHER ENDING IN MIND.
IT BEGAN WITH THE TWO OF US, THAT NIGHT IN THE ARDENNES--
--IT ENDS WITH US AS WELL.
BOTH AWAKENED--BOTH TRANSFORMED--BOTH DESTROYED.
NOW, AT LAST, WE BOTH MAY REST.
KRACK

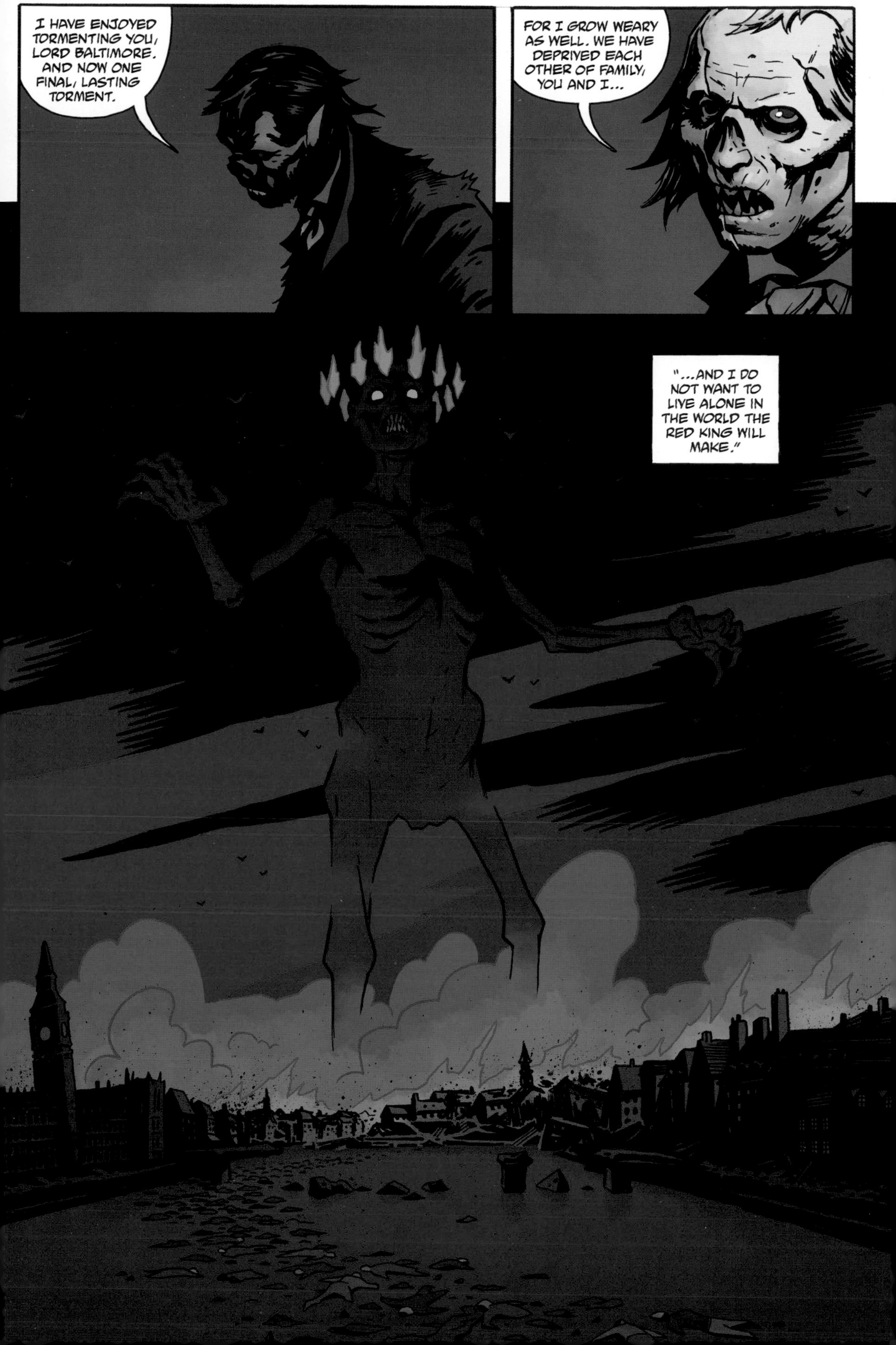
I HAVE ENJOYED TORMENTING YOU, LORD BALTIMORE. AND NOW ONE FINAL, LASTING TORMENT.
FOR I GROW WEARY AS WELL. WE HAVE DEPRIVED EACH OTHER OF FAMILY, YOU AND I...
"...AND I DO NOT WANT TO LIVE ALONE IN THE WORLD THE RED KING WILL MAKE."

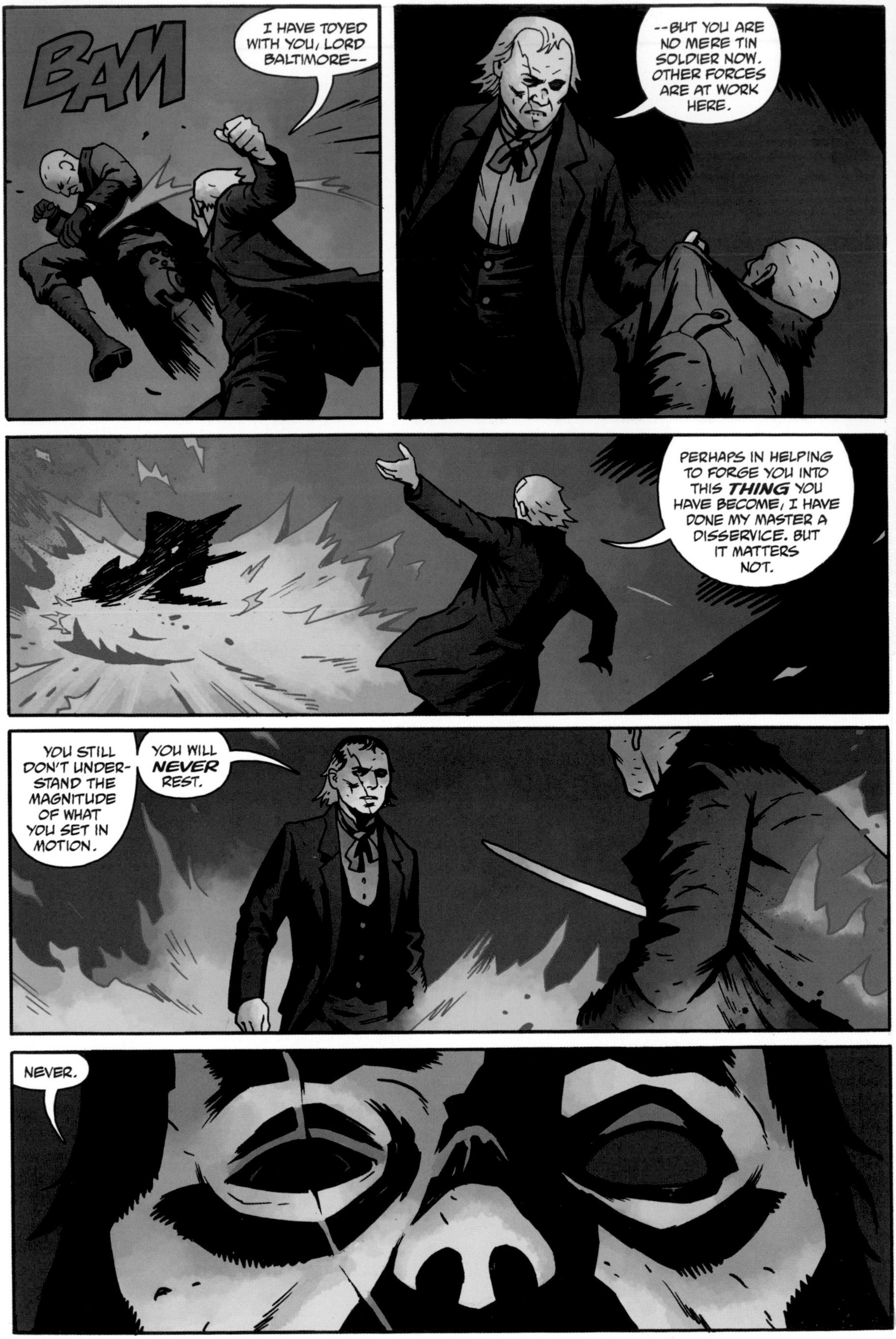
BAM
I HAVE TOYED WITH YOU, LORD BALTIMORE--
--BUT YOU ARE NO MERE TIN SOLDIER NOW. OTHER FORCES ARE AT WORK HERE.
PERHAPS IN HELPING TO FORGE YOU INTO THIS THING YOU HAVE BECOME, I HAVE DONE MY MASTER A DISSERVICE. BUT IT MATTERS NOT.
YOU STILL DON'T UNDERSTAND THE MAGNITUDE OF WHAT YOU SET IN MOTION.
YOU WILL NEVER REST.
NEVER.

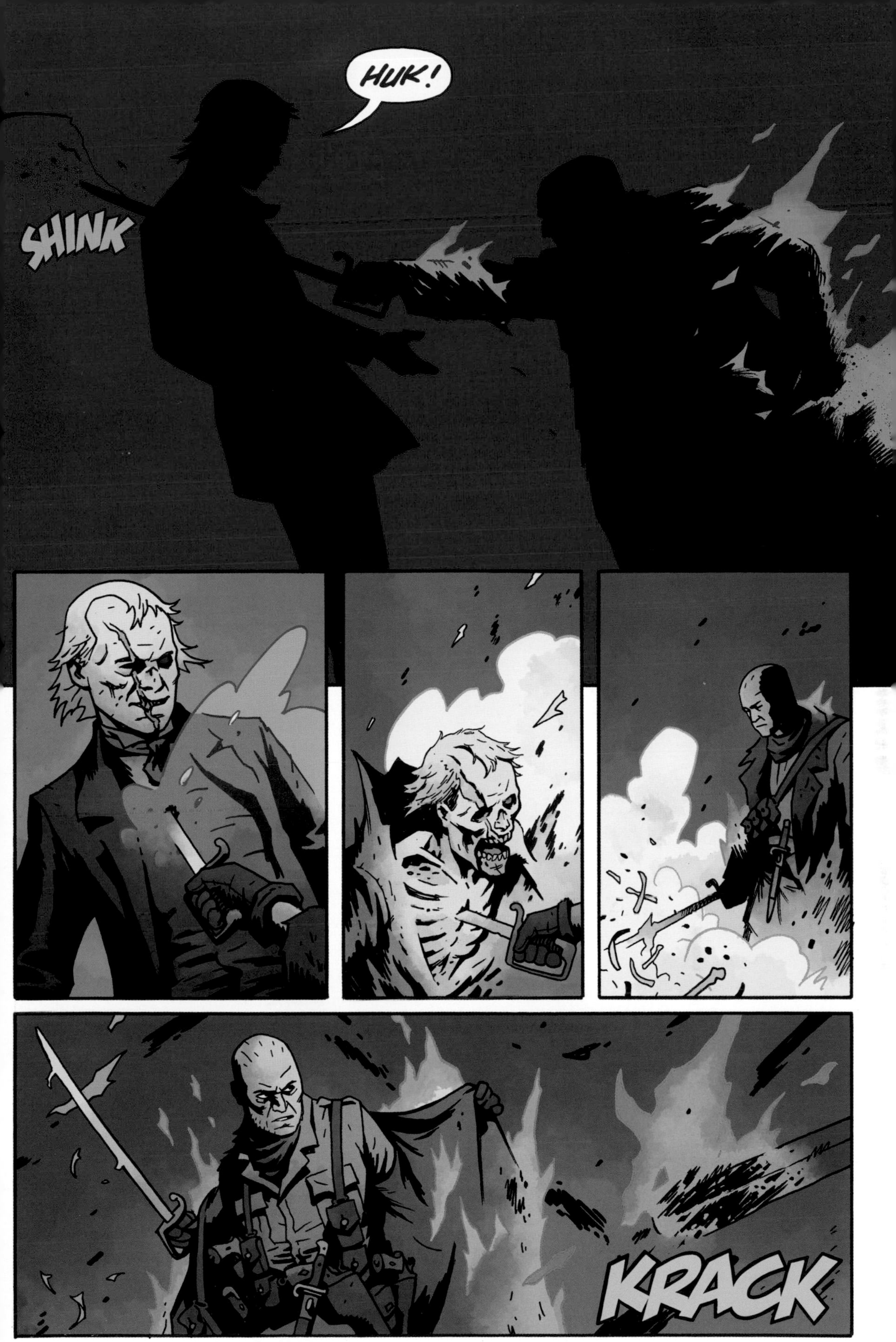
HUK!
SHINK
KRACK

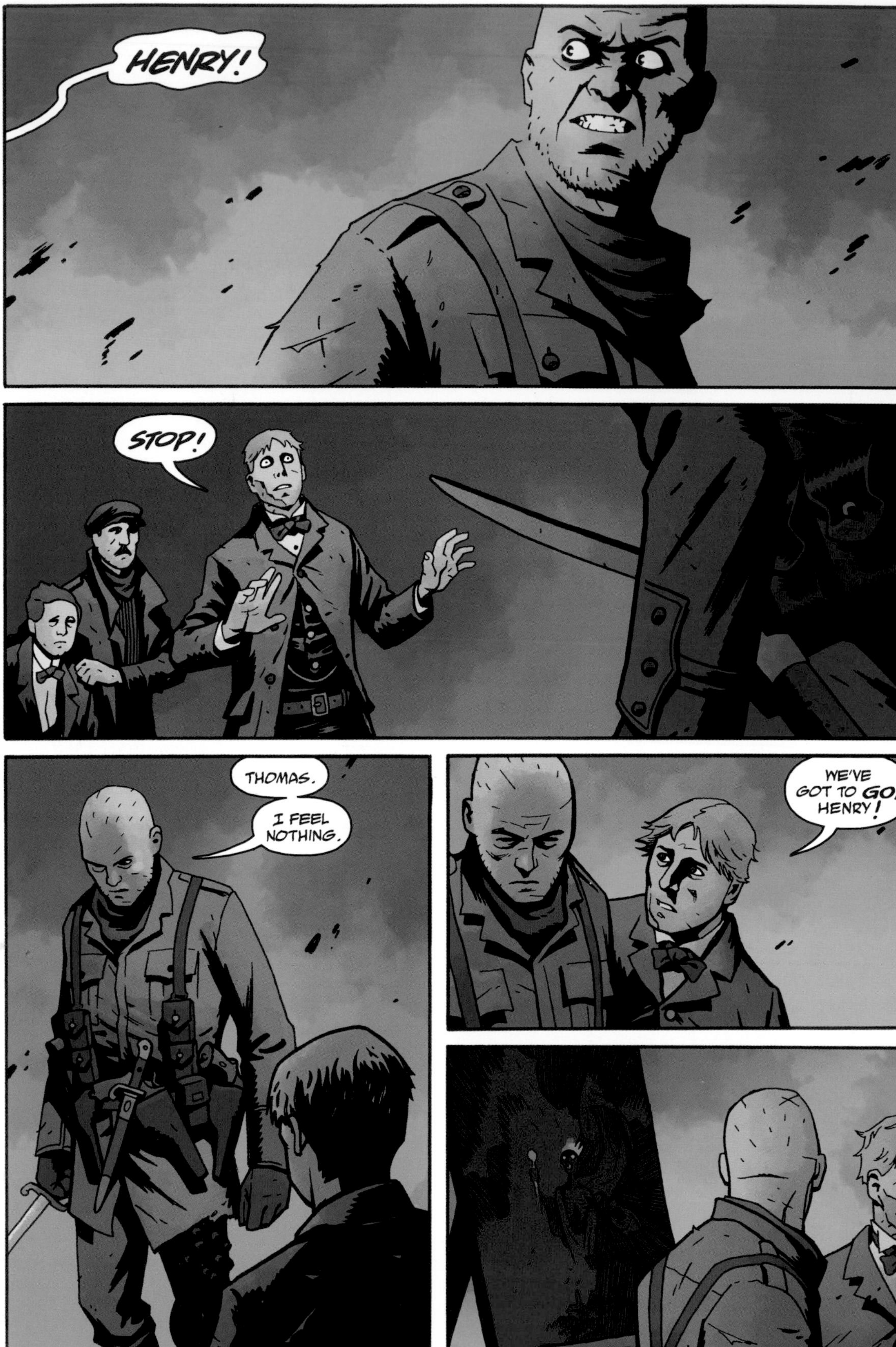
HENRY!
STOP!
THOMAS.
I FEEL NOTHING.
WE'VE GOT TO GO, HENRY!

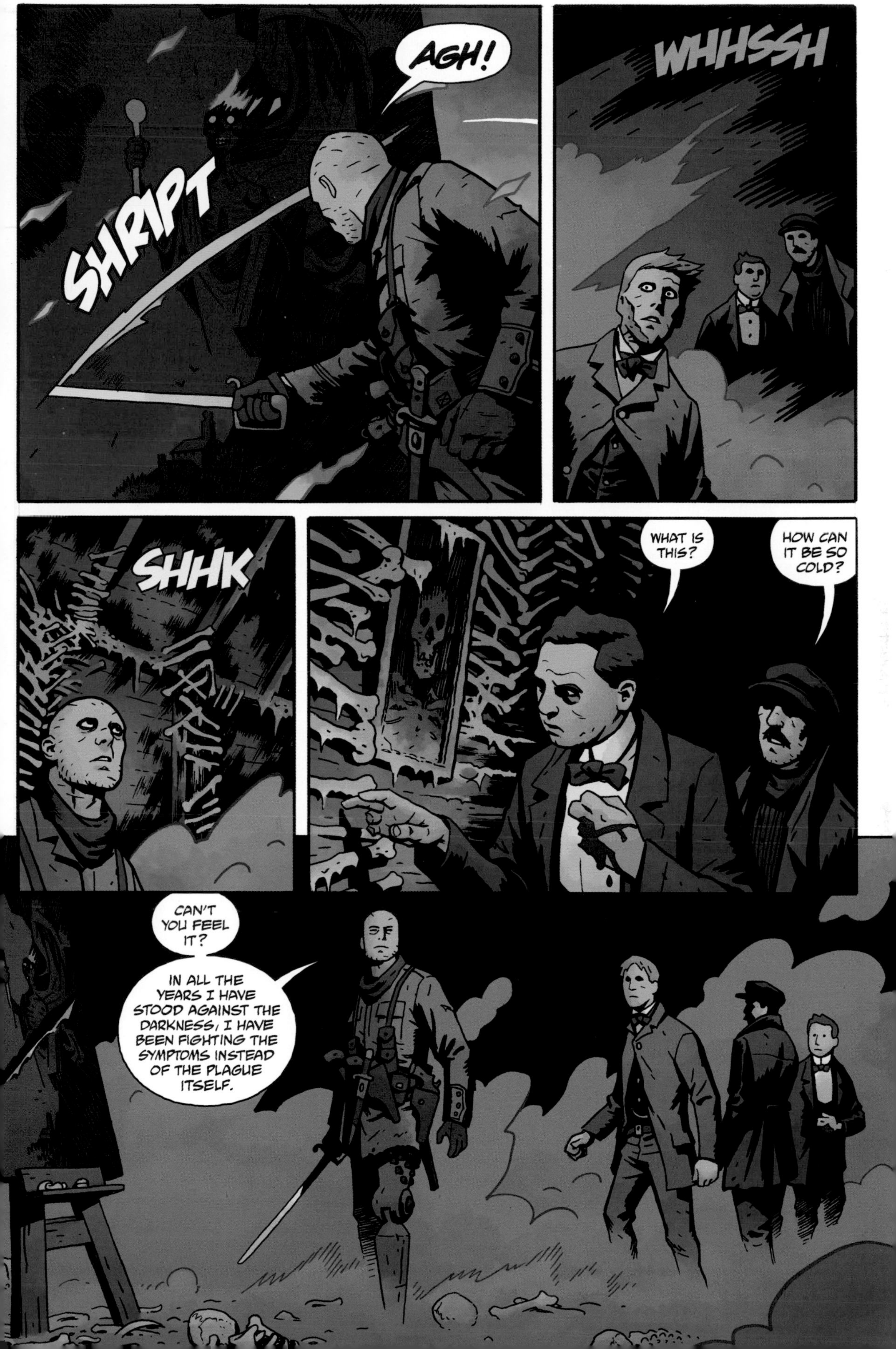
AGH!
SHRIPT
WHHSSH
SHHK
WHAT IS THIS?
HOW CAN IT BE SO COLD?
CAN'T YOU FEEL IT?
IN ALL THE YEARS I HAVE STOOD AGAINST THE DARKNESS, I HAVE BEEN FIGHTING THE SYMPTOMS INSTEAD OF THE PLAGUE ITSELF.

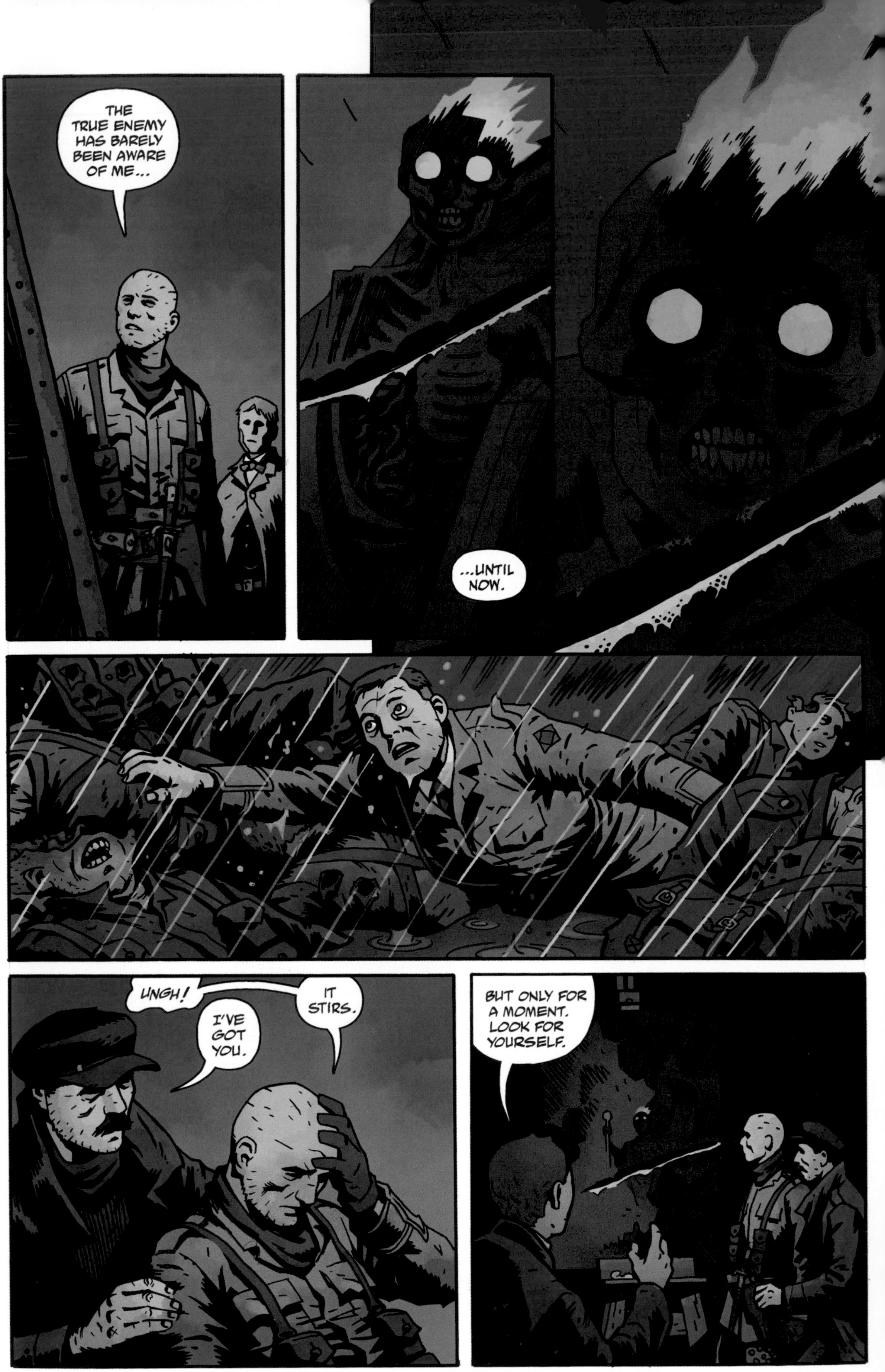
THE TRUE ENEMY HAS BARELY BEEN AWARE OF ME...
...UNTIL NOW.
UNGH!
I'VE GOT YOU.
IT STIRS.
BUT ONLY FOR A MOMENT. LOOK FOR YOURSELF.

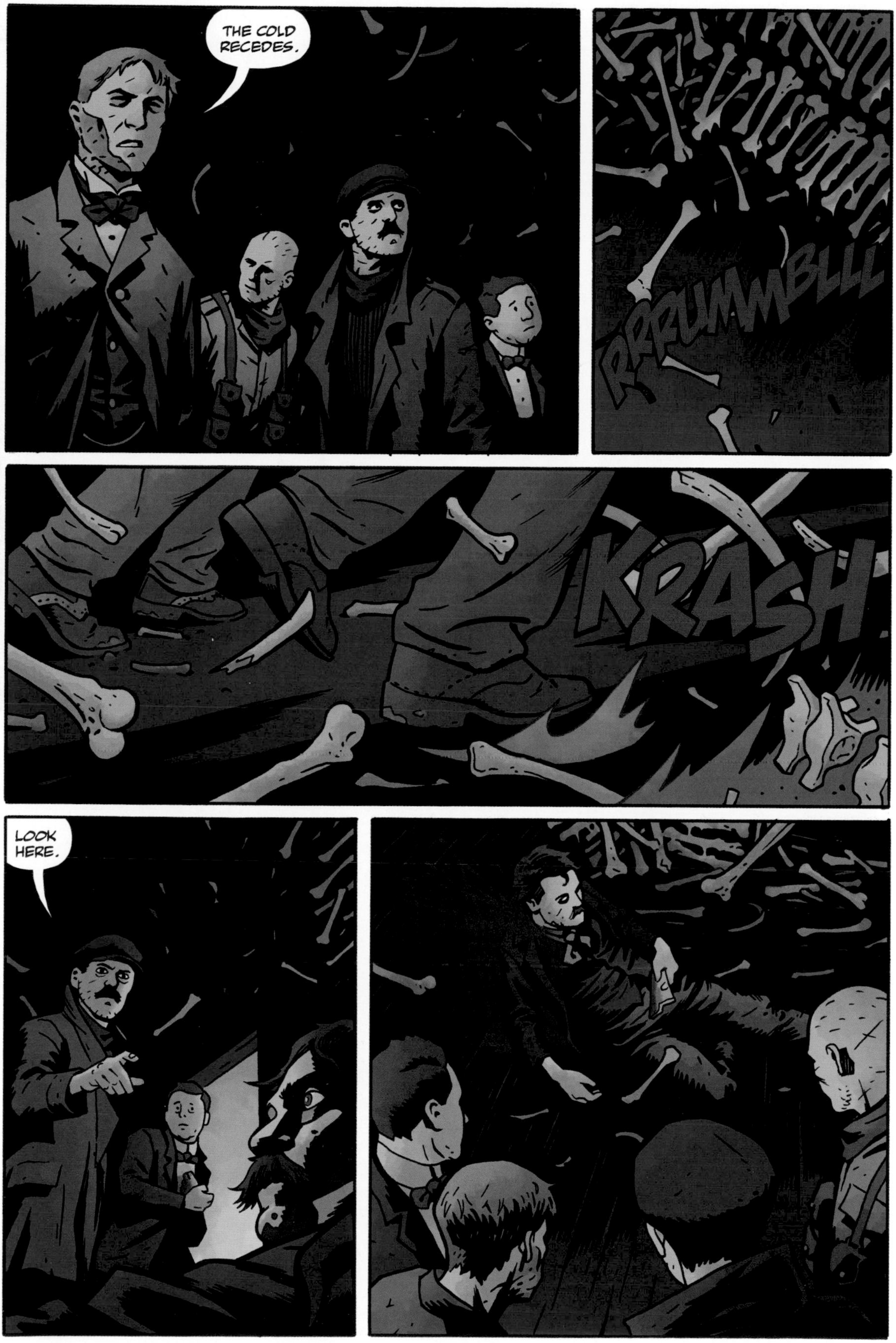
THE COLD RECEDES.
RRRUMMBLLL
KRASH
LOOK HERE.

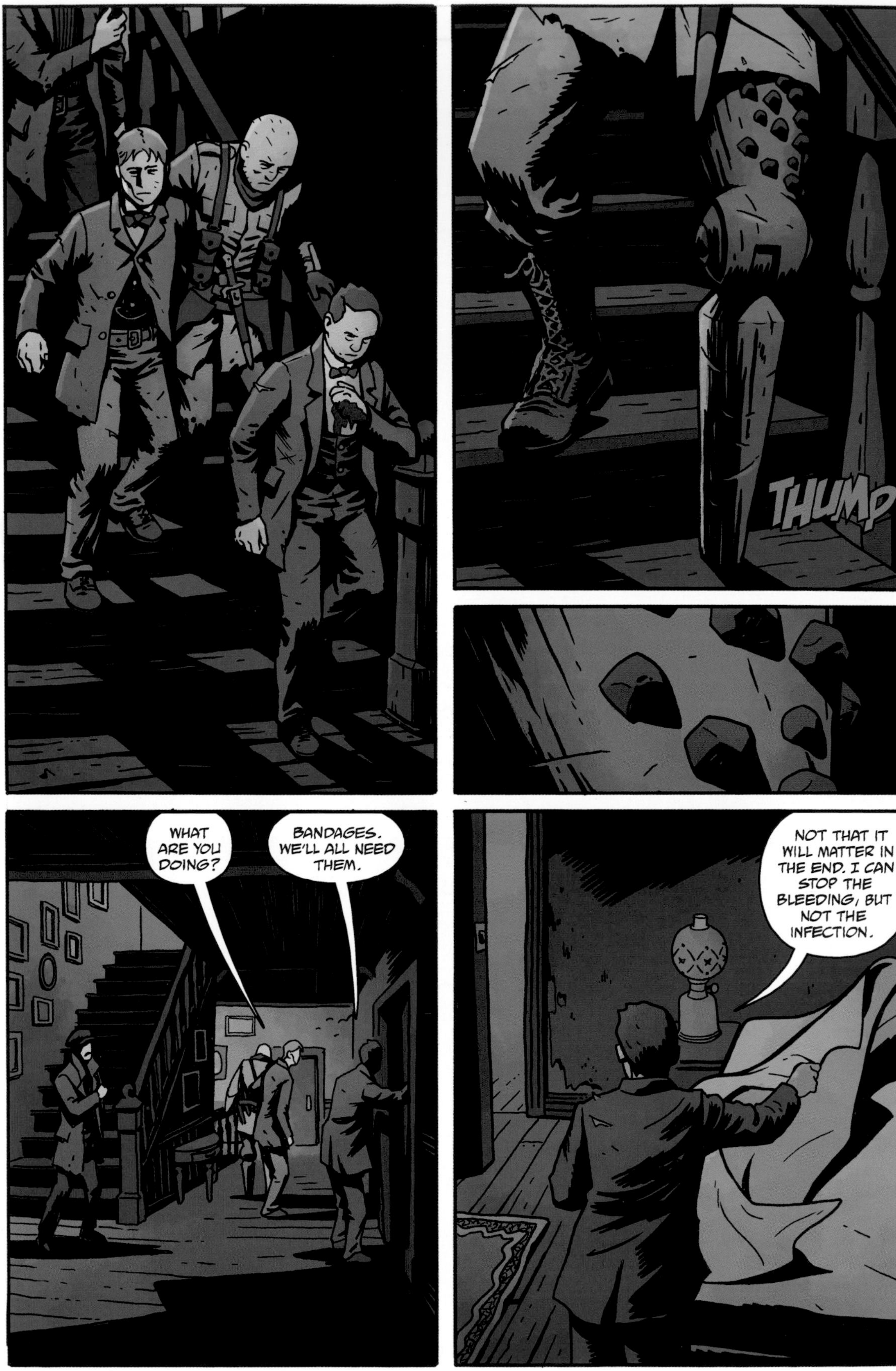
THUMP
WHAT ARE YOU DOING?
BANDAGES. WE'LL ALL NEED THEM.
NOT THAT IT WILL MATTER IN THE END. I CAN STOP THE BLEEDING, BUT NOT THE INFECTION.

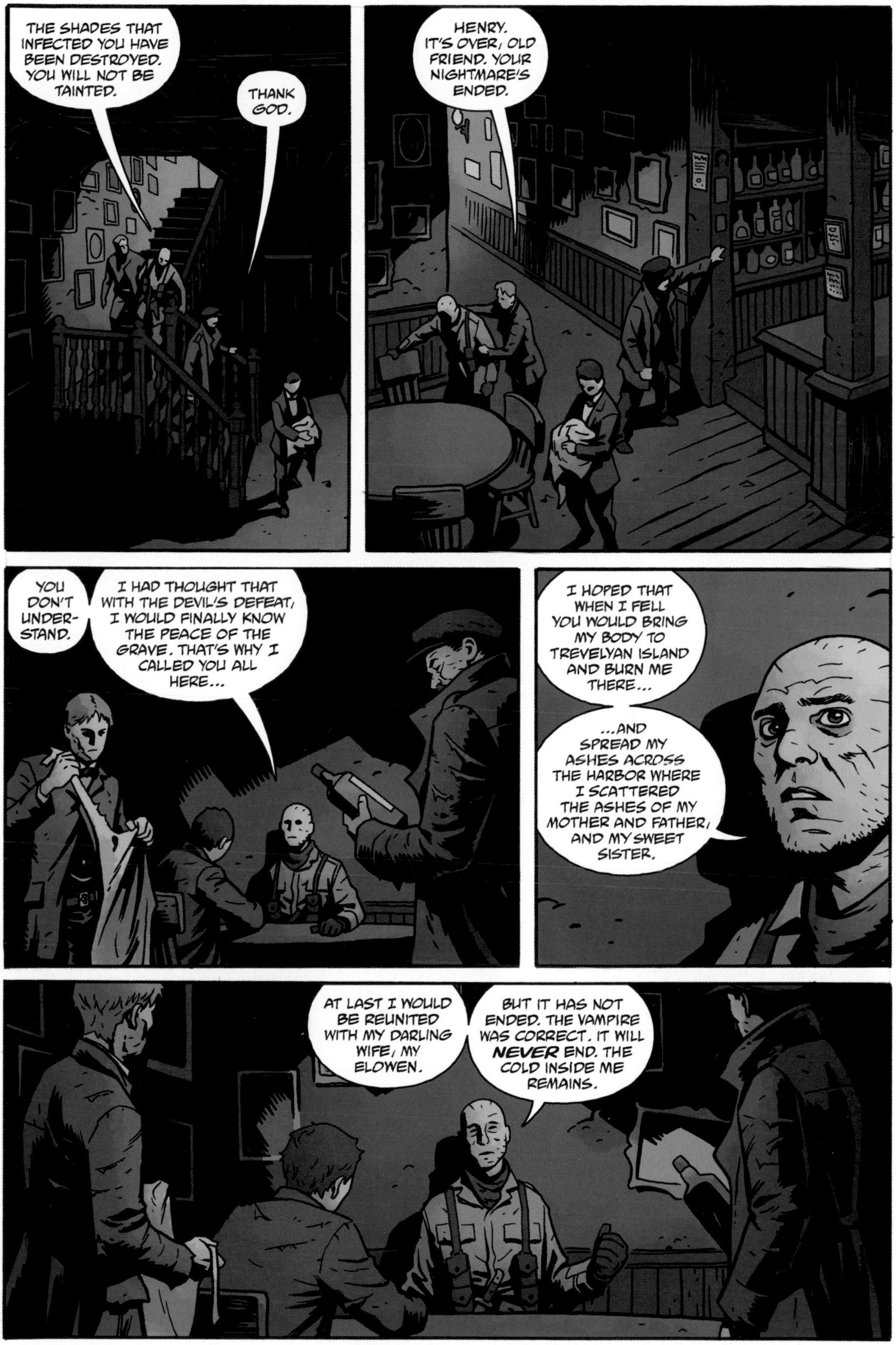
THE SHADES THAT INFECTED YOU HAVE BEEN DESTROYED. YOU WILL NOT BE TAINTED.
THANK GOD.
HENRY. IT'S OVER, OLD FRIEND. YOUR NIGHTMARE'S ENDED.
YOU DON'T UNDER-STAND.
I HAD THOUGHT THAT WITH THE DEVIL'S DEFEAT, I WOULD FINALLY KNOW THE PEACE OF THE GRAVE. THAT'S WHY I CALLED YOU ALL HERE...
I HOPED THAT WHEN I FELL YOU WOULD BRING MY BODY TO TREVELYAN ISLAND AND BURN ME THERE...
...AND SPREAD MY ASHES ACROSS THE HARBOR WHERE I SCATTERED THE ASHES OF MY MOTHER AND FATHER, AND MY SWEET SISTER.
AT LAST I WOULD BE REUNITED WITH MY DARLING WIFE, MY ELOWEN.
BUT IT HAS NOT ENDED. THE VAMPIRE WAS CORRECT. IT WILL **NEVER** END. THE COLD INSIDE ME REMAINS.

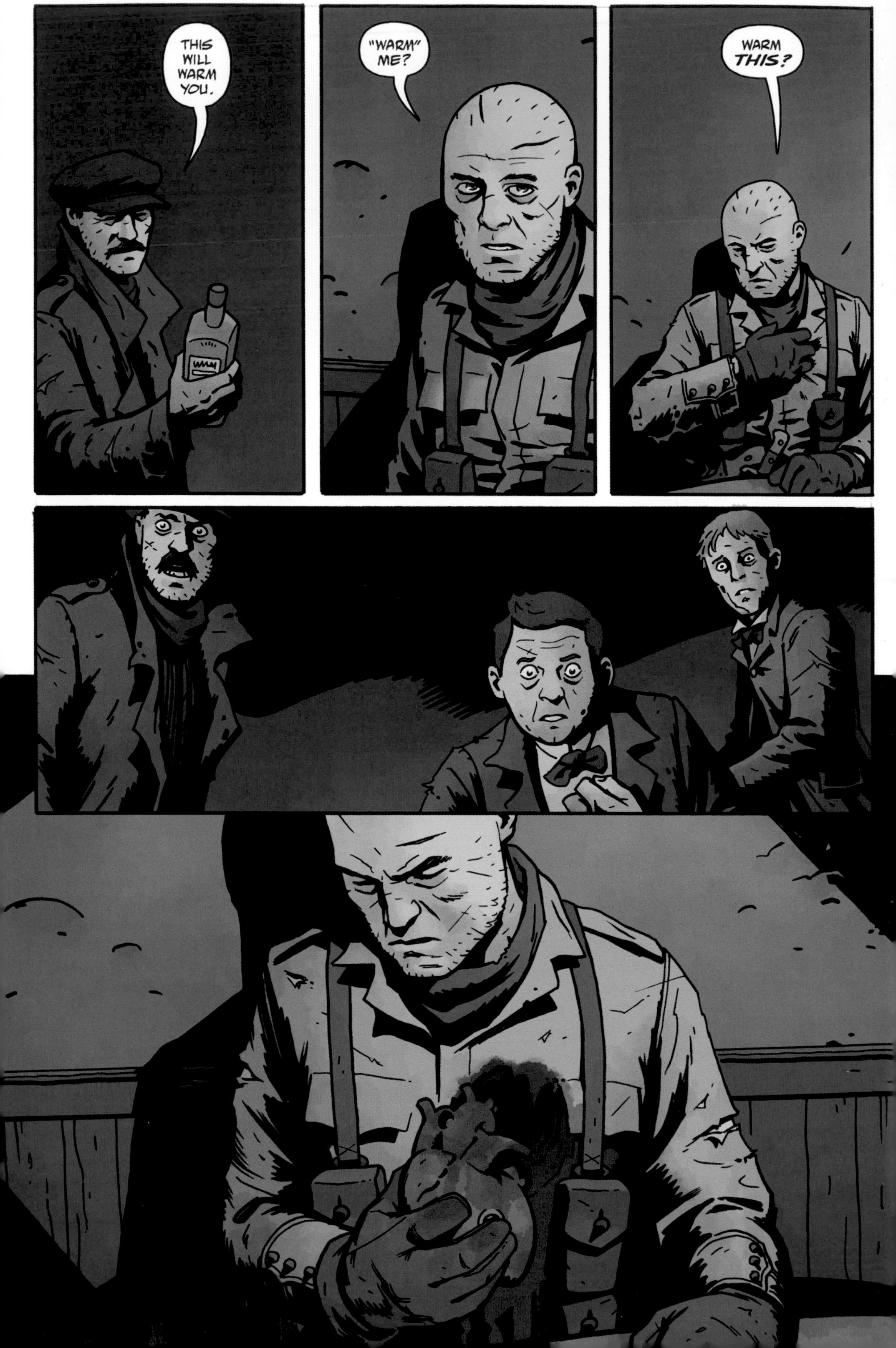
THIS WILL WARM YOU.
"WARM" ME?
WARM THIS?

KLUNK

I HAD THOUGHT MY QUEST WOULD END HERE...

...BUT IT IS MY ENDURING CURSE.

I UNDERSTAND, NOW, WHAT FATE HAS FORGED OF ME.

SO LONG AS THE RED KING REIGNS, THERE MUST ALWAYS BE LORD BALTIMORE.

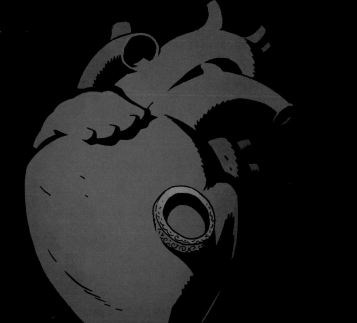

"When the maid cleared out the ashes next morning she found the soldier melted into the shape of a little tin heart, but all that remained of the dancer was her spangle."

—**The Steadfast Tin Soldier**
Hans Christian Andersen

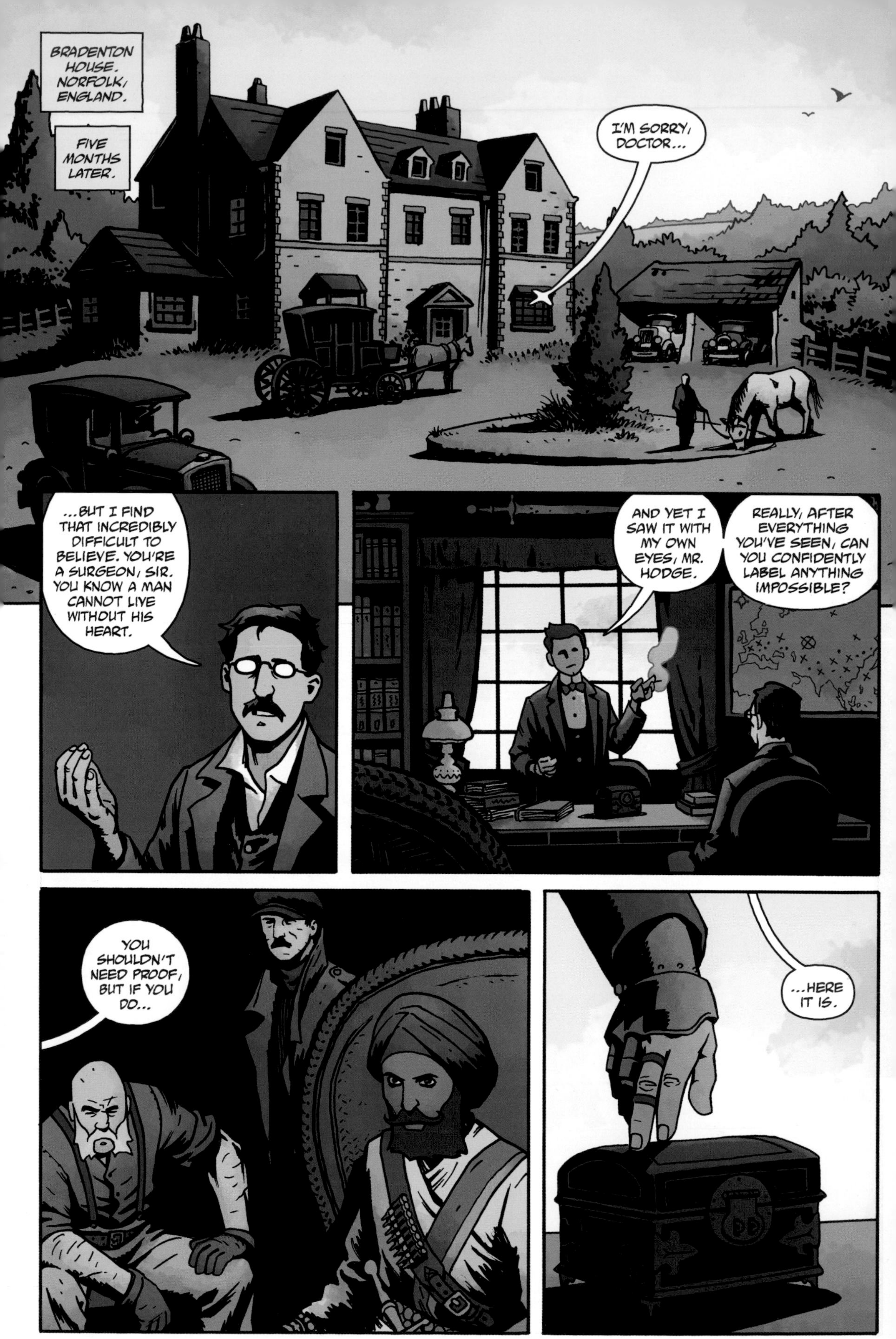
BRADENTON HOUSE. NORFOLK, ENGLAND.
FIVE MONTHS LATER.
I'M SORRY, DOCTOR...
...BUT I FIND THAT INCREDIBLY DIFFICULT TO BELIEVE. YOU'RE A SURGEON, SIR. YOU KNOW A MAN CANNOT LIVE WITHOUT HIS HEART.
AND YET I SAW IT WITH MY OWN EYES, MR. HODGE.
REALLY, AFTER EVERYTHING YOU'VE SEEN, CAN YOU CONFIDENTLY LABEL ANYTHING IMPOSSIBLE?
YOU SHOULDN'T NEED PROOF, BUT IF YOU DO...
...HERE IT IS.

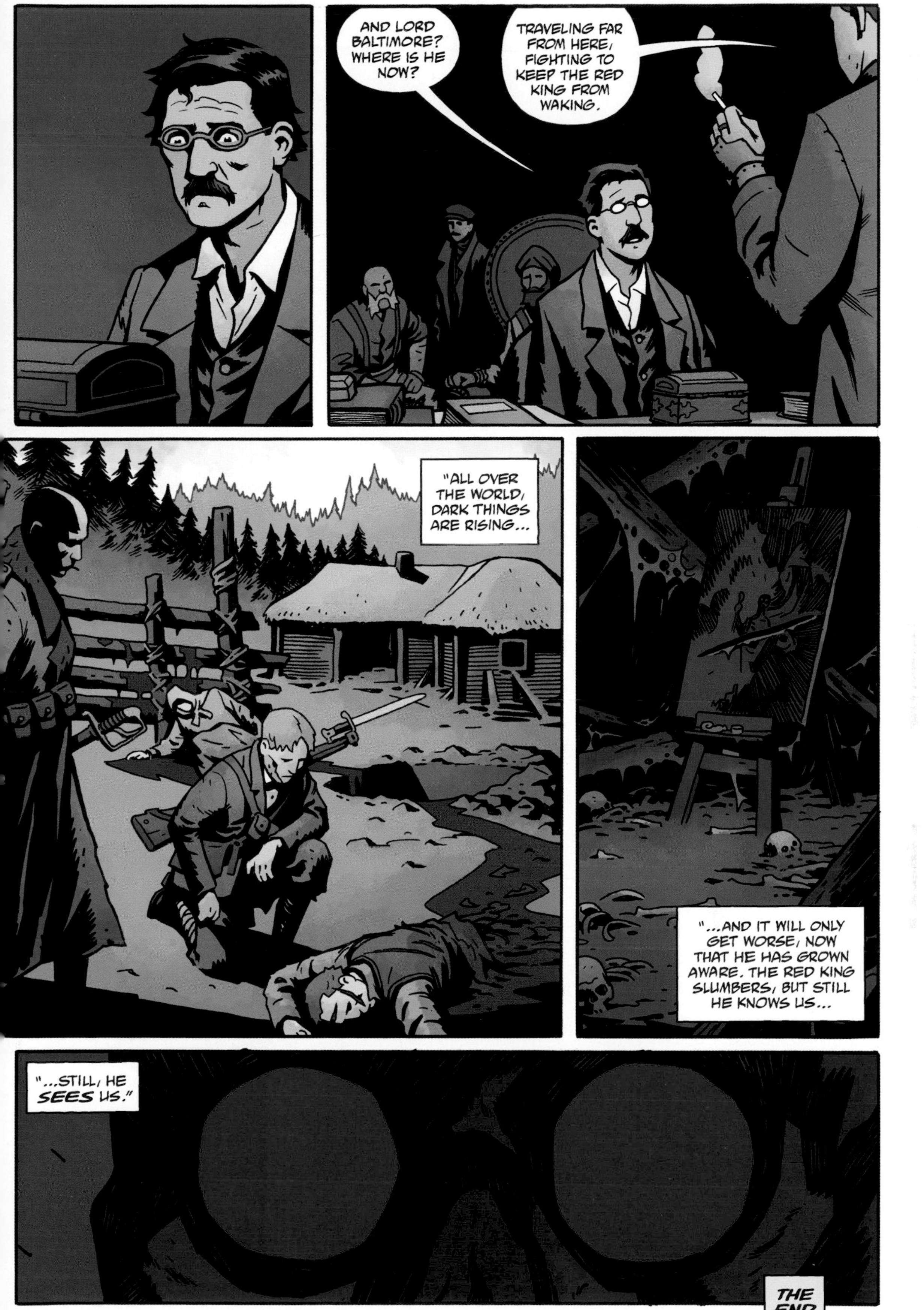
AND LORD BALTIMORE? WHERE IS HE NOW?
TRAVELING FAR FROM HERE, FIGHTING TO KEEP THE RED KING FROM WAKING.
"ALL OVER THE WORLD, DARK THINGS ARE RISING...
"...AND IT WILL ONLY GET WORSE, NOW THAT HE HAS GROWN AWARE. THE RED KING SLUMBERS, BUT STILL HE KNOWS US...
"...STILL, HE SEES US."
THE END

BALTIMORE™
CHAPEL OF BONES

SKETCHBOOK

Notes by Scott Allie

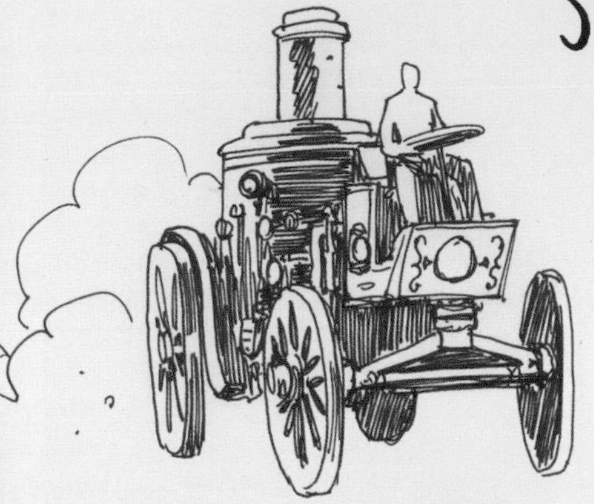

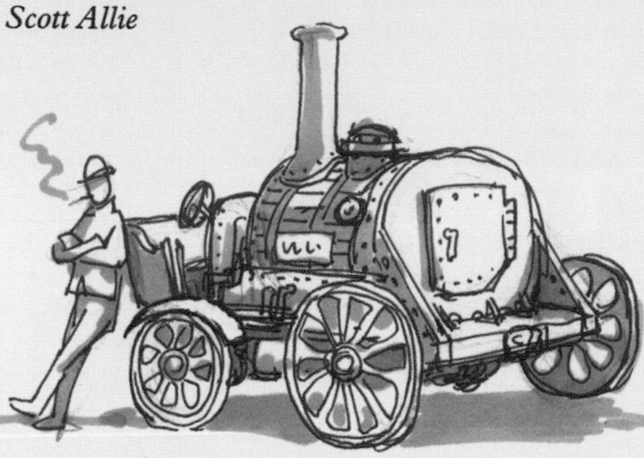

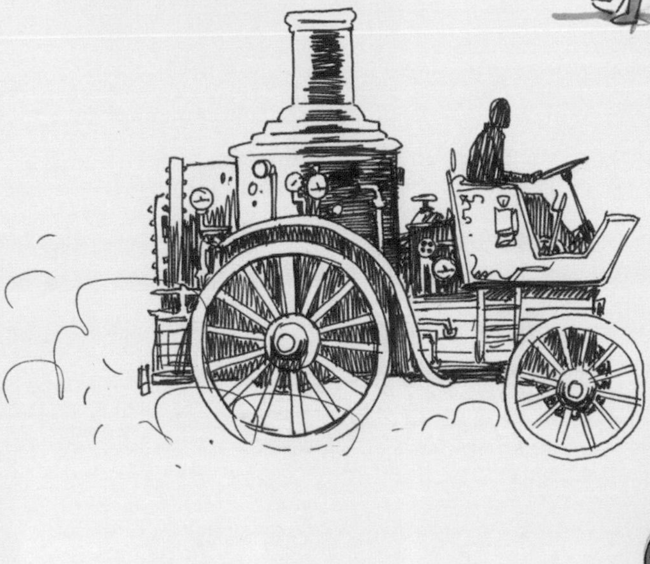

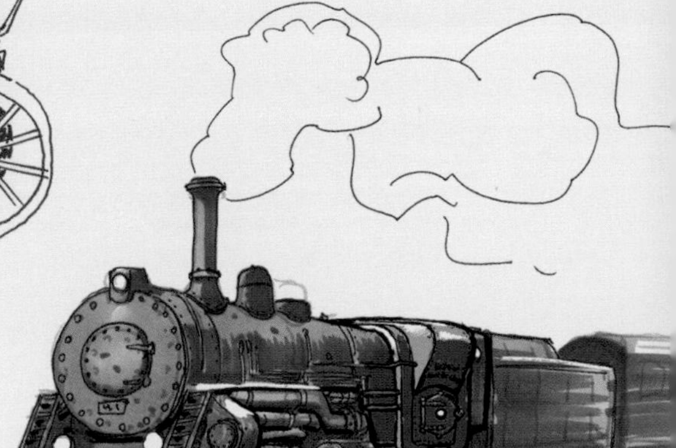

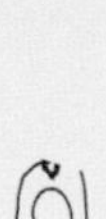
Tall/Thin

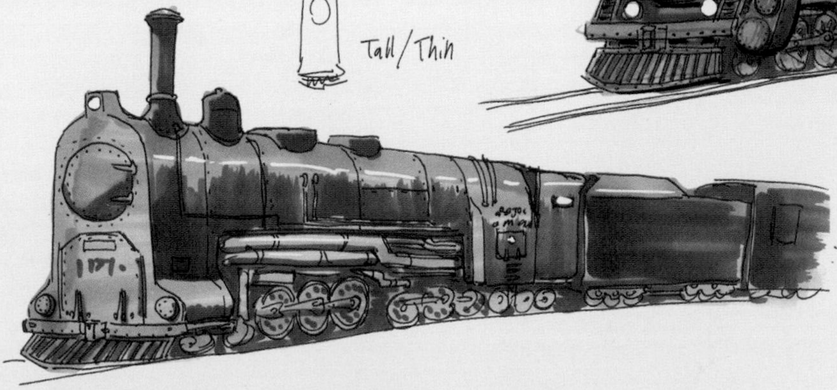

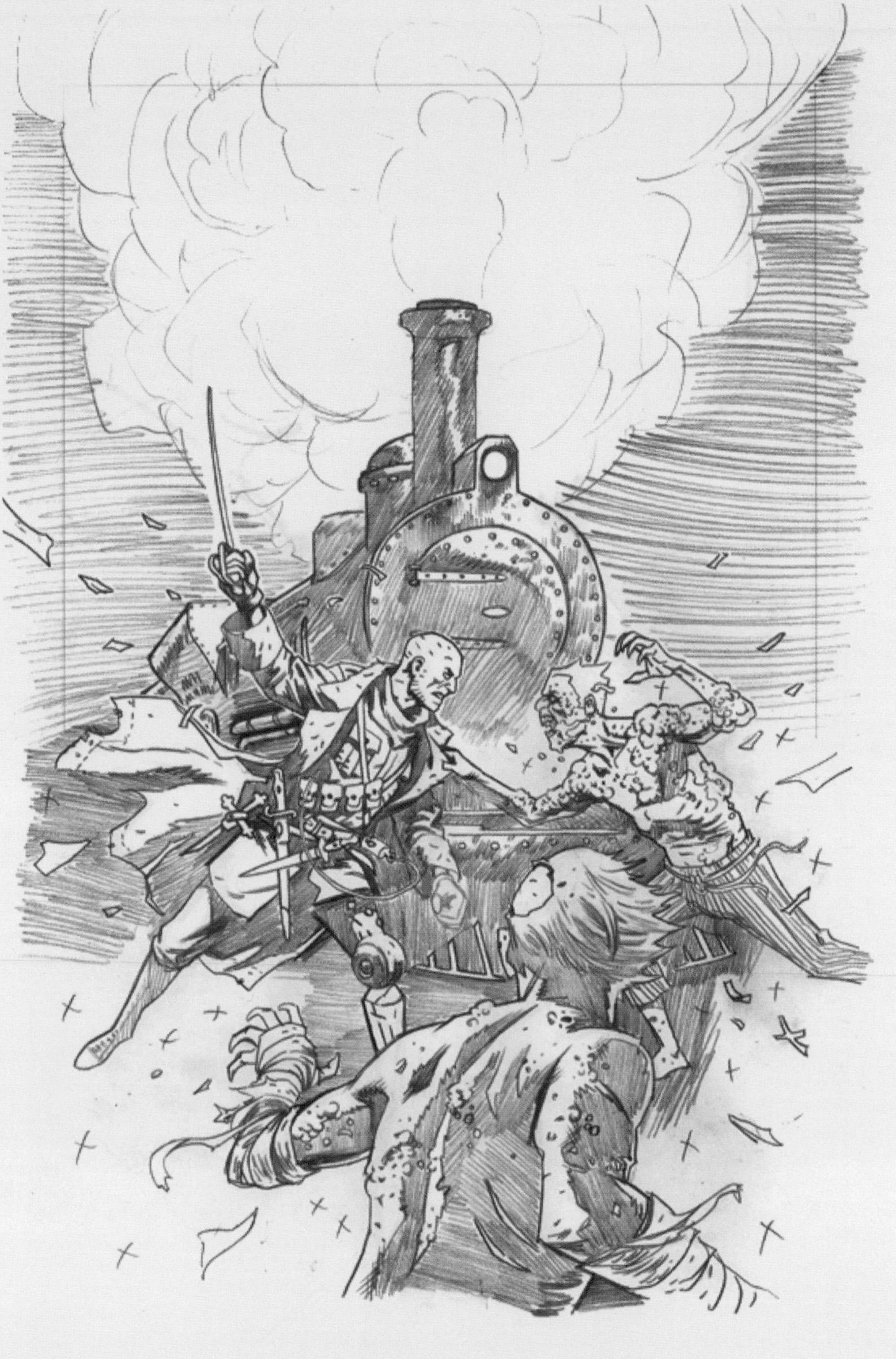

Studies for vehicles (facing) and Ben's pencils for the *Infernal Train* #1 cover.

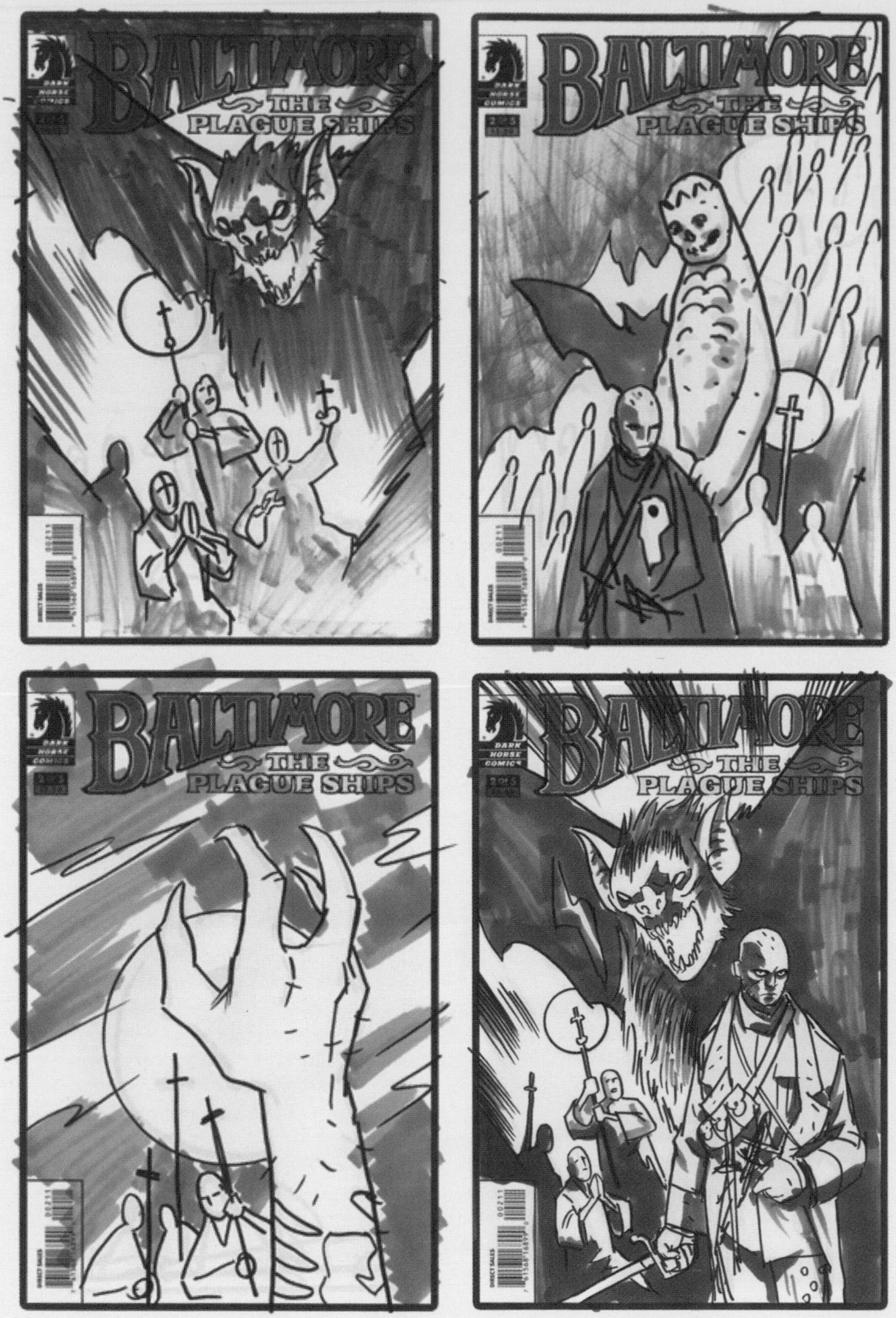
BALTIMORE
THE
PLAGUE SHIPS
BALTIMORE
THE
PLAGUE SHIPS
BALTIMORE
THE
PLAGUE SHIPS
BALTIMORE
THE
PLAGUE SHIPS

Sketches for the *Infernal Train* #3 cover (top and lower left); the revised sketch (lower right); and the final pencils (facing).

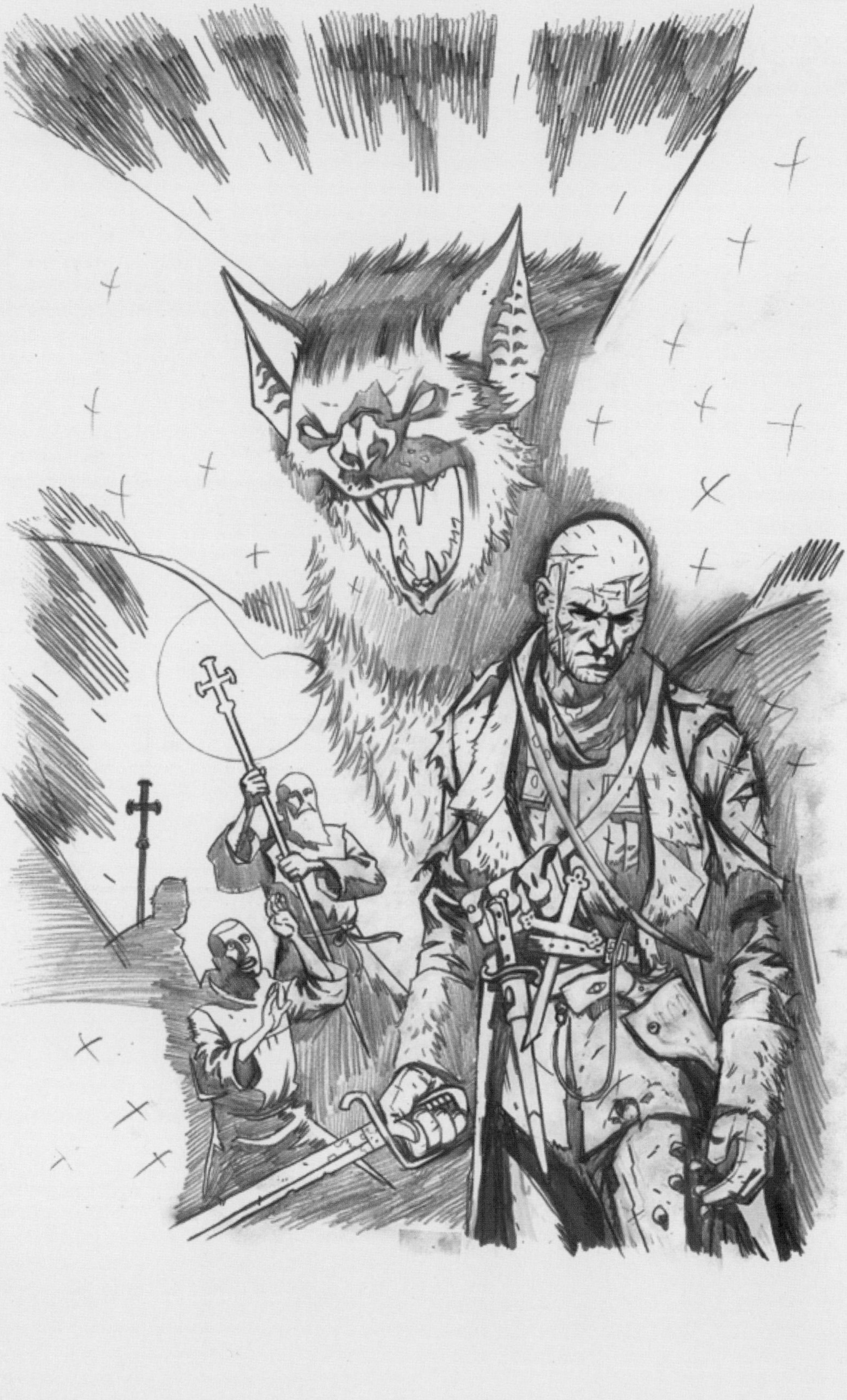

Red King's Tower
close on window
weird Fused Guardians
Guardians
Vague/Ambiguous sleeping Red King

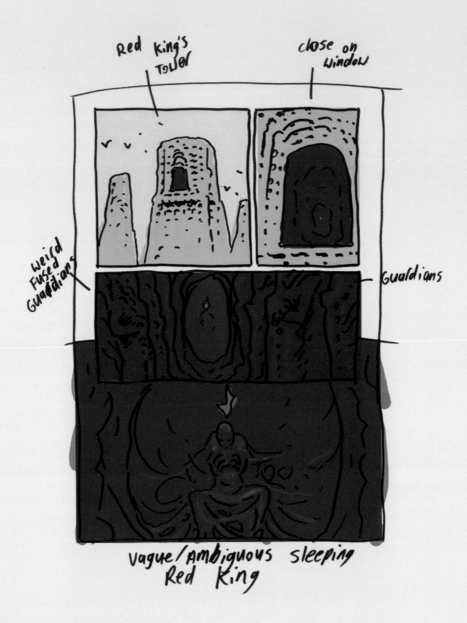

During one of Fulcanelli's speeches in *The Infernal Train*, Ben wanted to show the Red King sleeping in his limbo world. He drew this before the issue was written. As Ben says, "Then Chris wrote it differently. And then I drew it different to that. But this is where it started."

Facing: Ben's design for Duvic as a werewolf.

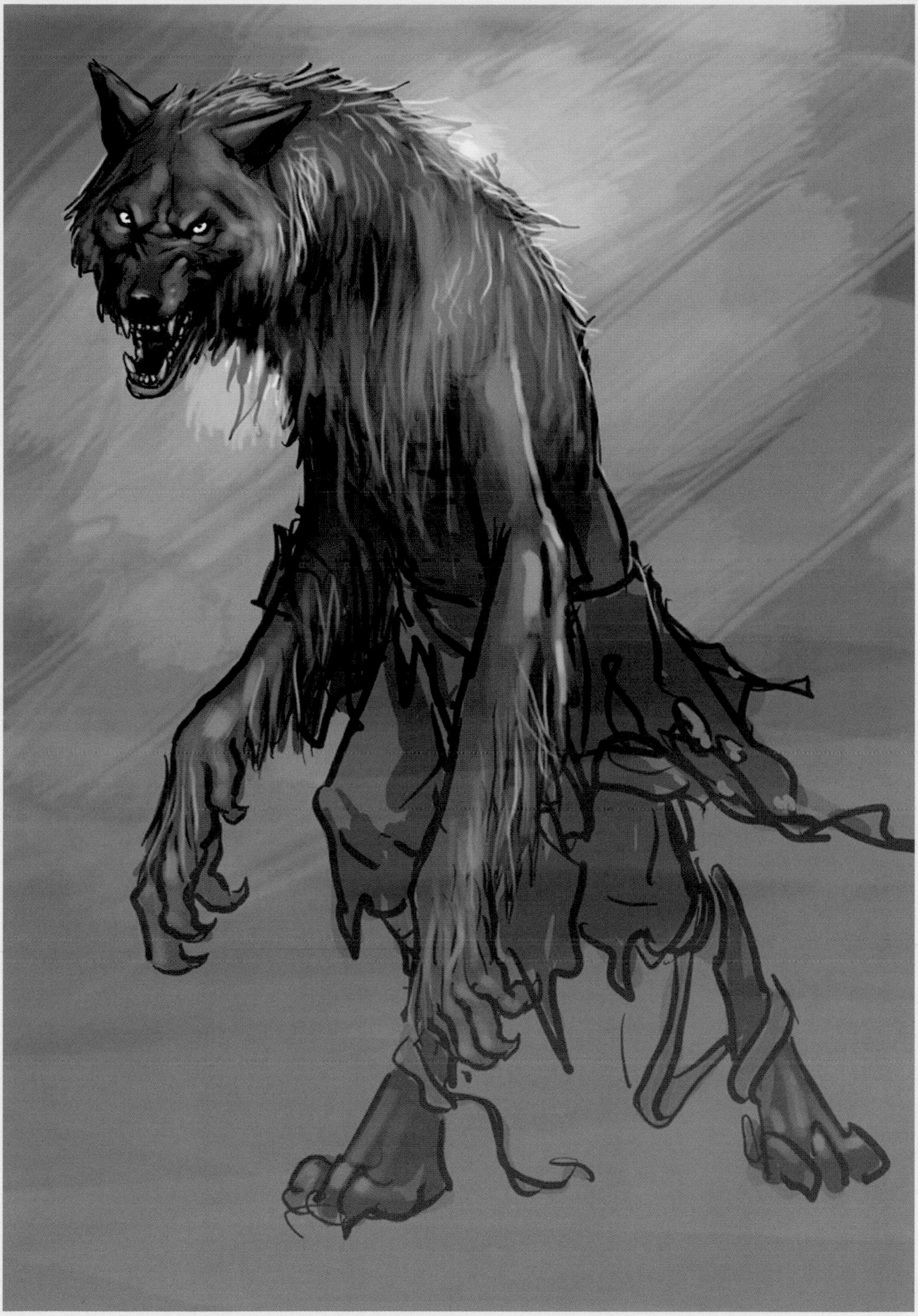

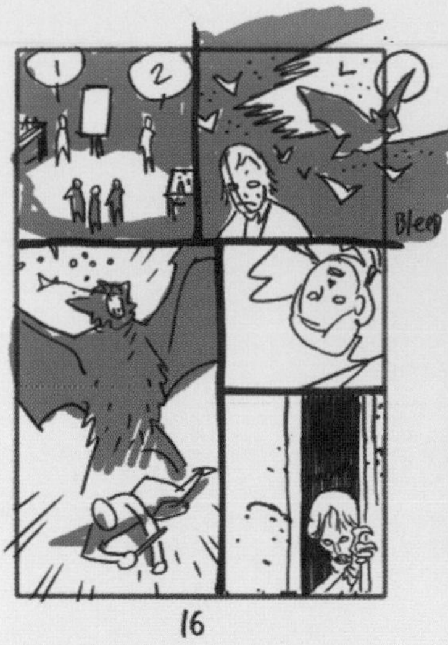
Bleed
16

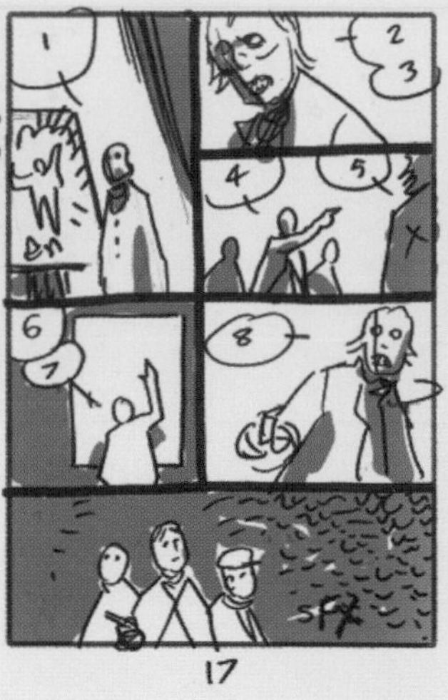
SFX
17

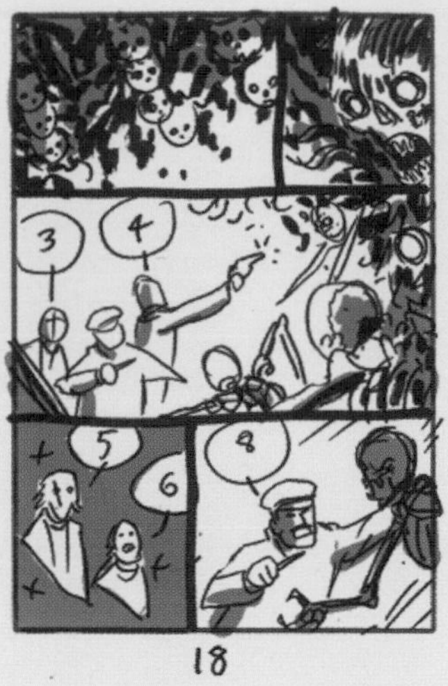
18

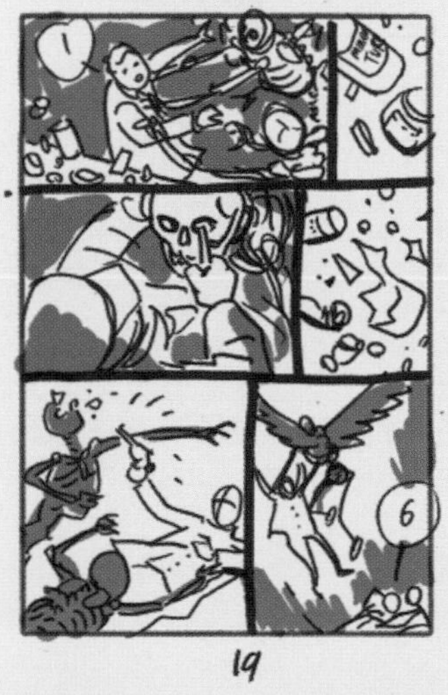
19

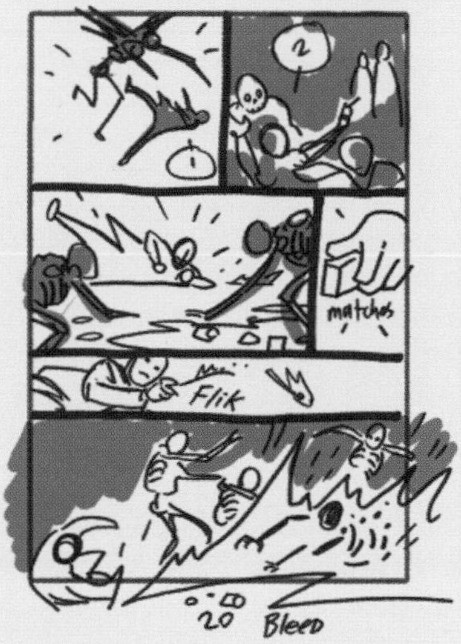
matches
Flik
20 Bleed

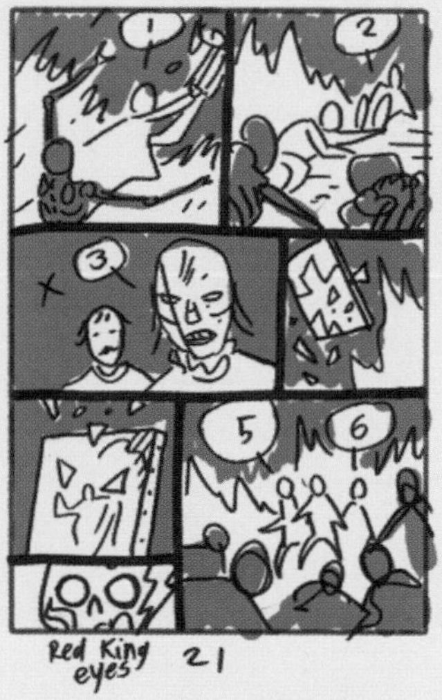
Red King eyes
21

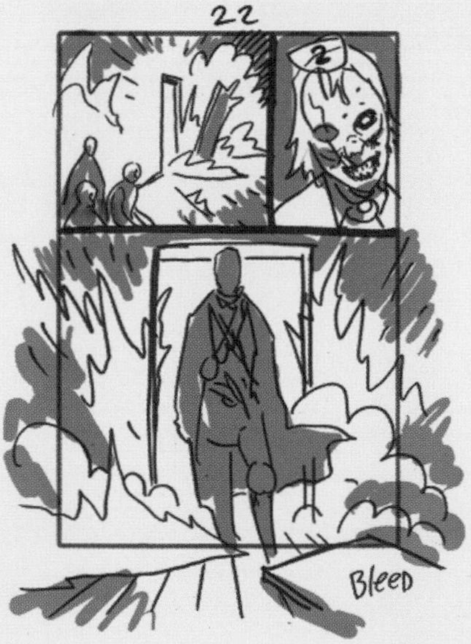
22
Bleed

Ben's layouts for the end of *Chapel of Bones* Part 1.

Facing: Illustration by Sebastián Fiumara (for fun).

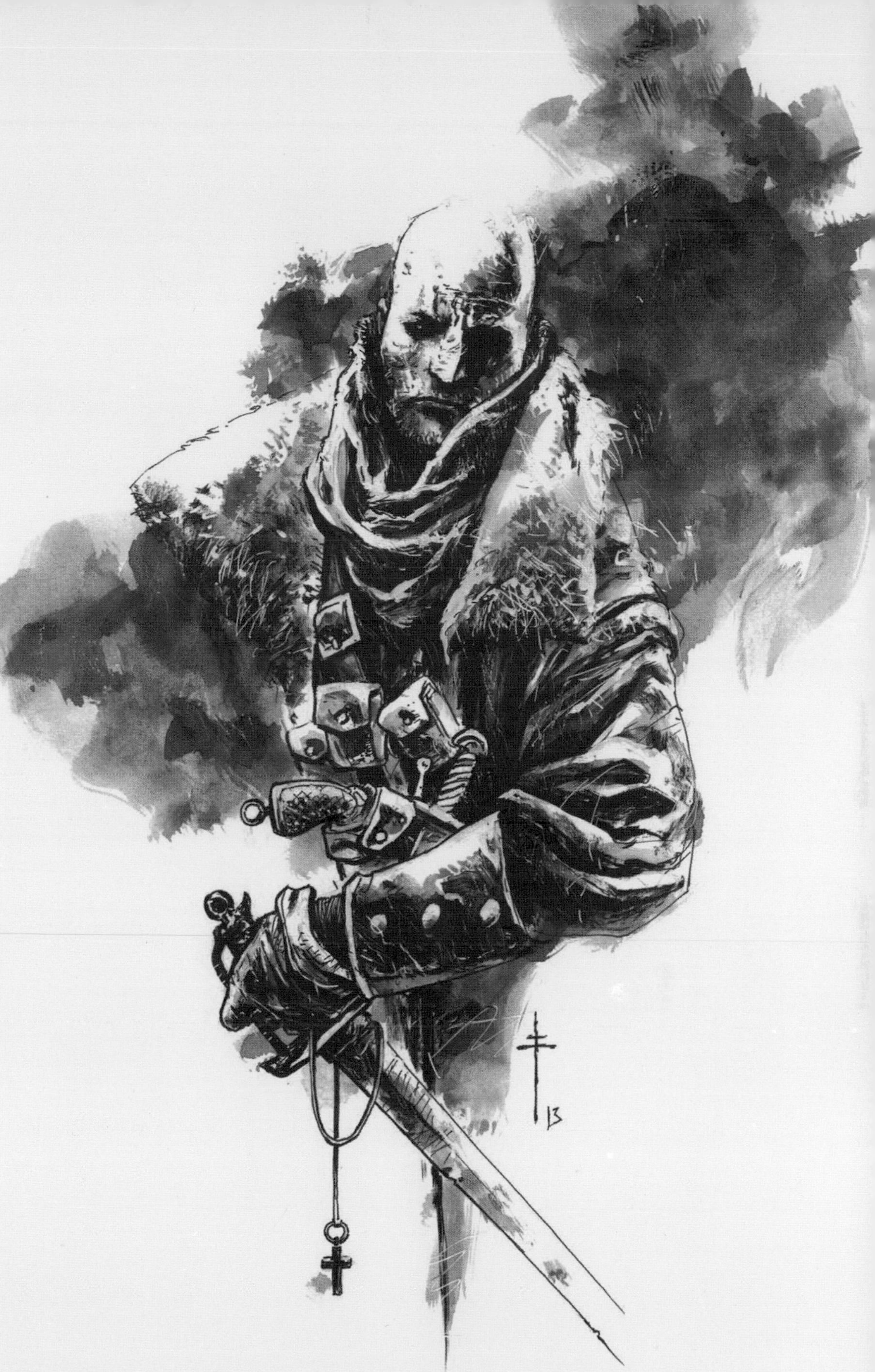

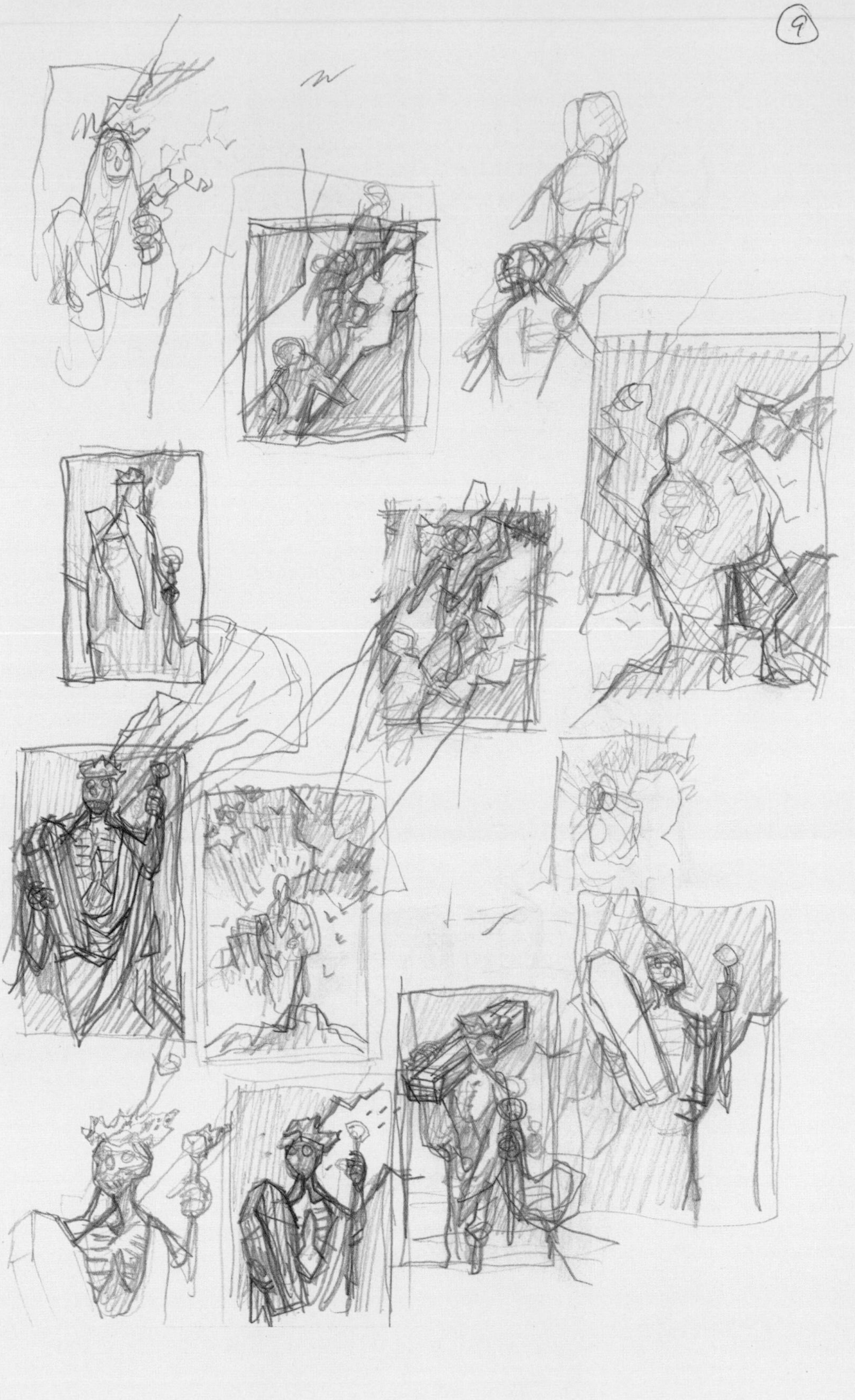

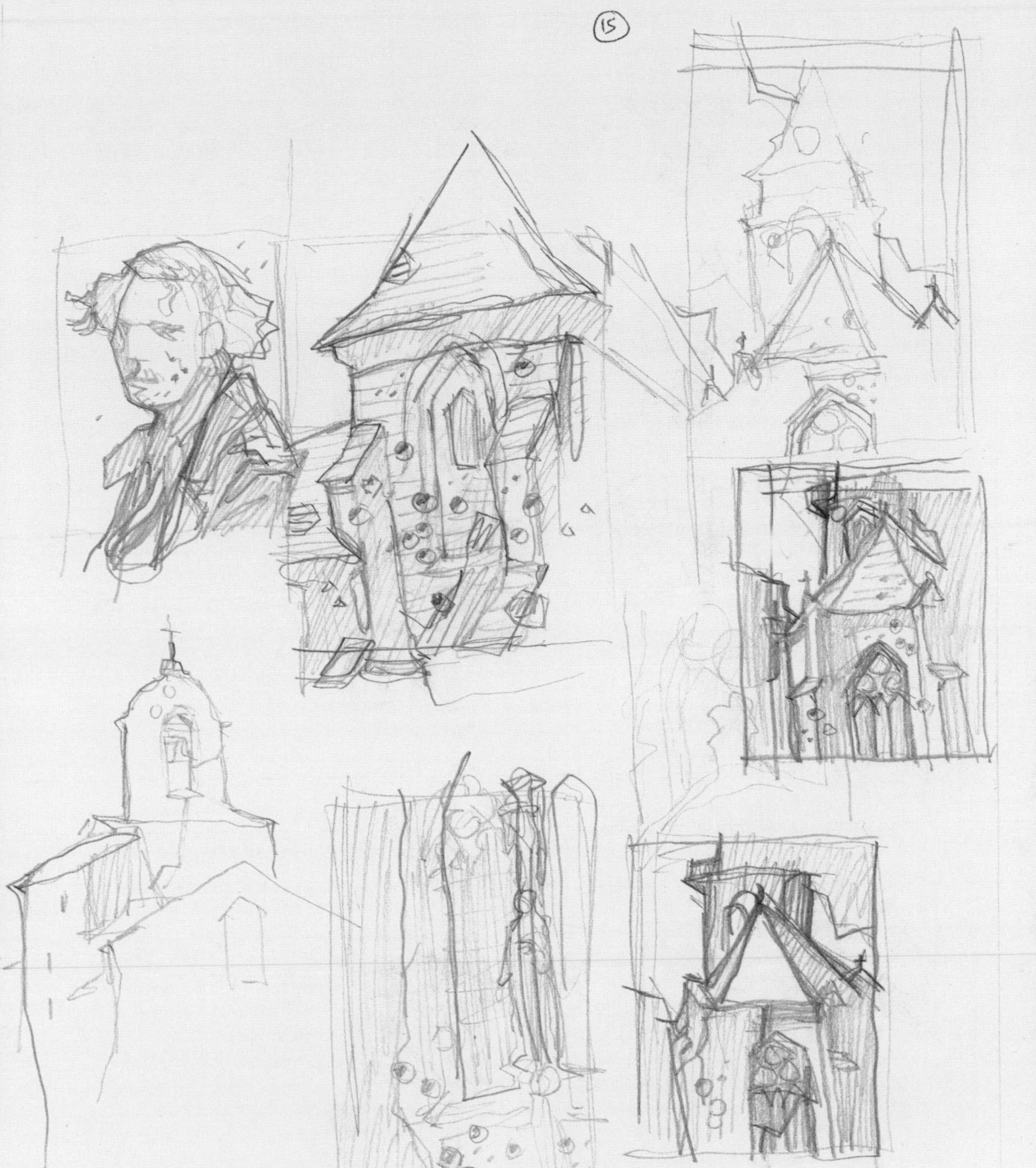
15

Mignola's sketches for the *Baltimore* novel, many of which provided the basis for the comics.

Facing: These sketches were for two different drawings of the Red King. One, early in the novel, was a vision that a monk described to Aischros. Later in the novel the artist, Bentley, has painted a similar image, which Ben copied for *Chapel of Bones*.

28 (p 32)   33~34

34~35
27 (p32)

Mike's drawings, from the novel, of Childress, Rose, and (from a sketch on the preceding page) Bentley.

Facing: Ben based his drawing of Baltimore's approach to London in the comic (bottom) on Mike's drawing of Aischros approaching (top) in the novel.

Bentley   236~237
135 (p 240)

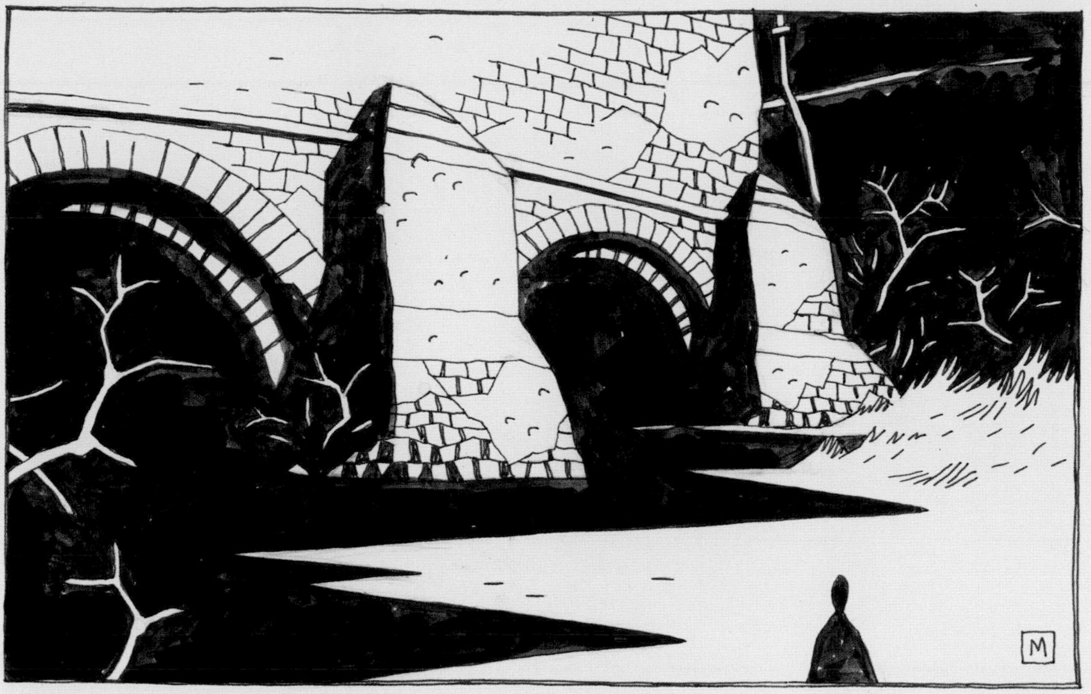
M

MIGNOLA

Entrance into city ~~27~~ 28(p27) - Bottom half of page

92 #71

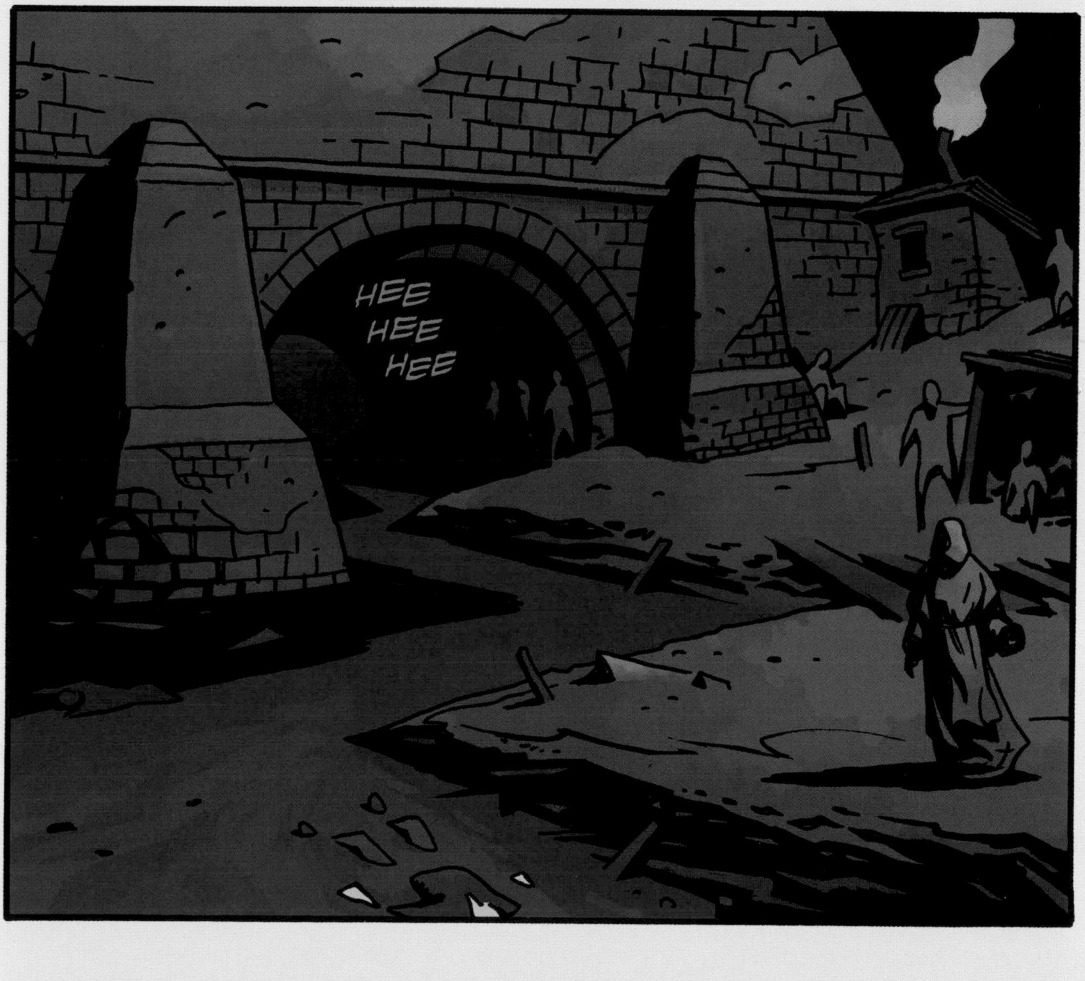
HEE
HEE
HEE

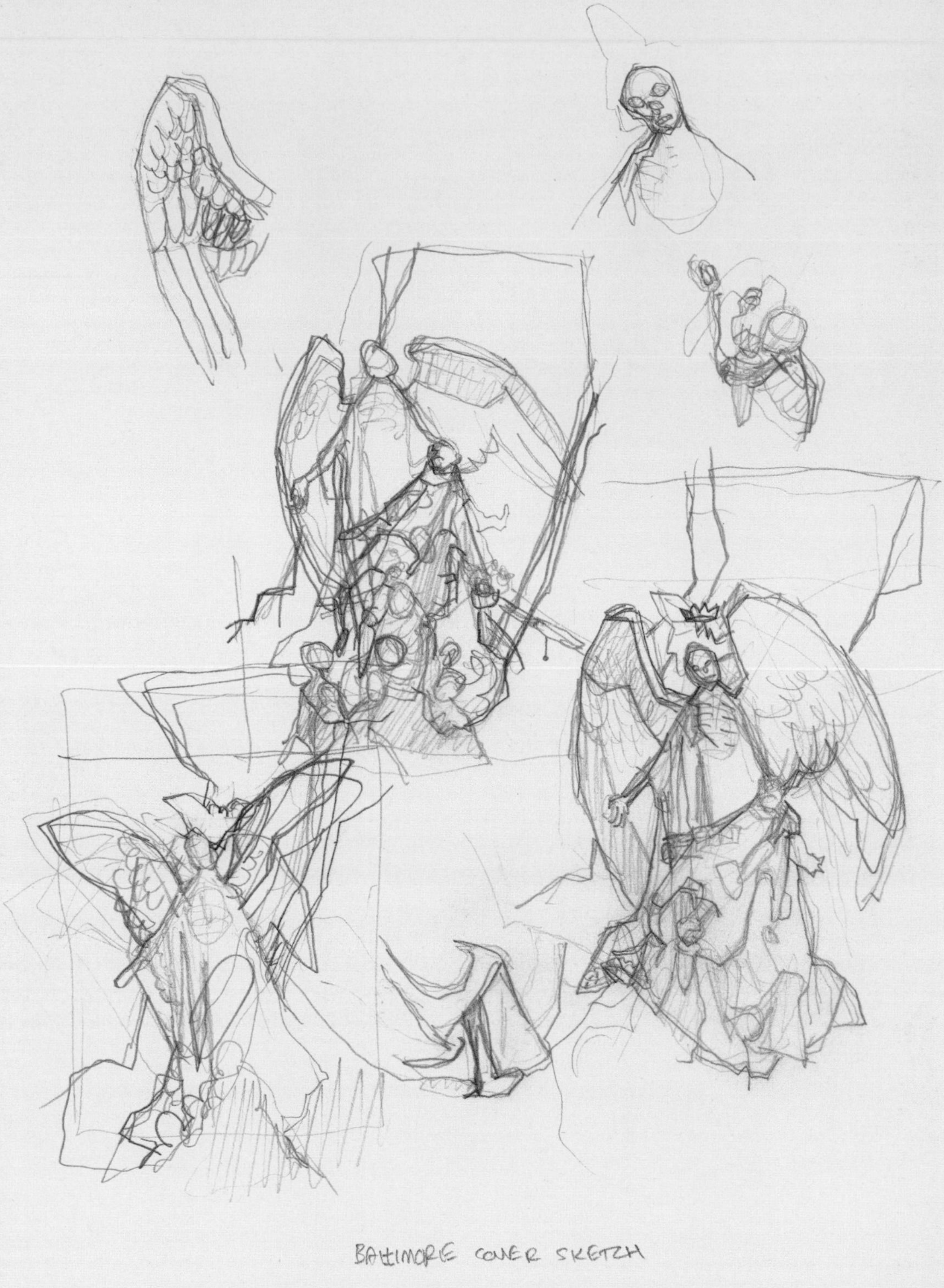
BALTIMORE COVER SKETCH

Mike's sketches for the cover of this collection.

Also by MIKE MIGNOLA

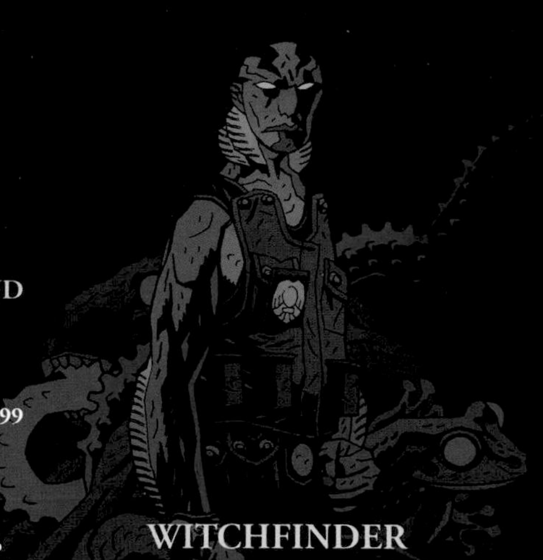

B.P.R.D.

PLAGUE OF FROGS
Volume 1
with Chris Golden, Guy Davis, and others
ISBN 978-1-59582-609-1 | $34.99
Volume 2
with John Arcudi, Davis, and others
ISBN 978-1-59582-672-5 | $34.99
Volume 3
with Arcudi, and Davis
ISBN 978-1-59582-860-6 | $34.99
Volume 4
with Arcudi and Davis
ISBN 978-1-59582-974-0 | $34.99

1946
with Joshua Dysart and Paul Azaceta
ISBN 978-1-59582-191-1 | $17.99

1947
with Dysart, Fábio Moon, and Gabriel Bá
ISBN 978-1-59582-478-3 | $17.99

1948
with Arcudi and Max Fiumara
ISBN 978-1-61655-183-4 | $17.99

BEING HUMAN
with Arcudi, Davis, and others
ISBN 978-1-59582-756-2 | $17.99

VAMPIRE
with Moon and Bá
ISBN 978-1-61655-196-4 | $19.99

B.P.R.D. HELL ON EARTH

NEW WORLD
with Arcudi and Davis
ISBN 978-1-59582-707-4 | $19.99

GODS AND MONSTERS
with Arcudi, Davis, and Crook
ISBN 978-1-59582-822-4 | $19.99

RUSSIA
with Arcudi, Crook, and Duncan Fegredo
ISBN 978-1-59582-946-7 | $19.9

THE DEVIL'S ENGINE AND THE LONG DEATH
with Arcudi, Crook, and James Harren
ISBN 978-1-59582-981-8 | $19.99

THE PICKENS COUNTY HORROR AND OTHERS
with Scott Allie, Jason Latour, Harren, Max Fiumara, and Becky Cloonan
ISBN 978-1-61655-140-7 | $19.99

THE RETURN OF THE MASTER
with Arcudi and Crook
ISBN 978-1-61655-193-3 | $19.99

A COLD DAY IN HELL
with Arcudi, Peter Snejbjerg, and Laurence Campbell
ISBN 978-1-61655-199-5 | $19.99

ABE SAPIEN

THE DROWNING
with Jason Shawn Alexander
ISBN 978-1-59582-185-0 | $17.99

THE DEVIL DOES NOT JEST AND OTHER STORIES
with Arcudi, Harren, and others
ISBN 978-1-59582-925-2 | $17.99

DARK AND TERRIBLE AND THE NEW RACE OF MAN
with Allie, Arcudi, Sebastián Fiumara, and Max Fiumara
ISBN 978-1-61655-284-8 | $19.99

LOBSTER JOHNSON

THE IRON PROMETHEUS
with Jason Armstrong
ISBN 978-1-59307-975-8 | $17.99

THE BURNING HAND
with Arcudi and Tonci Zonjic
ISBN 978-1-61655-031-8 | $17.99

SATAN SMELLS A RAT
with Arcudi, Fiumara, Joe Querio, Wilfredo Torres, and Kevin Nowlan
ISBN 978-1-61655-203-9 | $18.99

WITCHFINDER

IN THE SERVICE OF ANGELS
with Ben Stenbeck
ISBN 978-1-59582-483-7 | $17.99

LOST AND GONE FOREVER
with Arcudi and John Severin
ISBN 978-1-59582-794-4 | $17.99

THE AMAZING SCREW-ON HEAD AND OTHER CURIOUS OBJECTS

ISBN 978-1-59582-501-8 | $17.99

BALTIMORE

THE PLAGUE SHIPS
with Golden and Stenbeck
ISBN 978-1-59582-677-0 | $24.99

THE CURSE BELLS
with Golden and Stenbeck
ISBN 978-1-59582-674-9 | $24.99

A PASSING STRANGER AND OTHER STORIES
with Golden and Stenbeck
ISBN 978-1-61655-182-7 | $24.99

CHAPEL OF BONES
with Golden and Stenbeck
ISBN 978-1-61655-328-9 | $24.99

NOVELS

LOBSTER JOHNSON: THE SATAN FACTORY
with Thomas E. Sniegoski
ISBN 978-1-59582-203-1 | $12.95

JOE GOLEM AND THE DROWNING CITY
with Golden
ISBN 978-1-59582-971-9 | $99.99

DARK HORSE BOOKS
DarkHorse.com

AVAILABLE AT YOUR LOCAL COMICS SHOP OR BOOKSTORE! • To find a comics shop in your area, call 1-888-266-4226.
For more information or to order direct visit DarkHorse.com or call 1-800-862-0052 Mon.–Fri. 9 AM to 5 PM Pacific Time.
Prices and availability subject to change without notice.

HELLBOY

by MIKE MIGNOLA

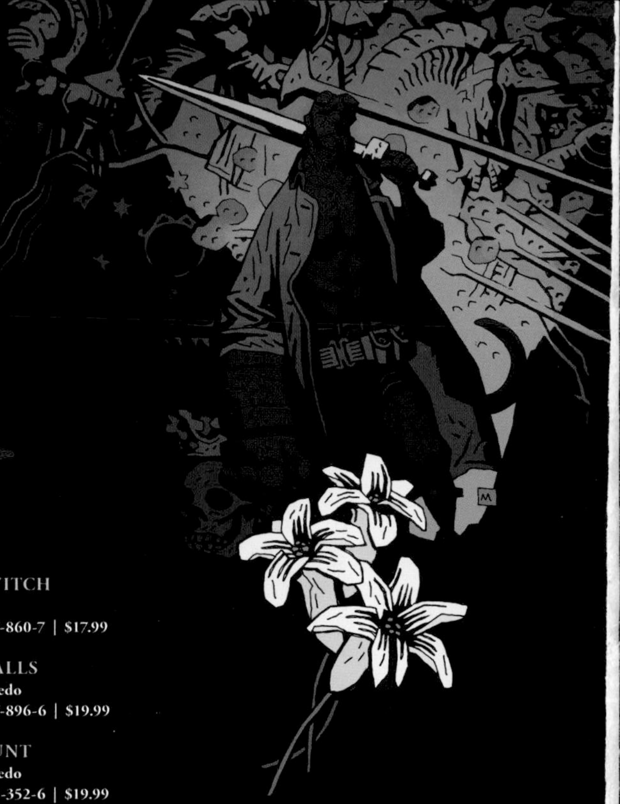

HELLBOY LIBRARY EDITION VOLUME 1:
Seed of Destruction and Wake the Devil
ISBN 978-1-59307-910-9 | $49.99

HELLBOY LIBRARY EDITION VOLUME 2:
The Chained Coffin and The Right Hand of Doom
ISBN 978-1-59307-989-5 | $49.99

HELLBOY LIBRARY EDITION VOLUME 3:
Conqueror Worm and Strange Places
ISBN 978-1-59582-352-6 | $49.99

HELLBOY LIBRARY EDITION VOLUME 4:
The Crooked Man and The Troll Witch
with Richard Corben and others
ISBN 978-1-59582-658-9 | $49.99

HELLBOY LIBRARY EDITION VOLUME 5:
Darkness Calls and the Wild Hunt
with Duncan Fegredo
ISBN 978-1-59582-886-6 | $49.99

HELLBOY LIBRARY EDITION VOLUME 6:
The Storm and the Fury and The Bride of Hell
with Duncan Fegredo, Richard Corben, Kevin Nowlan, and Scott Hampton
ISBN 978-1-61655-133-9 | $49.99

SEED OF DESTRUCTION
with John Byrne
ISBN 978-1-59307-094-6 | $17.99

WAKE THE DEVIL
ISBN 978-1-59307-095-3 | $17.99

THE CHAINED COFFIN AND OTHERS
ISBN 978-1-59307-091-5 | $17.99

THE RIGHT HAND OF DOOM
ISBN 978-1-59307-093-9 | $17.99

CONQUEROR WORM
ISBN 978-1-59307-092-2 | $17.99

STRANGE PLACES
ISBN 978-1-59307-475-3 | $17.99

THE TROLL WITCH AND OTHERS
ISBN 978-1-59307-860-7 | $17.99

DARKNESS CALLS
with Duncan Fegredo
ISBN 978-1-59307-896-6 | $19.99

THE WILD HUNT
with Duncan Fegredo
ISBN 978-1-59582-352-6 | $19.99

THE CROOKED MAN AND OTHERS
with Richard Corben
ISBN 978-1-59582-477-6 | $17.99

THE BRIDE OF HELL AND OTHERS
with Richard Corben, Kevin Nowlan, and Scott Hampton
ISBN 978-1-59582-740-1 | $19.99

THE STORM AND THE FURY
with Duncan Fegredo
ISBN 978-1-59582-827-9 | $19.99

HOUSE OF THE LIVING DEAD
with Richard Corben
ISBN 978-1-59582-757-9 | $14.99

THE MIDNIGHT CIRCUS
with Duncan Fegredo
ISBN 978-1-61655-238-1 | $14.99

HELLBOY: THE FIRST 20 YEARS
ISBN 978-1-61655-353-1 | $19.99

THE ART OF HELLBOY
ISBN 978-1-59307-089-2 | $29.99

HELLBOY II: THE ART OF THE MOVIE
ISBN 978-1-59307-964-2 | $24.99

HELLBOY: THE COMPANION
ISBN 978-1-59307-655-9 | $14.99

HELLBOY: WEIRD TALES
VOLUME 1
ISBN 978-1-56971-622-9 | $17.99
VOLUME 2
ISBN 978-1-56971-953-4 | $17.99

HELLBOY: MASKS AND MONSTERS
with James Robinson and Scott Benefiel
ISBN 978-1-59582-567-4 | $17.99

NOVELS

HELLBOY: EMERALD HELL
By Tom Piccirilli
ISBN 978-1-59582-141-6 | $12.99

HELLBOY: THE ALL-SEEING EYE
By Mark Morris
ISBN 978-1-59582-141-6 | $12.99

HELLBOY: THE FIRE WOLVES
By Tim Lebbon
ISBN 978-1-59582-204-8 | $12.99

HELLBOY: THE ICE WOLVES
By Mark Chadbourn
ISBN 978-1-59582-205-5 | $12.99

SHORT STORIES

Illustrated by Mike Mignola

HELLBOY: ODD JOBS
By Poppy Z. Brite, Greg Rucka, and others
ISBN 978-1-56971-440-9 | $14.99

HELLBOY: ODDER JOBS
By Frank Darabont, Guillermo del Toro, and others
ISBN 978-1-59307-226-1 | $14.99

HELLBOY: ODDEST JOBS
By Joe R. Lansdale, China Miéville, and others
ISBN 978-1-59307-944-4 | $14.99

AVAILABLE AT YOUR LOCAL COMICS SHOP OR BOOKSTORE! • To find a comics shop in your area, call 1-888-266-4226.
For more information or to order direct visit DarkHorse.com or call 1-800-862-0052 Mon.–Fri. 9 AM to 5 PM Pacific Time.
Prices and availability subject to change without notice.

DarkHorse.com